Praise for THE **S**ECOND OBJECTIVE

"*The Second Objective* recalls *The Day of the Jackal*, and is just as likely to become a movie. The suspenseful mystery in a war-time setting, with more turns in the plot than a mountain road, is likely to satisfy both mystery fans and World War II buffs."

—*The Des Moines Register*

"Perhaps best known as a writer and producer on David Lynch's TV series *Twin Peaks*, Mark Frost also has considerable chops as a novelist." —*Las Vegas Review-Journal*

"Frost's ability to transport readers both to 1944 and to the chilly, frantic front lines of World War II . . . is worth the book's price alone. By the time the second caper pops up in the last third of the book, *The Second Objective* turns into a flat-out page-turner, moving as fast as the frenetic characters do." —*Ventura County Sunday Star*

"Frost delivers solid, no-nonsense action livened with double and triple crosses and loyalties that are tested and strengthened . . . This is an old school thriller that will satisfy readers with a yen for stories where the good guys win against seemingly impossible odds."

—Richmond.com

THE
Second
Objective

THE
SECOND
OBJECTIVE

Mark Frost

New York

The Library of Congress has catalogued the hardcover edition of this book as follows:
Frost, Mark
   The second objective / Mark Frost. — 1st ed.
     p. cm.
   ISBN 1-4013-0222-X
   ISBN-13 978-1-4013-0222-1
   1. Eisenhower, Dwight D. (Dwight David), 1890–1969—Assassination attempts—Fiction.
2. Attempted assassination—Fiction.   3. World War, 1939–1945—Commando
operations—Fiction.   4. Ardennes, Battle of the, 1944–1945—Fiction.   I. Title.

PS3556.R599S43 2007
813'.54—dc22   2006043683

Paperback ISBN 978-1-4013-0952-7

Hyperion books are available for special promotions, premiums, or corporate training. For details contact Michael Rentas, Proprietary Markets, Hyperion, 77 West 66th Street, 12th floor, New York, New York 10023, or call 212-456-0133.

Design by Renato Stanisic
Map by Laura Hartman Maestro

FIRST PAPERBACK EDITION

10 9 8 7 6 5 4 3 2 1

FOR LYNN

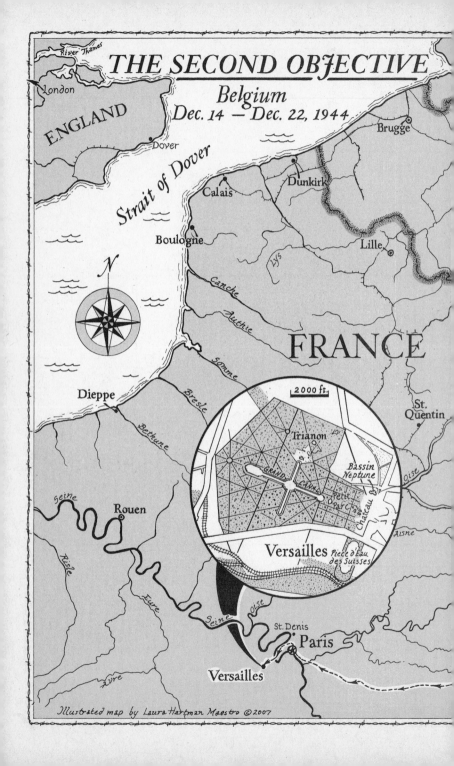

The Wolf's Lair, Rastenburg, East Prussia
OCTOBER 22, 1944

At half past midnight, Lieutenant Colonel Otto Skorzeny left the command bunker. He walked alone down the corridor outside, buried twenty feet belowground, bleak with artificial light. The poorly ventilated air still smelled of musty concrete and earth. The Führer had named his new field headquarters, one of ten structures linked by underground passages, *Die Wolfsschanze*: The Wolf's Lair. To Skorzeny, in that moment, it felt more like a tomb.

Skorzeny stared at the medal he held in his hand, the German Cross rendered in gold. He had just received the Reich's highest decoration for his most recent paramilitary operation, a bloodless coup that replaced the regent of Budapest with a Fascist cipher. Only a year before, Skorzeny had rocketed to fame after his first triumph, the daring rescue of Italian dictator Benito Mussolini from imprisonment on a remote Italian mountaintop. He had since led his personally trained special forces brigade on half a dozen other suicidal assignments, and was known and feared throughout Europe as "Hitler's commando."

The order he had just received made those missions seem like a training exercise.

Madness. This is madness.

The staff told him afterward that no one had seen the Führer in such a positive mood for months. He seemed at last to have shaken off the ill health and depression that had beset him after the nearly successful attempt on his life by a cadre of aristocratic German officers in July.

The amphetamines must be working, thought Skorzeny, who was burdened by few illusions about Adolf Hitler or any other human being.

The Führer's enthusiasm appeared unhinged from reality. In less than six months the German Army had been driven back from the shores of Normandy to their own borders. With the Soviets advancing from the east, and the Allies preparing to attack from the west, most military leaders privately believed the war was already lost. All that remained for the Wehrmacht was a brutal, grinding defensive collapse toward Berlin.

But as his empire crumbled around him, Hitler now proposed to mount the most ambitious offensive of the entire war. He had just outlined for Skorzeny his secret plan for a savage counterattack against the Western Allies. He would hurl all his remaining divisions at a lightly defended section of Belgium and Luxembourg. Entitled Operation Autumn Mist, the attack was designed to drive a wedge of steel between the American and British armies all the way west to the Atlantic. If they succeeded in cutting off the British north of Antwerp and trapped them in a second Dunkirk, the Führer believed that the English would sue for peace, and that the Americans would have no stomach for invading Germany on their own. Only then could he turn his entire war machine loose on Russia and destroy the Bolshevik menace he considered the one true enemy of Western civilization.

Genius shares a common border with insanity, thought Skorzeny. *Since I've last seen him he's crossed over.*

Skorzeny waited for the rant to end. Hitler put both hands on the table and sagged forward. His skin looked jaundiced under the room's sickly fluorescents. He inhaled deeply, spittle collecting at the sides of his mouth. As he raised his left hand to brush back an unruly forelock of hair, Skorzeny saw that it shook with a violent, involuntary tremor. The Führer took a few steps toward him with a shuffling gait, an old man's walk, his hand searching for support. In moments all his vitality had drained away, leaving this brittle husk.

Yes, amphetamines. Time for another dose.

On instinct Skorzeny reached out a hand. Hitler gripped the blond giant's immense right forearm and seemed to gather strength from it. Or perhaps this weakness was a ploy to elicit Skorzeny's sympathy. In either case, it stirred awake his loyalty to the man who had lifted him from obscurity to glory.

"How may I help?" asked Skorzeny.

When he learned what his own role was to be in Operation Autumn Mist, Skorzeny couldn't speak.

He was to raise a new brigade from throughout the German armed forces to take part in the invasion: two thousand men with one specialized ability in common. None could know the true nature of their mission until the night before they embarked. They were to be sworn to a blood oath under pain of death, trained in secrecy, turned into an effective commando unit, and sent to fulfill an objective that would mean almost certain death.

In six weeks' time.

That wasn't all. From within that brigade he was to select another group of men, no more than twenty of the most qualified he could find.

They would be given a second objective.

1

Grafenwöhr, Bavaria, Germany
NOVEMBER 3, 1944

ernie Oster arrived in Nuremberg after traveling through
the night alone on a passenger train. He carried classified,
stamped orders handed to him the previous day by his commanding officer in Berlin. He had been told to pack nothing and
change into civilian clothes before soldiers escorted him directly
from that meeting to the train. After showing his papers to the SS officers at Nuremberg Station, he was led into an empty holding area
and left there without explanation. At noon, after a dozen other men
had joined him in isolation, they were loaded into the back of a
blacked-out transport truck.

They were ordered to keep silent. The men exchanged only wary
looks and nods. None of his fellow passengers wore uniforms either,
but Bernie surmised from their appearance and manner that they
were all soldiers or sailors. Sitting alone in a corner, he chain-smoked
cigarettes, wondering where the other men had come from, what they
all had in common. His CO had given him no details during his briefing, only that Bernie had "volunteered"—without being offered the
choice—for a special assignment that required immediate transfer.
Fifteen hours and hundreds of kilometers later, he found himself in a
part of Germany he'd never seen before.

Soon after they started driving, the most agitated passenger blurted the questions they were all thinking: "What are we doing here? . . . What do they want with us?"

Bernie didn't answer. The risk that any of these other men could be an SS plant, placed among them to monitor their conversations—or provoke them by asking those same questions—was too great. He already had reason enough to fear for his life. Perhaps these other men did as well; none of them answered.

Peeking through a seam in the canvas, Bernie saw they were on a highway moving through stark gray countryside—bare trees, fallow fields, barren wilderness. Halfway through their second hour, they turned onto a remote road threading through a dark wood. Half a mile on, they approached the entrance to an elaborate compound, surrounded by steel-framed gates and barbed-wire fences that stretched into the trees as far as the eye could see.

It looked like a prison camp. Guards in unfamiliar uniforms patrolled the parapets and blockhouses above the walls. Machine guns had been placed on the towers, their barrels pointed to the interior. His stomach turned over.

So that's it. I've been found out.

The truck braked to a stop just short of the gates. The back canvas parted and two armed guards waved the passengers out at the point of a bayonet, their eyes flinching at daylight after the long, dark ride. An SS officer waited to escort them through the open gates. Bernie noticed that the guards on the walls and towers all had broad Slavic features. He heard an exchange between two of them in some unfamiliar, guttural language. The gates clanged shut behind them. Bernie wondered if these walls had been put up to keep others out or to keep them in.

The compound appeared to have been built for military purposes. He could see deep tank tracks in the mud, an artillery range in the distance. The guards led them into a low, empty barracks built from freshly cut logs, where sandwiches and bottles of beer had been set out for them. They sat on crude wooden beds and ate in silence as the guards watched. After a brief rest, they were led, one by one, to another cabin that Bernie could see through a window across the compound. None of them returned. Bernie was one of the last men summoned.

Two SS officers, a lieutenant and a captain, waited behind a desk in the building's only room, facing a single empty chair. Black-jacketed SS grenadiers stood sentry at the door, holding MP40 submachine guns.

The lieutenant ordered Bernie to empty his pockets on the table, including his military identity card, traveling papers.

"Your paybook, as well," said the lieutenant.

He collected the items in an envelope and put the envelope in a desk drawer. Without them, Bernie knew that as far as the army was concerned, he no longer existed. His heart thumped in his chest, and he was sure that the fear he'd been struggling to suppress showed on his face. He'd been dreading a moment like this for months: discovery, torture, execution.

The captain didn't look up at him once from his notes while the lieutenant ordered him to sit and began asking questions, in German, reading from a dossier.

"Private First Class Bernard Oster."

"Yes, sir."

"What is your unit?"

"The 42nd *Volksgrenadier* Division, sir. Mechanized Brigade."

"Your duties there?"

"I'm a mechanic in the motor pool, sir. Attached to central command headquarters in Berlin. I take care of the officers' cars."

"Is that your only responsibility?"

Here it comes, thought Bernie.

"No, sir. For the last month I've worked in the radio room. As a translator."

The lieutenant showed something on the dossier to the captain. He looked up at Bernie for the first time. A slender man in his early thirties, with slicked black hair and steel-gray eyes that stared through Bernie like an X-ray. He gestured to his lieutenant: *I'll take it from here.*

"You were born in the United States," said the captain, in crisp English.

"Yes, sir," said Bernie, trying not to look surprised.

"Your parents emigrated there in the early 1920s, after the last war. Why?"

"As I understand, there was little or no work in Germany then," said Bernie. "Economic hardship."

"Your father is an industrial chemist. He worked for Pfizer, on Long Island."

"That's right."

"And you were raised and educated in New York."

"Brooklyn. Yes I was, sir."

"When did your family return to Germany?"

"In 1938. I was fourteen."

"Why?"

Bernie hesitated. "For the same reason we left in the first place. My father lost his job in the Depression. He had no way to support his family. As a scientist and a German citizen, he got an offer from the new government to go home and work here."

The captain betrayed no reactions. Judging from the man's shrewd manner, he knew the answer to every question he was asking. His steady, unblinking gaze sent waves of fear through Bernie. When the SS took an interest in someone, he had a way of disappearing, even if he had nothing to hide. Bernie felt sweat dripping down under his arms.

"Your father works for IG Farben, in Frankfurt," said the captain.

"Yes, sir."

"Has he ever discussed his work with you?"

Is that what this is about? My father? Not what happened in Berlin?

"No, sir. I believe it is classified."

"You began military service sixteen months ago," said the captain. "When you turned eighteen. You made no attempt to enlist prior to that."

"I was still in school, sir—"

"Nor were you ever a member of the *Hitlerjugend*."

The captain's eyes bored into him. Bernie felt rattled to his core, certain the man could read the thoughts he tried to keep from his mind. Did he know that within months of returning to Nazi Germany, his father had been warned by his bosses at IG Farben that if he ever

tried to leave, his family would be killed? Or that Bernie's own hatred of the Nazis had only grown greater after he was drafted? He'd
come to Germany against his will, with an American teenager's skep-
ticism intact, immune to the Nazis' nationalist fantasia. With their
fixation on pomp and ritual, he'd thought them coarse and buffoon-
ish. Then he and his family had watched in horror as they brought
Europe to its knees.

Bernie's mind raced to the one question that mattered: Did this
man know that when they learned about his language skills and
moved him to the radio room, Bernie had twice altered his translation of intercepted American intelligence reports about troop movements, trying to mislead his superiors about their intent? Fighting
his own private resistance, probably ineffectual, certainly reckless.
He'd waited a month before trying again, sure they were watching
him. His second attempt had come just a week ago.

Had they only been waiting for him to stick his neck out again?
Why else would they have brought him here?

"I was older than the compulsory age when we returned from
America," said Bernie. "My father wanted me to finish my education."

The captain stood up and walked around the table. "Why has
your father never joined the National Socialist Party?"

"I'm afraid you'd have to ask him, sir—"

"Is he a patriotic man?"

"He's always thought of himself as a German first. That's why he
came home when he had the chance—"

The captain pulled his pistol and held it firmly to Bernie's forehead.

"And how do you think of yourself, Private?"

Bernie swallowed before answering. "As my father's son."

"You are an American citizen."

"I have dual citizenship, German and American."

"And if you had to choose?"

"I've never been given a choice—"

"I'm giving you one now."

Bernie never took his eyes away from the captain's, convinced
that the slightest slip would make him pull the trigger. "Speak with
my commanding officers if you think my allegiance is in question."

The captain kept staring at him. Bernie remained at attention, eyes forward, trembling.

"We have spoken with them. Isn't there anything else you wish to tell me?"

Bernie looked right at him. "No, sir."

Another moment, then the captain lowered the pistol and holstered it. Bernie had passed the test. His knees nearly buckled.

"You've volunteered to become part of a new brigade. English is a requirement. Yours is excellent, for obvious reasons. Is it safe to say you also have knowledge of American culture? Movie stars. Baseball. Current events."

"I've been away for six years, sir."

"You read newspapers, don't you? America is still of interest to you. You can answer the question honestly, son; it's only natural. It was your home for fourteen years."

Bernie saw the trap beneath the question, and asked neutrally, "Why, sir?"

"Your experience can be of value during our training. We may call upon your expertise in this area."

"I'll help any way I can, sir."

"I am Captain Stielau. You will report directly to me. You look relieved."

"Do I? I suppose I am, sir."

Stielau seemed amused by Bernie's reaction, then turned to his lieutenant: "Category One."

The lieutenant wrote Bernie's name on a roster with four columns. Bernie saw that his was the first name in the first column.

"May I ask the purpose of our new brigade, sir?"

"Yes," said Stielau.

Bernie hesitated. "What is the purpose of our new brigade, sir?"

"I said you could ask. I didn't say I would tell you. You're dismissed, Private Oster."

2

Grafenwöhr
NOVEMBER 1944

ernie tried to bury his fear by losing himself in the camp's routine. Over two thousand men from every corner of the Reich arrived during the following week. Bernie helped conduct their initial interviews, asking questions to determine their level of competence in English, both speaking and comprehension. They were then classified into four categories. One: fluency in English and working knowledge of American slang. Two: fluency without knowledge of specific American idioms. Three: general comprehension and the ability to conduct limited conversations. Four: restricted comprehension, men who had studied English in school without real-world application.

Bernie quickly realized that most of the "volunteers" had vastly overstated their abilities. By the end of the week, as the last men arrived, he had picked fewer than twenty to join him in Category One. Fifty went into Category Two. The third category had about one hundred men in it, and the fourth another two hundred. As for the rest, over two-thirds of the men who had been summoned to *Grafenwöhr*, their English was limited to single-word responses. Bernie barracked with the rest of the Ones and Twos; Threes and Fours occupied separate quarters across the yard, and the rest stayed on the far side of the compound.

The men were issued neutral olive-green uniforms without in-signia. All previous ranks were erased, and officers received no pref-erential treatment. They dined together in the same large mess hall, eating meals that far surpassed normal army fare. Contact with friends or family was forbidden. Every man signed an oath of si-lence, and letters home had to pass a censor's strict review. Medicine and prescription drugs were dispensed freely to prevent illness, since no one was allowed out of camp to see a doctor. This taut atmosphere fueled rumors and speculation about their brigade's reason for being, which flew through the camp, mutating on a daily basis. Their true purpose remained a mystery.

They heard their first explanation when Bernie and the rest of the brigade were called one day at dawn to a general assembly in the compound. Captain Stielau addressed them. They were now part of the 150th Panzer Brigade, he said, operating under the command of Colonel Otto Skorzeny. The mention of his name sent a ripple through the yard; he was without rival the most notorious figure in the German armed forces. Stielau told them their mission was called "Operation *Greif*," and they were being trained to defend Cologne when the Allies attacked across the Rhine. It sounded plausible, but Bernie found it impossible to reconcile with what they were being taught.

Their training began each morning with English lessons, focus-ing on American slang, and tutoring to eliminate native accents. Bernie helped craft a crash course on American culture, using news-papers, magazines, sports sections, and comic strips. Tests were given each day to drill this information into long-term memory. The men were ordered to use only English; anyone heard speaking German was disciplined with solitary confinement.

Each afternoon they were put through Skorzeny's commando train-ing: demolition, communications, reconnaissance, special weapons, light artillery, night fighting in both urban and forest environ-ments, hand-to-hand combat. They were schooled in map reading, the basics of movement under combat conditions, camouflage tech-niques, and communications. They were taught how to drive and ser-vice captured American jeeps, scout cars, half-tracks, and tanks. Each man in Categories One and Two was issued an M1 rifle. Ammunition was too scarce for target practice, but they learned to carry, field strip, and maintain their rifles as rigorously as any GI.

After dinner they gathered in the mess hall to listen to U.S. Armed Forces Radio. Beer was served and they were encouraged to sing along with the popular songs of American recording artists. On some nights they watched American films, in English, with orders to observe and mimic the actors' mannerisms. Seeing these familiar faces again, the first Hollywood stars he'd seen in years, made Bernie desperately homesick. His dread about what Skorzeny was really preparing them for grew with each passing day; only exhaustion kept it from overwhelming his mind.

At the end of the second week, the fluent English speakers, about eighty men, were placed directly under the command of Captain Stielau. Except for meals, they now spent their days apart from the others, and their language training intensified. Whenever shipments of new Allied material arrived—uniforms, boots, weapons—Stielau's men received it first. Bernie believed that the future objectives of the two groups, whatever they might be, had begun to diverge.

Bernie met one other American-born man in Category One, a U.S. Army deserter named William Sharper. He had served in the American Army until after the invasion of Normandy. Sharper took a lead role during training, teaching the men specific GI behaviors; the way they slouched, chewed gum, how to rip open a pack of cigarettes with a thumbnail, and the fine art of swearing. Bernie stayed clear of him, disturbed by the violence he saw in the man's eyes. A handful of others were former members of the German diplomatic corps who had learned English serving in foreign embassies. The rest came from the merchant marine, itinerant seamen who at some point had worked on American or English ships. One was a former porter on the *Queen Mary*. Their isolation, intense physical training, and the airtight atmosphere of secrecy brought them quickly and closely together as a unit.

At the start of the third week, each man in Bernie's unit was assigned an American name. American dog tags were issued bearing these names, along with a new rank, and they were ordered to refer to one another only by these new names and ranks. They were told to create and memorize a fictional American history: place of birth, family members, education, hometown history, favorite pets, girlfriends left behind, baseball teams, local geography. Bernie decided the only way to create a life story he could remember under pressure was to keep it as close as possible to his own. A New Yorker from Brooklyn, the son of immigrant parents, he became Private James Tenella.

That Tuesday Bernie was summoned to the interview cabin. A new arrival sat joking with Stielau's lieutenant, waiting to go through the evaluation process. Unlike the hundreds who'd preceded him, he still wore his German uniform: the crisp black tunic of a *Waffen*-SS lieutenant. He was in his mid to late twenties, wiry, compact, with close-cropped blond hair and a ready, dazzling smile.

Stielau's lieutenant waved Bernie into the room: "Private Tenella, meet our latest arrival, SS *Untersturmführer* Erich Von Leinsdorf."

Von Leinsdorf stood up to shake his hand, and looked him in the eye. "A pleasure. They tell me you may be able to iron the starch out of my plummy Mid-Atlantic tones."

Von Leinsdorf spoke perfect English, with a crisp upper-class British accent.

"Whatever it takes, sir," said Bernie.

Stielau's lieutenant handed Bernie the clipboard and left the room. Von Leinsdorf perched on the edge of the table and opened a sterling silver cigarette case engraved with his initials.

"I suppose I'll have to start smoking Lucky Strikes," he said. "No more English Players for me."

Von Leinsdorf torched his cigarette with a matching silver lighter and smiled again. He smoked like a movie star, or someone who had studied movie stars smoking. Despite his easygoing charm, Bernie felt a visceral wariness of the man. He seemed to take up more space than he physically occupied. The superior airs seemed characteristic for someone from his class, but Bernie was reacting to something starker than the aristocratic "Von" in his name. He pulled back the chair Von Leinsdorf had been using and sat down facing him.

"How was your trip?" asked Bernie.

"Appalling," he said with a smile, making no effort to keep the conversation going.

"Where'd you come in from, Lieutenant?"

"Where are *you* from, if you don't mind my asking? Your English is astonishing."

"I'm from New York. Brooklyn."

"Is that a fact? How fascinating. Born and bred?"

"That's right. How about you?"

"Munich, but as you may have gathered, I spent my formative years in England. Father was in the diplomatic corps, stationed to the embassy in London. We went over in twenty-eight. I was ten at the time. Father enrolled me at Westminster, public school. All those incestuous aristocratic family trees, it's a breeding ground for degenerate half-wits. So in I waltzed from the hinterlands, armed only with my meager schoolboy English. Bit of a wonder I survived."

"Hope the education was worth it."

"Oh, I got an education, all right. Where were you at ten, Brooklyn?"

"Fifth grade. PS 109."

"Of course you were. How charming."

"So you spoke only English in school?"

"Not just in school, old boy. At home, in the park, in the bath with my proper English nanny. Even family dinners. Father didn't want any guttural German consonants ruffling the feathers of our hosts."

"When did you come back to Germany?"

"Once the unpleasantness broke out, the tea bags ushered us straight to the door. Imagine my father's disappointment. He'd spent the better part of his life trying to penetrate this ironclad veil of courtesy. He never realized that's the reason for their obsession with manners: a coat of paint covering a hatred of all things foreign. And they seem so polite until you get to know them." Von Leinsdorf flashed a smile, stood up, and walked to the window. "So we both came back to Germany at the same age. Strange, feeling the outsider in your own country, isn't it?"

You don't know the half of it, thought Bernie.

"Where the devil are we, by the way? I was hoping I might be headed to Berlin. Has anyone told you what this is about?"

"Not a word," said Bernie.

"Very hush-hush all this, isn't it? Have they tipped their hand about what we're doing here, Brooklyn?"

"All they told us is that this guy Colonel Skorzeny's running the show."

Von Leinsdorf spun around. "Skorzeny? Otto Skorzeny?"

"That's what they said."

"Have you seen him? Has he been here?"

"No. Why?"

"I tried to transfer into his commando unit last year—"

"Where you been stationed?"

"Dachau," he said casually, flicking his cigarette.

Bernie had heard about the Munich suburb the SS used as a training center. Lurid stories about their concentration camp had been circulating through Berlin, but he knew better than to ask. He'd learned never to ask an SS man anything.

"I'm going to write up this report that your English is first rate," said Bernie. "They'll probably put you in Category Two."

Von Leinsdorf leaned over to glance at Bernie's notes. "That sounds suspiciously like a demotion. Why not Category One?"

"That's only for guys who come in knowing a lot of American slang."

"But you could teach me, couldn't you?"

"If that's what they want—"

"It's what *I* want," said Von Leinsdorf, sharply. He softened his tone and turned the charm back on. "Just between us, old boy, I hate thinking I'm not good enough for the top category. Sheer vanity, really."

"It's not up to me."

"I'm not asking for much. Wouldn't want the officers to think you're reluctant to help a fellow soldier. All this cloak and dagger, they must be watching you more closely than the rest of us. I'm sure they'd take a dim view of wobbly loyalties."

Bernie smiled, trying not to let him see that he'd even heard the threat. "I'll try to help you out, sure, what the fuck."

"What the fuck?"

"Most popular word in the GI language. Fuck this, fucking that. Fucking camp—"

"Fucking Krauts—"

"Now you're cooking with gas."

"What the fuck does that mean?"

"Means you're on the money, on the beam, moving down the right track."

"Right. So, Category One, then. I'll make it up to you, Brooklyn, see that you're assigned to my squad. We should fucking stick together, don't you think?"

"Sure, what the fuck."

Both men laughed. Bernie couldn't help liking the man, in spite of his initial reservations.

"What took you so long getting here?" asked Bernie. "They brought the rest of us in two weeks ago, you don't mind my asking."

"Haven't a clue. I assume it was some bureaucratic foul-up."

"A snafu."

"Pardon?"

"It's a whatchamacallit, a word you make from initials, an acronym? Situation Normal: All Fucked Up."

"Yes, brilliant. Snafu, indeed. The thing is, Brooklyn, I only heard about this two days ago. We were near the end of a major project, so they couldn't bear to part with me."

"At Dachau."

"That's right," said Von Leinsdorf, smiling as he lit another cigarette.

"So did you finish it? Your project?"

"A ways to go yet. Afraid they'll have to carry on without me."

Von Leinsdorf motioned with his head for Bernie to follow, and they walked into the darkening evening, back toward the dining hall. Von Leinsdorf tossed away his half-smoked cigarette and asked Bernie for one of his Lucky Strikes.

"Do you mind?" he asked. "I should get used to these."

"Help yourself."

Von Leinsdorf pulled the cigarette from the pack with his lips and torched it. "What do we call these? Smokes?"

"Smokes, nails," said Bernie.

"Nails?"

"Coffin nails. Sticks, butts."

Von Leinsdorf nodded, then lit and studied his cigarette. "So what are they training us for, Brooklyn? I get a different answer from everyone."

"They say we're going to defend Cologne when the Allies invade—"

"Come on, that's pure codswallop. All this trouble just to have us dig and wait for Patton to cross the Rhine? This is a Skorzeny mission. Hitler's commando. Start with the name: Operation *Greif*—the griffin. You remember what it looks like? Half German eagle, half Allied lion. Our purpose is in that image. We're going to cross the line disguised as an American brigade, a surprise attack. Something to shock the world."

"Maybe you're right," said Bernie, trying to sound casual as he heard his worst fear realized.

"I'm sure of it. And I've got a good idea what our target might be."

Bernie's eye caught a metallic flash of light above them in the darkness, from a guard tower directly above the courtyard.

"Somebody's up there," he said.

Von Leinsdorf turned to look. A tall, sturdy officer in uniform leaned forward, lighting a cigar, his face visible in the flame of the lighter a soldier held for him.

"It's him," said Von Leinsdorf.

"Who?"

"Skorzeny's here."

3

Grafenwöhr
NOVEMBER 20, 1944

The entire 150th Panzer Brigade was called into the commons at six-thirty A.M., before the morning meal. Bernie, Von Leinsdorf, and the rest of Captain Stielau's commando group stood in the first two rows facing the dining hall as a light mist fell from an overcast sky. Five minutes later the brigade snapped to attention as the camp's brass marched out ahead of Colonel Skorzeny. He wore his dress uniform but no overcoat, unlike the rest of the officers, and a confident smile that seemed oblivious to bad weather and any other adversity. Skorzeny stopped and surveyed his men for nearly a minute, studying faces, before he uttered a word. The Iron Cross hung at his throat, between the lightning SS runes and insignia of rank on his high, stiff collar. His bright eyes and sharp features suggested to Bernie the image of a hyper-intelligent fox.

"We are not here to turn you into soldiers," he said in English, his voice ringing out over the yard. "That was someone else's job. If they failed, there's nothing we can do for you now. Nor is there time to train you properly as commandos; the urgency of our mission is too great. It is the responsibility of every man to do the best he can with what we give you. Your principal weapons will be intelligence, ingenuity, and cunning.

"What I do expect from you is this: the willingness to change your entire pattern of behavior. Nationality, race, and culture are qualities you express unconsciously in your basic instincts, habits, and attitudes. They are much more deeply ingrained in your mind and body than you know. As far as the outside world is concerned, these qualities, these 'German characteristics,' have to change if you have any hope of surviving what lies ahead. It is no use dressing you in olive green and teaching you American slang if you click your boot heels and snap to attention like a Prussian grenadier the first time one of their officers barks out an order."

He gave a comic, self-deprecating demonstration, like one of the boys in the ranks. A big laugh spread through the assembly. Bernie glanced over at Von Leinsdorf, standing down the row. He watched Skorzeny with almost religious rapture. Skorzeny smiled and waited for the laughter to subside with the polished air of a co-median.

He's got them in his hands. They're ready to die for him right now.

"No similar operation of this size has ever been attempted in the history of warfare. I won't minimize the dangers you face. But I as-sure you the Führer has entrusted us with a responsibility on which the future of our country depends. You have his full support and ab-solute confidence. I know in my heart that you will not let him, or Germany, down. The rest is up to God and chance. Heil Hitler!"

Skorzeny turned with a click of his heels and marched away, his adjutant and officers falling into step behind him. He radiated command and iron confidence, tempered by empathy for his troops and self-deprecating humor. Von Leinsdorf and the others around him glowed with patriotic zeal; they looked ready to burst into song.

Skorzeny watched the brigade's military division go through maneuvers that morning on the training ground. Two captured American Sherman tanks and twelve German Panthers, which had been retrofitted to resemble Shermans, rumbled through their paces. In the afternoon, Stielau's commando company conducted a sabotage demonstration, blowing up a mock bridge ahead of sched-ule against a running clock. Skorzeny appeared pleased with their performance.

. . .

When Skorzeny returned to the officers' quarters for the evening, his adjutant was waiting for him outside. "Sir, a lieutenant from the commando company has requested a word with you."

"I don't have time for that now."

The adjutant lowered his voice. "He is SS. From a diplomatic corps family."

Skorzeny looked past him into the next room, where a young, upright man with close-cropped blond hair waited.

"All right, leave us," said Skorzeny.

Skorzeny walked in to join the man, who snapped to attention and saluted. "*Untersturmführer* Erich Von Leinsdorf, sir. It is an honor to meet you."

"What can I do for you, Lieutenant?"

"Sir, as a fellow SS officer, I take the liberty of speaking directly. The wildest rumors are circulating through camp regarding the mission. Once the men learned you were in charge, imaginations ran riot."

"Give me an example," said Skorzeny.

"We are going to rush across France to liberate our trapped garrison at Brest. Some have us crossing the Channel to invade London. There's even one that claims we're to cross the Atlantic by submarine and attack Roosevelt in the White House."

Skorzeny shook his head, amused. "And what do you think, Lieutenant?"

"I believe I know the real objective of the 105th Panzer Brigade, sir."

The man radiated such conviction that for a moment Skorzeny wondered if his seconds had disobeyed orders and taken him into their confidence. Skorzeny poured a drink, stood in front of the fire, and listened as Von Leinsdorf explained his theory. Hiding his astonishment at what the man told him, Skorzeny rolled the brandy in the snifter, a grand master with his hand poised over a suddenly useful pawn. He said nothing when Von Leinsdorf finished, letting him squirm.

"I will share this much with you," said Skorzeny finally. "The Führer has given us a specific military objective, the details of which I am not at liberty to disclose."

"I understand, sir," said Von Leinsdorf.

"He also gave us a second objective," said Skorzeny, moving closer. "No one else knows about it, not even your superior officers. Never mind how, but you've hit on it exactly. Let me tell you my problem, Lieutenant."

Von Leinsdorf tensed. "I didn't mean to cause any trouble—"

Skorzeny held up a hand for silence. "For some time I have been looking for an officer capable of leading this phase of the operation. I've found my man."

"I'm honored, sir."

"Choose a few others from your company. The best English speakers, three men, each qualified to lead a small squad. Do any come to mind?"

"Yes, sir."

"Take them into your confidence, but without the particulars we've discussed. Have each of these men assemble his own four-man team. Then consider this objective carefully and work out the tactical details yourself."

"What guidance can you give me, sir?"

"None. The rest is up to you. I don't like to limit a talented young officer's initiative. In the meantime, to help morale, introduce a rumor of our own into camp. Three American commandos were recently captured wearing German uniforms near Aachen. They were given safe passage back across the American line by the SS a few days later."

"Is that true?"

"Of course not. They were shot immediately." Skorzeny opened the door for him. "We'll meet again on the eve of the attack and finalize your plan. Good luck to us all."

"You may count on me, sir." Von Leinsdorf saluted, spun on his heel, and exited the room. Skorzeny's adjutant entered moments later.

"Bring me that man's dossier," said Skorzeny. "Ask Captain Stielau to come in."

Skorzeny watched the fire as he waited, and felt the threads of three different fabrics bind into one satisfying whole. The adjutant and Stielau returned together. Skorzeny quickly scanned Von Leinsdorf's dossier, while Stielau stood by.

"How did he end up here? His father was one-quarter Jewish."

"Yes, on the mother's side. According to Party standards that still made him half-caste, *Mischlinge.*"

"And he was Ambassador Ribbentrop's right-hand man in London at the time?" asked Skorzeny. "I remember hearing about this. A minor scandal."

"Ribbentrop shipped him off to an obscure post in Sweden. The mother took ill, went home, and died shortly after. When the father committed suicide a few months later, the boy, Erich, became a ward of the state."

"How did he kill himself?"

"The rope. A coward's death. Fit for a Jew."

Skorzeny read something in the file. "Erich found the body."

"Yes. He was sent back to Germany, and enrolled in the *Hitlerjugend*. He so excelled in every youth program they put him in—the Hitler School, the Political Institute—that he was transferred to the *Ordensburgen*. It's for only the most fanatical young National Socialists. Intense physical discipline, military instruction, education in the racial sciences, and the Jewish question—all under SS."

"In spite of his Jewish blood."

"The mother's line was pure Aryan, so he's only one eighth, slightly more than twelve percent. In special cases one can argue the Aryan blood is more dominant. For all that, he seems determined to eradicate his father's heritage. The lieutenant's creativity at Dachau has been nothing less than astonishing."

Skorzeny knew about the extermination program at Dachau and other death camps, but offered no comment. Senior officers working at a remove from the Final Solution never discussed what they knew in any way that required expressing an opinion. Stielau interpreted his silence as disapproval.

"In any case, since he is of such concern to you," said Stielau, "we'll have the man executed tomorrow."

"No, Stielau, you miss my point entirely. He's perfect."

"If I may ask, in what way, sir?"

"It's all very well to send our little brigade across enemy lines. If the stars align, and we catch them napping, there's even a slight chance we might succeed."

"Sir, I think you're discounting a very good chance we might change the course of the war—"

"I appreciate your enthusiasm, Captain Stielau, and your devotion to our cause. But realism is the harshest discipline. The longer view suggests that a bleak future awaits us all, regardless of our interim efforts."

Stielau said nothing, and Skorzeny instantly regretted his frankness.

"We are soldiers, nevertheless," said Skorzeny, closing Von Leinsdorf's dossier. "We play the hand we are dealt. And this man could turn out to be a wild card."

Bernie saw the change in Von Leinsdorf as soon as he returned to the barracks. A hard set in his eyes, jaw taut. He recruited his first two squad leaders that same night: a fellow SS officer, *Untersturmführer* Gerhard Bremer, and an Army Intelligence translator named Karl Heinz Schmidt. Bernie watched these conversations take place. When Von Leinsdorf returned to his bunk, Bernie asked what was going on but got no answer. *He's following new orders*, thought Bernie. *From Skorzeny himself*.

Von Leinsdorf recruited his third squad leader the next morning, the former American Army sergeant William Sharper. After four years as a GI in North Africa and France, Sharper had deserted to the Wehrmacht three months earlier after beating his superior officer half to death during a barracks poker game. He'd spent those months in the custody of German Intelligence, before being cleared and released for this mission. Von Leinsdorf sized up Sharper as a working-class hooligan, more suited to life as a Nazi storm trooper than in the conformist U.S. Army. He authorized each of the three men to recruit his own four-man squad. When Karl Schmidt pressed for details about this "second objective," Von Leinsdorf said it had to remain classified until the night before the mission.

That night Von Leinsdorf asked Bernie Oster to join his squad, along with a middle-aged merchant seaman named Marius Schieff and a former bank clerk from Vienna named Gunther Preuss, both Category Two men. Von Leinsdorf told them nothing about what the new assignment involved, but it was clear to Bernie that his status within the brigade had changed for the worse. He no longer feared discovery for what he'd done in Berlin. The path Von Leinsdorf was leading him down now felt far more dangerous.

A week before the launch, Otto Skorzeny attended a final briefing with the Army General Staff at the Reich Chancellery in Berlin. Skorzeny walked through his brigade's role in the invasion, and they agreed on procedures to protect his commandos from German attack. His disguised American tanks would bear two yellow triangles within the unit insignia stenciled onto their armor. If any regular Wehrmacht and commando units met on the battlefield during daylight, the men of Operation *Greif* were to remove their American helmets and hold them over their heads. At night, when encountering regulation German forces, they were to use pistol-fired flares, known as Verey lights, to reveal their identities.

Skorzeny was told that weather forecasts for their target day appeared favorable, calling for heavy cloud cover that neutralized Allied air superiority. All signals were go.

The counteroffensive into Belgium and Luxembourg known as Operation Autumn Mist would begin at dawn on December 16.

4

Grafenwöhr
DECEMBER 10, 1944

hortly after dark on December 10, the men of Operation *Greif* left their camp at Grafenwöhr and loaded onto a special transport train. Bernie saw that the cars had been camouflaged to resemble a shipment of Christmas trees being delivered to troops along the Western Front. Their vehicles, freshly painted and accessorized as American, were loaded on covered flatbeds at the rear of the train. Outfitted in their GI uniforms, Skorzeny's men were not allowed to leave the crowded boxcars during the two-day journey. A Gestapo detachment came on board to protect the train and deflect questions from outsiders about its secret manifest. Bernie knew the heavily armed Gestapo was also there to prevent any of the brigade from deserting.

The 150th Panzer Brigade detrained just before midnight on December 12 near an infantry training grounds at Wahn, southwest of Cologne, where they quartered for the night. To avoid contact with regular Wehrmacht units, they remained confined to the buildings throughout the following day. That night, under blackout conditions, the brigade convoyed in their own vehicles to the town of Münstereifel, twenty miles closer to the Belgian border. Stielau's commando group continued ten miles farther west, near the town of Stadtkyll. During that trip, camouflage netting slipped from a half-track in front of Bernie's transport, revealing its white five-pointed Allied star. A Wehrmacht patrol tried to intercept what appeared to be a column of American vehicles. They were taken into custody by the Gestapo escort and weren't seen again.

The commandos spent the rest of the night around a remote forester's cottage, organizing into their patrol units and receiving fuel, ammunition, and last-minute supplies. As dawn approached, Bernie could make out the vast bunkers and ramparts of the German Western Wall. Since their arrival at Wahn, he had caught glimpses around the border of a massive Wehrmacht buildup that dwarfed their brigade.

At six A.M., Otto Skorzeny arrived and the company assembled outside the cottage. The only soldier present in German uniform, Skorzeny ordered them to circle around him, informally, in the American manner. He told them their appearance and manners reflected a complete and convincing transformation: They were GIs now. Shivering in the frigid predawn air, Bernie learned for the first time the full scope of Operation Autumn Mist, and their own primary objective. Not as bad as he'd feared, but he knew Von Leinsdorf had something far worse in store. Skorzeny tried to rally them with stories of the German Army's long history of successes in the Ardennes, and how thinly it was now held by the Allies. He told them to be prudent about their use of gasoline, to scrounge any they could while in the field. They were to avoid at all costs any hostile engagement with the enemy.

"Every patrol must remain in radio contact with our corps command," said Skorzeny. "Our mission depends on the intelligence you provide. Make note of everything you see and hear. Trust your training. Take no unnecessary risks."

One man asked the question that was on all of their minds: "Will they treat us as spies if we're captured?"

"I have consulted with experts on international law. If you are captured, we believe that if you wear your German uniform underneath, or change into it beforehand, you will be granted the same protection as any other prisoner of war."

Before they had time to question that, Skorzeny wished them luck and shook every man's hand. Following behind him, his adjutant handed every commando a silver Zippo lighter. Bernie noticed it gave off a faint smell of bitter almonds. They were told each lighter contained a glass vial of hydrocyanic acid, and that the poison could be used offensively to subdue an opponent. The implication that they were expected to use it on themselves in the event of capture was inescapable.

Skorzeny called Captain Stielau and Lieutenant Von Leinsdorf into the cottage. He asked to hear a summary of Von Leinsdorf's plan for executing the Second Objective, listened quietly, made suggestions but appeared satisfied with his overall strategy. He asked Von Leinsdorf to call in the squad leaders he had selected. Skorzeny chatted briefly with each man, addressing them only by their adopted American names.

Skorzeny's adjutant presented each squad leader with a packet of specially forged documents, including U.S. Army ID cards, high-level American security passes, letters of transit, and detailed maps of various cities in France. They were also given a cache of customized weapons, explosives, and ammunition prepared at Skorzeny's request by the Technical Criminal Institute of Berlin. These included piano wire garrotes, concealed knives, and a new technology: a metallic silencer that attached to the end of their American officer's handgun. He then drew their attention to a map of the Belgian border his adjutant laid out on the table.

"Your squads will be the first to cross, through these gaps in their line," said Skorzeny, showing points of infiltration. "Begin your reconnaissance assignments. Your reports will be vital to us during the early hours. Avoid capture at any cost."

Then Skorzeny for the first time detailed their second objective. When he finished, no one broke the silence. From their shocked reaction Skorzeny knew that Von Leinsdorf had followed orders and refused to discuss the mission with them.

"Sir, at what point are we expected to attempt this?" asked Karl Schmidt.

"I will explain when the colonel leaves," said Von Leinsdorf to silence him.

"I would prefer to hear the colonel's views firsthand," said a defiant Schmidt.

"Your orders are perfectly clear," said Skorzeny. "For the next two days, reconnaissance and support for the invasion. At midnight on the seventeenth, regardless of whether or not our brigade has reached its first objective, proceed with the second."

"What should we tell the men in our squads?" asked Schmidt.

"Tell them nothing," said Skorzeny. "Until you have to."

"That was my advice as well," said Von Leinsdorf, making clear his irritation.

"What kind of support will we have from the rest of our brigade?" asked Schmidt.

"That depends on the progress of the entire offensive," said Skorzeny. He gestured to his adjutant to pack up, eager to leave.

"No more questions," said Von Leinsdorf.

"But should we expect them, sir?" asked Schmidt, ignoring Von Leinsdorf. "Is anyone else involved or are we acting alone?"

"If all goes according to plan," said Skorzeny, "help will be waiting when you near your target."

"How much help?" asked Schmidt.

"A fifth squad," said Von Leinsdorf.

"There, you see?" said Skorzeny with a smile. "Support will be there when you need it the most. On the other hand, as I always tell my men, expect nothing and you won't be disappointed."

Skorzeny wished them luck and walked out toward his waiting transport, followed by his adjutant. Their vehicle was parked on the edge of a clearing, near where the commandos' twenty American jeeps were being serviced and fueled. The paint on the jeeps' unit insignia was still drying.

"Keep no records of that meeting," said Skorzeny firmly to his adjutant. "As far as Autumn Mist is concerned, it never occurred."

Skorzeny climbed into the transport where his bodyguards waited and drove off to the north.

In the cottage, standing over the various maps of Belgium and France on the table, Von Leinsdorf walked them one last time through their first two days. "On the seventeenth I'll contact each of you by radio. If you don't hear from me, assume we are going ahead and work your way south. We'll stage the operation from here, on the evening of the nineteenth."

He pointed to a prominent old cathedral city, an hour and a half northeast of Paris.

"We need a place to meet," said Von Leinsdorf. "Any suggestions?"

"I was stationed there for a couple weeks," said William Sharper, the American.

"In which army?" asked Schmidt.

"Fuck you, Schmidt. There's an old movie house here, on an old square on the east bank of the canal," said Sharper, pointing to the area. "The Wehrmacht showed films during the Occupation. GIs are using it now."

"Mark it on your maps. Meet at this cinema between nine P.M. and midnight on the nineteenth," said Von Leinsdorf. "Wait no longer than that. Even if you're the only squad, move forward on your own initiative."

Von Leinsdorf shook each man's hand before they all exited the cottage and went their separate ways. He placed a hand on Schmidt's shoulder, holding him back.

"I realize that in our former positions we hold equal rank," said Von Leinsdorf, once they were alone. "And that you've held yours slightly longer than I have mine."

"That's correct."

"Be that as it may, Colonel Skorzeny has put me in charge of this mission. I take that responsibility seriously. If you ever question my authority again, I'll kill you."

Von Leinsdorf stared at Schmidt until he recognized the terror he had over the years grown so accustomed to seeing in weaker men's eyes, then walked outside.

The men of his squad, Bernie Oster, Marius Schieff, and Gunther Preuss, were waiting for him near their own jeep, loading in supplies.

"Good news, gentlemen," said Von Leinsdorf. "We're going across tonight."

Northeast Belgium
DECEMBER 14, 1944, 8:40 P.M.

Shivering under a sky thick with stars, three GIs manning the Frontier Control Station lit a fire in a discarded oil drum, in violation of blackout orders. Their tin-roofed hut offered no relief from the arctic air riding in behind a storm front. Winter hadn't officially arrived, but the season's first storm had dropped six inches of snow the night before. Although they were less than four miles from the German border, and occasionally heard engines gunning in that direction, only sporadic skirmishing had broken the calm during the weeks they'd been stationed there. So each night after dark they lit a fire behind their hut and took turns warming their hands, while the others sat inside, playing cards by the light of a Coleman lantern.

They were green recruits—a sergeant and two privates—drafted in the last six months and hastily trained. Their 99th Infantry Division had deployed in the Ardennes only a month before, thrown in beside new units too raw for combat and veterans too beaten down for more. The men's regiment, the 394th, had dug in along a twenty-mile perimeter that paralleled the Belgian-German border, a craggy, forested gap between two mountainous ridges. Stationed at thousand-yard intervals, the soldiers of the 394th spent their days and nights in bone-chilling foxholes, staring at a silent forest, protected from the elements only by rough ceilings of pine branches.

By comparison these three men of Rifle Company F, Squad "D," had drawn a plush assignment, guarding this checkpoint on an old logging road a mile north of the village of Elsenborn. Ten miles to the rear their base camp offered hot meals and showers, Hollywood movies, and touring swing bands that played weekly USO dances swarming with grateful Belgian girls. A conviction had spread through their barracks that the war was all but over. A month of frigid nights hunkered down in the Losheim Gap seemed an easy way to work off your part in the war effort. They might even sail home without firing a shot in anger.

"Sarge," said Private Anderson, from behind the blockhouse.

"What is it?" answered Mallory from inside.

"Something coming."

Headlights washed over the blockhouse window. Sergeant Vincent Mallory of South Boston grabbed his Garand M1 carbine, and Private Jack Ellis followed him out the blanket hanging over the open doorway. Private First Class Chick Anderson stationed himself at the gate beside the striped wooden arm that crossed the dirt road.

A single vehicle drove toward them from the direction of Kalterherberg, a crossroads four miles north, near the German border. Mallory recognized the round headlights and straining gearbox; a Willys Jeep, pack mule of the American Army. He stepped forward and waved the lantern, flagging them down. Ellis readied his rifle and flanked his sergeant in the road ten yards ahead of the gate.

The jeep slowed as it approached. Top down, windscreen flipped up. A GI in the front passenger's seat stood up and frantically waved his arms at Mallory.

"What the fuck—where the hell is this?"

When the jeep stopped a short distance away, Mallory could see that the GI wore a private's stripe. Skinny, agitated, barely out of his teens, black curly hair peeking out from a helmet shoved back on his head. The driver beside him kept his head down, eyes straight ahead on the road.

"Where you coming from?" asked Mallory.

"Jesus, I got no idea—we been driving around out here for I don't know how fuckin' long—how long, Lieutenant?"

He turned to an officer behind him in the backseat. Mallory swung the lantern around.

Four men in the jeep.

The lieutenant with the bar on his collar leaned forward: compact, blond, good-looking, mid-twenties, a confident big-man-on-campus smile.

"And he's supposed to be our fucking navigator," said the lieutenant. "Show him our pass, dummy."

"All fucking night like this," said the jittery private, handing over their trip ticket to Mallory, then turning to Ellis. "You got any smokes, buddy?"

Mallory read the trip ticket, which looked in order, then scanned the unit markings stenciled on the jeep's hood. "You fellas are a long way from Twelfth Army, sir."

"Tell me about it," said the lieutenant, a slight Southern twang in his voice. "We left HQ in Luxembourg eight hours ago. Supposed to hook up with the 106 in Vielsalm at eighteen hundred."

Mallory handed back the pass as he watched the fourth man, in the back beside the lieutenant, unfold a large map.

"You overshot it, sir," said Mallory. "Vielsalm's twenty miles southwest of here."

"That's fuckin' beautiful news," said the private, as Ellis handed him a cigarette. "I tried to tell you, sir, we should've turned left about two hours ago— Hey, thanks, man; you got a match?"

"You don't want to light that here, son," said Mallory.

"Right, shit, what am I thinking?" The private stuck the cigarette behind his ear; Mallory noticed his hands were shaking.

"Probably don't want to be running your headlights either," said Mallory. "Didn't they give you blackouts?"

"Is that why you stopped us, Sergeant?" asked the lieutenant.

"This is a roadblock, sir. We've got orders to stop everybody."

"Well, I'm glad you did. Maybe you can give Private Knucklehead here some pointers on reading a map."

"If I ever get it back— Would you please let me see that?" the private pleaded with the fourth man, who had just flicked on a flashlight, buried his face in the map, and showed no interest in handing it over.

"You're coming from the direction of the Kraut line," said Mallory.

"No shit," said the private. "Why do you think we turned around? You could smell the fuckin' Wiener schnitzel."

"Kind of unusual to see four men in a jeep," said Mallory.

"We're escorting Captain Conway here," said the lieutenant, nodding to the man beside him. "New intelligence officer for the 106."

"Captain." Mallory saluted the man, who didn't respond, still shining his flashlight over the map, looking for something.

"Aren't you supposed to ask me for the password, Sergeant?" asked the blond lieutenant.

"That's right. If we're not sure of the men."

"So what do you do if somebody doesn't know it? I mean, Christ, I don't know it myself."

"Don't worry about it. Password's 'Betty Grable.' They'll ask you for it at the next roadblock outside the village."

"I want to ask these guys a *question*—would you please give me that back, sir?" said the private to the intelligence officer.

Thinking the kid seemed a little out of line talking like that to an officer, Mallory signaled Anderson to raise the gate. In his peripheral vision Mallory noticed that the jeep's driver had no unit insignia on the shoulder of his field jacket.

"So what unit you guys with anyway?" Mallory asked the driver. "Hey, buddy?"

The driver turned toward him but didn't answer. The man looked older than he expected, lined and weathered, forty if he was a day. He smiled and nodded at Mallory, but it seemed like a rehearsed response, furtive and uncomprehending.

This guy's not right, whispered some primal instinct.

Mallory felt a surge of adrenaline kick in. His index finger reconnected with the trigger of his M1.

"We're Field HQ, Radio Company," said the blond lieutenant,

smiling again. "Could I trouble you to give us a hand reading our map?"

The driver gave an awkward wave and turned away from Mallory, training his eyes straight ahead again. In one smooth move the lieutenant stood up in the back and snatched the map from the private's hand just as he wrested it away from the intelligence officer.

"No problem, sir. You know, our radio's on the fritz," said Mallory, moving no closer to the jeep. "Maybe one of you could take a look at it?"

"We're already running pretty late—"

"Sure it'll just take a second, sir. Get it working, we could hail the 106 for you, let 'em know where you're at."

Neither man moved as the lieutenant looked down at Mallory for a long moment; then he smiled again. "Private Tenella, grab your kit."

The lieutenant slipped over the edge of the jeep, landed like a cat, and stopped to fold the large map down to a manageable size. Mallory tried to catch Ellis's eye, but he was helping the private fish out some tools from the back of the jeep.

"Betty Grable," said the lieutenant, shaking his head, as he passed Mallory, headed for the blockhouse. "What'll they think of next?"

"I don't know. Can you believe that bombshell married Mickey Rooney?" asked Mallory.

"I heard it, but I don't believe it," said the lieutenant.

Mallory ran a last visual check on the driver, who was rummaging for something on the front seat. His finger firmly on the trigger, Mallory raised the muzzle toward the lieutenant's back as he turned to follow him, when the man pivoted in his direction.

All Mallory saw was the map, taut in front of his face, moving straight at him. A muffled pop, and the lines and shades of Belgium burst inward. The first bullet caught Mallory under the right ear, shattering his jaw, glancing off the bone, and tearing through the other side of his mouth. Choking on blood and shattered teeth, he dropped his rifle and was reaching for his throat when Von Leinsdorf fired again, catching him in the right shoulder, spinning him around.

The intelligence officer, Gunther Preuss, stood up and hit Private Ellis in the face with the flashlight. Bernie dropped his toolbox and backed away from the jeep.

The driver vaulted out of the jeep and ran toward Anderson at the gate.

Preuss jumped down after Ellis from the jeep, a knife in his hand. They landed with a heavy thud, Ellis underneath giving a groan as Preuss's full weight compressed him.

Anderson turned at the gate to see the driver with a machine pistol in his hand, ten feet away, closing fast. Anderson raised his rifle. They fired simultaneously: Anderson squeezed off two shots; the driver emptied his magazine.

Von Leinsdorf fired once more at Mallory as he toppled over, then turned casually away as if bored with a conversation. Preuss had his knife buried in Ellis's ribs, bearing down on him, using his left hand to push the barrel of Ellis's rifle away from his chest. Grunting with effort, Ellis stubbornly held the gun with both hands, trying to inch a finger toward the trigger. Eyes wild, Preuss looked up at Bernie, standing a few feet away.

"*Das Gewehr!*" he said. "*Halte das Gewehr!*"

Bernie didn't move. Von Leinsdorf marched over, pointed the pistol, with a long steel cylinder attached to the muzzle, at Ellis's head, and fired twice. Once the American went slack, Preuss slapped the rifle away and rolled off the body, breathing heavily.

Bernie felt shock stun his system. He'd never seen anyone die before. He couldn't think; he couldn't move.

"What the fuck?" whispered Bernie. "What the fuck?"

"Get hold of yourself," said Von Leinsdorf; then he turned to Preuss and pointed. "Drag the bodies into those woods."

Von Leinsdorf jogged back toward the gate. Private Anderson lay dead, sprawled facedown in the dirt, bleeding from half a dozen wounds. The driver—merchant seaman Marius Schieff, from Rostock—had propped himself up against the base of the gate, pistol still in hand, looking down at a dark stain spreading across his field jacket.

Von Leinsdorf knelt down beside him and spoke to him gently. "Marius? How bad is it? Can you walk back to the line?"

Schieff smiled grimly. "Walk five miles?"

"We can't turn back, my friend," said Von Leinsdorf.

"*Ich weiss,*" said Schieff. "Go on, leave me here, maybe someone finds me—"

Von Leinsdorf stood up and without hesitating fired twice into Schieff's head at close range. He unscrewed the silencer as he glanced into the guardhouse, then holstered the weapon and walked back to the jeep. Gunther Preuss was already on his feet, grunting with effort as he dragged Ellis's body toward the nearby woods. Bernie hurried toward Von Leinsdorf.

"Jesus Christ, what the fuck did you do?"

"I told you to be quiet. Collect their tags, get the bodies off the road—"

"You know the orders, god damn it, we're not supposed to engage, somebody must've heard those shots—"

Von Leinsdorf walked past him to Mallory's body, flicked open his lighter, and fired up a Lucky Strike as he looked at the dead American. "Who's married to Betty Grable?"

"Betty Grable, the movie star? Fuck if I know—"

"Mickey Rooney?"

"No, it's not him—wait a minute, let me think a second—it's that bandleader, Harry James—what difference does it make?"

"I gave him the wrong answer. He was about to do something heroic." Von Leinsdorf picked up Mallory's legs and glared at Bernie. "Are you just going to stand there, Brooklyn?"

Bernie grabbed Mallory's arms, and they carried him toward the woods. "But how did you know that? How could you possibly know that?"

"There's no radio in the shed," said Von Leinsdorf.

Gunther Preuss, the overweight former bank clerk from Vienna, stomped past them on his way from the woods back toward the guard gate.

"*Was sollen wir mit Schieff tun?*" asked Preuss.

"Take his papers, empty his pockets, put him with the others," said Von Leinsdorf.

"Kann ich seine Stiefel haben?"

"For Christ's sake, Preuss, the body's not even cold—"

"Mine . . . they fit no good," said Preuss elaborately.

"That the best you can do?" asked Bernie. "You sound like fucking Frankenstein."

"Then take one of the American's boots," said Von Leinsdorf.

"Danke, Untersturmführer—"

"And speak English or keep your mouth shut, you fat, fucking, useless piece of shit."

Preuss dropped his shoulders and broke into a harried trot. Von Leinsdorf looked over at Bernie, with a sly smile. "What do you think? My slang is improving, yes?"

Bernie glared at him. "You said 'kit.'"

"What about it?"

"It's not a 'kit,' it's a toolbox."

"You're right," said Von Leinsdorf. "Kit's British. Fuck all."

"And you're on Preuss's case? You're fuckin' nuts, you know that?"

Von Leinsdorf laughed, blew smoke, enjoying himself. Twenty yards into the woods, they dropped Mallory's body beside Ellis under a thick stand of evergreens. A gust of wind stirred the branches overhead, dropping clots of wet snow on them.

"Why'd you have to kill Schieff?" asked Bernie.

"He was gut shot, he wouldn't have lasted an hour—"

"We could've treated him, taken him for help—"

"He knew the risks. Besides, you heard what our friendly sergeant said back there," said Von Leinsdorf, tapping Mallory's boot with his. "Americans ride three men to a jeep. You'd think our fearless leaders might have picked up that little detail, eh, Brooklyn?"

Von Leinsdorf leaned down, opened their shirts, and slipped the dog tags off Mallory and Ellis.

"Cover the bodies," he said, tossing the tags to Bernie. "Take their ID, jackets, weapons, anything else we can use. You're driving."

Bernie caught the tags and dropped them into his pocket. His nightmare had come to life; American blood on his hands. Four men dead in less than five minutes. And Von Leinsdorf seemed to like it. He was practically humming as he walked away. But how long now before they became the hunted?

He saw Mallory's foot twitch once as he rifled through the man's field jacket. He leaned down and realized Mallory was still breathing.

Once Von Leinsdorf was out of sight, Bernie took a sulfa packet, bandages, and an ampule of morphine from his pocket, and knelt down beside the gravely wounded sergeant.

6

Southwest of Liège, Belgium
DECEMBER 14, 9:00 P.M.

arl Grannit leaned out the window of the engine car and looked back along the length of the U.S. Army transport train, eleven freight cars trailing behind them as they rounded a broad turn. He gazed out at the smooth moonlight glancing off the Meuse River as it flashed through the trees, then at his watch under the bare bulb of the cab. He shoveled more coal into the firebox while he waited for his engineer to finish a call on the radio, talking to dispatch.

"How close are we?" asked Grannit, over the roar of the engine, when the call ended.

"Four miles," said the engineer. "Next station's Clermont."

"What about our backup?"

"Says they're all in place. Ready to go."

"Famous last words," said Grannit.

"Think they're gonna make a move, Earl?"

"I'll take a look."

Grannit swung outside on the handrail, found his footing, and inched back along the ledge rimming the coal car. He stepped across to the first freight car, climbed the ladder to the roof, set himself, and looked ahead down the tracks. He could already make out the Clermont station lights piercing the night in the distance. Then he spotted a crossing in the foreground, where two cars were flashing their headlights toward the oncoming train. The engine had already started to slow; he heard the whining steel grind of the brakes.

At least half a mile short of the station.

"Shit. Shit, shit."

By the time Grannit worked his way back to the engine car, the train had nearly come to a complete stop.

"That was the signal, wasn't it?" asked the engineer, looking wide-eyed. "I was supposed to stop, right?"

"Yeah, Ole," said Grannit. "You were supposed to stop."

Four men were moving toward them alongside the tracks from the crossroads, flashlight beams zigzagging. Grannit grabbed a lantern and jumped down to meet them.

"Hey, how's it going there?" said the man leading the way.

The others behind him hung back. Two wore trench coats with raised collars, peaked hats silhouetted black against the sky. Officers.

The advance man stepped into the light of Grannit's lantern. He was short, energetic, pounding a wad of gum, the flat rasp of Jersey or Philly in his voice. Grannit eyed his insignia; corporal, battalion quartermaster's staff.

"Eddie Bennings, Company C," he said, offering a glad hand. "You new to the unit?"

"Just last week. Me and Ole," said Grannit.

"Welcome to the 724. Let me tell you something, pal: You landed in clover. You been to our billet in Paris yet?" Grannit shook his head. "You'll see. They don't call us the 'million-dollar outfit' for nothing, know what I'm saying?"

"We heard some talk."

"So they put you on the milk run up from Matelot, huh?" Bennings waved to the officers, letting them know he had the situation under control. They headed back to the cars.

"Who's the brass?" asked Grannit.

"Interested parties. We look out for each other in the 724. What the Frogs call 'es-pree de corpse.' I'll explain the drill—what's your name?"

"Earl Grannit. Like I said, that's Ole. Ole Carlson."

"Okay, Earl, there's a side rail coming up on your right about a hundred yards. We'll switch you over. Take the whole rig onto that side rail. Uncouple the stock you're carrying after car eight then head into the station."

"Just leave 'em?"

"Right. We'll take it from there."

"What if the depot asks questions, the end of our run?"

"That ain't gonna be a problem—"

"We come in three cars light they might—"

"I'm telling you, they won't have a problem," said Bennings. "You're covered, okay? This ain't our first clambake."

Earl Grannit toed the dirt for a second, thinking it over. "So what's our end, Eddie?"

"Listen to you, all business all of a sudden. This ain't gonna take long. We'll hook up on the platform after; you'll make out. Piece a cake. Easy as Betty Crocker."

"Everything after car eight."

"You got it, pally," said Bennings, patting him on the arm and shaking his hand again. He shoved a roll of twenties wrapped around a couple packs of Chesterfields into Grannit's shirt pocket and handed him a box of cigars. "That's just a taste. Wait'll you see the setup in Paris. The 724 takes care of its own, my friend. Our guy Jonesy'll ride in with you, make sure everything's square."

Bennings bounded away down the tracks after the officers. Grannit heard their cars starting up. The fourth man from the cross-road, Jonesy, a hulking, beady-eyed noncom, walked after Grannit toward the engine. Grannit swung back up into the cab ahead of him and stashed the contraband goods in the tender.

"You get all that?" asked Earl quietly.

"The PX cars," said Ole Carlson.

"You signal the station?"

"They're at least five minutes away."

Jonesy climbed up into the cab behind them. Grannit turned to him.

"Ole," said Grannit. "Jonesy."

Carlson nodded, friendly, ready to shake hands. Jonesy stuck a toothpick in his mouth, and put a hand on his hip, showing the holstered, pearl-handled .45 on his belt. Making it clear he wasn't there to chitchat.

"Let's take her in," said Grannit.

Ole Carlson engaged the throttle and eased the train forward at five miles an hour. They passed Corporal Bennings, standing by the switch at the crossroads. He gave a jaunty little wave as they rolled past him onto the side rail. Grannit leaned out of the cab and checked the stock behind them, signaling Carlson to brake again once the last car cleared the main track.

"You want to let the station know we're delayed?" asked Grannit.

Carlson had picked up the transmitter, when two more GIs walked out of the shadows near the engine car, carrying Thompson machine guns. Jonesy grabbed the handset from Carlson and hung it back up.

"Let 'em worry," said Jonesy. "Let's get it done."

Grannit jumped down and headed back along the train. Jonesy followed him a few paces back. A dozen other uniforms stepped out of the woods around them, converging on the end of the train. Two five-ton cargo trucks pulled up alongside the last few cars, men rolling up their canvas backing, ready to load in.

Like vultures, thought Grannit. *Like they can smell it.*

The first eight cars carried artillery ordnance. They'd been told exactly where the commissary cars started. By the time Grannit reached the coupling, the crew had already pried open the locks and thrown back the sidings. They swarmed inside, foraging through the boxes and crates, looking for cigarettes, liquor, chocolate, soap, coffee. Designated for front-line battalions, this cargo, Grannit knew, would disappear by daybreak into the burgeoning black markets of Paris and Brussels. In the last few months thousands of Allied soldiers had deserted to join this gold-rush racket, siphoning off army supply trains, selling to the French, Belgians, even stranded Krauts with cash. Once the American Army marched into Paris, the situation spiraled out of control. Fortunes were being made. The high-end players were said to be living in style on the Left Bank, like Al Capone and Dutch Schultz. By December over 40 percent of the luxury goods landing at Normandy, the staples of corps morale, never made it to the front-line soldier.

From what Grannit saw in front of him, an entire U.S. railway battalion had been infected, swarming over this train like locusts, their
officers standing by to supervise. He'd witnessed enough human im-
perfection that few variations on the tune surprised him, but this put a
fist in his stomach.

Grannit pulled out a heavy coupling jack wedged into the freight
car's slats. As he inserted the jack into the joint to uncouple the cars,
the train's steam whistle blew: three short bursts, then three long,
three short.

Ole sending an SOS. If they were paying attention, their backup
at the station would double-time it down the tracks.

Grannit looked over at Jonesy. He had turned around, staring
back at the engine, trying to decide what that whistle signified,
whether he should worry or not.

Grannit covered the five steps between them and tomahawked
Jonesy in the back of his knee with the coupling jack. He buckled and
dropped to one knee. Grannit caught him with a second shot on the
crown of the right shoulder, paralyzing his gun arm before he could
reach his holster. Grannit shoved him and Jonesy hit the ground,
whimpering in pain, trying to roll off the damaged shoulder. Grannit
pulled Jonesy's Colt and knelt down on top of him, grabbing his neck,
driving a knee into the big man's kidney.

"Stay down, Jonesy," he said.

"Fuck, what'd you hit me for?"

"You're under arrest, you dumb shit. Put your hands in front of
you and your face in the dirt or I'll blow your head off."

Jonesy complied. Grannit slipped a homemade sap out of his
pocket—a black dress sock filled with twelve-gauge shot—and cracked
him behind the ear. Jonesy went limp. Grannit stood up and turned
toward the PX cars. The train whistle hadn't appeared to alarm the
scavengers, and none of them had seen him take Jonesy down in the
dark, but more than a few glanced his way. He spotted the two officers
he'd seen earlier with Eddie Bennings beside the cargo trucks, looking
a lot more concerned.

Grannit walked straight at them, holding the gun at his side. As
he got close, the two officers and Bennings headed for their car,

parked nearby. When the engine started, Grannit raised the .45 and shot out the left front tire. The concussion cut through the night. He reached the driver's side, smashed the window with the barrel of the Colt, reached in, and yanked the keys out of the ignition. The man behind the wheel, a captain, looked at him, red-faced and indignant, and made a feeble swipe at Grannit's hand.

"What the hell you think you're doing, soldier?"

Grannit grabbed the captain by the collar, pulled his head out the window, and shoved his neck against the edge of the roof, knocking off his hat. By now he had the whole unit's attention, soldiers coming toward him with weapons drawn, others scattering. Eddie Bennings scrambled out of the backseat, staring at Grannit like he'd seen a ghost.

"Easy, Earl, buddy—" said Eddie.

Grannit jammed the Colt in the captain's cheek and spoke right into his ear. "Name and rank."

"Captain John Stringer."

"Captain, tell your boys to drop everything and lie down where they're standing, right now."

"Who the fuck are you?"

"Military Police, CID." Stringer didn't respond, eyes wide. Grannit leaned in closer. "Criminal Investigation Division."

"What the fuck is that?"

"Bad news for Company C." Grannit spotted Bennings in the corner of his eye, edging away. "Get on the ground, Eddie—all you 'million dollar' sons of bitches!"

Grannit fired a shot in the air and two more at the nearest cargo truck, shredding a tire and blowing off the driver's side mirror. Eddie hit the ground, and most of the others around him followed suit. A few sprinted for the woods.

He heard MP whistles trill in the distance, and heavy footsteps, twenty men running toward them on cinders. Ole and their backup.

"Can't we work something out here?" asked Stringer.

"Sure," said Grannit. "How about twenty years?"

7

Elsenborn, Belgium
DECEMBER 14, 9:30 P.M.

Betty Grable," said Erich Von Leinsdorf.

The young MP manning the heavily fortified checkpoint just outside the village gave a cursory glance at the three men in the jeep.

"Can I see your trip ticket, sir?" he asked.

"Of course."

Von Leinsdorf tapped Bernie Oster on the shoulder. He handed over a flawless forgery of an American military road pass, detailing their itinerary from Luxembourg City to Vielsalm. A smudged thumbprint obscured the ink around the day, date, and authorizing stamp.

The MP held it under his flashlight, trying to make it out. "You're from Twelfth Army HQ?"

"That's right," said Bernie.

"I don't mean to be an asshole, but we're running an errand for old man Bradley," said Von Leinsdorf. "It's time sensitive."

"Go on through," said the MP, handing back the pass.

"Have a good night," said Von Leinsdorf.

Bernie dropped the jeep into gear and drove past a sandbag installation protecting an unmanned .50-caliber machine gun and an M-10 tank destroyer. The one-lane village crawled with rowdy

GIs, more than a few of them drunk. The snow had turned to slush, and Bernie slowed behind two men weaving down the middle of the road, dragging a freshly cut fir behind them toward a brightly lit tavern in the center of the town, soldiers crowding the door.

"Can we stop to eat?" asked Preuss.

"You can't honestly be that stupid, can you?" said Von Leinsdorf. "Put some distance between us and that checkpoint."

Bernie slammed on the brakes as another GI wandered right in front of the jeep. He carried an open wine bottle and banged on the hood as they jerked to a halt a few feet away.

"Hey, watch it!" the man said.

Bernie waved apologetically. The soldier staggered around the jeep and hung on the passenger side, leaning in to talk to Preuss.

"You hear the latest fuckin' morale booster?" the American asked, "Frankie Frisch, Mel Ott, buncha hotshot ballplayers and some tootsie from the movies, what's her name, that Kraut broad—"

"Marlene Dietrich," said Von Leinsdorf.

"That's the one. Driving all around, visiting wounded and shit—"

Bernie leaned across the front seat, trying to get the drunk to focus on him instead of Preuss. "Mel Ott, how about that? We gotta get a move on now, buddy—"

The drunk leaned in closer toward Preuss, who had a witless smile frozen on his face. Bernie caught a glimpse of Von Leinsdorf drawing his pistol and holding it against the back of Preuss's seat. Ready to shoot if he gave them away.

"But y'know what that means, don't you?" said the drunk. "Letting big shots so close to the line? Means the fuckin' Krauts are done. Kaput."

"Don't be so sure," said Bernie.

"Any luck the turkey shoot's over by Christmas and we're on a gut bucket home. Cheers, buddy."

The drunk offered his bottle to Preuss. Preuss stared at him blankly. Von Leinsdorf leaned forward and grabbed the bottle.

"To Christmas in Connecticut," he said, and took a hearty swig.

"Yes, sir, Lieutenant," said the drunk, trying to straighten as he realized he was talking to an officer. "Didn't see you there."

Von Leinsdorf handed back the bottle. The drunk saluted him, and nearly fell on his ass. Von Leinsdorf watched the drunk stagger away, then looked at the boisterous soldiers stacked outside the noisy tavern, most with open bottles in hand.

"There's your civilian American Army, Brooklyn," said Von Leinsdorf. "Stinking drunk, in uniform, within sight of the front. Bloody amateurs."

The two soldiers finally dragged the fir tree off the road, pausing to toast the three men in the jeep with their bottle.

"Merry Christmas, assholes!" they said.

"Bottoms up, fuckers," said Von Leinsdorf quietly.

"Up your bottoms!" Preuss said to them, half-standing in his seat.

Von Leinsdorf shoved Preuss back in his seat. "I ought to just shoot you right now."

Bernie looked over at Gunther Preuss, his face like putty, panting for breath, mopping the sweat off his forehead in twenty-degree weather. Von Leinsdorf gave Bernie an exasperated glance and Bernie knew they were thinking the same thing: *This shithead's going to get us killed.*

"Hey, you picked him," said Bernie.

"In camp, the model soldier. In the field: a nitwit." Von Leinsdorf cuffed the back of Preuss's head and slid down into his seat. "Get us the hell out of here."

Five miles down the road they crossed the Warche River and entered Butgenbach. For the first time since they'd crossed the Allied lines, their wheels hit two-lane pavement. This town, much larger than Elsenborn, was all buttoned up, not a soul on the streets. A heavy fog crept in, enshrouding the empty streets. A few dim lights glowed through it from the row of tidy businesses they passed.

"These signs are in German," said Bernie.

"This *is* Germany," said Von Leinsdorf. "Over eight hundred square miles. Don't you know your history?"

"It's not my neighborhood," said Bernie.

"This was never part of Belgium; they just gave it to them. Versailles, 1920. Reparations, that was the polite word. A proud moment for the West, putting the Hun in his place. They carved up the German empire like birthday cake. Here. The Saar to France, the Polish corridor, the Southern Tyrol. Crippled our economy and punished a race of innocent people for the crimes of a corrupt monarchy. The Allies' idea of fair play." He gauged Bernie's reaction. "Wasn't this in your American schoolbooks, Brooklyn?"

Bernie let that go. "They still speak German?"

"That's right. When we took it back in 1940, they lined the streets and cheered that they were part of the fatherland again."

"Yeah? What'd they say when the Americans took it back? Heil Roosevelt?"

Bernie glanced back in the mirror at Von Leinsdorf, who couldn't keep the superior smirk off his face.

"Irony. You're aware that's a well-known Jewish trait, Brooklyn."

Bernie didn't answer. Halfway through the town, they dead-ended into the International Highway that ran due west from the German border. Von Leinsdorf signaled Bernie to pull over, then stood in the backseat, surveying both ways down the empty road.

"The panzers will drive straight through here," he said. "Fifty miles from the border to the river and nothing in our way but a rabble of drunken fraternity boys. By God, the plan will work."

Not if I have anything to say about it, thought Bernie.

"So we keep going?" he asked.

"The next village," said Von Leinsdorf.

Three miles west they entered the town of Waimes. Von Leinsdorf signaled Bernie to slow down. He took out his officer's notebook and paged through it.

"What are we looking for?" asked Bernie.

"There's a curfew," said Von Leinsdorf. "We can't stay on this road too late."

"*Ich bin hungrig,*" said Preuss, the first words he'd uttered since Elsenborn.

"I didn't hear that," snapped Von Leinsdorf.

"I have hungry," said Preuss.

"I *am* hungry," said Bernie, correcting him.

"Yes. Me also," said Preuss.

"Speak German again," said Von Leinsdorf, "and I'll feed you your own leg."

Von Leinsdorf scanned the buildings as they continued through the encroaching fog. A lettered sign in the shape of an oversized pink pig loomed out of the mist on the right. Von Leinsdorf told Bernie to pull over beside the butcher's shop beneath it. Preuss looked up at the sign and his mood brightened.

"We eat now," he said.

Von Leinsdorf banged on the front door. Bernie peered through the front display window. A massive shape carrying a lantern appeared inside and moved behind the door.

"We close," said a woman's voice.

"Der Phoenix steigt. Der Pfeil fliegt," said Von Leinsdorf.

The Phoenix rises. The Arrow flies.

The woman shuffled to the window and held up the lantern to look at them. She stood over six feet tall, wrapped in a cheap housecoat. Bernie shrank back on instinct as she appeared in the light.

Her enormous head looked oblong, misshapen, and her skin was flushed with ragged scarlet patches—a peasant's face, absent a healthy glow of outdoor labor. Bright, small eyes peered out from beneath a thick ridge of simian bone. A fringe of lank, mousy brown hair hung down in greasy clumps. Her tongue darted out between thick sensual lips as she sized them up. With a sidestep she vanished again, and the door opened.

"Willkommen," she said.

"Park the jeep around back," said Von Leinsdorf to Bernie.

Von Leinsdorf and Preuss followed her into the shop. A smell of onions and fried meat wafted off her. With every step waves of cascading fat shimmied down her upper back. She led them through a storeroom behind the sales counter, into a small abattoir with a stained concrete floor. Two bare bulbs provided the only light. A butchered animal carcass hung from a steel hook suspended on a chain connected to a bolt in the ceiling. Judging by the shape, Von Leinsdorf thought it might be a dog. A sharp scent of blood and offal thickened the air. The woman turned sideways to wedge her girth behind the cutting block. She opened a hidden hatch in the wall, then slid out a small shelf revealing a crystal wireless shortwave radio.

"*Das ist zu Ihrer Verwendung,*" she said to Leinsdorf.

"Please, fräulein, may we speak English?" asked Von Leinsdorf, indicating Preuss. "My friend needs the practice."

"The *Amis* come here, but never find this radio," she said. "I speak with my contact every day. They tell me you come."

"Good; that's what they were supposed to do. The *Abwehr* was also supposed to leave a package for us here. Do you have it with you?"

"No package. No one comes."

"Did they contact you about it?"

"No. No *Abwehr* comes. The *Amis* take all the food, from all the village. They leave me nothing." She picked up a large meat cleaver from an array of cutting instruments on the chopping block, which was covered with a mass of some half-minced internal organ. "They don't tell me you dress like the *Amis*."

The cleaver posed both a question and a threat. Von Leinsdorf tried to keep her focused on him, and not Preuss.

"And you mustn't tell anyone either, fräulein," said Von Leinsdorf, turning on an authoritative charm. "It is fräulein, isn't it?"

The big woman blushed, the scarlet patches on her cheeks glowing like embers. "Frau. Frau Escher."

Bernie entered the house through the back after parking the jeep and came face to face with Frau Escher, clutching the meat cleaver.

"Whoa, what the fuck," said Bernie.

Von Leinsdorf signaled Bernie to stay calm. "What is your Christian name, my dear?"

"Lisolette," she said, smiling coquettishly.

"What a pretty name. And might I ask, where is Herr Escher?"

"German Army. Four years. I see him last time two years."

After a while looking at her, he probably ran all the way to the Russian Front, thought Bernie.

"Four years without your husband is a terrible sacrifice," said Von Leinsdorf. "We're proud of you, working for our cause, giving us information with your radio. Risking your life during this American occupation. You've done a great service for your country."

She blushed again. "So kind of you to say."

Bernie couldn't tell if she was crazy or just simple. Maybe it was both.

"Another favor, Frau Escher," said Von Leinsdorf. "We were told you could give us something to eat. And shelter for the night."

"I would be happy," she said; then she frowned and re-gripped the cleaver. "But why you dress like the *Amis*?"

"A top secret assignment," said Von Leinsdorf. Then whispering: "On orders from the Führer himself."

"No."

"I swear to you, it's true."

"*Mein Gott*. I go now. You eat."

Frau Escher laid down the cleaver, flashed a travesty of a schoolgirl smile at Von Leinsdorf, and waddled into the front room. Von Leinsdorf signaled the others to follow, while he turned to the radio. He fingered the tuning knobs; their slotted grooves were slippery with clotted animal fat.

Disgusted, Von Leinsdorf took out his handkerchief and wiped off the knobs. He dialed in the frequency for their corps command post, twelve miles east of the border. He spoke in prearranged code, broadcasting less than a minute, letting headquarters know they were safely across. He made it clear their other jeep squads should steer clear of the Elsenborn logging road, but made no mention of the shooting at the checkpoint. He also let them know the package they'd expected to find from the *Abwehr* in Waimes had not arrived. After a pause, the dispatcher told him to return to the butcher shop the next day and try again.

Report of their success encouraged Colonel Skorzeny to step up deployment of their remaining commando squads. Before dawn, nine more advance teams of Operation *Greif* would infiltrate the American line.

Then there would be only twenty-fours hours until it began.

8

Spa, Belgium
DECEMBER 15, 2:00 A.M.

Shortly after Earl Grannit and Ole Carlson arrested Captain John Stringer and his squadron of thieves near the Clermont station, two platoons of MPs raided the 724th's barracks at Liège and dropped a net over the rest of C Company. MPs herded the suspects into the ballroom of the Hotel Britannique. Set on top of a ridgeline to the north of the Losheim Gap, this marshy plateau around Spa had been uninhabitable until the Romans discovered natural thermal baths percolating up from under the barren sulfuric soil. Over the centuries, as the city of Spa grew to accommodate the well-heeled travelers who came to bask in those beneficial waters, the name became the generic term for all such pleasure-seeking temples. Since early October, Spa's ornate nineteenth-century resorts had all been commandeered by First Army.

When he arrived at the hotel, Grannit was pleased to see over ninety anxious GIs cooling their heels in the ballroom. The two officers, and three others who'd been hauled in from the barracks, including the battalion commander, had been confined to private rooms upstairs. Grannit and Carlson filled out their paperwork in the hotel's ornate lobby, smoked cigarettes, and ordered coffee and sandwiches from the kitchen, while they waited for their superiors and counterparts in Army Intelligence to arrive.

"What the heck is this, Spam?" asked Carlson, scrutinizing the contents of his sandwich.

"Pâté," said Grannit.

Carlson kept staring at it. "Sure looks like Spam."

"I'm pretty sure they use some of the same parts."

"Of what?"

"Of whatever goes into Spam. Pig, cow," said Grannit, taking another big bite.

Eyeing the meat spread suspiciously, Ole took an exploratory sniff.

"It's not going to bite back, Ole."

"Smells iffy," said Carlson.

"You eat Spam, don't you?"

"Sure. Spam's great. Breakfast, lunch, and dinner. Fourteen different ways."

"Trust me on this," said Grannit. "Whatever parts of those pigs or cows that's in Spam? What's in here is from higher up."

Ole put the sandwich back together, took a small, cautious bite, and rolled it around in his mouth for a while.

"You're right, Earl," said Carlson. "That is a whole lot tastier than Spam."

They'd only been partnered a few weeks. Carlson had been an insurance investigator and volunteer fireman back home in Sioux Falls. Grannit liked how that prepared him for both the quick, unpredictable action and the crushingly dull aftermath of police work. Ole had gone through training as an MP before being transferred to CID, where he specialized in forgery and document work, the area of insurance fraud that he'd trained in. Ole was religious, always went to chapel on Sundays, and said his prayers but never threw it at you. He liked Ole for his flat, halting Midwestern voice, too, his blond brush cut on a head like a shot put, and his straight-ahead nature.

"Man, I like this French coffee," said Carlson. "Got some hair on it. Makes you want to stand up and say hello."

"That's Belgian coffee," said Grannit.

Ole just nodded. He watched two uniformed MPs lead another

group of GI suspects through the lobby. "You gonna handle interrogating these boys?"

"Many as they'll let me," said Grannit.

"That the kind of thing you do back in New York, Earl?"

"That's right, Ole."

"Thieves and murderers and rapists—"

"We didn't turn anybody away."

"Man oh man oh man. Life in the big city." Ole pondered for a
moment. "Could I watch you interrogating these fellas?"

"That's not up to me," said Grannit.

"I figure I could pick up a lot from that. About detective work
and what have you."

"Nothing personal, okay? This ain't night school. Just keep your
eyes open and don't pass up an opportunity to shut the hell up. What
you do with it after is your business."

"Sure, okay," said Carlson. "I can tell you're mad, though.
Makes me mad, too, these railroad bums. Thinking about what they
did."

"Don't lose any sleep over it."

Grannit finished his sandwich, stretched out on the sofa, pulled
his hat down over his eyes, and folded his arms. Carlson had watched
him do this before, grabbing short bursts of shut-eye, and figured it
for an old detective's trick, catnapping when he got the chance. Ole
decided to give it a try and squirmed to get comfortable in the big
overstuffed chair. Grannit cocked open an eye and watched Ole decide whether or not he should park his muddy boots on a heavy
gilded table. Then he got up, spread out an edition of *Stars and
Stripes* on the table, sat back down, and eased one boot down and
then the other on the folded page.

Grannit pulled his hat back down. There was the occasional shit
about Ole that drove him nuts, too.

A young captain and lieutenant from Army Intelligence showed
up at five in the morning, throwing their weight around, while their
adjutants ran around for coffee and donuts. When they started
bitching about how hard they were going to have to work to keep

the whole stinking Railway Battalion story out of the *New York Times*, Grannit turned over a table in their laps.

"We just broke the biggest criminal case of the war trying to solve a front-line morale problem, so I don't give a fuck it's a public relations headache for some rear-echelon horse's ass. You got that?"

Grannit's superiors from CID showed up in time to hear that and let it drop that Lieutenant Grannit had fifteen years in NYPD robbery-homicide. The hotshots from Intelligence seemed eager to tidy up their paperwork and hit the road.

At daybreak, over breakfast, the CID prosecutors laid out what they hoped to hear from these suspects before their courts-martial. Grannit liked what he heard about due process in a military tribunal: They required less burden of proof during wartime, which meant no lawyering bullshit from defendants' counsel. But Supreme Command wanted this mess scooped up and thrown out with the trash, and no ink spilled in the press with the war headed into the final innings. Home-front spirits were riding high, and nobody wanted to spoil Mom and Pop's Sunday dinner dwelling on the sordid details about these greedy, thieving pricks.

"How we going to do that, Earl?" they asked.

"You need confessions," said Grannit.

"What we're hearing so far," said one of the senior MPs, "is that none of 'em wants to cooperate."

None of them had a solution. Grannit held back, reminding himself that CID was a brand-new unit, less than four months in the field, organized to handle major felony crimes committed by GIs against fellow soldiers or civilians. With such limited time to get on its feet, they'd barely had a chance to print manuals, let alone train their personnel. To keep peace at home when the war broke out, Uncle Sam handed every working American cop a draft exemption. Grannit had tried to enlist during the first weeks of the war, but NYPD brass said he was too valuable to let go. Twenty-seven months and one pricey midtown lawyer later, he had argued his way off the force and into the army without forfeiting his pension. The next day they shipped him to the new Criminal Investigation Division training base in Michigan.

His superiors had never worked a day in civilian law enforcement. They were career soldiers in the Military Police, straight as their standard-issue neckties. You wanted traffic control in a crowded staging area, a fight in a dockside bar suppressed, or chain of custody maintained on prisoners of war? That played to the MPs' strengths—logistics, discipline, and security; all beat-cop talents—but they were ill equipped for felony detective work. In less than a week the men trying to run CID realized Grannit knew more about organizing a criminal investigation force than they did. The railroad case had taken six weeks to crack, and Grannit had quarterbacked the effort. Now they were waiting for him to send in the next play.

"What you got here is a massive racketeering operation," said Grannit. "Organized crime, like we had on the Brooklyn docks."

"You work those cases?"

"A couple."

"How'd you break 'em?"

"Hook a small fish. Small fish gives up a bigger fish. Roll 'em over like that all the way up the line."

"HQ needs this to go away today," said the senior CID man.

"Then for starters," said Grannit, "let me talk to 'em."

Grannit strolled through the holding area in the ballroom, studying faces. He picked out six men, including Corporal Eddie Bennings. They were hustled upstairs to the fourth floor and tossed into a room. Grannit had some MPs empty out the furniture, turn off the heat, and open the windows to the balcony. He let the suspects stew for an hour in the freezing cold, with orders to keep silent. The first time the MPs outside heard one of them say a word, they marched in and took away their matches and cigarettes. Whenever one of them dozed off, the MPs kicked him awake.

Two hours later, Grannit walked into the hotel room, followed by the three biggest MPs in the unit, swinging their nightsticks. Grannit wore a brown civilian suit with no badge or insignia. He explained to the prisoners that during the next fifteen minutes they were each going to write and sign a confession detailing their involvement in the battalion's black-market activities. He set paper and pens down in the middle of the floor and lit a cigarette. The six men looked at him and one another, but no one moved toward the pens.

Grannit finished his cigarette, walked over to the toughest-looking guy in the group, slammed his head into the wall, and went to work on his kidneys. By the time he finished, the man was urinating on himself and four of the other five suspects had pens in their hands. Each was escorted to a separate, heated room down the hall, where they were told a hot meal and a cocktail of their choice would be served as soon as they finished their confessions.

Grannit stayed in the cold room with Eddie Bennings, the one man who hadn't picked up a pen.

"You're not going to write a statement?"

"Fuck you," said Bennings.

Grannit ordered the other MPs out of the room and lit another cigarette.

"I know you from someplace, Eddie?"

"Where the fuck would I know you from?"

"You ever been fingerprinted in a New York police station? Done any time? Eduardo DiBiaso, that's the name you were born with, isn't it?"

"Where'd you get that?"

"Right here on your paperwork, Eduardo. Why is that, you change it for the draft board to get the stink of garlic off you? Or were you dodging a warrant?"

Bennings narrowed his gaze, working hard to show how little he cared. Grannit had known this pissant had a rap sheet the moment he laid eyes on him, strictly small potatoes, a wannabe who'd clocked enough time around the mob to lose his moral compass.

"You got a wife and kids back home, Bennings?"

"I got a wife."

"That where you're sending the money? Home to the wife?" No response. "Which makes her an accessory after the fact. We could go after her, too. Send the NYPD to her door. What's her taste been so far, five thousand? Ten?"

"I got nothing to say till I talk to a lawyer."

"Lawyer? Where the fuck you think you are, Hoboken? There's no justice system here. There's no neighborhood capo back home taking care of the family 'cause you kept your mouth shut. Military courts don't work that way. This ain't some penny-ante beef, pinching rum off the back of a Seagram's truck. These are war crimes, pal. People go to jail for life or face a firing squad. We got you on ice. You don't play ball, you're never gonna see your wife again."

"Bullshit."

"And once word gets around how you guys ripped off our troops in the field? Life in the brig is gonna be some hard fucking time."

The first crack showed in Eddie's practiced tough-guy facade. "What about it?"

"We know you got a relationship with the officers running this show. You brought some experience from home; they trust you 'cause you got things done. You're a key man for them. You want to tell me anything different?"

Eddie didn't.

"Help us put those big shots in the pokey and the system's gonna treat you better. That's common sense. Your boys are soldiers, not gangsters, so nobody's coming back at you if you roll over, you might not even stand trial. A slap on the wrist, maybe. They transfer you into another unit with no jail time."

"What, so I can get killed on the front line? Thanks but no thanks."

"Okay, Eddie. So we'll go with choice number three."

Grannit stubbed out his cigarette, grabbed Eddie by the collar and wrist, and marched him through the balcony doors.

"What's that? What the fuck you doing?"

"I turn my back for a split second, you were so despondent you threw yourself over the rail. Tragic waste of life. No death payment, no gold star in the window, no folded flag for the missus—"

"Wait a second, wait a second—"

"You don't think I'm pissed off enough? I'd be doing a favor for everybody in your life you're going to fuck over if you live through this—"

Eddie grabbed hold of the wrought iron balcony with both hands for dear life as Grannit muscled him to the edge.

"Okay, okay, I'll write it, I'll write it, I'll cooperate—"

"You sure about that?" Grannit yanked hard on his arms.

"I'm sure, I'm sure, Jesus Christ!"

Grannit let him drop to the floor of the balcony, panting like a puppy, slick with sweat.

"Fifteen minutes," he said, and walked out of the room.

By six o'clock that night the urge to confess had spread through the 724th like old-time religion. Whenever Earl Grannit returned to the ballroom, he found more willing volunteers to take upstairs. He'd seen this before, panic spreading through a pack of crooks on some silent animal wavelength. By midafternoon, he no longer needed to speak to suspects personally and handed them off to teams of junior CID officers like Ole Carlson, who needed the experience. As confessions piled up on their desks, the Army Intelligence men in charge felt as if they'd witnessed Grannit turn water into wine.

The CID brass organized dinner for their investigators that night in the hotel's private dining room. Grannit made it clear he didn't want anybody making too big a deal, but there was no doubt about who they were celebrating. CID had cracked its biggest case of the war, and Earl Grannit made it happen.

During the main course, a radio message came into the communications center downstairs for CID's commanding officer. Three GIs from the 394th stationed at a checkpoint outside a small village called Elsenborn fifteen miles due east had gone AWOL overnight. Local MPs were on their way to investigate, so the radio operator didn't feel it was important enough to interrupt the dinner.

An hour later, the radio man burst into the room during coffee and dessert with a second dispatch: The missing men's bodies had been found in the woods a mile outside of town.

9

The Road to the Meuse, Belgium
DECEMBER 15, 7:00 A.M.

The three other commando teams working under Erich Von Leinsdorf crossed into Belgium before midnight and passed through American lines without incident. Gerhard Bremer's team spent the night with a family of German sympathizers in the town of St. Jacques. American deserter William Sharper's team, posing as a forward recon unit for Fifth Army, reached their safe house in Ligneuville. Karl Schmidt's team lost their way, fell in behind a convoy of American vehicles heading west, then peeled off after midnight and spent the remainder of the night hidden in a forest. All three teams were up and on the road, heading west, before first light.

Von Leinsdorf's squad spent the night on the floor in the parlor of Frau Escher's apartment over her butcher shop in Waimes. Bernie Oster drifted between sleep and consciousness, disturbed by a persistent vision of their fleshy hostess storming into the room with her meat cleaver while they slept. Every time a floorboard groaned, a blast of adrenaline went off in his gut like a firecracker. By five A.M. Bernie couldn't lie still any longer and went downstairs to piss.

The woman was already working at the bench in the shop's back room. He could see her distorted shadow splashed against the far wall and heard the rough rasp of a bone cutter. He stepped quietly outside into the frigid morning air, his feet crunching on a crust of muddy frost. Their jeep sat just around the corner. The International Highway stretched out in front of him. The impulse to bolt hit him so hard he couldn't catch his breath.

But which way should he run? Back toward the German line, into the teeth of the offensive that was about to be unleashed? Not as long as Erich Von Leinsdorf had access to a radio; they'd shoot him as a deserter, or take him for a GI and kill him on sight. Maybe if he lay low for a day and changed into civilian clothes, he could slip across once the attack began. But the odds of making his way home to Frankfurt without papers or travel passes were low. He tried to put the thought from his mind, but after months of Allied carpet bombing, for all he knew his parents were already dead.

No, he should head deeper behind the American line, try to hook up with one of their units, and tell them the Krauts were about to invade. Would they buy it? Wasn't that what they'd trained him for these last three months? To pass as an American? In his heart of hearts, in his mortal soul, he was still a kid from New York who wanted his old life back. But what if he broke down under questioning, and the truth came out?

Who was he kidding? Betting his life on the mercy of the U.S. Army with the Germans about to rain holy hell down on them? He'd be court-martialed and shot in no time flat. So how could he warn them without dying for it?

One other way occurred to him. They had stashed their regulation Wehrmacht gear in four jerricans strapped to the jeep. He could take off in the jeep, change into his German uniform, then walk west waving a white flag and surrender as a deserter who'd just come across the lines. Tell them everything he knew about the coming attack, and live out what was left of the war as an Allied prisoner. That was his best chance, but only until zero hour. As soon as bullets started flying, his bargaining chip lost its value. But did he know enough about the offensive beyond what his own brigade was doing? His knowledge about even that was sketchy; Von Leinsdorf had kept them in the dark.

His mind raced back and forth, stuck on a final question: Was it worth the risk of giving Erich Von Leinsdorf a reason to hunt him down?

"Did she feed you breakfast?"

He turned sharply. Von Leinsdorf stood six feet behind him.

Jesus, I didn't even hear him coming.

Bernie worked to keep the traitorous thoughts he'd been dancing with off his face. Von Leinsdorf took a piss, supremely casual, a cigarette on his lip.

"Fuck no," said Bernie. "Not after that dinner she fed us. Bet my left nut this fucking village is missing some cats."

Von Leinsdorf chuckled, and buttoned his pants back up. "Go tell Preuss we're leaving."

"She said the Americans took all her food? Jesus, how fat was she before the war started?"

"Get Preuss."

Bernie worried for a moment that the man had read his mind.

"What, you don't want to see her again either?"

"Fuck no," said Von Leinsdorf, and smiled slyly.

He found Preuss hunched over the table in the kitchen, greedily scarfing down a thin fried egg and another plate of sausages from Frau Escher's display case of mystery meats. The woman sat on a stool in the corner polishing Preuss's new GI boots.

"Well, ain't this a cozy picture of domestic bliss," Bernie said.

Preuss looked up at him, half-chewed food in his mouth, slack-jawed and clueless. Frau Escher offered Bernie a plate for himself, but his stomach turned at the thought of it. He pulled Preuss out the back door, still carrying his boots, to where Von Leinsdorf had backed up their jeep.

The woman waved from her doorway as they drove off. Preuss waved back. Bernie saw her wiping her eyes with a handkerchief.

"She's set her cap for you, Preuss," said Von Leinsdorf.

"Cap? What is this?" asked Preuss.

"She's in the market for a husband."

"You want to fill that position, Preuss?" asked Bernie.

"I like her cooking," said Preuss.

Bernie meowed like a cat.

"Here pussy, pussy, pussy," said Von Leinsdorf. "Here pussy, pussy, pussy."

"I don't appreciate," said Preuss, turning red. "I don't appreciate."

Bernie and Von Leinsdorf broke out laughing.

The highway filled with routine morning traffic as they traveled west. Allied security loosened, and the road took on the look and feel of an ordinary day; citizens going about their business, soldiers minding theirs. They passed a major crossroads outside Malmédy, then worked southwest through Stavelot to the bridges over the Ambleve River at Trois-Ponts. The Ambleve was the last geographic obstacle before the ground graded down toward the Meuse River valley. Bernie watched Von Leinsdorf make coded entries in his notebook, detailing each defensive position they passed. The deeper they drove, the more encouraged Von Leinsdorf became; the Allies had no idea what was about to hit them.

By late afternoon, as daylight faded, they drew within sight of the Meuse River and the bridge at Amay. They pulled off the road on a steep bluff above the river, into a stand of woods. Heavy clouds rolled in as they made camp, a new weather system lowering the ceiling and reducing visibility, exactly as forecast. Allied aircraft would be neutralized by those skies, attack planes and reconnaissance alike. Preuss broke out packets of American K rations they'd taken from the dead GIs. Bernie activated their field transmitter, adjusting the antennae until he secured a signal. Preuss came over to show him one of the K rations.

"Look here," said Preuss. "Can you believe this?"

"It's just a slice of cheese, Preuss."

"No, look, it have bacon in it," he said, pointing to the cheese, then taking a bite. "Real bacon. Here, try."

Bernie took a bite to humor him. The cheese was hard, dry, and bland as wax, but carried an insistent odor of rancid pork.

"That's okay, Preuss."

"An army which can do this," said Preuss, shaking his head in admiration. "Cheese *mit* bacon."

Von Leinsdorf climbed a nearby embankment, unfolded a map, and studied the bridge below through field glasses. Light traffic, half of it American military, flowed in both directions. Sandbags surrounded an antiaircraft gun emplacement and a single machine gun on the eastern shore, manned by what looked like a single platoon. He saw no forces at all on the western shore. Bernie joined him, while Preuss sat a short distance away with a pad and pen. Trained as the reconnaissance officer for their squad, he began sketching in details of the bridge on a hand-drawn map.

"That's why we're here?" asked Bernie. "That bridge?"

"Our first objective," said Von Leinsdorf. "We take and hold it, and two others between here and Namur, before the Americans can destroy or defend them."

"Just me, you, and lard-butt over there."

"The entire commando company. Tomorrow, after our recon. Bremer, Schmidt, and Sharper's teams are scouting the other two."

Bernie thought about it for a moment. "You said first objective."

"Did I?"

"Does that mean there's a second one?"

Von Leinsdorf didn't look at him. Bernie felt him hiding something, and tried again.

"All those crazy stories flying around camp. We went through all that training just to take a few bridges and sit on our hands?"

"What are you asking?"

"You know what I'm asking," said Bernie. "Are we supposed to do something else?"

Again Von Leinsdorf kept quiet.

"Doesn't take a genius to figure it out," said Bernie, trying to keep the alarm from his voice. "Skorzeny gave you another assignment. You picked the other squads."

"What if he did?" said Von Leinsdorf.

"Then come on, at least tell me what it is."

Von Leinsdorf bent over the radio to transmit a coded report of their progress.

"When our tanks cross this bridge," said Von Leinsdorf, "all that stands between them and the coast at Antwerp is seventy miles of open highway. Once they're past here, we move on to something else. And that's all I can say."

He stared at Bernie, hard, then turned back to the radio.

Okay, asshole, thought Bernie. *Keep your secret. But I'm going to find out what it is.*

East of Elsenborn
DECEMBER 16, 1:00 A.M.

"Their relief detail showed up as scheduled at fourteen hundred hours yesterday afternoon," said the MP, "but the squad's position couldn't be immediately ascertained."

"You mean they weren't here," said Grannit.

"That's correct, sir."

The MP walked Grannit from the jeep toward the cinder-block guardhouse. The young soldier—too eager to please—had been first on the scene with jurisdiction ever since he'd arrived a few hours ago. Once the bodies were discovered, a crowd had descended. Grannit could already see they'd made a hash of it, two dozen soldiers trampling the crime scene. What was left of the snow had melted into thick slurry and frozen again during the night. Grannit picked up a stick and ran it along the ground.

"What's your name, son?"

"Chester Brosh, sir."

"Chester, take a deep breath, blow your whistle, and get that giant cluster fuck over here behind this line I'm drawing," said Grannit.

"Right now, sir?"

"Yes, right now."

Chester blew his whistle. It took five minutes to clear traffic in front of the blockhouse. Grannit had the drivers line up all the vehicles in a semicircle and turn on their headlights. Once the blockhouse was lit up and secure, he walked around and studied the scene from different angles, knelt down to look at some tire tracks, pointed out areas he wanted Ole and the other MPs to comb over, then told Chester to lead him to the bodies.

Grannit used a flashlight to follow the ground toward the woods as they walked. Under a dense copse of fir trees, many of the branches still laden with snow, three bodies lay next to one another. They were stiff with cold and rigor mortis. Each had been stripped of his jacket and dog tags. One was missing his boots.

"Anybody ID these men?" asked Grannit.

"Guys from their squad say this is Private Anderson and that's Private Ellis," said Brosh, pointing to the man without boots. "They had a third man out here with them, Sergeant Mallory, but we can't find him."

"So who the hell is this guy?"

"They didn't know him, sir."

Grannit looked at the third man. Near forty. Weathered, wind-burned face and a working man's hands. He studied the man's right hand, then examined his wounds. A single shot, left torso, with a large exit wound through the back, probably a rifle round. Double-tap gunshot wound to the head, small-caliber, close-range, the same as Ellis. He had a small tattoo on his right shoulder, a nautical anchor and rope. Grannit looked into the man's mouth, then took out a plastic bag and secured it around the man's right hand.

Grannit lit a cigarette and settled back on his haunches. All three men had been killed out by the road; then, judging by the boot prints, they were dragged back here by three fellow GIs. As he examined the ground, he noticed another faint drag line in the dirt moving away from this spot deeper into the woods. He followed it with his flashlight. About fifty yards into the trees the beam flashed on another pair of combat boots. Grannit pulled his pistol and hurried toward them.

A fourth man had dragged himself away from the others. He had scooped out a shallow depression to keep himself warm, and covered himself with downed branches, which Grannit hurriedly tossed aside. The soldier still wore his field jacket and lay on his side, curled up, unconscious. Grannit felt for a pulse.

"This man's still alive," said Grannit.

A medic summoned to the scene covered him in blankets and pumped four units of blood into Sergeant Mallory as they drove him to a field hospital ten miles away in Malmédy.

At five in the morning Grannit completed his sweep of the checkpoint. The other soldiers hadn't been any help, but Ole Carlson collected eight shell casings from around the guard gate, six small-caliber and two copper-jacketed M1 rounds. Ten yards short of the gate, where Grannit found tire tracks in the mud, he turned up three more pistol rounds. Grannit also bagged a broken cigarette, a Lucky Strike, unsmoked. He pinpointed a number of bloodstains—one on the base of the road gate itself—and a few more footprints, all of them regulation GI combat boots.

Before they took the bodies away, Grannit asked the medic to have the hospital remove any bullets before they were turned over to a graves detail. He needed them for forensics, and if it wasn't too much to ask, he also wanted autopsies. The medic said he'd try, and told him to come by the field hospital later that morning when they'd have a clearer picture of Sergeant Mallory's condition. Grannit agreed. If Mallory made it, Grannit wanted to be there when he came around.

Ole Carlson brought him a cup of coffee from a supply wagon and they stood near the blockhouse, stamping their feet to stay warm.

"What do you think happened, Earl?" asked Carlson.

"They drive up in a Willys out of the north, down the logging road. Pull up short of the gate. The detail's playing cards inside; they step out to question them. Whatever the beef was, it starts here, next to the jeep. Mallory, Ellis, and the third man are tapped by the same shooter. Somebody else kills Anderson over by that gate. The third man's hit first by a second shooter, in the chest, with an M1. Then he was shot in the head afterward like the others. The third man's the only one of them who discharged his pistol."

Carlson stared at him with his mouth open. "Geez, you think he killed the other two?"

"No, Ole," said Grannit patiently. "He got shot the same as Ellis, right? In the head."

"Right."

"I think the third guy ran toward the gate and shot Anderson—he's got six small-caliber rounds in him—and Anderson shot him back with the M1. Won't know for sure till I see the bullets, if they don't fuck that up at the hospital, which is a big if."

"Okay," said Carlson. "So we got GIs shooting GIs. Maybe it's a robbery. Maybe the parties knew each other. Maybe the killers drove out here to settle some score, or a gambling debt—"

"Facts first, theories later." Grannit stepped forward, setting the scene. "Our third man came in on the jeep with three others. One of those men is the main shooter."

"They shoot 'em, drag the bodies, dump 'em in the woods, and just drive off?"

"That's right. With one of 'em wearing a new pair of boots," said Grannit. "Ask the MPs in Elsenborn if any jeeps came through there last night that fit the profile. See if any infantry dug in around here heard anything. The trail's already cold."

Carlson hurried off toward the other MPs. Soldiers carried the bodies by him on three stretchers, covered by ponchos. Grannit asked them to hold up. He uncovered the third man, looked at the tattoo on his arm again and the dental work in his mouth. Then he examined his boots. He wore them without leggings, against dress regulations, but not unheard of in the field. Reaching inside, he found a small photograph tucked in the calf of the man's right boot and held it up to his flashlight. A casual Kodachrome snapshot with scalloped edges, probably taken with a Brownie, of a woman in her mid-thirties standing on a dock near a waterline. An ordinary brunette in a swimsuit, overweight, her arms folded self-consciously across her middle, forcing a smile for the camera. Bright midday sun overhead, shining in the woman's eyes, causing her to squint.

The man's wife or girlfriend at some vacation spot, probably the last one they spent together. A row of buildings lined the shore to the right, a couple of street vendors visible in soft focus behind her. The developer's stamp on the back was slightly smudged, but it looked like "August 1944." Grannit kept looking at it. Something about the photograph felt wrong, although he couldn't put his finger on why.

Grannit shined the flashlight on the face of his watch: 5:30. Daylight wouldn't break for another hour. He caught a flicker of bright light out of the corner of his eye to the east, miles in the distance. As he looked up, more pinpricks of intense light blossomed, like an immense panel of flashbulbs going off. The thick cloud cover on the eastern horizon began to glow as if a full moon had just lit up the sky.

It occurred to him in that split second that the last few hours had passed silently, none of the distant small-arms fire you heard this close to the front. Not even a dog barking.

Grannit ran toward the ring of vehicles, calling for Carlson, looking for their jeep. He jumped in behind the wheel, shouting at Ole to get in—

Just then a roar like a hundred distant thunderstorms filled the night from the east, shattering the silence with a series of cascading booms that stepped toward them in intensity.

Then the barrage hit and obliterated time.

The first fourteen-inch shells whistled overhead and crashed through the highest trees. A shower of others landed and detonated across a thousand-yard range, shaking the earth in a continuous shudder. Grannit saw a string of explosions and flame rising to the east, closer to the border, lines of trees uprooting in eruptions of fire. High above, at a piercing frequency above the rumbling artillery, he heard the deadly whine of V1 missiles. On top of that, screaming engines of aircraft flying low, headed west, emitting a sonic roar unlike any planes he'd ever heard before. White blossoms, small solid clouds, hundreds of them, mushroomed in the gray clouds above. It took a moment for Grannit to register that he was looking at a sky full of parachutes.

Carlson jumped into the jeep as Grannit stepped on the gas. As they skidded onto the road, a shell landed where Grannit had been standing thirty seconds earlier and demolished the cinder-block guardhouse.

10

Stavelot, Belgium
DECEMBER 16, 6:30 A.M.

Erich Von Leinsdorf's squad had been on the road for three hours, working their way back from the Meuse, when they heard the artillery barrage begin in the east. Von Leinsdorf patted Bernie on the shoulder as he drove, and showed him the time: Operation Autumn Mist had begun exactly on schedule. With the offensive under way, their task on its first day was to disrupt the American reaction. Moving east, they had already reversed or removed half a dozen road signs at key intersections to confuse Allied troops who would soon be swarming toward the invading forces. They also severed three telephone and telegraph trunk lines between Spa, Liège, and the American Front.

Bernie huddled over the wheel, unable since hearing about it the night before to shake the idea of a "second objective" out of his head. They were trying to injure or kill more Americans, and it made him sick. The thought of what Von Leinsdorf would do to him if he tried to interfere paralyzed him.

The barrage from the east ended abruptly at 0630 hours. Bernie knew that was the signal for the three army groups to begin their advance into Belgium and Luxembourg. If all went according to plan, German paratroopers and assault squads would already be swarming through the Losheim Gap, ripping holes in the Allies' defenses, opening the way for the tanks.

A light appeared on the road ahead of them as they entered a clearing. Bernie slowed when he caught sight of it. The overcast sky had begun to turn gray with the approach of dawn, and he could make out what looked like a farm boy standing by the side of the road, swinging a lantern. The boy waved at them and stepped into their path.

"Keep your distance," said Von Leinsdorf.

Bernie stopped the jeep about fifty feet in front of the boy. He waved his hands again and walked toward them.

"American?" the boy shouted. "American?"

"Whoa, hold up there. What do you want, kid?" asked Bernie.

"American, yes?"

"That's right. What do you want?"

The boy glanced nervously to his left, toward a tangled, over-grown hedge to the right of the jeep. Something rustled in those branches. Von Leinsdorf grabbed his rifle and dropped down in the seat.

"Drive, drive!" he shouted.

Bernie stepped on the gas and ducked, just as a rifle barrel pointed at them out of the dense branches. He heard two loud booms. The jeep fishtailed in the mud then righted itself and skidded forward. The boy on the road pulled out a pistol and pointed it at the wind-screen, but the jeep's right front fender clipped him on the leg, spun him around, and knocked him to the ground before he could fire. Von Leinsdorf came up from the floor of the backseat firing an M1, emptying an entire clip at the brush behind them.

"Stop!"

Bernie slammed on the brakes. Von Leinsdorf jumped out of the jeep and ran toward the trees, slamming another clip into the rifle.

"Get the boy!" he shouted.

Bernie pulled his pistol and jumped down, crouching low around the jeep. The boy on the ground was writhing in pain, whimpering, trying to reach the pistol lying a few feet from him in the snow. Bernie hurried over and kicked the gun out of his reach. The boy glared up at him, pain and raw hatred contorting his face.

"*Amis*, fuck you!"

"Easy," said Bernie. "Take it easy, you little shit. You all right?"

The boy spat at him.

"*Ami*, I hate fucking *Amis*," he said. "Fuck you."

Von Leinsdorf came around the hedge dragging a second boy by the collar, carrying an old shotgun. He manhandled him to the ground next to the first boy. As he went down, the boy's coat came off in Von Leinsdorf's hand. Something he saw made him laugh.

"What's so funny?" asked Bernie.

Von Leinsdorf moved and Bernie saw that the boy wore a red armband with a Nazi swastika around his left arm. Bernie stripped the coat off the wounded boy on the ground; he was wearing a swastika as well.

"God damn," he said. "Fucking Hitler Youth."

"I told you this was more Germany than Belgium." Von Leinsdorf spoke to the boys in German. "*Meine kleine Hitlerjugend*. So tell me, you pick up a signal the invasion is about to begin and try to pick off some Americans with your father's bird gun, *nicht wahr*?"

The boys stared at him in shock. Von Leinsdorf broke down the ancient double-barreled shotgun and popped out the spent shells.

"You are German?" asked the second boy, in broken English.

"That's right. Not that we don't appreciate your enthusiasm," said Von Leinsdorf, "but you nearly shot my head off."

"Are you really soldiers?" the wounded boy asked.

"What are you, the village idiot?" asked Bernie.

"Where's your father?" asked Von Leinsdorf. "In the army?"

"He was killed. In Russia."

"He'd be proud to know his son is a patriot. Even if you don't know which side to shoot at."

They heard a rumble of heavy vehicles rolling up behind them along the same road. Headlights flashed through the woods. Von Leinsdorf yanked the wounded boy to his feet.

"Go home, get the hell out of here," he said. "Those are real Americans coming now."

"You better think twice before taking any more potshots if you want to live till dinner," said Bernie.

The second boy put an arm around his injured friend and helped him limp toward the trees.

"And don't forget your blunderbuss," said Von Leinsdorf, hurling the old gun after them. The boy picked it up and they helped each other stumble out of sight.

Bernie and Von Leinsdorf hurried back to the jeep and saw Gunther Preuss slumped forward in the backseat. He turned to look at them, a pinched, fearful hangdog stare. His left hand gripped his right shoulder, blood seeping between his fingers.

"Oh shit," said Bernie.

"It's nothing," said Preuss. "It's nothing, Erich, I swear."

"Let me see," said Von Leinsdorf.

He pried Preuss's hand away from the wound. The uniform was shredded across his unit patch, the flesh of his shoulder peppered with shot. Other pellets had sprayed him across the neck and the right side of the face. All three areas were bleeding copiously.

"God damn it," said Leinsdorf.

"Please, Erich," said Preuss, tears running down his face. "Don't kill me. Don't kill me."

Bernie could see Von Leinsdorf weighing the odds, and his hand moved toward his pistol.

"It's not that bad," said Bernie.

"Get out of the jeep," said Von Leinsdorf.

"I can patch him up," said Bernie. "It's not going to kill him, he won't slow us down—"

"Out of my way. Preuss, get down—"

Von Leinsdorf reached for Preuss. Bernie grabbed his hand.

"Don't do it."

"Let go of my hand, Brooklyn—"

Before they started to struggle, both men were caught in the convoy headlights; eight vehicles—jeeps, transport trucks, and a towed antitank gun—turned into the clearing behind them. Von Leinsdorf shook off Bernie's grip and stepped toward the oncoming vehicles waving his arms. Bernie could see a platoon of rifle infantry hunched in the trailing canvas-backed trucks.

The lead jeep pulled up alongside Von Leinsdorf. An American captain in the backseat stood up.

"What's the holdup?" asked the captain.

"Somebody fired on us when we drove in," said Von Leinsdorf. "One of my guys is hit."

"Let's take a look at him," the captain said, then turned and called to the rear. "Get a medic up here!" A man jumped out of one of the transports and jogged toward their jeep. "Was it Krauts?"

"We couldn't see. We returned fire, I think they moved off—"

"You a recon unit?"

"That's right, sir."

"Well, don't go after 'em, all hell's broke loose up ahead—"

"We heard shelling. What's going on?"

"Who the hell knows? We're getting reports they started coming at us in force soon as that artillery knocked off. Radio's saying there's Kraut paratroopers up along the ridgeline—"

"No shit—"

"We've got units strung out all along this road; everybody's ass is hanging out. They want us to hook in and form a line at Malmédy—"

The medic opened his haversack and stepped up on the jeep's sideboard to take a look at Preuss. Bernie hovered next to him.

"He can't even talk," said Bernie. "Think he's hit pretty bad."

Taking his cue from Bernie, Preuss rolled his head back, moaning as the medic ripped the arm of his jacket down and probed the wound. Preuss didn't respond to any of the medic's questions; Bernie answered in his place.

"We heard they might try a spoiling attack," said Von Leinsdorf.

"Hell, you hear those planes overhead, the V1s? They're throwing the works at us. It's no fucking spoiling attack—"

"He needs a field hospital," said the medic, sifting a packet of sulfa powder onto Preuss's shoulder.

"We were on our way to Vielsalm," said Von Leinsdorf.

"Screw that, I'm overriding it, you're coming with us," said the captain. "Two hundred ninety-first Combat Engineers. Got orders to drag every able body we can muster in there. Fall in behind me, Lieutenant. We're about five miles from Malmédy."

The medic jumped into the jeep beside Preuss, unrolling a bandage. Bernie looked for guidance at Von Leinsdorf, who nodded at him to climb in. Bernie steered their jeep into line behind the captain and they continued down the road.

"One hell of a morning, huh?" said the medic to Von Leinsdorf.

"You said it, pal."

Malmédy, Belgium
DECEMBER 16, 6:30 A.M.

Earl Grannit's jeep covered the mile back to Elsenborn at top speed, dodging through a moving wall of vehicles as the artillery barrage continued behind them. The village was in an uproar, hungover soldiers roused from sleep running in every direction. Frantic citizens clogged the roads, belongings in hand, evacuating to the west. Grannit pulled up next to the checkpoint at the edge of town, waved over one of the young MPs trying to control the traffic spilling in from the east, and flashed his CID credentials.

"Were you on duty here night before last, son?" asked Grannit.

"I guess I was, sir," said the MP.

"A jeep came through, sometime between nine and midnight, three men. Anything come to mind?"

"Coulda been ten like that, sir."

"I'm only looking for one. Think about it. Something stand out?"

Another shell burst, closer to the village, less than a hundred yards from where they were parked. The MP ducked down; Grannit didn't flinch. "Yeah, maybe. There was one came through from Bradley's headquarters, Twelfth Army. Seemed like they were a little off course."

"Who was in it?"

"Couple of officers. A lieutenant, I think, that's who I talked to. They had a private driving."

"Was their pass in order?"

"I think it was."

"Where were they headed?"

"Somewhere south of here."

"You get any names?"

"Sorry, Lieutenant, that's all I remember." Another shell exploded, even closer, and the MP ducked again. "Jesus, what the hell's happening?"

"There's a war going on," said Grannit.

He steered them past the checkpoint, getting bogged down in traffic and mud on the main road halfway through the village.

"I never been shelled before," said Carlson. "You been shelled before?"

"No. I'd say once is enough."

"Yeah, I don't need to go through that again."

"Next chance you get at a radio, call Twelfth Army," said Grannit, "see if they've got any patrols in this sector answers to that description."

Carlson wrote it down.

"Where we headed, Earl? We going after them?"

"Has our job changed in the last ten minutes?"

"I guess not."

"These are wrong guys, Ole."

"Okay, so we're going after 'em. So where we going?"

"You remember the location of that field hospital where they took Sergeant Mallory?"

Carlson searched his notebook. "I think I wrote it down."

"It was Malmédy, wasn't it?"

Just as Carlson found it in the book. "Sixty-seventh Evac."

67th Evacuation Hospital, Malmédy
DECEMBER 16, 8:00 A.M.

When the artillery barrage began at dawn, no one at the hospital paid it much mind: By the time it ended an hour later, shells had started to land near Malmédy, word came in that the Germans had punched a hole through the American line, and paratroopers had been spotted on the ridge less than three miles away. The operating theater, which had been running at less than a third of capacity during the recent lull, was put on full alert.

A wave of ambulances arrived within minutes—front-line soldiers with blunt trauma and shrapnel wounds. Many had suffered puncture wounds when shells shattered the trees, firing splinters in every direction. A number of civilians were injured when a rocket hit near the town's medieval Catholic cathedral after morning mass, knocking down a wall and ringing the bells.

Earl Grannit and Ole Carlson entered the large tent complex on the outskirts of Malmédy just after 7:30 A.M. They moved past a crowd of wounded GIs stacked in the prep area, located the surgery ward, and found the senior nurse on duty, Dorothy Skogan, working in postop recovery. Grannit showed his credentials and asked about Sergeant Vincent Mallory. Skogan didn't know the name, but recognized him from Grannit's description.

She told them Mallory had arrived earlier that night, without dog tags, just after 3:00 A.M., accompanied by a medic and a pair of MPs. He had been shot three times and his complicated surgeries lasted over two hours. By the time they finished, the soldier had stabilized, his severe blood loss restored by transfusion. The surgery team had just wrapped out of the OR when the bombs started flying.

"What's his condition?" asked Grannit.

"Critical but stable. Severe blood loss, shock and hypothermia. Gunshot wounds to the right shoulder, left hip. His jawbone's shattered, most of his teeth fractured."

"Is he conscious?"

"No. Won't expect him to be for hours, if then."

"Well. We really need to talk to him."

"That may be difficult, Lieutenant. The bullet tore up his tongue, and we had to wire what was left of his jaw to a plate. I didn't even know his name until you just told me; he didn't have his tags."

Grannit looked at Carlson, frustrated. He quickly told her that Mallory had been shot and left for dead with three other men for over twenty-four hours before they'd found him. "Anything strike you as unusual about him?"

"When I was prepping him, I found an empty ampule of morphine in his field jacket. There was sulfa on all three wounds. I found bandages compressed against the wounds on his hip and shoulder that stopped him from bleeding out."

"So the medics took care of him during transport," said Grannit.

"No, that's my point. The medic in the ambulance said that's how they found him."

"We're the ones who found him," said Grannit, puzzled.

"And you didn't notice this?"

"No. You're saying somebody gave him first aid before we got there?" asked Grannit.

"That's what the medic said," she replied. "I don't think the sergeant was in any shape to do it himself, do you?"

They had reached Mallory's cot in the recovery tent. His lower face and neck were encased in a yoke of bandage, an IV drip fed his arm, oxygen tubes straddled his nose. His face looked swollen as a football. Skogan wrote Mallory's name on a strip of tape and fixed it to his cot.

"Least we know his name now," she said. "He was lucky that bullet hit him in the jaw. It was headed toward his brain."

"You didn't happen to save the bullets, did you?"

"We're a little busy right now."

"It's important. Ole'll give you a hand," said Grannit.

"Where you from, Dorothy?" asked Carlson, as he walked away with her.

"A long way from here, kiddo," she said. "Madison, Wisconsin."

"No kidding. I'm from Sioux Falls."

Grannit moved to take a closer look at Mallory. He studied the angle of the wounds, visualizing him back at the checkpoint, trying to re-create the encounter.

He was behind you. You turned and he fired point-blank. He thought the first shot took you out. The second and third were afterthoughts, as you fell. Then he got distracted by the other men and assumed you were dead. He killed Private Ellis, while the second shooter took care of Anderson. Then he killed the second shooter, his own man.

Why?

Because he was hit. Private Anderson returned fire and shot him before he went down. Chest wound from an M1. Possibly fatal, but not right away. So our man didn't want to take a chance and leave one of his own behind.

Two head shots. No hesitation. Kills his own man. They toss his body next to the other vics, take all their tags, placing a big bet nobody would notice this stranger among them. Drive on to Elsenborn.

Two officers, one private driving the jeep. One lieutenant who does the talking, and probably the shooting. All the way from Twelfth Army, Bradley's HQ in Luxembourg, almost a hundred miles south.

So who treated Mallory's wound before we got there?

Grannit shook his head to stay awake and rubbed a hand over his eyes, waves of fatigue washing through him. He'd been gunning for forty-eight hours straight; it was a sudden struggle to keep his thoughts on track.

Fuck it. The trail was cold. Now the Krauts launch this offensive. That tipped over the fucking applecart. No chance he'd ever get to the bottom of this now.

The idea burned a hole in him. He never let go of a case while he was on the job. Why should it be any different over here? Because life was cheaper? Did that make these murders any less important?

Vince Mallory lying there, hanging by a thread, his life shattered. Somebody did this to him. Find out who.

No excuse not to finish the job. He'd made that promise a long time ago, and backed it up ever since.

His mind kept working through the fatigue. *Don't let go. There's more to this than you can see.*

He needed coffee. He went to look for some.

Captain Hardy of the 291st Engineer Combat Battalion led his small convoy into Malmédy at 7:45 A.M. They found the tent complex of the 67th Evac Hospital on the outskirts of town. Bernie pulled up outside next to a line of ambulances. Hardy stopped his jeep alongside them and barked directions.

"Get your man squared away. Our rally point's near the cathedral on the eastern approach."

"We'll be there," said Von Leinsdorf, snapping a salute.

Hardy's jeep pulled away. The medic helped Bernie guide Preuss down from the back of their Willys.

"We'll get him inside," said Bernie. "Thanks for your help."

The medic swung onto the back of one of the convoy trucks as it drove off. Preuss stumbled and Von Leinsdorf grabbed his other arm. They propped him up between them, through the traffic congesting the front of the tent. Preuss moaned, half-conscious, in a morphine haze.

"What the hell do we do?" asked Bernie.

"We can't leave him here," said Von Leinsdorf. "For obvious reasons."

Two nurses stationed at the entrance trotted out to help.

"Where's he hit?" one of them asked.

"Right shoulder," said Von Leinsdorf.

"Bring him this way."

Holding Preuss between them, they followed the nurses into the tent, then set him down on a stretcher in a waiting area overflowing with wounded. A passing nurse kneeled down to take a look at Preuss just after he hit the canvas.

"He's had first aid already," said Dorothy Skogan.

"Medic gave us a hand on the way in," said Von Leinsdorf. "What's the procedure?"

"We'll take him, but there's going to be a wait. There's a lot of wounded ahead of him."

She stood up briskly and moved on. A young, moonfaced MP with a blond brush cut walked after her, and took a passing glance at Von Leinsdorf and Bernie. Von Leinsdorf met his eye, deep concern evident on his face, which the MP, Ole Carlson, took for worry over their wounded friend. Preuss moaned again, drifting in and out of the morphine clouds, head rocking from side to side.

"*Schiesse . . . Schiesse . . .*"

Bernie knelt down next to Preuss and laid a hand over his mouth. "Easy, easy, don't talk."

"He'll come out okay, buddy," said Carlson.

"Thanks," said Bernie, lowering his head.

Carlson walked away following the nurse. Von Leinsdorf knelt beside Bernie.

"Take his tags," said Von Leinsdorf.

"What?"

"Put these on him," he said, slipping another set of dog tags from his pocket. "Take his ID and anything else that could tie him to us."

Bernie reached into Preuss's shirt and yanked off his tags as Von Leinsdorf stood watch. Bernie slipped the second set of tags into Preuss's pocket, then pulled his forged ID card out of his jacket.

"Where's his lighter?" asked Von Leinsdorf, as he tucked the card away.

"How should I know?"

"Find it."

Bernie realized what he was asking. "I'm not doing that."

"Then wait outside."

"I know what you want it for; I'm not letting you do that—"

A young admitting nurse with a clipboard walked up to them. "I need some information before we take him to the ward."

Von Leinsdorf reached past Bernie into Preuss's pocket, fished out the tags they'd just put there and handed them over. "He's not with our unit. We were driving by, he flagged us down and passed out in the jeep, so we brought him in."

The nurse examined the tags and wrote down the name. "Sergeant Vincent Mallory."

"See, we didn't even know his name," said Von Leinsdorf, continuing to rummage through Preuss's pockets. "Maybe we can find something else to help you." He fished out a silver Zippo lighter and a pack of cigarettes. "Don't suppose he'll be needing these for a while, huh?"

"You don't know anything else about him?"

"You know as much as we do," said Von Leinsdorf, pocketing the lighter.

The nurse printed the name on a strip of white tape and attached it to the stretcher. "You did a good thing just getting him this far." She signaled a couple of orderlies, who lifted Preuss's stretcher and carried him toward an adjoining tent.

"Where you taking him?" asked Bernie.

"To prep him for surgery. If you don't know this guy, there's no reason to wait, it's going to be a while."

The nurse moved off, following the stretcher.

"Shit. He's going to come out of it and start crying for his *Mutter*," said Von Leinsdorf.

"Let's get out of here."

Von Leinsdorf looked around, thinking, before he answered.

"Wait here," he said.

Von Leinsdorf followed Preuss into the next tent. As he entered, he picked up a clipboard hanging next to a bulletin board, pretending to study it as he tailed the stretcher. The orderlies set Preuss down in the busy prep center, where two dozen wounded lay waiting, separated by screens, attended by an assembly line of nurses and orderlies.

Standing near a busy nurses' station by the entrance to the operating theater, Von Leinsdorf watched them strip off Preuss's jacket and shirt and plug him into an IV. Moments later, Von Leinsdorf buried his face in the clipboard when Dorothy Skogan walked up to the desk with Ole Carlson and a supervising orderly.

"I don't have time for this shit now," said the orderly.

"He just wants the bullets we pulled from the maxillofacial we did this morning," said Dorothy.

"We got a hundred people shot to shit, what's the rush?" asked the orderly.

"Criminal investigation," said Carlson, showing his badge. "There's a harder way to do this, you want to give that a try?"

The orderly sighed. "Patient's name?"

"Mallory, Vincent Mallory. He was brought in late last night."

Von Leinsdorf was about to move toward Preuss when he heard that name, and stopped to listen.

"Where is he now?"

"He's in recovery. I've got to get back to work," said Dorothy.

"That's fine, I can take it from here," said Carlson. "Thanks for your help, Dorothy."

Skogan left for the operating theater. The orderly sifted through a pile of paperwork on the desk, looking for Mallory's.

"Your chances ain't good. We usually toss everything when we scrub down," said the orderly.

"Anything you give us is really appreciated," said Carlson, smiling patiently.

Neither of them noticed Von Leinsdorf walk out of the prep tent. He stopped a passing nurse to ask: "I'm looking for a man from my unit just came out of surgery, where would he be?"

She directed him outside to an adjoining tent. Von Leinsdorf carried the clipboard with him, sloshed through the mud, and parted the flaps of the recovery tent. Quieter in here, fewer lights, sharp contrast to the chaos in the OR. Patients rested on cots in cubicles created by curtains. Two nurses moved from one man to the next, making notations, monitoring medication. Von Leinsdorf slipped on a white coat, kept his focus on the clipboard, and drew no attention as he walked by. He glanced in each cubicle he passed, reading the names on strips of white tape attached to the foot of their cots.

He found Mallory's name but didn't recognize the man on the cot as the sergeant he had shot at the checkpoint. His face was bloated by surgery and covered with bandages. Another man stood to the right of the cot, arms folded, looking down at Mallory. Broad shoulders, rangy, weathered—a "tough customer" was the slang that came to Von Leinsdorf's mind. The man wore a regulation uniform with no insignia. That may have been the privilege of an officer, but this one had the leathery aura of a seasoned noncom. Von Leinsdorf walked past the cot, stepping in to look at a patient two beds down.

Von Leinsdorf pieced together a scenario: Someone found Mallory where they'd left him in the woods. Alive, against all odds. He might have talked about the shooting but his condition suggested otherwise. Von Leinsdorf had learned as much as anyone alive would ever want to know about the nuances of dying. He knew exactly how to gauge death's approach, when it was ready to make its final embrace.

This man was hanging by a thread. A whisper would nudge him into its arms.

The man standing over Mallory rubbed his face and headed for the exit. They nearly collided; Von Leinsdorf let him pass. As soon as the man left, Von Leinsdorf stepped back to Mallory's cot and took Preuss's Zippo lighter from his pocket. Opening a pocketknife he pried away the wick and flint and removed a small glass vial from the cavity. He used the knife to cut a slit in the IV bag attached to Mallory's arm. Snapping the head off the vial, he poured the clear contents through the slit into the bag. A nurse walked into the ward. He pocketed the empty vial and walked away without looking back. Stepping out of the tent, he dropped the vial and crushed it into the mud.

A minute later Grannit walked back into the tent with a cup of coffee, saw the man's legs bucking and kicking, his arms twitching, head whipping from side to side, his breathing rapid and labored. He called out for the nurses and used all his weight to restrain Mallory on the cot. The man's eyes opened, the pupils fixed and unseeing. Bright cherry-red blood streamed from his nose and mouth. By the time a trauma team arrived, Mallory's limbs had gone rigid and he had stopped breathing. Grannit stepped back and let them work.

Bernie sat on his helmet beside a Christmas tree near the entrance of the admitting tent. Every time an officer passed, he agonized about whether he should take him aside and identify Von Leinsdorf as a spy. Once they had the German in custody, he might be able to blend into the chaos and fade away. But the thought of a second objective held him back. Von Leinsdorf wouldn't crack even if they tortured him, of that he was sure; he'd sneer at a firing squad while they tied the blindfold on. Bernie didn't know how many others in their brigade had been assigned this second objective, so unless he found out what it was, he couldn't do a thing to stop it. Until then he needed Von Leinsdorf alive and in the clear. But how many others would he kill before then? That was the equation he had to live with. Now that the attack had started, trying to surrender would only get himself shot. He kept his head down, picked up a newspaper, and tried to shrink into the corner.

It was the American service paper, *Stars and Stripes*. His eye was drawn to a headline on the front page.

ALLIES BOMB IG FARBEN

German Industrial Giant Near Frankfurt Hit Hard
Daylight Raid Leaves Nazi War Machine Reeling

His father still worked at IG Farben. He'd had no contact with his family since leaving for Grafenwöhr in October, at which point both his parents were alive. That suddenly seemed in doubt.

Bernie's gaze drifted to the improvised Christmas tree, gauze serving as tinsel, surgical clamps and scissors hung like ornaments. The meager attempt at holiday cheer, his own peril, and the growing crowd of wounded arriving for treatment brought him to the verge of tears. A nurse's aide offered him a cup of coffee. He declined, and his forlorn look drew her sympathy.

"Hard being away from home this time of year, isn't it?" she asked.

He looked up at her. She was a plain girl, early twenties, with crooked teeth and a one-sided smile.

"I guess you could say that," said Bernie.

"I love Christmas. Never spent one like this before. Where you from?"

"Brooklyn," he said, surprised when it came out of his mouth.

"Really? We sailed out of the Brooklyn yard on our way over a few weeks ago. You'll be happy to know it's still there. I'm from Wichita. That's a long way from New York. Might even be farther away from it than where we are now."

"I don't think you can get any farther away than this."

"Don't worry now, you'll be going home soon," she said.

She patted him on the back. Her kindness made it hard for him to say anything more. He spotted Von Leinsdorf coming toward him through the room, wearing a doctor's white coat, and stood up.

"Get in the jeep," said Von Leinsdorf. "Keep the engine running."

"Where are you going?"

"Make sure you're pointed toward the road," he said, taking off the coat and heading back toward the prep tent.

"I want an autopsy," said Grannit. "I need to know what killed him."

"Could have been any number of things," said the surgeon who'd worked on Mallory, not eager to oblige. "Postoperative trauma, delayed reaction to anesthesia—"

"His original wounds were enough to kill him," said a second doctor.

"We were told he'd come through that surgery, that he'd recover," said Grannit.

"The truth is, Lieutenant, these things aren't predictable," said the surgeon. "We see it every hour of every day. Each man has a different breaking point. Sergeant Mallory reached his."

Grannit looked at the weary doctors in their blood-soaked gowns—decent men, trained to heal, not kill. He could hardly expect a different reaction: What was one more dead soldier? After watching so many young men lose their lives, what else could they do but turn up their hands?

A passing nurse overheard the name. "Did you say Mallory?"

"That's right," said Grannit."

"But he hasn't even gone into surgery yet."

"Yes he did, he was postop."

"When did they operate?"

"Last night when he came in."

"But I just admitted him fifteen minutes ago."

"What's the first name?" asked the surgeon, looking at the chart. "We can't be talking about the same Mallory."

"First name's Vincent," said Grannit. "Vincent Mallory."

"Sergeant Vincent Mallory, that's him," said the admitting nurse. "I just took the information off his tags—"

"Where is he now?"

"In the prep tent."

"Show me," said Grannit.

They hurried toward the tent, burst through the flaps, and searched down the busy rows, the doctors following.

"Did he come in alone?" asked Grannit.

"No, a couple of soldiers brought him in—"

The admitting nurse pulled back the curtain isolating his cubicle. Gunther Preuss lay on the cot, an IV in his arm, bright red blood sliding from his mouth and nose, his body racked with convulsions.

The nurse and doctors hurried to the patient's side, calling for help. Grannit caught movement out of the corner of his eye. An officer in uniform walking against traffic out of the tent at a rapid pace. Grannit took off after him, pulling his Colt, holding it aloft so people would notice.

"Out of the way!"

The crowd parted, some hitting the floor in alarm. The officer heard the shouts and, without looking back, sprinted out the front of the tent. Grannit hurdled a cot, bowled over a couple of soldiers, and jammed his way out after him.

A jeep was pulling out of the parking area, wheels skidding in the mud. Two men on board. Grannit saw the officer he'd followed haul himself into the front seat as it slipped away. The glint of silver bars on his collar. A lieutenant. No stripes on the driver's jacket, a private.

Grannit gave chase to the edge of the parking area, aiming the pistol but unable to sight a clear shot. He waved down a motorcycle dispatcher, flashed his badge to the driver, then yanked him off the bike when he slowed and jumped on. Jacking the bike around, he downshifted to gain torque in the mud and slid onto the narrow road heading into Malmédy. He spotted the jeep a quarter of a mile ahead crossing a small bridge into town. Grannit downshifted again and opened the throttle.

"Keep going," said Von Leinsdorf to Bernie. "Head southeast."

"What happened? Where's Preuss?"

"Just do as I tell you," said Von Leinsdorf, glancing behind them.

Bernie whipped the jeep around the town center, a welter of narrow, ancient streets, avoiding collisions, wheeling around obstacles, ignoring traffic signs. The sidewalks were packed with citizens carrying suitcases and bags, pushing carts full of possessions, fleeing from the German advance. Twice he narrowly missed civilians who darted suddenly into the street, one carrying a bright green parrot in a cage. As they reached a narrow bridge leading out of town, they came face-to-face with an American half-track headed the other way. Bernie steered to the right without slowing and accelerated past it, only inches to spare, the jeep's right fender sending up sparks as it scraped against the stone wall.

Behind them, Grannit dodged through oncoming traffic, weaving around slower cars and trucks. Crossing the first bridge into town, he veered into an intersection and nearly collided with a stalled wagon. Turning hard right, he jumped the bike up onto a sidewalk, leaned on the horn, and shouted for people to clear out of his way. He skirted a group of Allied soldiers organizing a defense along the town's eastern perimeter on the near side of a second bridge. Halfway across the bridge, he slammed on the brakes when a column of American vehicles barreled into the village. Grannit stood up on the bike, looked ahead, and caught sight of the jeep across the bridge, moving down a long straightaway into the country. Some MPs jumped out of a jeep to set up a roadblock and direct traffic. Grannit shouted at them, showed him his badge.

"Clear this bridge, god damn it!"

The MPs waded into traffic and cleared a path for him. Soldiers riding into the village shouted at Grannit that he didn't want to head that way. Paratroopers had taken the towns to the east, and columns of panzers were coming up behind them.

As their jeep cleared the outskirts of town, Bernie steered onto the shoulder. American military vehicles crowded the westbound side of the road, carrying soldiers on hoods of jeeps and hanging off the sides of trucks. The men wore the haunted look of battle fatigue and many were wounded. Bernie could hear the boom of artillery and the rattle of small arms to the east. Von Leinsdorf lit a cigarette and couldn't keep a smile off his face.

"Quite a sight, Brooklyn," said Von Leinsdorf. "Your amateur American Army. What did I tell you? Retreat's too dignified a word—they're bugging out after only four hours."

Bernie didn't respond, alarmed by an image he was picking up in the rearview mirror.

The moment the MPs opened a path, Grannit muscled the bike across the bridge, accelerating through the gearbox as he roared past the retreating American column. He caught sight of the jeep again, at the top of a rise less than a mile ahead, where the road headed into a stretch of gently rolling hills. He tried to coax more speed out of the jeep as they crested another hill.

"Somebody's following us," he said.

Von Leinsdorf looked back and saw the motorcycle clear the hill behind them. He picked up his rifle. When they reached the top of the next rise, the bike had closed the gap to less than half a mile.

"Who is it?" asked Bernie.

"I don't know. Maybe we forgot to pay our bill at the hospital," said Von Leinsdorf, screwing a telescopic sight onto the rifle. "Pull over at the bottom of the next hill."

When they reached the base of the hill, Bernie pulled off the road onto a hidden drive that led to a farmhouse in a stand of pines. Once they were out of sight, he cut the engine. Dust settled. Over the country silence, they could hear the buzz of the approaching motorcycle. Von Leinsdorf steadied the barrel of the rifle on the back of the windscreen and waited. The buzz grew louder. He looked down the sight, settling the crosshairs on the peak of the hill.

Bernie swiveled around when he heard a clatter of breaking dishes from inside the farmhouse. The face of a GI appeared in a window, then the door swung open; a group of six young soldiers hurried toward them.

"Jesus Christ, get out of sight," said one of them. "What the hell are you doing?"

Von Leinsdorf took his eye off the sight and looked over, annoyed.

"They're right on top of us, get out of sight!"

A rumble shook the earth, along with it the high-pitched whine of steel grating on steel. On the far side of the woods to the east three Panther tanks appeared and wheeled to a stop on the summit of the next hill, straddling the road. Walking alongside and behind them, in skirmish formation, were a column of black-jacketed soldiers. On their collars Bernie saw the double-lightning insignia of the SS *Panzergrenadiers*.

Aboard the bike, Grannit hit the top of the incoming hill and skidded to a halt when he saw the tanks astride the next rise, a quarter of a mile in front of him. Behind them, stretching as far as he could see, was a solid column of soldiers, mounted artillery, and half-tracks filled with infantry. In a hollow below and to the right he spotted the jeep he'd been chasing. A squad of GIs was trotting toward it from a nearby stone farmhouse.

Von Leinsdorf found Earl Grannit in his sights as he crested the hill, and nestled him right in the center of the crosshairs. As he was about to fire, Bernie grabbed the barrel, yanking it off target.

"I think that's one of ours, Lieutenant," he said, for the benefit of the approaching GIs.

Von Leinsdorf glared at him but didn't respond. Bernie refused to let go of the rifle.

"You don't want the Krauts to know we're down here, do you?"

The soldiers from the farmhouse reached the side of their jeep. They were all Bernie's age or younger, frightened and confused.

"You got to get us out of here," one of them said.

"Who the fuck are you?" snapped Von Leinsdorf.

"Rifle company, 99th Infantry," said their sergeant. "We were mining a logging road near the Skyline Drive. Krauts started coming out of the woodwork. Our jeep got hit. We've been dodging 'em for hours, trying to get back to our line."

"They're all over the fuckin' place," said another. "What the hell are we supposed to do, Lieutenant?"

One of the young Americans, wearing a bandage on a leg wound, started crying. They all looked to Von Leinsdorf for guidance, like a lost pack of Boy Scouts. Von Leinsdorf could barely conceal his disgust.

"They haven't spotted us yet," said Bernie. "Hop on, we'll make a run for it."

The six GIs crowded into the backseat and jumped onto the running boards as Bernie turned the engine over.

Looking down into the valley, Grannit saw the officer he'd been chasing since the hospital stand up in the jeep and hold up his rifle. The man met his eye and waved jauntily, just as the jeep turned and headed onto a dirt road behind the farmhouse.

As Grannit turned back to the hill, a turret on one of the tanks turned in his direction. He spun the bike around and accelerated down the hill back toward Malmédy, just as the first tank round came whistling over his head and exploded off to the side of the road.

11

67th Evacuation Hospital
DECEMBER 16, NOON

The naked body of Gunther Preuss lay on a stainless steel countertop behind curtains near the back of the surgery tent, a makeshift morgue. Vincent Mallory's corpse, already examined, lay on a second counter, covered with a blood-stained sheet. Earl Grannit had persuaded the head surgeon he'd spoken with earlier to examine both men's bodies. While the doctor opened them up, Grannit sat off to the side and lit a cigar to kill the stench, a technique he'd learned during visits to the New York City morgue.

After making his way back to the hospital, Grannit had sought out a senior combat officer and given him a detailed report about the German battalion he'd seen on the road east of Malmédy. Returning to his own assignment, he found that Ole had secured the scene, quarantined evidence before it got tossed, and collected statements from witnesses. Among the evidence, Grannit took particular interest in the two plastic IV bags. Both had been cut open in identical fashion.

The doctor called Grannit over and pointed out unnaturally bright pink mucous membranes lining the man's exposed throat and lungs. Even over the cigar, Grannit noticed a faint odor of bitter almonds emanating from the body.

"They were both poisoned," said the doctor. "Some toxin caused the hemorrhaging that destroyed all this soft tissue."

"What do you think it was?"

"Judging from the smell, if I recall my rudimentary chemistry correctly, hydrocyanic acid. Prussic or cyanide."

"Something you could pour into an IV bag," said Grannit.

"Comes in liquid form. It's a clear substance, so nobody'd notice."

"How big a dose?"

"Wouldn't take more than a few drops—don't get too close with that cigar smoke, Lieutenant, or you're gonna get a nasty taste in your mouth; that stuff forms a bad compound with tobacco."

Grannit stood back. "You keep that here in the hospital?"

"No, we do not, sir." The doctor snapped off his gloves and looked at him sharply. "You're a cop, aren't you? Back home."

"That's right."

"You like to tell me what's going on? We don't have enough carnage, some sick son of a bitch has to come into my hospital and kill wounded soldiers? Why in the hell should that happen?"

"I'll have to get back to you."

"I'm going back to work," said the surgeon. "They're saying we got big trouble out there. That what you saw?"

"Trouble doesn't cover it."

"There's talk we might have to pull out of here, if the damn army doesn't chase its tail around before they're on top of us. My staff can't save lives in a German prison camp."

The doctor left him alone with the bodies. Grannit set the cigar down and took a close look at the false Vincent Mallory. A second soldier with no ID killed in two days. Wearing a captain's bars. Soft hands, a wedding ring. A new pair of boots, taken off one of the dead GIs at the checkpoint.

This was that second officer the MP spotted in the jeep at Elsenborn.

So why'd you kill this one, Lieutenant? He gets tagged along the way to wherever you're going, all of a sudden he's expendable, too? A superior offi-

cer? This wasn't a fatal wound like your other man—buckshot in his shoulder and neck—but still you took him out.

Then why run the risk of taking him to a hospital? If you wanted him dead, why bring him here when you could just shoot him by the side of the road?

Unless you were still after the real Mallory. Is he what brought you here, you needed to finish the job? But how could you have known he survived Elsenborn? The way you left him, what were his chances? And why would you give this other man of yours his tags unless you thought the real Mallory was dead?

Because the sergeant's surviving was a loose end you didn't realize you'd left hanging until you got here, when your friend checked in wearing Mallory's tags. Once you were inside, you found this out and killed them both.

He could leave the why for later. Grannit had seen the man who'd done this. The blond lieutenant. Standing in that jeep, waving at him.

Five murders in two days. A killer with the nerve to cut open Mallory's IV and pour that poison into him, then do the same to his own man on his way out before Mallory was even dead.

Grannit's eye was drawn to a magnifier mounted on a stand attached to the autopsy table, and he remembered the photograph he'd found in the other man's boot. That led him back to this man's boots, sitting under the table. He searched through them, found nothing inside; then, following a hunch, he pulled his knife and pried away at the heels.

The right heel came away in his hand. Hidden inside he found a folded piece of paper. On it was a hand-drawn map of a river and a bridge crossing, detailing access roads on both sides and defensive emplacements. A few words had been scribbled hastily in the margins, but Grannit couldn't make them out. Arrows pointed to two other bridges, on either side, that were only sketched in, without detail.

Ole Carlson hurried into the tent, excited, holding up a plastic bag. "It took some doing but I found 'em, Earl. These are the bullets from Mallory. The real Mallory, not the fake Mallory."

"I get it, Ole."

Carlson's eyes settled at the body on the table and turned away as if he'd been hit in the stomach, blood draining from his face. He opened his eyes and was looking straight down at Mallory on the other table. "Oh Lord."

"You all right there, Ole?"

"Not so good, actually."

"Close your eyes and breathe."

"I would, but the smell is sort of a problem."

"Can't help you there," said Grannit.

Grannit put the spent shells under the magnifier. One was badly damaged, little more than a shapeless lump, probably the shot that shattered Mallory's jaw. The others were pistol rounds, and at first glance he knew they were .45s from a Colt, a U.S. officer's sidearm. But they also bore peculiar rifling, as if they'd passed down an unusually long barrel.

"They pulled some buckshot from the fake Mallory there," said Carlson, trying not to retch, keeping his eyes off the bodies. "Kind of strange, isn't it? Who the heck is using shotguns out there? It ain't duck season, I know that much. Dang, that smell could take down a bull."

"You want a cigar or something?"

"No, thanks, a cigar would definitely make me puke."

Grannit pulled out the photograph he'd found on the first John Doe and held it under the magnifier.

"Anyway, I finally got through to Twelfth Army," said Carlson. "The phone lines are down; they think that's the Krauts' doing, so I got through to Twelfth Army dispatch on the radio. Krauts are coming at 'em down there, too—"

"Did you ask about the patrol?"

"Yeah. The Twelfth has no record of any patrol in this sector answering that description."

"There's a reason for that," said Grannit.

"What is it?"

Grannit waved Carlson over to look at the photograph of the woman at the seaside scene under the magnifier.

Among the structures lining the dock behind her was a civic office building, probably the port's customs house. Carved into the stone entablature over its entrance, in the center of a laurel wreath clutched in the talons of the German imperial eagle, was an elaborate swastika.

"Because they're Krauts," said Grannit.

12

Dwight Eisenhower was nursing a same-day champagne hangover. His valet, an ex-bellhop named Mickey Mc-Keough, had married his Women's Army Corps sergeant girlfriend that morning in the gilded Louis XIV chapel of the Trianon Palace Hotel on the grounds of the Versailles compound. Eisenhower told a friend that the diminutive bride and groom looked cute enough to decorate the top of their own cake. The reception went into the early afternoon, and when the bubbly ran out they dipped into the general's private wine cellar. With only nine days left until Christmas and the front firmly in Allied control, few of the overworked staff at Supreme Headquarters of the Allied Expeditionary Forces needed an excuse to let off steam, but wishing Mickey and his wife well was better than most.

General Eisenhower had a more personal reason for indulging himself. A cable had arrived that morning informing him that President Roosevelt had placed his name in nomination before Congress for the post of General of the Army. This new rank would bring with it a fifth star and sole authority over the Allies' entire armed forces in Europe. That much power had not been conferred on one soldier since the First World War. After sixteen years as a desk-bound major, Eisenhower had risen from lieutenant colonel to the army's highest rank in a little over three years. The affable fifty-four-year-old

Kansan had planned a private dinner that night to celebrate with some drinking buddies, among them one of his best friends and colleagues, General Omar Bradley. Bradley had arranged for a bushel of Ike's favorite oysters to be flown in from the Normandy coast. Given their recent successes in the field, for the first time in two years, Eisenhower felt he could allow the weight of the war to slip slightly off his shoulders.

Eisenhower, Bradley, and four staff officers were in the Clemenceau Ballroom of the Trianon Palace at Versailles, which they used as their tactical map room. They were halfway through a relaxed meeting about how to speed up training and delivery of replacement soldiers from the States. Eisenhower drank coffee, chain-smoked, popped a handful of aspirin, and ate a big lunch, trying to negotiate away his headache from the morning's champagne before the evening's Scotch. He was already on medication for high blood pressure and stress. His left knee, sprained two months earlier and slow to recover, ached with the arrival of an early winter cold front. Outside, heading into the shortest days of the year, the sky was already beginning to darken.

The meeting was interrupted by the arrival of a brigadier general, deputy to Eisenhower's chief intelligence officer, British Brigadier General Kenneth Strong. The man appeared grim and called Strong out of the room. Eisenhower saw the same look on Strong's face when he returned, and asked him to share what he'd learned. Strong moved to one of the large maps that adorned the walls.

"We're getting fragmented reports that the enemy counterattacked this morning across a broad front," said Strong. "Here, in the Ardennes, First Army sector, all the way down into Luxembourg."

Eisenhower looked to Bradley, whose headquarters were in Luxembourg City. "What do you know about this?"

"I was in Spa with General Hodges yesterday, but I didn't see any of this myself," said Bradley.

"Didn't you hear anything, Brad?"

"Some early reports came in as we were leaving. My first thought was it's just a spoiling attack. That's what I still think. They're trying to disrupt our move across the Rhine."

Eisenhower stood up to join them at the map and pointed at the Losheim Gap. They called this sector the "Ghost Front," for it had seen no heavy action since Hitler's panzer blitz to Paris four years earlier. Eisenhower also knew that this same sleepy seven-mile corridor had served as the fast lane for Germany's first-strike invasions of France in 1914 and 1870. Concentrating their effective forces to the north and south after pushing the Germans out of France, the Allies had rolled the dice that in winter the harsh terrain and broken roads of the thinly held Ardennes offered no strategic advantage or tactical temptation to the reeling Nazi army.

"We're spread pretty thin in here, aren't we, Brad?"

"Four divisions."

"Fairly green, aren't they?"

"Two of them are replacements. The others we've pulled off the line after heavy action."

"So it's half nursery, half old folks' home."

"That's the risk we've taken."

"How many divisions have they committed; do we have a count?"

"Not yet," said Strong. "But Jerry's put together a steady buildup on the other side of the Siegfried, as many as ten divisions already—"

"And intelligence always indicated that was purely defensive, in anticipation of our moving against them," said Bradley, slightly irritated.

"Well, it isn't defensive now."

"This has to be a local attack, to distract us from Patton's move into the Rhine."

They had all been stunned by the news, but Eisenhower was the first to recover. His headache was gone, swept away by alarm and clarity. "This is our weakest point. Why would they hit our weakest point in force?"

"I don't know the answer," admitted Bradley. "He's not after a terrain objective. That ground doesn't mean anything."

"This is no spoiling attack. Not with those kind of numbers."

"Then what kind of attack is it?" asked Bradley.

"I don't know yet, Brad, but we're not going to wait to find out.

First Army doesn't have any reserve; they've caught us with our pants down."

"I'm sure Hodges would've let us know by now—"

"Maybe he can't. Mobilize 7th Armored out of Holland, get them moving toward Spa by morning. And I want three more divisions on stand-by to support this sector until we get it sorted out," said Eisenhower. "What's available to us?"

"We've got the 82nd and 101st bivouacked near Reims," said Strong.

"They're still being refitted," said Bradley.

"Cancel all leaves, get 'em back in camp and ready to move in twenty-four hours," said Eisenhower. "Patton'll have to give us one of his for the third."

"That's going to hurt his move across the Saar," said Bradley. "George isn't going to like it."

"George isn't running this damn war," said Eisenhower.

They wouldn't learn until the following day that General Courtney Hodges, commander of First Army, headquartered in Spa, had been trying since early morning to alert Allied headquarters in Versailles that German forces were rolling over his forward positions.

His phone lines had all been cut.

The foul weather hovering over the Ardennes worsened during the night. Cold winds pushed through a front with heavy cloud cover that discharged sleet storms and sporadic snow. Across the Channel, all of England remained socked in as well, grounding Allied fighters and bombers that might have blunted the initial German advance. C-47 transports were unable to take off from British bases, denying reinforcements and fresh supplies to the troops under siege throughout the expanding front.

By dawn the disjointed communications received by Supreme Allied Command had coalesced into an alarming realization that the weakest sector in their front line was under assault from thirty-six divisions, over half a million men, the largest German offensive of the entire war.

13

The Ardennes
DECEMBER 16, 10:00 P.M.

Bernie powered the jeep along a logging road into the cover of a nearby forest. Hearing more German troops headed their way, he pulled off the road and the six young soldiers of the 99th Infantry covered the jeep with evergreen branches downed by an artillery barrage. Bernie, Von Leinsdorf, and the Americans waited in silence as the forward line of German infantry and scout cars swept past them, visible twenty yards away on the edge of the woods. Von Leinsdorf had to order the agitated engineers to stay down and keep silent. Those were battle-ready German veterans; if these green kids drew fire, they were all dead. Once the Germans passed—Von Leinsdorf identified them as a reconnaissance company—they climbed back on the jeep and cautiously drove deeper into the woods to the east.

An hour after dark they came across an abandoned woodcutter's cabin. Bernie parked the jeep in a small shed out back and shut the doors. Inside, they pulled the curtains to black out the one-room cabin, lit a kerosene lamp, and settled in for the night. Bernie helped tend the injured GIs with the jeep's med kit. The crump of artillery, rockets flying overhead, and the crackle of small arms continued through the night. The riflemen shared their K rations, eaten cold. Von Leinsdorf learned as much as he could from the Americans about their company and its movements during the last day. It was clear the German attack had taken the Allies completely by surprise.

Von Leinsdorf assigned a sentry rotation for the platoon, to get them through what remained of the night. The first man stood his post at the door while the rest bunked down around the room. Von Leinsdorf asked the platoon sergeant for a look at their maps, which he spread out on the room's crude table. Von Leinsdorf held the lamp close and tried to pinpoint their position.

One of the American kids, a baby-faced private, crawled over next to Bernie and offered him a smoke, then lit it for him, cupping his hand to hide the flame.

"You're from New York, ain'tcha?" the kid asked.

"Yeah."

"Thought so. Heard it in your voice. Me too. Charlie Decker."

"Jimmy Tenella," said Bernie.

"Pleased to meetcha, Jimmy. I'm from the Bronx, Grand Concourse up near Van Cortlandt Park?"

"Yankees fan?"

"Only since birth."

"I'm from Brooklyn."

"Dem bums. Too bad for you." They shook hands awkwardly. "So how long you been over here, Jimmy?"

"Too long," said Bernie. He noticed Von Leinsdorf watching them from across the room.

"You in the first wave? Since D-day, huh?"

"Feels like longer."

"Wow. We been here three weeks. Fresh off the banana boat," said Charlie, trying to sound hardened and indifferent. "I graduated high school six months ago. I never been anywhere before."

"You're someplace now."

"You guys know how to handle yourselves. You've seen the hellfire and brimstone, am I right?"

Bernie looked at him. "I've seen a few things."

"You probably went through basic, too. They hardly gave us any training. Then they stick us out here, saying we won't even see any action? I don't even have the right socks."

Charlie smiled and slowly shook his head. With his unlined face and wide eyes, he seemed eerily matter-of-fact about their predicament. Bernie felt an urgent impulse to get away from him.

"You got a girl back home, Jimmy?"

"No, not really. You?"

"Ann Marie Possler. Real sweet kid. I got a letter from her the other day. Finally wrote her back last night." He took an envelope out of his jacket, smiling as he looked at it. "She's in Queens. I'd like you to get this to her."

"Just keep your head down, you'll be okay."

"I'm going to die today."

Bernie didn't know what to say, but the hollow look on Charlie's face put a chill through him. *Maybe he knows. Maybe he's right.*

"See, a guy like Bobby Dugan"—Charlie pointed at the wounded soldier across the room—"he catches some shrapnel today, falls all to pieces? He's gonna grow old and die in bed." He nodded at two more of his men. "Rodney and Patchett. They're not gonna see home again either."

"Come on, knock it off, how could you know that?"

"I've heard the words of the Prophet. Even a heart of stone can be turned into a heart of flesh, if you don't reject the teaching. The new covenant will be unbreakable. It will be written on the heart. Redemption is at hand."

Charlie held the envelope out to him. Bernie saw the madness in his eyes.

"Say but the word, cleanse your soul of sin, and you shall be healed, and you shall have new life," said Charlie, and then without changing expression: "Just make sure this gets into the mail for me, okay?"

"Sure thing, Charlie." Bernie took the letter and stuck it in his pocket. "I'll take care of it."

"You got a Bible, Jimmy?"

"Not on me."

"I'd like you to have mine. Here, take it."

"Why don't you hang on to it."

"You mail the letter," said Charlie, lying back down on his bedroll. "I got a good feeling about you."

Bernie walked away from him and stood by the door, trying to shake the kid's voice out of his head. When Von Leinsdorf finished at the table, he joined Bernie outside for a smoke. The air was dead still, a frozen pool. They moved out of earshot from the cabin. A thick fog crept in and snow fell silently around them.

"Have you talked to these guys?" whispered Bernie. "At least one of 'em's a fucking lunatic."

Von Leinsdorf looked at his watch. "We have to be somewhere in a few hours."

"Where, for what?"

"To pick up something we need."

"Is this about the bridge, or the other thing?"

Von Leinsdorf glared at him. "The other thing. And they're not coming with us."

"Leave 'em here. Tell 'em we're going for help—"

"I'm not asking for suggestions." Von Leinsdorf loaded a fresh clip into his pistol.

"So wave down one of our patrols, identify ourselves—we've got signals for that, right? Let 'em surrender."

Von Leinsdorf chambered a round. "You're getting sentimental on me, Brooklyn."

"Look, they don't have any idea who we are or what we're doing. What can they say that could give us any trouble? You don't have to kill them."

"If you're not willing to help, I'll do it myself."

They heard the cabin door swing open behind them. One of the riflemen walked outside to take a piss. Von Leinsdorf raised the gun on instinct. The man in his sights wasn't looking their way and gave no indication that he knew they were there. Bernie stepped between Von Leinsdorf and the target.

"I need to know what the fuck we're doing here," whispered Bernie. "What are we picking up?"

"Security passes. From the *Abwehr*."

Bernie's heart jumped at the mention of the German secret intelligence organization. "Why didn't they give 'em to us before we left?"

"They were supposed to be with that fat woman the night we came across. They'll be there now."

"What the fuck do we need 'em for?"

"I can't tell you any more," said Von Leinsdorf. "Are you going to help or wait out here?"

"We can't shoot 'em. What if there's a patrol in the area?"

Von Leinsdorf answered by taking the silencer out and screwing it on the pistol.

Bernie saw the rifleman go back inside. "At least let 'em fall asleep first. It'll be easier then."

"Not if there's two of us." Von Leinsdorf saw the look on his face and relented. "All right. We'll wait till they're asleep."

Bernie followed him back inside. He told the soldier at the window to catch some rest, that he'd take the last watch. The American joined his friends on the floor. Three were already sleeping; the other two were playing cards by the light of the lantern. Bernie looked at Von Leinsdorf. Both men lit cigarettes and waited.

As snow accumulated outside, the fog reduced their field of vision to less than twenty yards, a white void surrounding the cottage. The first hint of dawn was in the sky before the soldiers finally turned off the lamp and lay down. Von Leinsdorf drew his pistol and signaled Bernie. Bernie picked up a rifle sitting by the door and looked down at Charlie Decker lying asleep at his feet.

You could shoot Von Leinsdorf instead, he thought.

No. Not without knowing what his mission was first. But he couldn't shoot these GIs either.

Von Leinsdorf pointed his pistol at the first man's head. Bernie heard something outside and waved his hand to stop him. He cracked open the window and gestured Von Leinsdorf over.

The faint sputter of motorized diesels. Moments later, they both heard faint shouts coming toward them in the distance. Charlie Decker woke when he heard the voices and saw Bernie and Von Leinsdorf at the window.

"Who is it?" asked Charlie. "Who's out there?"

Von Leinsdorf gestured urgently for quiet. They waited. More shouts, closer, then the squeak of footsteps running in the snow outside. A few isolated gunshots, then bursts of automatic fire. The rest of the soldiers woke in the room behind them. Then came the unmistakable grinding of heavy gears. Bernie recognized the distinctive rumble; German tanks were moving their way.

"They're ours," said Bernie to Von Leinsdorf, before he could censor himself.

Thinking he meant Americans, Charlie Decker threw open the front door and ran outside before Bernie could stop him.

"Hey! Hey, guys! Hey, we're Americans! We're over here!"

From somewhere in the fog a stream of .50 bullets chunked across the front of the cabin, cutting down Charlie Decker at the door, ripping open his chest. He fell back through the doorway, dead before he hit the floor at Bernie's feet. Everyone inside scrambled for cover. Bernie looked down at Decker, a faint smile on the kid's face, as his eyes glassed over.

Moments later, GIs slashed out of the fog right in front of the cabin, a platoon in headlong retreat, most without weapons, running for their lives. A tank shell hit the cottage with a massive, dull thud, but didn't detonate, a hissing dud, the tip of its nose poking out between logs. At the sight of it, two of the riflemen broke out the back door, out of their heads with fear. Heavier gunfire erupted, bullets piercing the wattled walls of the building. Screams issued from behind the building.

Von Leinsdorf and Bernie dove to the floor as more bullets whistled overhead. The wounded American kid crawled against the rear wall and began screaming for his mother as more rounds kicked through the room.

Bernie crawled to the open door and pushed it almost shut. A ghostly line of German paratroopers in white parkas and winter camouflage emerged from the fog, submachine guns firing. From behind them, the muzzle of a white panzer appeared, and then, moments later, the hulking body of the tank, painted a ghostly white, drove into the clearing. Von Leinsdorf crawled over to Bernie.

"I told you we should have fucking killed them," he said in Bernie's ear.

The panzer rolled toward the cottage as paratroopers trotted past the building, picking off survivors running ahead of them. Von Leinsdorf crawled to the wounded American boy and held a hand over his mouth. Pressed against the base of the wall, the last two riflemen looked to Von Leinsdorf for orders, close to cracking, ready to bolt like the others. He gestured at them to stay put.

Bernie saw the parka of a German soldier who was peering in through the cottage window. He pressed his face forward trying to see through the crude glass and his breath condensed on the pane. The Americans huddled directly under the window below him, unseen, terrified. Von Leinsdorf kept his hand clamped over the wounded GI's mouth, pulled his knife, and held it to his throat. A moment later the German soldier moved away. Bernie raised onto his knees to peer out the same window. What he saw coming drove him to dive down away from the wall.

The barrel of the panzer's cannon smashed through the window, penetrating halfway across the room. It paused for a moment and then swung violently to the right, toppling furniture, knocking over shelves. Bernie flattened himself against the wall closest to the tank, away from where the machine gun was mounted. He heard the engine engage as the barrel swung back to the left. Muffled shouting issued from inside the tank. Someone reloaded the machine gun.

The Americans panicked and ran for the back door. Bernie turned in time to see Von Leinsdorf cut the throat of the wounded GI. He heard the crew in the tank crank another shell into the chamber, and sprinted for the door as the cannon fired. The shot blew away the back wall of the cottage just as Bernie and Von Leinsdorf hurled themselves out the doorway. Bernie felt the concussion ripple through his body from behind, and the crack of the explosion deafened him.

Bernie landed facedown in the snow. He turned and looked up, groggy, lost in a white, silent world. His senses haywire, he staggered to his hands and knees, trying to remember where he was. A shrill, bell-like tone screamed out of the deep silence and pierced his mind. He felt someone grabbing for him, tugging him to his feet by the sleeve—Von Leinsdorf—then pulling him into the fog. Bernie saw the spinning tracks of the panzer, reversing away from the shattered cottage wall. A boot landed in the snow near him, with a leg still in it.

He felt something wet on his face, wiped at it, and his hand came away smeared with blood, the bright red shocking amid all the white.

They lurched into the fog, Bernie trailing Von Leinsdorf, trying to keep him in sight. He knew he was shouting, but he couldn't hear his own voice. Von Leinsdorf vanished ahead of him in the fog. Bernie turned his head to look for him, and a tree hurtled at him out of the white. He had no time to stop or change course—a low-hanging branch clotheslined him across the neck and everything went black.

14

The order came down from First Army headquarters in Spa shortly after 7:30 A.M. to abandon the 67th Evacuation Hospital. The situation to the east had grown steadily worse during the night, as waves of new wounded continued to arrive, overwhelming the facility. Confirmation that *Waffen*-SS panzer divisions were moving toward Malmédy hastened the decision to withdraw; stories about their atrocities to female prisoners preceded them. Doctors and nurses were ordered to drop everything and take only what they could carry. The hospital's chief surgeon asked a skeleton staff of five volunteers to stay behind and tend the few men who were too critically wounded to transport. Every nurse in the ward raised her hand, so they had to choose by drawing lots.

Earl Grannit and Ole Carlson had worked through the night on a borrowed typewriter, piecing together the investigation until they'd condensed it to five pages. After placing repeated calls on deteriorating phone lines to Spa and Liège, Grannit finally got through to a reconnaissance officer at First Army headquarters shortly after dawn.

"There's a hundred damn rivers in this part of Belgium," said Grannit. "We're trying to figure out which one we're looking at here."

After describing in detail the map of the river he'd found in the boot of the dead German, Grannit held on the line while the officer consulted his charts.

"Sounds like the Meuse," said the officer. "There's three bridges southwest of Liège at Engis, Amay, and Huy."

"How far apart are they?"

"They're all within twenty miles of each other. You got any maps with you?"

Carlson handed him one, folded to that section of the river. "I'm looking at it. What's their tactical significance?"

The officer thought for a moment. "If Jerry's looking to get across the Meuse, that'd be a damn good place to try—"

"How so? What good does it do them to cross that far south?" asked Grannit.

The line crackled and went dead. Grannit jiggled the receiver but couldn't reestablish the connection. Another shell exploded nearby outside. Ole ducked instinctively, but Grannit didn't move, lost in thought.

"Earl?"

"Let's go," he said finally, heading outside. "Bring the maps."

A fleet of trucks and ambulances lined up behind the tents to convoy patients and staff back toward Liège. V1 rockets and German planes continued to scream westward above the clouds overhead. Red crosses were being hastily painted on the canvas tops of the transports, as the staff hoped to ward off attack from the air.

Grannit climbed behind the wheel of their jeep, and they fought their way out of the congestion surrounding the hospital. He headed west, dodging around a brigade of American armor moving toward Malmédy. Their CO, standing up in a Willys at the rear of the column, shouted at them for directions. Grannit pointed them toward Malmédy, moved the jeep off to the shoulder, and kept driving.

"I was thinking, shouldn't we tell somebody what we know?" asked Carlson.

"What do we know, Ole?"

"You know, about the Krauts and the murders and—" Ole stuttered for a moment.

"And what?"

"I don't know what. But somebody at HQ ought to hear about this."

"We tried, Ole. Nobody's answering the god damn phone."

"Well, we should just drive over there."

"They've got their hands full. For all we know they're not even there anymore."

"But these guys are killing GIs, Earl."

"There's a lot of that going around today."

"But they're Krauts—"

"I know that, Ole, and you know that, and we're gonna tell 'em soon as we know what the hell they're doing here. That's our job now. Make sense of it first."

Grannit swerved as another shell landed by the side of the road.

"Everybody's got their job today and we got ours, okay? And, by the way, mine doesn't include having to cheer you the fuck up," said Grannit.

Baugnez Crossroads, Belgium
DECEMBER 17, 1:00 P.M.

"Private Tenella! Private Tenella!"

Bernie came to lying on the worn wooden floor of a small café. An American sergeant was staring down at him, holding his dog tags in one hand, shaking him by the shoulder with the other. The man's voice sounded muffled, as if Bernie had cotton stuffed in his ears. It took him a moment to connect himself to the name the man was using. He tried to answer, but his own voice came out as a dry croak he couldn't hear. His throat throbbed where he'd collided with the tree, and his head pulsed in painful disjointed rhythms. He felt a bandage on his forehead as he sat up and looked around.

At least thirty other GIs were huddled nearby in the room, crouched or sitting. None carried weapons. Two American medics moved from man to man, tending to the injured. Bernie thought he recognized some faces, then looked at their shoulder patches and

realized they were part of the same unit they'd ridden into Malmédy
with only the day before, the 291st Combat Engineers. Then Bernie
saw the half dozen black-jacketed SS grenadiers holding submachine guns near the door. Their commanding officer, a tall, whip-
thin captain, stood nearby, jabbering angrily at a middle-aged male
civilian.

"Where are we?" Bernie asked in a harsh whisper.

"Who the fuck knows?" said the sergeant. "Keep it down. You
gotta keep quiet, for Christ's sake, you were moaning so loud. They
just beat the piss out of a guy for less."

"How'd I get here?"

"We found you in the woods, 'bout half a mile back, and carried
you in." Bernie had to concentrate, reading the man's lips to understand him. "We were about to saddle up when this big column
of Kraut tanks rolls up on us so fast we couldn't even put up a
fight."

"You seen my lieutenant? I was with somebody—"

"Sorry. Just you and a bunch a dead GIs, kid. Keep your voice
down. I can hear you just fine."

Bernie noticed the attention of the other prisoners in the room
drifting toward the door. The SS captain was shouting at the civilian,
who had his hands up, flinching at every word. He wore a white shirt
and stained white apron. Bernie guessed he owned the café. The captain pulled his handgun and pistol-whipped the man across the face,
knocking him to the ground. He covered his head with his hands,
pleading for his life. The captain twisted the barrel of the gun into
his ear, toyed with shooting him but didn't. He shoved the man to the
floor with his boot, then turned to his soldiers and barked a series of
orders.

The SS men at the door fanned out toward the prisoners, gesturing with their guns. *"Raus! Raus! Ausenseite!"*

The GIs stumbled to their feet and pressed together as a unit
toward the front door. Swept up with the men around him, Bernie
tried to maneuver near one of the grenadiers to try to say something
in German, but he couldn't get close enough. Even if he'd caught
the man's attention, what would he say? All he had with him was

American identity papers. He didn't know if any other divisions involved in the invasion even knew about their brigade. Without Von Leinsdorf to back him up, what if they didn't believe him?

The SS men herded the GIs outside. A main highway passed in front of the café, intersecting with a smaller road that fed down from the north around a tight corner. Both arteries were jammed with German military vehicles—artillery, rocket launchers, tanks, scout cars, troop transports—entire armored divisions pouring in from the north and east. Two SS officers stood at the intersection, shouting frantically, trying to direct the columns as they merged toward the west. The traffic stretched out in either direction as far as the eye could see.

In a meadow to the east of the café, just south of the main road, stood a larger group of American prisoners, over fifty of them bunched together in the trampled snow and dead grass, under heavy Wehrmacht guard. Bernie and the GIs from the café were funneled down into the meadow to join them, forming a solid mass. German soldiers riding along the road shouted curses and laughed at the Americans as they passed. When one of the massive German Tiger tanks slowed to negotiate the sharp turn, an officer—Bernie thought he was a general—stood on the turret of his tank and called out to the prisoners in crisp English.

"How do you like us now, *Amis*? It's a long way to Tipperary, boys!"

The other SS men riding on the general's tank roared with laughter and gave the Americans mock salutes as they drove past the clearing. A burly American sergeant standing in front of Bernie raised his middle finger at them, which only made the Germans laugh harder.

"Nice to know they took care of that little morale problem they been having since we kicked their ass in France," said the GI defiantly, moving toward the road and shouting after them. "We'll see you again, you Prussian pricks! Go shit in your hat!"

Some of his buddies stepped in front of him to head the man off and shepherd him back into the crowd. Bernie didn't like any part of what he felt brewing. The Germans were riding on a belligerent high that felt reckless and unpredictable. He worked his way to the southern edge of the crowd, away from the road, and looked back toward the café.

Bernie thought he spotted a green American field jacket among the black-shirted soldiers. He took a few steps closer. When the SS blocking his view shifted, he realized that Von Leinsdorf was standing next to them. He had his American helmet propped against his hip, talking to two SS officers. The two men laughed at something he said; Von Leinsdorf clearly hadn't had any trouble explaining his identity.

Bernie took a few steps toward the café, waving his arms at Von Leinsdorf. He raised his helmet over his head, their brigade's signal to alert other German divisions, and tried to call out, but he couldn't make himself heard above the traffic from the road. Two Wehrmacht soldiers stepped toward him as soon as he moved out of the cluster in the meadow. He showed his helmet and raised it even further as he continued toward them, hoping they knew the signal.

"Ich bin deutsch! Ich bin ein deutscher Soldat!" he said as loudly as he could.

Von Leinsdorf never looked in his direction. Bernie saw Erich and the officers shake hands and part. The SS captain issued a fresh set of orders to the grenadiers around him. They hurried toward the meadow, while the captain followed Von Leinsdorf back into the café. Bernie pointed after Von Leinsdorf as the two guards closed in on him.

"Der ist mein dominierender Offizier! Ich muß mit ihm sprechen!"

The first soldier speared him in the stomach with the butt of his rifle, doubling him over. The second man struck him a glancing blow behind the ear. Bernie hit the ground and covered his head.

No other blows fell. He thought for a moment that he'd gotten through. When he chanced a look up, the soldiers had turned back toward the road. The SS grenadiers from the café entered the meadow, shouting orders to every soldier in the area. The two privates dragged him back to the main body of prisoners, dropping him near the perimeter.

Bernie heard the sound of breaking glass from the café, and moments later flames sprouted from the windows. The SS captain pushed the café owner ahead of him out the front door, shoving him to the ground, kicking him, pistol in his hand again.

The grenadiers from the café waved down two troop transports. They pulled to the side, out of the flow of traffic. A dozen heavily armed *Waffen*-SS jumped down from the back of the trucks, listened to the grenadiers, and then spread out along a fence that ran the full length of the meadow. Bernie heard a loud crack. He looked back over to the café; the owner was loping down the street, comically unsteady on his feet. The SS captain fired his pistol at him a second time, laughing, shooting for sport rather than trying to hit the man in earnest. Bernie didn't see where Von Leinsdorf had gone, but he was no longer in sight.

The Americans in the meadow shifted restlessly in place. Bernie could smell the bloodlust in the air, and when the SS men turned to face them, he knew exactly what was coming. He backed slowly away from the rear edge of the group, the mass of prisoners between him and the guards near the road. Then he bent low and sprinted straight for the line of trees behind the meadow, fifty feet away.

One of the *Waffen*-SS standing along the road stepped forward, pulled his handgun, and fired three shots point-blank at an American private in the front rank of the crowd. The GI fell to the ground, clutching his chest in surprise, crying out for help.

Time seemed to slow; no one on either side moved. The prisoners around the man stepped back in horror and watched him drop.

Bernie dug in his feet to gain traction with every step, as if he were running in place, his legs heavy and unresponsive. As the first fatal shots cut sharply through the meadow, all he could hear was his own labored breathing. The logic of what the SS was about to do hit him in an oblique flash of intuition.

They don't want prisoners. They're moving forward too fast. They don't want anything to slow them down—

The meadow filled with bullets. Machine guns opened up all along the edge of the road. Gunners on top of half-tracks turned their barrels into the meadow and fired away. As the first rows of prisoners went down, the stunned Americans behind them scattered in all directions, but the relentless fire from the SS grenadiers covered every angle. Cries of anguish and terror rose from the field as panic spread. Many tried to follow Bernie toward the woods but couldn't catch him. Only a handful covered more than twenty paces before they were cut down, blood splattering the snow. A few close to the front line never even moved, but helplessly stood their ground; some fell to their knees and prayed while they waited to die.

Bernie reached the tree line. Bullets nicked the trunks and naked branches around him, buzzing like hornets. He didn't know if any of the shooters had him in their sights, but he didn't dare look back, plunging into denser stands of evergreens until he was gasping for air. He didn't stop for half a mile, when the enfilade behind him finally ended.

Bernie fell to his hands and knees. All he heard from the meadow now were single shots and occasional bursts. The SS killers were walking in among the bodies, finishing off survivors. He turned back and held perfectly still, but he couldn't see or hear anyone moving through the woods behind him.

The snow was deeper here, slanting drifts of cold, fresh powder. Bernie's body began to shake uncontrollably, chilled to his core, on the brink of going into shock. He pushed his back against a tree, wrapped his arms around his middle, and tried to breathe deeply. His feet and hands felt numb; his ribs ached where the soldiers had clubbed him. Some deep animal instinct told him he had to keep moving or his body might shut down. He willed himself forward, the trail of footprints behind him his only point of reckoning.

It began to snow again, flurries thickening to a heavy shower. He darted through the woods for another mile, until he heard traffic and caught sight of another road and tried to get his bearings. A steady line of German vehicles moved along it, heading right to left; if they were going west, he was facing north. Farther down the road to the right he saw the edge of a small village. He kept going inside the tree line until he could see the first buildings more clearly.

The town looked deserted. A few houses had been hit by shells. One structure was still burning. A vague idea drove him—that he could crawl into an abandoned basement, find some warmth and maybe something to eat—but he knew he couldn't chance crossing the road in daylight. Just then the dull drone of a plane passed overhead, slower and lower than any he'd heard all day.

Moments later, a shower of paper fluttered down around him. He looked up, as hundreds of white pages descended like oversized snowflakes. He plucked one out of the air as it neared him, held it up in front of his face, and willed his eyes to focus.

It was an illustrated leaflet, written in English. It featured a line drawing of two handsome, tuxedoed men, with their arms around three sexually exaggerated women in evening gowns and jewelry carrying open bottles of champagne. Next to these decadent figures, and oblivious to them, three American GIs stood over the dead body of another soldier in the snow. The title underneath the drawing read: YOUR FIRST WINTER IN EUROPE.

"EASY GOING HAS STOPPED" read the headline to the flyer.

*Perhaps you've already noticed it: The nearer you get to
the German border, the heavier your losses.
Naturally. They're defending their own homes, just
as you would.
Winter is just around the corner, hence
diminishing the support of your Air Force. That places
more burdens on the shoulders of you, the infantry.
Therefore, heavier casualties.
You are only miles from the German border now.
Do you know what you're fighting for?*

Bernie laughed bitterly. The absurdity of it lifted enough of the weight he carried that somehow he felt he could keep going. There were at least two hours of light left, and he prepared to settle in among a stand of trees to wait. His vantage point gave him a view down the main street of the village. He couldn't understand why it looked familiar.

He found himself staring for almost thirty seconds at something hanging from one of the buildings that he knew he should recognize, before he remembered where he'd seen it before.

A sign in the shape of a large pink pig.

15

arl Grannit pulled out the German's hand-drawn map and compared it to the bridge crossing in the town of Engis, but it didn't match the picture. He climbed back in the jeep, where Ole Carlson waited, and continued along the road fronting the east bank of the Meuse.

"There's another bridge ten miles south," said Carlson, who had been studying their regulation map. "Town's called Amay."

They had made slow progress west on the roads out of Malmédy that morning, which were choked with Allied vehicles. At every checkpoint, they encountered GIs who knew less than they did, and who held them up with questions about the German offensive. Coherent orders had yet to filter down from First Army headquarters to company levels. The officers they ran into were acting solely on their own authority, without any overview of the field. There was no consensus at ground level about what the Krauts were up to, where their attack was headed, or how the Allies were going to respond.

As they rounded a turn in the river and the nineteenth-century stone bridge at Amay first came into sight, Grannit ordered Carlson to stop the jeep. He pulled out the hand-drawn map again, and compared it to the scene in front of them.

"This is it," said Grannit.

Carlson craned out of his seat to look. "Think the Krauts are here already?"

"I don't know, Ole. Let's drive up and ask."

"But what if they've taken the bridge already?"

"Then we'll ask in a more subtle way."

They found a platoon of GIs manning an antiaircraft battery on the eastern approach to the two-lane bridge. A single .50-caliber machine gun and some sandbags completed its defenses, another match to the map. Grannit waved over the sergeant in charge as they drove up in front of the bridge. Grannit showed his credentials and asked the sergeant what orders he'd received since the offensive began.

"Stay on alert," said the sergeant, his cheek plumped with a wad of tobacco. "Increase patrols. Company said they were sending reinforcements, but we ain't seen squat. Thought that might be you."

"What's the new vice president's name?" asked Carlson.

"What?"

"The new vice president. What's his name?"

"What do you want to know for?"

"I just want to know," said Carlson, his hand on the butt of his pistol.

"Harry S Truman, from my home state of Missouri," said the sergeant, spitting some tobacco. "What the hell's wrong with you, son?"

"I think he's okay, Earl," said Carlson.

"Thanks, Ole."

Grannit told the sergeant what they'd run into at Malmédy. Other men from the platoon drifted forward to listen. He skimped on detail, but it was still the most news they'd had since the attack began.

"What's backing you up on the other side of the river?" asked Grannit.

"Backing us up? Not a damn thing. Everything's supposed to be in front of us. We're it, brother."

"So what's over there?"

"Cows, dairy farms, and a shitload of pissed-off Belgians."

"Where's this road lead?"

"Once you're across, about fifteen miles west it ties into their main highway. Straight shot from there to Brussels, about forty miles, then another thirty to Antwerp."

Grannit held the hand-drawn map out to the sergeant. "You have any idea what angle you'd have to be looking at your bridge to draw this?"

"Up on that bluff, most likely," said the sergeant, pointing to some low hills to the east. "Where'd you get this?"

Grannit ignored the question. "Any jeeps come through here the last two days with guys saying they're from Twelfth Army?"

The sergeant canvassed his platoon. "Don't ring a bell, Lieutenant."

Grannit looked up toward the hill behind them. "Your boys know the way up there?"

"Sure, we patrol it all the time." The sergeant ordered one of his men into the jeep with Grannit and Carlson. "Duffy'll take you up."

It took ten minutes up a steep dirt switchback road to reach the summit. Grannit climbed out and walked along the ridge until he found an opening in the trees that offered a view down at the bridge. He compared it to the map. The angles and perspectives matched perfectly. Grannit signaled to Ole and the private.

"Spread out and search this area," he said.

A short distance away, Carlson found some tire tracks that had pulled off the road. They followed them fifteen yards into the woods and in a small clearing found the remains of a campsite: discarded K-ration wrappers, a few soggy cigarette butts. Grannit examined them.

Lucky Strikes. The brand he'd found at the Elsenborn checkpoint, smoked down to the nub.

"They were here," said Grannit. "Before the attack even started. That's the reason for the American uniforms, that's why they came over the line. They sent teams in to scout these bridges."

"Why's that?"

"Because this is where they're headed. They don't give a damn about Malmédy or Liège or Spa—"

"Earl—"

"This isn't about taking back ground or engaging us where we stand. They're going to cross this river and drive straight for the coast—"

"Hey, Earl," said Carlson. "There's a jeep coming down the river road."

Carlson handed Grannit his field glasses. He steadied them on Carlson's shoulder, found the road, then picked out a Willys heading south, slowing as it approached the checkpoint at the bridge.

There were four men in the jeep.

Grannit ran for their own jeep, shouting for the others to follow.

Waimes, Belgium
DECEMBER 17, 4:30 P.M.

Traffic slowed as daylight began to fail, German vehicles passing now in clusters instead of a steady stream. Bernie could see their oncoming headlights splash across the side of a barn at the corner just before they turned right and exited the village. He waited until the barn went dark, then burst out of the trees toward the road. The barn lit up again just before he reached the front of the pavement. Ten seconds to cross over and reach the shadows behind the barn.

The approaching vehicle leaned around the corner at high speed before he was halfway across. Bernie picked up his pace, cleared the far side, and sprinted for the barn. The headlights swept across him just as he flattened his back against the wall, but the German scout car shooting past him down the road never hesitated. He caught his breath, then crept along the dark side of the barn toward the edge of town.

He heard footsteps crunching in the snow, voices speaking German just around the corner, and he froze in place. Two soldiers walked around the building ahead of him, rifles on their shoulders. Bernie was about to step out and speak to them in German when he saw the double-lightning insignia of the SS on their collars. Images of the shooters who'd gone to work in the meadow flooded his mind. He leaned back into the dark and waited for them to pass out of sight.

He crept cautiously down an alley in the failing light until he found Frau Escher's butcher shop. He tried the back door, but it was locked, and he saw no lights inside. Bernie moved around the side until he found a narrow casement window at ground level that fed down into the cellar. He leaned down, broke the pane with his elbow, brushed the splinters out, reached in to undo the lock, and lifted the frame. He lay down on his belly and shimmied backward into and through the opening, feeling for the ground inside with his feet.

When he dropped to the floor, Bernie pulled out his lighter, turned up the wick, and waited for his eyes to adjust to the faint, flickering light. He was in a storage room with a dirt floor, and a pile of firewood and a variety of cans, boxes, and tools stacked against the walls. He moved to the room's only door, opened it quietly, and stepped into a short hallway covered with filthy, chipped linoleum.

On the left, a steep flight of open stairs without a banister led up to the first floor and ended at a door. A second door was straight ahead of him at the end of the hall he was in. In the gloom of the basement he could see at least one other door, possibly to a closet. He started up the stairs. They creaked loudly under his feet. As he was about to reach the door at the top, he heard something move in the room at the end of the hallway down below.

Bernie stopped midstep, held his breath, and listened. A few moments later he heard the sound again. A slight rustling, some substantial mass shifting in place against the floor. It sounded heavy and alive. An animal most likely. Maybe she kept livestock down here. He remembered the unidentifiable carcass he'd seen earlier hanging in the woman's abattoir. He tried to erase that picture from his mind as he reached for the doorknob.

A low, keening moan issued from the room down below and sent chills crawling across the back of his neck. Startled, Bernie turned toward the sound; the flame wavered in the air, burning his hand, and he dropped the lighter. It clattered through the gap between the stairs; the flame went out as it fell from sight, and the basement plunged into absolute darkness.

The sound again. He realized that his first instinct had been wrong; it wasn't an animal. A terrible sound of pain and despair—only a human voice could express such suffering.

Bernie stopped in place, trying to orient himself in the darkness. He turned carefully and reached his hands ahead of him for the door at the top of the steps, located the knob, and turned it. Locked. He leaned forward and pressed his full weight against it. The door felt substantial, unyielding. He wouldn't be able to attack it successfully in the dark.

Another pitiable moan issued from the room below.

Despite the cold, he felt sweat break out all along his brow. He felt his hands shaking. Afraid he might lose his balance, he turned and sat down on a step below him, trying to settle his nerves.

Who was in that room? The woman, Frau Escher? Maybe the SS had come through and injured her, or worse, then left her to die.

He used both hands and feet to slide down one step, then another, and work his way back down to the floor. On his hands and knees, he felt his way around the stairs, to the back of the risers, heading toward the spot in his mind's eye where he'd watched the lighter fall from sight. He spread his hands out ahead on the floor as he edged forward, trying to cover every inch of ground.

One of his hands came in contact with something smooth and fleshy and he scuttled back away from it, grunting in disgust. Another moan issued from the room behind the door at the end of the hall. Much louder and closer, and in the deep darkness the sound cut right through him.

What had he touched? He waited, but sensed nothing moving toward him. He reached out his hands again, angling in another direction, slowly at first, then more frantically as fear wormed deeper into his mind, until his thumb grazed something metallic on the floor. He chased after it with clawing fingers and finally got his hands around the lighter. Trying to stave off panic, he flicked it once, twice, but got no spark. He shook the lighter in his hand, breathed deeply, waited, then tried again. The small flame sprouted into the air and held, a pinpoint of light in a sea of black.

The geography of where he was faded back into view. His eyes took in everything in snapshots, turning to look in each direction until he fixed his position.

The stairs. The short hallway. The door from which he'd entered from the storage room. The second door at the end of the hall.

Under the stairs near where he was crouched, a pile of gnawed and weathered bones.

Lying next to them, the object he'd grazed in the dark—a human hand.

Bernie scrambled backward across the floor, away from the thing, until his back collided with a wall. His heart thumped in his chest; adrenaline pumped through his gut. He stood up without realizing it. As his back bumped against the wall again, the door behind him swung open. Bernie turned when he heard the hinges yawn.

He stepped back from the open door and held the lighter out in front of him, waiting for the flame to penetrate the gloom inside. Two long shapes lay on the floor inside the small space. He took a step closer and saw that they wore olive green field uniforms. One rested motionless, and he knew on instinct the body had no life in it. The other moved slightly, seemed to sense his presence, then moaned again and feebly raised an arm in his direction. The arm ended in a bloody black stump.

Bernie heard the sharp bang of a door slamming shut upstairs, followed by heavy, shuffling footsteps crossing the room directly over his head, and the sound of something heavy dragging across the floor. Keys rattled in the lock of the door at the head of the stairs. Bernie killed the lighter, left the small room where the two bodies lay, and retreated back down the hall to the storage room. Hiding behind the closed door, he eased it open a crack and looked out.

The door at the top of the stairs swung open and a wedge of yellow light sliced down into the basement hallway. He saw her shadow first, then the woman's bulk appeared on the landing, almost obliterating the light. She clumped down two steps, then turned and reached back for something. She proceeded to back down the stairs, dragging a body behind her feet first, face up. Bernie saw black boots and the green field jacket of a GI. The head bounced heavily on each step as she yanked the body after her like a sack of cement. She was wheezing with effort, and muttering under her breath in German.

"*Sehen Sie, Amis, wie Sie es jetzt mögen.*"

When the body hit the basement floor, she turned and noticed the open door behind her to the room with the other soldiers. She dropped the feet of the body she'd just dragged down and entered the smaller room. She pulled a string to turn on a naked overhead bulb, setting it swinging. Bernie saw a concrete floor with a drain in the middle, dried blood on the walls. Hanging from a line, apparently to dry, he saw what looked like a stretched, mottled sheet of skin. The woman leaned down over the soldier who was still alive and viciously kicked him with her boot, prompting another moan.

"You open this door, *Ami*? You open this door? What I tell you? Maybe now I took your other hand, yes?"

She marched back into the hall. Bernie shut the door quietly and leaned back, feeling ill and weak. He thought about trying to identify himself, in the hope she'd remember him from the other day, but what he'd seen in that room made that unthinkable. Not in the dark hell of that basement, not in an American uniform. She'd crossed a border human beings never came back from. He heard the woman's weight burden the stairs as she made her way back up.

Bernie glanced around the room in the dim light from the broken window. The line of tools against the wall. A shovel. A pickax. A hatchet planted in a small stack of cut wood under the window. He moved over to pick up the hatchet and caught movement out of the corner of his eye.

Her bright, vacant blue eyes were staring down at him through the broken window. Then, in an instant, she was gone.

Bernie tried to pull out the hatchet, but it was wedged so deeply into the wood that he couldn't dislodge it. The woodpile collapsed around him, sending logs rolling across the room. He stepped over them, his hands found the shovel, and he threw open the storage room door. He heard her footsteps stomping across the floor above. He closed the door behind him, ran underneath the staircase, and planted his back against the wall.

He saw her shadow first, thrown down against the basement floor by the sharp yellow light as she stood at the top of the stairs. She held a meat cleaver in her hand.

"You come to steal my food again, *Ami*?" she called toward the closed storage room door. "Like those other boys?"

Bernie didn't move. He wasn't even sure he was breathing.

"Maybe I lock you in down here. See how you like that for a week, yes? No food? No water? You like that, *Ami*? With your friends here?"

She waited, then took a step down onto the first riser. Bernie heard the nails groan above him as they held her weight.

"They all lying in a meadow, *Ami*. All dead. All your friends. We take care of them good, huh? Like I take care of you. You come into our village. You kill my livestock. Take my food. We see how you like it."

She stepped down to the next riser. Now Bernie could see the back of her feet and thick, booted ankles through the open stairs.

"Come out, *Ami*. I have something for you," she said, her tone changing to a playful sing-song. "You must be hungry, yes? Come here, boy, I fix you something nice."

As she stepped down onto the third stair, Bernie reached both hands in from behind, grabbed her fat right ankle and yanked it toward him with all his strength. Her left foot lifted off the stair, and she struggled to maintain her balance. She planted her left leg and nearly pulled her right foot out of his hand. Leaning forward, she made a small hop to the left, then tried to skip down to the next stair onto her left foot. Bernie twisted the foot he still held in his grasp and felt it turn her body in midair. She toppled forward, arms extended, landing heavily on her left side down the rest of the stairs with a loud yelp. She slid the rest of the way, then rolled onto the floor on top of the dead soldier.

Bernie gripped the handle of the shovel, leaned out from under the stairs, and waited. The woman groaned, her breath rising and falling in a ragged rasp. He edged forward until he caught sight of her heaped form in the edge of the light. Bernie took a deep breath.

The woman jolted to life, scrabbling along the ground at him like a rabid dog, the cleaver in her hand, gibbering incoherently. Bernie stumbled away from her until he slammed into another door. It crashed open behind him and he fell back into a narrow room lined with shelves on either side. The woman crawled after him. He kicked the door shut with his foot; it slammed into her face and bounced off, but she kept coming. Bernie crabbed backward, pulling down shelving between them. Glass jars exploded on and around her as she advanced. The room filled with noxious smells; he didn't want to know what was in those jars. He jumped to his feet, made his way around the shelving to the right, saw another door ahead, and threw himself at it. The door flew open. He slammed it shut and bolted it just as she drew herself up and threw her mass at the other side. The entire wall shuddered. She shrieked and hit it again, then went quiet.

Bernie looked around. He was back in the first room he'd entered. He peered through the door to the hallway. He could see the stairs. He glanced at the casement window he had broken, but didn't think he could climb through it in time.

Bernie made a break for the stairs, and she came running out of the darkness, cutting off his angle. He tried to leap up to the third stair, caught his toe on the edge, and landed hard, facedown on the stairs. She closed in behind him, the cleaver going up in her hand. Bernie turned, whipped the shovel around, and the cleaver scraped down along its shaft, sparks flying, metal ringing on metal. He swung the shovel back the other way and struck a glancing blow to the side of her head, but she shook it off and kept after him.

Bernie pulled himself up onto the next riser, parried another blow from the cleaver, then jabbed the blade at her fleshy mass to keep her at bay. She knocked the shovel aside and brought the cleaver down again, missing Bernie's hip by two inches, splintering the wood of the riser as he rolled out of its way.

Bernie swung the shovel again, but couldn't put much weight behind it. The blow struck her in the ribs and she hardly seemed to notice. She pinned the handle under one arm, turned her body, and wrenched the shovel out of his hands, letting it fall. Bernie turned and crawled frantically up the stairs.

Someone stood in the open doorway at the top, silhouetted. He saw an arm point toward him, holding a pistol. Bernie threw himself flat on the stairs, turning his head away, and from the corner of his eye he saw her nightmare figure lurching up the stairs behind him, the cleaver high in the air. Then came the sharp report of the gun, twice, three, four shots, echoing harshly.

The bullets stopped the woman on the stairs, blossoms of blood spreading across her chest. She looked at Bernie in disbelief, wobbled in place, gave a soft, low groan, crumpled, and collapsed off the side of the staircase, hitting the concrete floor with a heavy crunch.

Bernie felt a hand on his shoulder. He raised his head up to look.

"Jesus Christ, Brooklyn," said Von Leinsdorf. "I leave you alone for a minute, look what you get yourself into."

"What the fuck. What the fuck."

Von Leinsdorf continued down the stairs. He walked into the room at the end of the hall where she'd stashed the bodies. Moments later, Bernie heard another shot.

16

The Bridge at Amay
DECEMBER 17, 4:30 P.M.

Grannit downshifted sharply, the gearbox of the Willys grinding in protest, fishtailing the rear tires around the hairpin turns. They'd taken ten minutes to drive up the hill. Going down, they reached the river road in five.

As they accelerated toward the bridgehead, they could see the other jeep parked alongside the checkpoint. All four passengers were still in their seats. An officer in the back was talking with the sergeant in charge of the bridge.

"Don't you want to slow down a little, Earl?" asked Carlson.

Grannit looked at him, annoyed. "Do you want to drive, Ole?"

"Just thought you'd want to come in slow so we don't tip 'em off."

"You want me to pull over so you can drive?"

"No."

"Why don't I just stop right here and you can take us in at the right speed?"

"Forget it. Sorry I asked."

"Jesus, you'd make coffee nervous."

Grannit hit the brakes before they made the final turn and reached the bridge emplacement ten seconds later. Grannit gave a casual wave to the sergeant as he pulled in front of the other jeep, cutting off their way forward. A captain in the passenger seat of the second jeep turned to look at them with a wave and a friendly smile.

"Everything okay, Sergeant?" asked Grannit.

"This is Captain Harlan," said the sergeant, turning to the new arrivals. "Did I get that right, sir?"

Harlan nodded. Grannit hopped out of the jeep and saluted.

"How are you doing today?" Harlan asked Grannit, returning the salute. "Where you fellas from?"

None of the four men appeared unduly nervous. Two wore their boots without leggings, like the dead German they'd found at the crossing, and one lacked a regulation belt. Only one man wore a unit patch on his shoulder. Keeping an eye on their movements, Grannit casually moved around their jeep. He noticed that the lettering on their hood looked freshly stenciled, showing no wear and tear. Four spare jerricans were tied to the back.

"We were near Liège this morning," said Grannit, taking out a pack of cigarettes. "Where you coming in from, sir?"

"We were in Holland yesterday, Eindhoven. Signal Corps, Third Armored. Orders to move came down in the middle of the night. It was hell just getting everybody on the road."

Grannit tried to light a cigarette, deliberately mistiming his roll of the flint. "See any Krauts on the way down?"

"We sure didn't. Guess the heavy stuff 's still to the east, huh? Is it really as bad as they're saying?"

"Where you guys headed? Hey, you got a light?" asked Grannit.

Captain Harlan fished out his silver Zippo. "They said they wanted the whole outfit in Malmédy by tonight. Our CO told us to divert west and head down to Bastogne. We're looking for the turn to get us back on the highway, just stopped to ask directions—"

As the captain held out his lighter, ready to flick it on, Grannit grabbed his hand and took it from him. He pulled his .45 with the other and held it inches from the captain's head.

"Have your driver toss the keys to my partner," said Grannit.

On the other side of their jeep, Carlson pulled his handgun and covered the driver. The sergeant and his platoon stepped forward, training weapons on the other men in the jeep. None of them moved.

"What's this all about? What's the problem?" asked Harlan.

"Do it," said Grannit.

The driver looked at his captain, who nodded, then pulled the keys from the ignition and threw them to Carlson.

"You want to think about what you're doing, Lieutenant?" said Harlan. "Don't make yourself any trouble—"

"Climb down, all of you. Leave the weapons. Get on the road, hands and knees."

The men in the jeep obeyed.

"Don't do something you'll regret, Lieutenant," said Harlan. "There's obviously some kind of misunderstanding. I know tensions are running high—"

"Put your sidearm on the ground and slide it to me," said Grannit.

Captain Harlan did as he was told. "You want to check our ID again? Our pay books, what? We already showed our trip pass to these fellas; what more do you need?"

Grannit holstered his Colt and yanked the cover off the captain's Zippo. A small glass vial of clear liquid had been packed in next to the saturated wadding. Grannit pulled it out and took a sniff.

Bitter almonds.

Harlan saw the glass vial in Grannit's hand, and his eyes betrayed him.

"*Sprechen Sie deutsch*, Captain?" asked Grannit.

Von Leinsdorf helped Bernie up the stairs and set him on a sofa in the front parlor. He locked the door to the cellar and closed the blinds before turning on a light. He laid out an assortment of cold K rations and opened two bottles of ale he'd found in the kitchen. Bernie drank and ate greedily.

"How badly are you hurt?" asked Von Leinsdorf.

"I'm fine," said Bernie, his voice scratchy and hoarse. "Everything's working. She never got a piece of me."

He met Von Leinsdorf's eyes and didn't look away, to make sure he was believed. Leinsdorf appeared satisfied. He leaned back in his chair, threw a leg over its arm, and lit a cigarette.

"I lost you in that fog," he said.

"An American patrol pulled me out of there," said Bernie, biting into some crackers and cheese. "Tree knocked me on my ass."

"Never seen pea soup like that before, even in London. At least it let me get our jeep back." Leinsdorf tapped down a cigarette on the face of his wristwatch and watched Bernie wolf down the rations. "Where'd they take you?"

"Baugnez."

"You were in Baugnez?"

"Yeah. Just before the tanks got there."

"That was our main column. *Obersturmbannführer* Peiper's command, the First SS Panzer Division. *Die Leibstandarte*. You know who they are, Brooklyn?"

"Hitler's bodyguard."

"Five thousand men. The most elite regiment in the army. Spearhead of the invasion."

"Is that why they don't take prisoners?"

Von Leinsdorf leaned forward. "You saw what happened?"

"Saw it, fuck, we were thrown in with 'em, I nearly got killed."

"For fuck's sake, Brooklyn, why didn't you tell them who you were?"

"I tried. Happened so fast I never got the chance. I saw you outside but couldn't get your attention. I made it into the woods when they started shooting."

"So you remembered this place."

"Regular four-star hotel. How'd you find me?"

"Not because I was looking. I met our *Abwehr* contact at that café. He said they left the package for us here this morning, so I came to find it. Lucky for you, old boy."

"So is it here?"

"I was about to take a look when I heard you romping around with your girlfriend. Christ, what a ghastly beast. What was she doing down there?"

Bernie shrugged, trying to deny the memory, but Von Leinsdorf read something on his face.

"You're not going to tell me she dragged those bodies here for . . . delicatessen purposes—"

"I don't want to think about it."

"Neither do I. But it makes you wonder about that meal she served us the other night—"

"I don't want to talk about that either."

"*La spécialité maison*: Frau Escher's secret recipe."

"Shut the fuck up."

"Her husband never joined the army," said Von Leinsdorf, trying to suppress a laugh. "That must have been him in the display case."

"It's not fucking funny," said Bernie, finishing his ale. "I could have ended up in a sausage."

"That's why we're always rushing through here on our way to France. No one comes to Belgium for the food." He tried to restrain himself and broke up even harder.

"Shut up!" As the alcohol hit his system, Bernie felt himself give in and slide over into laughter.

"Which explains her interest in poor old Preuss," said Von Leinsdorf. "That wasn't lust, it was hunger."

"There was a lot to love—"

"And she wanted to bring out the 'wurst' in him."

Bernie fell over on the sofa and banged his fists on the table until he rolled onto the floor. Both laughed until they had tears in their eyes.

"Oh shit," said Von Leinsdorf, drying his eyes.

"Fuck," said Bernie.

"Fuck, fuck, fuck. God damn it."

"So what do we do now?" asked Bernie when the laughter finally subsided.

"I'm going to find that package," said Von Leinsdorf, getting to his feet and searching the room.

"You make contact with corps command?"

"No. I talked to some of Peiper's men. They say Skorzeny and the rest of our brigade's stuck near the border."

"What's holding them up?"

"Logistical problems, across the entire front. We've broken through but can't get troops to the front. Half our divisions are still into Germany."

"What happened?"

Bernie followed him into the kitchen, where Von Leinsdorf rifled through the cabinets.

"Final shipments of fuel didn't arrive, so they're scavenging for gasoline. There's too much traffic for these country roads and the weather's turned them to skating rinks. The Americans blew some key bridges as they fell back; others can't bear the weight of the tanks. Now the roads are so congested the fuel can't get to the forward positions. Aside from that, everything's going splendidly."

"Snafu."

"Snafu is right. But Americans keep surrendering every time we make contact. Over ten thousand on the first day alone. Entire divisions."

"That's why they don't want prisoners. So they won't get slowed down. That's why those prisoners were shot."

"Maybe."

"You have any idea how the Americans are going to react when word gets out about that?"

"This is war. Happens all the time."

"Not to Americans it doesn't."

"It's the nature of the beast. On the Russian front neither side takes prisoners—"

"I got news for you, this isn't Russia, and your trigger-happy pals in the *Waffen*-SS can't go around killing American prisoners with impunity—"

"Take it easy, Brooklyn—"

"Take it easy? You know what this does to our chances if we're captured in these uniforms? If there was ever any doubt about a firing squad, forget it. We're in deep fucking water, both sides are shooting at us, we've lost half our squad—"

Von Leinsdorf moved into the workroom behind the kitchen and kept looking.

"The first thing they teach you in the military: Plans are only useful until the moment you meet the enemy."

"Here's a plan: Why don't we head back to Germany? I'm serious. If our brigade's not even across the border yet, what the fuck are we doing? Let's ditch these uniforms and get out of here."

"You're talking about desertion."

"That's just a word. It doesn't mean anything. Nothing means anything out here, it's just fucking chaos, and from what I've seen all it does is make people crazy. We're not going back to that bridge, are we?"

"No."

"Well, I don't see any point in getting killed for nothing, do you?"

"It wouldn't be for nothing, Brooklyn," said Von Leinsdorf. "You're forgetting. We have a second objective."

Bernie's heart thudded in his chest. Von Leinsdorf opened the cabinet where the woman hid her radio, reached to the back, fished around, and lifted out a large envelope. He opened it and looked inside.

"And now that we have these, we can get on with it."

"Why? What's in there?"

Von Leinsdorf showed Bernie four high-level U.S. Army security passes for Supreme Allied Headquarters.

"What did we need 'em for?" asked Bernie. "You already gave us one of these before we came over the line."

"There was a mistake in the printing," said Von Leinsdorf. "Our document team misspelled a word, but it wasn't discovered in time. These are the corrected versions. We can't use the old ones."

"Use them for what? Why are we even talking about this? Let's get the hell out of here."

Von Leinsdorf grabbed him by the collar and pulled him close. "I can be your friend, Brooklyn. In spite of our differences, after what we've been through I like to think that I am. But don't suggest that again."

Von Leinsdorf released him and put the passes back in the envelope.

Friend. That wasn't a word Bernie had ever used in relation to Erich Von Leinsdorf. There had been moments when he felt they could get along, even stumble toward some understanding of each other, and the man had just saved his life. But the question stuck: Did their mission demand this violence from him—seven killed now in two days—or give him an excuse to indulge it?

"This other objective," said Bernie. "You going to tell me what it is?"

"Why should I trust you, Brooklyn? Do you trust me? After Schieff and Preuss, I don't think so."

"Guy gets the sniffles around you, he ends up with a bullet in the head."

Von Leinsdorf pointed an emphatic finger at him. "They endangered our mission. Nothing else matters. We don't need them now anyway."

"What does that mean? You need me, so I get to live?"

"Put it any way you like," said Von Leinsdorf. "I can't complete the assignment without you. Go pack up the jeep, I'll use the radio."

Once Bernie left the room, Von Leinsdorf used the radio to contact his other squad leaders, Gerhard Bremer and William Sharper. Both squads had evaded capture through the first days of the invasion and picked up their corrected SHAEF security passes from the *Abwehr*. Von Leinsdorf told them that they were to move south into France, as scheduled, and pursue the Second Objective.

Karl Schmidt's squad failed to respond, but Von Leinsdorf considered that a plus; the man was a weak-kneed intellectual and chronic complainer. They were better off without him. He would have been no help at all where they were going.

17

Grannit and Carlson secured their four prisoners and sat them down behind the sandbag emplacement while the bridge detail stood watch. Carlson radioed headquarters about the arrests. Grannit searched their jeep. After assembling the evidence he found in an empty ammunition tin, he walked back to the prisoners.

"You're in charge, right?" he asked their captain.

The man nodded.

"Take a walk with me," said Grannit, gesturing toward the bridge.

The German stood up and started ahead of him. Ole Carlson hurried out of the radio tent as they neared the bridge.

"Command says bring 'em in to First Army Interrogation," said Carlson, falling into step with them. "They want Army Counterintelligence in on it, we should get 'em there ASAP—"

"I won't be long," said Grannit.

"They said they don't want to wait, Earl—"

"Give me a few minutes. And stand by for that other thing we talked about."

Carlson gave the German next to Grannit a long look. "Whatever you say."

Ole pulled his sidearm and walked back toward the other prisoners. Grannit waved the German on ahead of him. The man looked back at

Carlson, concerned. Grannit shoved him forward and told him not to turn around. By the time they reached the middle of the bridge, it was nearly pitch black.

"Stop here," said Grannit.

Grannit set the ammo box down on the ground between them, turned on a flashlight, and pointed it at the German. He had a long, intelligent face, and was trying at the moment to put up a hardened front.

"Let's get one thing straight. There's enough in that jeep to hang you five times. Unless you think you're going to pass these off as souvenirs." He held up a pair of red armbands with swastikas. "I ask questions and you answer them, got that? What's your name?"

"Karl Heinz Schmidt."

"What's your rank?"

"*Obersturmführer*. Lieutenant."

Grannit held up the dog tags he'd taken earlier from the man's neck. "Who's Captain Ted Harlan?"

"I have no idea."

"Did you kill him?"

"No."

"Why are you wearing his tags?"

"They were given to me. I assume he must be an American prisoner of war."

"What unit are you with?"

"The 150th Panzer Brigade."

"Who's your commanding officer?"

Schmidt hesitated. "Colonel Otto Skorzeny."

Grannit recognized the name from military briefings, but showed no reaction.

"So what brings you to Belgium, Karl?" asked Grannit. "Sightseeing? Little vacation?"

"Could I have a cigarette, please?"

Grannit handed him a pack. Schmidt's hands were shaking as he tried to light a match.

"My understanding under the accords of the Geneva Convention, to which both of our countries are a party, is that I am required to give you only the information you've already requested. Nothing more."

Schmidt tried to meet his eye with resolve. Grannit took a step closer to him.

"Here's the truth: I don't know shit about military procedure. I'm with a special investigative division and we do things differently, so let me put it on a plate for you: You got pinched behind our lines wearing an American uniform. The book says that makes you a spy and all bets are off. They teach you what that phrase means, Lieutenant Schmidt, all bets are off?"

Schmidt shook his head. Grannit took another step forward until they were nose to nose.

"It means I don't give a fuck. So you tell me what I want to know or I'm going to hurt you. I'll start with an easy question. How many other men are in your squad? How many were with you in that jeep?"

Schmidt appeared confused. "Three."

Grannit waved the flashlight back toward the edge of the bridge, switching it off and on. A moment later, a single shot rang out, followed by a scream, then another shot. Grannit turned back to Schmidt.

"I think it's two now," said Grannit.

Schmidt's knees buckled slightly. He backed up a step and went pale.

"You want a heads-up on your next few days? Military Intelligence questions you, you go before a court-martial and then a firing squad, and the court-martial's a formality."

Schmidt took another step and staggered when he felt the wall of the bridge behind him.

"Nobody on this side's going to defend you or care what happens to you, and nobody on your side's ever going to hear about it. The one chance you've got is to cooperate and tell us everything you know. If you don't come clean, I'll save everybody the trouble and drop your ass off this bridge right now."

Schmidt went down onto his haunches, head lowered, breathing in jagged bursts.

"You don't strike me as a stupid man," said Grannit. "I don't want to lean on you if I don't have to. You're not a soldier, are you, Schmidt?"

Schmidt shook his head. Grannit knelt down next to him and lowered his voice, radiating sympathy.

"I didn't think so. You have a family?"

"Yes," said Schmidt. "A wife. Two boys. Twins. They're not even ten years old."

Grannit took out a notebook and pen and waited. "That's who you should be thinking about now. I can't make any promises but this: I'll do what I can for you."

Schmidt rubbed his eyes, struggling to compose himself. "We were part of a special brigade. Those of us who came over in American uniform. Our company was going to assemble here."

"To capture the bridge?"

"And two others, nearby, by tonight."

"So where's the rest of your brigade?"

"I don't know. We were sent ahead to scout. When the others came, we were to secure the bridges for the main offensive. We had tanks. Some captured American. Panzers and Panthers disguised to look like Shermans. We have also motorized artillery, antitank guns, three mortar platoons, an armored reconnaissance group, a full supply column—"

Grannit could hardly write fast enough to keep up. "How many men are we talking about?"

"I would estimate two thousand? There was supposed to be a paratroop drop also, regular Wehrmacht, to support us against the bridges. The main columns were supposed to reach this position within a day. By tonight."

"The main objective being Antwerp."

Schmidt looked at him, mildly surprised. "That's right. If all went according to plan, they said it would fall within a week." He continued as Grannit kept writing.

"I want you to know I had no choice in this. I am not in the Nazi Party; I didn't even enlist. I despise what has happened to my country. It's only that I spoke your language, you see? I worked as a translator before the war, at a Berlin publishing house; I studied English in college. There were threats to my wife and children; they made me work as an intelligence officer, reading newspapers, interpreting reports; I've never been near the front line—"

"I'll be sure to note that," said Grannit. "So how many men in your company came over the line? How many were in the jeeps?"

"The commando unit? I don't know, maybe eighty men?"

"All in four-man teams."

"Yes, that was how they organized us."

"About twenty teams altogether?"

"That sounds right."

"Did you all have the same objective?"

"As far as the bridges were concerned? Yes, but different responsibilities. Some for reconnaissance, some trained for sabotage, others demolition."

"There's another team I'm looking for." Grannit described the two soldiers he'd tracked to the hospital and chased in the jeep. "I need to find the lieutenant in charge of that squad. You have any idea who I'm talking about?"

Schmidt's look hardened. "Yes, I do. I think I know exactly who that man is."

"What's his name?"

"I never knew his German name. He is using the American name Miller, Lieutenant George Miller."

"What else can you tell me about him?"

"He is SS. I think he came from Dachau."

"Where's that?"

"The SS training center. Near Munich."

Grannit wrote down the name, put his notebook in his pocket, and pulled the man to his feet.

"We can talk more while we're driving in," said Grannit. "You did all right, Schmidt. You did the right thing."

"What choice do I have? What choice have I had from the beginning?"

Grannit didn't answer. As they neared the bridgehead, he waved his flashlight. By the time they reached the emplacement, Carlson was waiting behind the wheel of a small transport with the engine running. Guarded by two soldiers from the bridge, the other three Germans sat in the open payload. None of them had been wounded or harmed in any way. Schmidt looked at Grannit, who couldn't tell if he was angry or relieved.

"You think I'd shoot a prisoner of war?" asked Grannit. "Where the hell you think you are, Russia? Get in."

He pointed Schmidt into the back of the captured jeep. Grannit took the sergeant in charge of the bridge platoon aside and relayed what Schmidt had told him about the impending attack.

"Radio your unit, tell them to get you reinforced fast. Maybe they're coming in force, maybe they're not, but you've got to hold this bridge."

"Yes, sir."

Grannit climbed into the jeep beside Schmidt. One of the bridge platoon GIs jumped in to drive, and both vehicles headed north along the river road.

"They really thought you could pull this thing off," said Grannit, after a while.

"They hoped," said Schmidt.

"But you didn't."

Schmidt shrugged. "Hope is all they have left." He watched the river for a moment, a plaintive look on his face. "Is it up to you? Whether I live or die?"

"I'll have something to say about it," said Grannit.

"But is it your decision to make?"

"Why do you want to know?"

"Our brigade was to capture that bridge," he said, studying Grannit's reaction. "We were also given a second objective."

Grannit waited. "Why don't you tell me what it was."

Schmidt watched him closely. "I'll wait. To speak to your superiors."

"Why not tell me now?"

"You made the choice to spare my life, and I appreciate that. But I need to speak about this with someone who can offer me a more substantial guarantee."

18

Waimes
DECEMBER 17, 10:00 P.M.

Before they left, Erich Von Leinsdorf poured out the kerosene from every lamp in the house and set Frau Escher's butcher shop on fire. By the time they drove away, *Obersturmbannführer* Peiper's main panzer column had advanced through to the west; the village was deserted. Fog curled in, and more snow began to fall as they picked their way south and west. Von Leinsdorf studied a road map with a flashlight.

"I made coffee," he said, holding up a thermos. "Drink a lot of it."

Von Leinsdorf poured him a cup, and Bernie choked downed the strong brew as he drove, blasting his senses awake. Von Leinsdorf handed him a new helmet.

"What's this for?" he asked.

"Some Americans have had a look at us. We're changing units."

"Fuck, I was just getting used to Jimmy Tenella."

"You don't have to change the name, just give me your helmet."

Bernie did, and Von Leinsdorf tossed it out of the jeep.

"We're with the 291st Combat Engineers now. Our CO sent us south with dispatches just before they pulled back from Malmédy." He held up a leather U.S. Army document tube.

"I'm supposed to remember all this?"

"You'd better, old boy, or we're fairly fucked."

"Where are we going?" asked Bernie.

"You drive, I'll get us there. The good news is we can take back roads the entire way. Left here."

Von Leinsdorf switched on the flashlight over the map again. Bernie glanced over and realized that at some point Von Leinsdorf had changed the color of his blond brush cut to a dirty brown.

"What'd you do to your hair?"

"Another of Frau Escher's secrets. Hair dye in the bathroom."

Von Leinsdorf put on a pair of square, black-framed glasses, which drastically altered his appearance, making him look years older.

"Where did you get all this stuff?"

"Downstairs."

Bernie fumbled off his helmet. "Jesus, this is from one of those stiffs in the basement?"

"The ones they gave us at Grafenwöhr were stamped with the wrong mark inside the shell, see here?" He showed him a factory insignia inside the rim of the new helmet. "It's a different stamp for officers and noncoms. Ours looked the same. I'd put that back on if I were you; there may be snipers out here."

Bernie uneasily set the helmet back on his head.

"I take it you lost your rifle, too," said Von Leinsdorf. "There's another M1 in the back. What do you think of this?"

He held a vicious-looking hunting knife into the light.

"The woman had it strapped to her thigh."

Bernie made a face. "You searched her thighs?"

"Be thankful she didn't use it on you," said Von Leinsdorf. "If anyone stops us or we hit a checkpoint, show them this." He handed Bernie another road pass. "If they ask you anything else, you defer to me."

"So what do you need me for?"

"In case they ask us some bullshit trick question about baseball or who's fucking Minnie Mouse. Then jump in with all deliberate speed. You are up to that, aren't you, Brooklyn?"

Bernie swallowed his frustration and kept driving; anxiety gnawed at him, his hands clutched the wheel. They reached the Ambleve River near midnight, crossing an ancient stone bridge pockmarked with bullets. The highway south took them into a shadowy forest. Ancient hardwoods crowded the road, their branches intertwining overhead to create a fog-enshrouded canopy. The stripped trees took on an unearthly silver glow, like twisted knots of human limbs in the mist. Visibility narrowed to a few yards.

Bernie had to brake suddenly to avoid slamming into a burned-out troop transport. A shell had hit the gas tank flush and the wheels had melted right onto the road. The charred corpses inside were impossible to identify as either German or American. They slowly drove around it and edged forward. Bernie thought he saw a line of men sprint across the road in front of them and disappear into the woods, but he couldn't tell what uniforms they were wearing. Von Leinsdorf crouched in the passenger seat and raised his rifle. A volley of bullets whistled by them out of the fog from that direction and shattered the rearview mirror. Von Leinsdorf returned fire, emptying his clip. Bernie stepped on the gas, taking a chance that nothing else lay hidden ahead of them in the dense air.

At three in the morning they emerged onto a high rocky plain, and Von Leinsdorf directed Bernie to follow signs toward Bastogne. Artillery boomed in the distance and drew closer as they approached. They cleared a checkpoint outside the village and entered an entrenched stronghold in the middle of town. MPs directed them to central command for VIII Corps, and they parked around the corner. Rifle companies were digging in all around, fortifying positions for mortars and machine guns. Bernie changed field jackets, putting on one that bore the insignia of the 291st Engineers.

"Stay next to me," said Von Leinsdorf. "Don't talk to anybody."

Holding up the document tube, Von Leinsdorf showed their new, corrected SHAEF security passes at the door, and they were sent toward the signal office. The command center, hastily thrown together in the middle of an old cathedral, hummed with frantic energy, officers shouting over one another. Housed in one of the chapels off the main nave, a battery of radio, telex, and telegraph operators relayed updated messages. Von Leinsdorf stood near the back and observed for a minute, getting a grasp of the command structure.

"Keep your head down," said Von Leinsdorf. "Look busy."

Bernie took out a pad and began to write. His hands could barely hold the pen. A signal corps sergeant barked at them as he walked past, gesturing at the document tube.

"You got something for us, Lieutenant?" he said.

"Already handed 'em off," said Von Leinsdorf. "Waiting on dispatches for the Twelfth."

"Don't wait too long," said the sergeant. "You might not get back out."

Listening to the chatter, Bernie learned that German forces were advancing rapidly to the north and south of Bastogne. The mood in the room ran just short of panic that they were about to be overrun; Bernie felt it fire his overwrought nerves. Von Leinsdorf studied the radio operators. He picked out a small corporal who looked close to exhaustion, then moved toward him the next time he came off a call, holding up the document tube. He had to shout to be heard over the din in the room.

"God damn it, they told us General Bradley would be here," said Von Leinsdorf. "I've got to get these into his hands."

"Bradley? He was supposed to be here an hour ago, but we lost the main road between here and Luxembourg."

"Christ, you're telling me he's not coming?"

"They might try to fly him in later, or get him back down to France. Ike wants both him and Patton for a pow-wow—"

"Where the hell's that going to be?"

"Maybe Verdun, maybe in Paris, they haven't said yet."

"Well, when the fuck is it scheduled?"

Bernie moved closer, listening and watching Von Leinsdorf. His sudden interest in Bradley's movements alarmed him.

"I don't think before tomorrow, and you can forget about getting to Luxembourg before that, sir, the Krauts are swarming down there—"

"Then god damn it, Corporal, I've got to get into France today. I need to know which crossings are still open and if it's gonna be Verdun or Paris as soon as you get word."

"I'll stay on it, sir."

"Where's your signal officer? I need the fucking passwords."

"We were just about to put out today's list," he said.

"Well, don't let me stop you," said Von Leinsdorf.

As the radio operator went to work, Bernie saw Von Leinsdorf step back and assess whether he'd been overheard. Every man in the room was so caught up in his own corner of the war that no one paid any attention. Ten steps away, Bernie watched a group of officers knotted around a red-faced general, who was shouting angrily at them. A shell landed outside, close enough to shake dust from the ceiling and momentarily dim the lights. During the blackout, Von Leinsdorf brazenly snatched the password list from the operator's desk—Bernie saw it in his hand when the lights came back on. Von Leinsdorf put it in his pocket, looked over, caught Bernie watching, and winked at him.

He's crazy. He's enjoying this.

Until he found a way to stop Von Leinsdorf, Bernie had resigned himself to the consequences of sabotage, reconnaissance, even espionage. That at least gave him a chance to avoid killing Americans.

Until that moment, assassination hadn't even occurred to him.

The telex station behind where Bernie was standing jumped to life, startling him.

Bernie leaned forward to read the message as it came through. It was an urgent signal from First Army HQ in Liège. The headline identified it as an emergency override, the highest level of Allied security alert.

First Army Interrogation Center, Liège
DECEMBER 18, 4:00 A.M.

The contents of Karl Schmidt's satchel, jeep, and pockets lay on the table between Schmidt and Major Moran from the 301st Counter Intelligence Corps Detachment. Schmidt's wrists were in handcuffs, secured through the slats of the chair behind his back, and he still wore the undershirt and trousers of his American uniform. Major Moran asked questions, while Earl Grannit and a team of intelligence officers watched through a one-way observation window in an ad-joining room. From there, a stenographer transcribed the conversation, which was conducted in English, although a translator was also present if the need for one arose. A wire tape recorder ran throughout the interview, so that when they reviewed and transcribed, no detail would be overlooked.

In a money belt concealed around his waist, Schmidt had carried $2000 in American currency, a thousand in counterfeit British pounds, and smaller amounts in Belgian, Dutch, and French notes and coins. American soldiers in Europe rarely carried cash and were instead issued printed scrip they called "invasion money," a detail that had escaped the scrutiny of Skorzeny's quartermaster. A shortwave military radio of German origin was found hidden in the back of Schmidt's jeep. They also found ten Pervitin tablets—caffeine-based energy boosters—an assortment of concealed weapons, including brass knuckles, hand grenades, and a stiletto; an American officer's field manual; and an English pocket-sized edition of the New Testament. Hidden in an empty fuel canister they found fuses, detonators, and six pounds of Nipolite, a malleable plastic explosive.

Other cans held four regulation German uniforms and a number of more exotic weapons, including a piano wire garrote and a silencer. Grannit took particular interest in the silencer, a silver cylinder that slid neatly over the barrel of Schmidt's standard American issue M1911 automatic. It also fit onto the end of a compact machine pistol they found, which converted to an automatic rifle with the addition of an armatured stock and telescopic sight. Among the ammunition for it they found a clip of seven bullets containing a poisonous aconite compound encased in the head, which was scored to split upon contact, causing certain death.

Because of his forgery training, Ole Carlson worked with two officers to examine Schmidt's collection of maps and documents. They included credible versions of the highest security passes issued by the Allied forces.

Early in his interview, Lieutenant Schmidt repeated the information he had given Grannit about the commando unit known as

Einheit Stielau. In earlier interrogations the other three captured members of his squad corroborated the basics of Schmidt's story. However, none of those men admitted knowing anything about a so-called second objective, even after being subjected to severe physical abuse.

Major Moran hadn't yet resorted to coercion with the talkative Schmidt, when negotiations stalled over this second objective. Schmidt offered to reveal what he knew about it, but only if given written assurance that he would not be executed as a spy. Major Moran refused. An agitated and emotional Schmidt refused to say anything more.

Furious, Moran came out of the room and ordered his men to beat it out of him. Earl Grannit asked if he could be left alone with Schmidt for a few moments. The major agreed. Grannit entered and took Moran's seat across from Schmidt.

"It doesn't matter what you dangle in front of them, Karl. They can't make that promise to you."

"But it's not fair. From the moment they brought us to that camp, we had to obey orders or they would shoot us. I haven't conducted espionage, I haven't killed Americans, I haven't committed any crimes—"

"That's not for me to decide. For all I know it may be true, but right now you have to do better."

"How?"

"Tell them you'll go out on patrol, help them look for the other commando teams. You know who or what to look for, don't you?"

"Would they let me do that?"

"Of course. But first you have to tell them what they want to know. We already grilled your squad about this. Nobody's backing you up. They say they don't know anything about a second objective—"

"They don't know because I never told them. We were ordered not to tell them anything—"

"Where'd that order come from?"

"From the officer in charge, the one who called himself Lieutenant

Miller, the man you asked me about. Please, they must believe me, I'm telling you the truth, but I'm fighting for my life."

Grannit hesitated. "Let me see what I can do."

Grannit left the room, and walked right past Moran and his men. "I gotta take a piss."

He went across the hall into the room where Ole Carlson was examining Schmidt's documents.

"These forgeries are high-quality," said Carlson. "I can't find a single fault that gives 'em away—"

Grannit leaned in and whispered, "Come into the other room. Wait for my signal after I go back in with Schmidt, then buy me a minute alone with him."

Carlson's eyes went wide, and he followed Grannit back into the observation room where the CIC officers had congregated, keeping an eye on Schmidt through the window. Grannit lit a cigarette.

"So?" asked Moran, in a foul mood. "Is he bullshitting us?"

"I don't think so."

"We're through fucking around with this asshole. If he's got something, let him put it on the table."

"I've got a good sense of this man, Major. We need to work him carefully—"

"Yeah, well, he can go fuck himself. I think he's full of shit, I think he's bluffing—"

"I respectfully disagree—"

"Well, who made you the fucking expert?"

"Colonel Otto Skorzeny put their unit together," said Grannit. "That name means something to you college graduates, doesn't it? You think Hitler sent them over here to play patty-cake?"

"So take a billy club and beat it out of him. That's how the NYPD likes to work, isn't it? Or do you prefer a rubber hose?"

Grannit pulled his sidearm and chambered a round. "Why don't I just pump bullets into him until he comes clean. You want to give me your okeydokey on that, Major? I'll make him confess to the fucking Lincoln assassination if that does the trick for you. Is that how you want to utilize our only asset?"

"You've got five minutes," said Moran.

Grannit stubbed out his cigarette on the doorjamb and walked back into the interrogation room. He sat down, glanced back at the one-way window, and rubbed the bridge of his nose. Seeing that signal, Ole Carlson stepped into the room, stumbled over somebody's foot, and spilled his coffee all over Major Moran's trousers. During the confusion that followed, Grannit leaned forward and switched off the hidden microphone under the table.

"Okay, Karl, I got you your deal, let's hear it," said Grannit.

"They won't prosecute me as a spy, they'll treat me like any other prisoner of war?"

"You have my word on it."

Schmidt leaned forward and cradled his head in his hands on the table, shoulders heaving with emotion. Grannit guessed he had less than a minute before the CIC smart-asses rushed in to turn the microphone back on.

"Save it for your family reunion, Karl, we're short on time. Now, you're going to have to ride along on those patrols we talked about; I told them you agreed to that—"

"Yes, of course—"

"And this whole thing stays between me, you, and the officer in charge, because it's against regulations. You can't mention it, even to him when they all pile in here, okay?"

Schmidt lifted his head up from the table. "Yes."

"What was your second objective?"

Grannit reached down and turned the hidden microphone back on.

"After the first two days," said Schmidt, "we are supposed to move south. Into France."

"How many men?"

Schmidt didn't blink. He reasoned that if he exaggerated the scope of the threat, he had a better chance at clemency, and that the right lie might save his life.

"All of us," said Schmidt. "Eighty men. The entire company of Skorzeny's commandos. We're to meet in Reims on the nineteenth, at a cinema, then move south to Paris."

"What's in Paris?"

"We rendezvous at the Café de la Paix with our local support and then move on Versailles. That's our objective."

"What is?"

"To attack Allied headquarters command."

Grannit felt his throat tighten.

"And to kill General Eisenhower."

19

VIII Corps HQ, Bastogne, Belgium
DECEMBER 18, 7:00 A.M.

J esus Christ, take a look at this."
The telex operator ripped off the printed cable and held it
out to the radioman next to him before Bernie could read it.
"Holy shit."

The corporal's reaction drew Von Leinsdorf's attention, and he
stepped toward them, taking a look at it before Bernie did. He
handed it back to the corporal, then smiled at Bernie.

"Read it, Corporal," said Von Leinsdorf.

"Let me have your attention!" The corporal stood up on his chair
and read it out loud. "First Army HQ, emergency override alert
for all units in Belgium, Luxembourg, and Holland. Be aware that
squads of German commandos in American uniform, driving American vehicles, are operating in combat zone behind Allied lines—"

Bernie froze in place. The room quieted and soldiers gathered
around them as the message continued.

"Be also warned brigade strength force disguised as same,
equipped with Sherman tanks and mobile artillery, believed to be
somewhere in the field, details to follow—"

Excitement radiated out around them. The corporal rushed the
cable toward the CO's desk. News of the bulletin ripped through the
room, generating an uproar.

Bernie backed up against the wall, out of traffic, trying to make himself invisible. He caught Von Leinsdorf's eye. Von Leinsdorf tilted his head toward the door and Bernie started toward the exit. A couple of HQ staff sergeants ahead of them looked like they were trying to stop people from leaving and to organize a stronger watch on the door. Von Leinsdorf grabbed one by the arm.

"Christ, can you fucking believe this?" asked Von Leinsdorf.

"I believe they'd do anything."

"But how are we gonna know the difference? How can we tell these fuckers apart? Nazis wearing our uniforms, what if they're standing right in front of us?"

"We'll know, sir. They can't pull something like this off."

"Jesus, I hope you're right. Station men here, check IDs coming in and out. We've got to secure our perimeter, get word to the MPs, let's jump on it."

"Yes, sir."

The sergeant hurried off. Von Leinsdorf grabbed Bernie behind the elbow, guiding him through the door. "Keep walking. Don't stop."

The MPs outside were just hearing the news. Von Leinsdorf barked at them, "CO needs you men inside, double time, move, move, move."

The news radiated out in front of them, jumping from man to man. Bernie kept waiting for someone to notice them, stop them, put an end to it, and some part of him half wished it would happen. As they reached the street, another artillery barrage began and lit up the morning sky, shells stepping progressively closer to the village.

"They caught one of us," said Von Leinsdorf. "Probably one of the scout teams."

"How much do you think they know?"

"Their alert didn't mention the Second Objective. So we keep going."

"To where?"

"Reims, France," said Von Leinsdorf.

"What are we doing there?"

"In Reims? We're going to the movies."

They turned the corner and saw an MP in the parking area examining the unit numbers on their jeep. Bernie saw Von Leinsdorf's hand move toward his belt as they approached.

"Corporal, what are you standing there for? Don't you know what's happening?" asked Von Leinsdorf.

"You from Twelfth Army, sir?" asked the MP.

"That's right," said Von Leinsdorf, climbing aboard and signaling Bernie to get in and drive, as he held up the document tube. "And we're heading back there now, got to get these to the Old Man."

The MP put a hand out and stopped Bernie from starting the jeep. "Where'd you come in from?"

"North," said Bernie. "Both roads to Luxembourg are cut off, case you haven't heard."

"I was just gonna say," said the MP. "Road north's cut off, too, if you planned on going back that way."

"How do we get out of here?" asked Bernie.

"You gotta head due west. I see your road pass, soldier?"

Bernie glanced at Von Leinsdorf and handed it to him. They waited while he shined his flashlight on it. Bernie saw Von Leinsdorf reach down into the seat for the hunting knife.

The MP took his time looking it over, then handed it back. "You better make tracks. Krauts just about got us buttoned up."

"Good luck to you," said Von Leinsdorf.

"You said something's going on inside?" asked the MP.

"Nothing to worry about," said Von Leinsdorf.

Bernie stepped on the gas and they drove due west out of Bastogne.

Liège
DECEMBER 18, NOON

They didn't turn off the tape recorders until Earl Grannit had squeezed every last detail out of Karl Heinz Schmidt. Less than three hours later, stripped of his uniform and dressed as a prisoner of war, Schmidt was handed over to a squad of Army Intelligence officers. They began roving patrols of the main highways south and west of the front lines, using Schmidt as their watchdog, looking for elements of what Schmidt had called Operation *Greif*.

Ongoing Allied communications problems prevented First Army Interrogation from notifying Counter Intelligence in the city of Reims, France, about Schmidt's final revelation: that the German assassination teams were planning to rendezvous at a cinema there on the evening of December 19. Earl Grannit and Ole Carlson drove out of Liège at noon and headed south to deliver that news in person.

Carlson held Karl Schmidt's forged blue SHAEF pass in his hand, studying it as they drove, then suddenly slapped it against his leg. "Staring me right in the face. That's what's wrong with this thing."

"What?" asked Grannit.

"This is U.S. government issue watermarked paper, and everything else is so well crafted you'da thought the Krauts'd catch this, it's just so danged obvious once you notice—"

"Notice what, Ole?"

"They transposed the e and a in 'headquarters.' They misspelled the doggone word."

Carlson showed it to him.

"Get on the radio," said Grannit. "Make sure they know that at the border. With luck we'll get there before they cross over."

Carlson cranked up the radio, trying to find a signal. "They're gonna execute him, aren't they?" he asked. "Schmidt?"

"That's right, Ole." Grannit glanced over as he drove. "What's the problem?"

"You promised him he wouldn't die for it."

"We don't even know he's telling the truth. Maybe he made the whole thing up to save his ass."

"Sounded pretty straight to me. How many more teams you think they sent over?"

"He said eighty men."

"They're desperate enough to try something like this. He had too many details. I think it's real and he got caught up without knowing what it was about—"

"Every bad guy's got a sob story, Ole."

"I'm just saying that if he's shot for it after helping us and us telling him different so he'd talk, it's a raw deal—"

"Guy comes over the line, wartime, in our uniform, confesses he's got orders to kill our commanding general, and you feel sorry for him."

"We lied to him, Earl."

Grannit said nothing.

"Well, how do you feel about it?"

Grannit took a long look at him. "Do I look troubled to you?"

Lieutenant Karl Heinz Schmidt would not see the other three men from his own jeep squad again until two days before Christmas. That night a group of captured German nurses were brought outside their cells and sang Christmas carols to them in their native language.

The four men were marched out at dawn the next day, Christmas Eve, tied to posts, and executed by an American firing squad. Schmidt's protests about a secret arrangement with Counter Intelligence that was supposed to have spared his life fell on deaf ears.

By noon on December 18, First Army Headquarters at the Hotel Britannique in Spa had been abandoned, retreating northwest toward Liège. Supply dumps in the area were ordered to pull back fuel and ammunition stores and destroy whatever they couldn't move to prevent them from falling into enemy hands. The German offensive had caught First Army so off guard and undermanned that every available able body was pressed into front-line action. Around Malmédy that included clerks and cooks with no combat experience, who called themselves "canteen commandos." First Army's commanding officer, General Courtney Hodges, issued one last order just before retreating toward Liège. All Allied military personnel currently in the brig for court-martial offenses were offered a one-time amnesty if they volunteered to join units fighting the increasingly desperate defense.

On the afternoon of December 18, Corporal Eddie Bennings and twenty-six other members of the 724th Railway Battalion accepted the offer. They were released from custody in Liège, re-armed, loaded onto a truck, and shipped toward Malmédy.

Fifteen minutes after being assigned to a front-line company, Eddie Bennings cut himself on the arm with his bayonet, spilling an impressive but inconsequential amount of blood. He feigned dizziness, and a medic walked him to a mobile field hospital. Bennings entered, slipped out the back of the tent as soon as he was alone, jogged half a mile down the road to the supply depot's fuel shed, came out carrying two cans of gas, hot-wired a parked jeep, and headed south toward France.

As the day wore on, the warning about Skorzeny's commandos paralyzed the American battle zone. Military police locked down every major intersection under Allied control. Effective immediately, no enlisted man or officer without the current password was allowed to pass through any checkpoint. Traffic piled up behind roadblocks, and movement of American troops, during critical hours of the offensive, came to a dead halt. Reinforcements were delayed, hundreds of soldiers ended up in custody, and important dispatches were held up for hours. Placards with information about the imposters appeared in every barracks. An army of men who had never felt any reason to distrust the American uniform now viewed one another through a lens of paranoia and suspicion. Like the rumors that had infected the Nazi camp at Grafenwöhr, wild speculation about the objectives of the 150th Panzer Brigade spread across the battlefield. Not even Otto Skorzeny would have dared to hope that the mere mention of his commando squads would create such chaos in the Allied ranks.

The bulletin that German spies were operating behind Allied lines was not the only news to hit hard on December 18. Late on the afternoon of December 17, three survivors of the massacre at Baugnez Crossroads were found by an American patrol and rushed to the field hospital in Malmédy. Two reporters from *Time* magazine encountered the survivors, heard their story, and rushed it to headquarters in

Liège. By nightfall, First Army senior staff released the story that invading SS forces had murdered a large group of unarmed American prisoners of war. Newspapers in the United States, which hadn't yet run a single story about the Ardennes offensive because of a blackout ordered by SHAEF, were encouraged to publish detailed accounts of the incident. Many compared the slaughter to the Japanese attack on Pearl Harbor. Anti-German sentiment spiked to a wartime high; war bond purchases and volunteer enlistments soared.

Americans all across the country were reading about the "massacre at Malmédy" before the bodies of the eighty-six victims had even been recovered, lying under a thick blanket of snow in the meadow at the Baugnez Crossroads.

20

Supreme Allied Headquarters, Versailles
DECEMBER 18, 10:00 A.M.

General Eisenhower spent the morning with his staff in his Map Room, trying to piece together fifty disjointed dispatches into a coherent overview of the invasion. This much was clear: Twenty-four Wehrmacht and *Waffen*-SS divisions had already been identified in the attack, striking toward Allied positions in three broad columns. While the northern and southern thrusts had met with makeshift but effective American resistance, the center through the heart of the Ardennes had not held. As Allied forces there crumbled and fell backward before the bludgeoning thrust of *Kampfgruppe* Peiper, tens of thousands of Wehrmacht and SS troops poured into the elastic middle behind them. The German attack flowed out to the south and west from there like water collecting in a basin, creating a distinct bulge on the map centering around the town of Bastogne.

During those early, uncertain hours, Dwight Eisenhower maintained a remarkable evenness of spirit. He had never led a battlefield unit but knew the first obligation of command was to set an example for the men around him. Despite the unsettling possibilities the attack presented, he never showed a moment's panic, and his calm attitude flowed through SHAEF and down the chain of command. As a portrait of the battle began to emerge, Eisenhower's tactical mind made an intuitive leap toward his enemy's intent. He picked up a captured

German sword, pointed to the center of the map, then slashed it west, all the way to Antwerp.

"They're trying to split our army groups with this central thrust, and isolate the British to the north," said Eisenhower. "These flanking columns are only there to screen the main push."

General Strong asked him how he wanted to respond. Eisenhower stepped closer to the map, bringing the sword back to the middle of the Meuse River.

"If we keep them on this side of the river, pinch them in along both shoulders, and confine the central column along this corridor, there's a chance we can choke them off here."

The point of the sword came to rest on a nexus of interlocking roads south and east of the Meuse. Eisenhower immediately ordered his reserve divisions, the 82nd and 101st Airborne, to proceed with all haste toward Bastogne.

No longer able to reach Bastogne himself, General Omar Bradley summoned General George Patton to Twelfth Army headquarters in Luxembourg City. He told Patton that his Third Army's offensive across the Saar River to the south, set to launch within days, had been officially called off. Bradley ordered Patton to have three of his divisions on the march toward the Ardennes within twenty-four hours.

During their meeting, Eisenhower sent word that he wanted to meet both his senior field commanders the following day in the French fortress city of Verdun, halfway between their headquarters, to finalize their response to the Ardennes offensive. Before they parted that evening, Bradley sympathized with Patton that his scheduled attack would not be going ahead.

"What the hell, Brad," said Patton. "We'll still be killing Krauts."

To the east of the German border, at their battle headquarters in Ziegenberg, news of the invasion's successes during the first two days heartened the Wehrmacht general staff. Hundreds of miles of forfeited Belgian territory had been regained, and thousands of American soldiers had surrendered. *Obersturmbannführer* Peiper's panzer column appeared to be relentlessly carving its way toward the Meuse.

The truth was more complicated. On the first morning after a crucial paratroop drop fell ten miles off course, the northernmost of their three panzer columns encountered stiff resistance and stalled in its tracks. Their inability to keep pace with the swift western progress of Peiper's central column left his northern shoulder exposed and vulnerable to attack if the Allies were able to regroup. Peiper's advance to the Meuse had turned into a race against time.

Since the offensive began, the main battle group of Otto Skorzeny's 150th Panzer Brigade had been stuck behind the massive traffic jam that backed up to the Western Wall. Despite the work of its advance commando teams, Operation *Greif*'s success depended on the main force making a clean break into open territory within the first few hours. Skorzeny's American tanks would not even reach Belgian ground until the early hours of December 17. Shortly after they did, Skorzeny's commanding officer, Lieutenant Colonel Hardieck, attempted to avoid the traffic jam by driving around it on secondary roads. His Willys Jeep hit a land mine on a logging road that had not been cleared by scout teams. Hardieck, along with his driver and adjutant, was killed instantly.

Colonel Skorzeny decided to take personal command of the brigade, but the roads were so snarled with traffic that Skorzeny was forced to abandon his jeep and walk ten miles to reach their forward position. By which point, at dawn on December 17, realizing his tanks had no chance to reach the river that evening on schedule, Skorzeny nearly called off Operation *Greif*. Only the encouraging intelligence from his lead commando units that the bridges at the Meuse were still undefended kept Skorzeny from issuing that order.

After consulting with his staff, he decided to try to keep their first objective alive for one more day.

At midnight on December 17, after speaking with Von Leinsdorf by radio, the two other commando teams he had recruited for the Second Objective cut off contact with Skorzeny's corps command and made their way south toward France. By late afternoon on December 18, disguised as a squad of MPs, SS *Untersturmführer* Gerhard Bremer's team was less than forty miles north of the French border. After driving into the middle of a firefight, William Sharper's squad had been forced to spend the night in the basement of an abandoned tavern. The delay put them two hours behind Bremer when they headed south again that morning.

Neither of them knew that the squad headed by Lieutenant Karl Schmidt had been arrested, that Schmidt had confessed, and that the alert was spreading behind American lines.

21

Twenty miles west of Bastogne, Bernie slowed the jeep as they neared an American battalion's encampment. Forward security posts were unmanned, exterior gates had been left open and the camp abandoned, leaving behind the battalion's bivouac and heavy gun emplacements. The German vanguard had not moved through yet, but artillery fire from the southeast suggested they were closing fast. In an eerie silence, the two men searched the tents to scrounge for rations and supplies.

The Americans had left in a hurry. Scores of uneaten breakfasts still sat on mess hall tables. Canisters of hot coffee and oatmeal bubbled over on field stoves. Von Leinsdorf helped himself to coffee and a slice of toast off a plate, then filled a knapsack with K rations and medical supplies. Outside they squeezed the last few gallons of gas from the camp's depot and strapped four extra cans to the rear of the jeep, enough fuel to get them deep into France. By the time they finished, they could hear German tanks advancing behind them, less than a mile away.

A short drive beyond the camp, they neared a river and spotted a platoon of American engineers working on the far side of an old stone bridge. Bernie drove toward the eastern approach, then slammed on the brakes when four armed GIs jumped out of the bushes, blocked the road, and pointed their rifles at them.

"What's the password?" shouted the lead corporal.

"Jesus," said Bernie. "You almost gave me a fucking heart attack."

"The password is 'stamp,'" said Von Leinsdorf. "What's the countersign?"

"Powder," said the man.

"That's incorrect," said Von Leinsdorf.

That response seemed to confuse them, and they conferred noisily for a moment.

"Hurry up, for Christ's sake. We're carrying important dispatches," said Von Leinsdorf.

"The Krauts are right on our ass," said Bernie.

"Hold your horses." They finished talking among themselves. "Is it 'smoke'?"

"That's right," said Von Leinsdorf. "Now get the fuck out of the way."

Another one of the soldiers stepped forward to ask: "What's the capital of Illinois?"

"Springfield," said Bernie.

"That's the wrong answer, search 'em."

The other soldiers moved toward the jeep. Von Leinsdorf stood up and pulled his pistol.

"It's Springfield, for Christ's sake, what the fuck's the matter with you?" shouted Bernie.

"The capital of Illinois is Chicago."

"Who says it is?" asked Bernie.

The corporal pointed to one of his other men. "He does."

"Is he from Illinois?"

They asked the man. He shook his head.

"He's a fucking moron, it's not Chicago, it's Springfield."

The soldiers discussed it heatedly among themselves, and couldn't reach a decision, but didn't move out of the road.

"God damn it, we don't have time for this shit," said Von Leinsdorf, pulling his pistol. "You're grilling us? You didn't even know the countersign. What are you fuckups doing here? Is that your bivouac we just passed?"

"Yes, sir, we're the last company out. We got orders to blow this bridge. The Krauts are supposed to break through any minute."

"No shit, Einstein, I just told you they're on our ass," said Bernie.

"We can help," said Von Leinsdorf. "We're engineers."

"That wouldn't be up to us, sir. Ask over there," said the corporal, pointing to the far side of the bridge.

"Then get out of the fucking way," said Von Leinsdorf.

The soldiers finally stood aside.

"It's Springfield, I'm telling you, anybody else comes through and you're gonna ask 'em that," said Bernie, as they drove past them.

When Bernie reached the far side of the bridge, Von Leinsdorf pointed to three other Allied vehicles and ordered him to pull over.

"What the hell for?" asked Bernie.

"Because I told you to," said Von Leinsdorf. "Come with me and keep your mouth shut."

Bernie followed Von Leinsdorf down a steep path that ran along the base of the bridge to the edge of the river below. Half a dozen American engineers worked underneath, planting M85 satchel charges, stringing fuses to the western shore beneath the single span.

"How can we help?" Von Leinsdorf shouted.

"You guys techs?" asked the sergeant in charge.

"That's right."

"You can rig those last two charges," he said, pointing them toward a pile of demolition supplies stacked against the stone.

Von Leinsdorf opened one of the boxes and handed Bernie two twenty-pound satchels, packed tight with block charges. They hammered two spikes in between the stones in the base of the rampart and suspended the satchels on them. Looking across the river, Bernie could see six other satchels strung under the bridge, connected by fuses leading back toward the western approach.

"What are we doing here?" whispered Bernie.

"Give me the priming assembly," said Von Leinsdorf.

Bernie watched as he appeared to attach the detonating cord clip to the booster charge running from the satchel, but at the last moment folded the connector underneath the clip with a pair of pliers, concealing it inside a fold of canvas. He then ran the fuse out to the main line running toward the shore.

"Here they come!" shouted one of the GIs on the far side of the bridge.

Moments later they heard the last patrol retreating over the bridge overhead. Bernie stepped out from under the span and looked east, but he was too far below the bank to see anything.

"Let's get the hell out of here," he said.

"Hold your horses," said Von Leinsdorf, working calmly.

He repeated the procedure on the second satchel. The other engineers had finished their work, running lines behind them as they backed toward the eastern shore. Von Leinsdorf tossed their fuse line to the sergeant who was making fast all the connections. Bernie turned to follow the engineers up to the road, looked back across the river, and saw a line of gray German scout cars advancing down the road, less than a mile away.

Instead of hooking their line to the main fuse, the sergeant stopped to check the connections on their satchels. Von Leinsdorf, who had started after Bernie, hesitated when he saw the man stop. He waved at Bernie to keep going. Bernie could see that the sergeant was about to come across their unconnected detonating cord. Von Leinsdorf pulled his knife, held it along his leg, and advanced toward the sergeant's back.

"Sarge, come on, they're closing in on the bridge," called Bernie.

The sergeant looked up and saw Von Leinsdorf ten feet away with the knife in his hand. Von Leinsdorf kept walking, trying not to appear threatening.

"I double-checked everything, Sarge," said Von Leinsdorf.

"Stop right where you are," said the sergeant.

The sergeant pulled a handgun on Von Leinsdorf. Von Leinsdorf turned to glance at Bernie, expecting him to react. Bernie slowly raised his rifle, unsure where to point it.

"Sarge, the Krauts are coming, what's the problem?" asked Bernie.

"Drop that knife, Lieutenant," said the sergeant. "Right now."

"Come on, Brooklyn," said Von Leinsdorf, glancing back at him. "What are you waiting for?"

"I'm counting to three, then I shoot," said the sergeant. "One, two—"

Von Leinsdorf dropped the knife and raised his hands. "Jesus, what are you so jumpy for, Sarge? Did I fuck up the connections? I didn't mean to—"

"Turn around and start walking."

"Brooklyn?"

"Drop the rifle, kid, or I'll fire. I'm not fucking around."

Bernie lowered the rifle, holding it to the side as he stepped toward them. "We lied, okay? So we're not engineers, we were driving past and saw the situation. He didn't mean to fuck up the fuse. We're just trying to give you a hand."

The sergeant hesitated, blinking his eyes, exhausted and anxious, trying to decide.

"For Christ's sake, what you gonna do, shoot one of your own?" asked Bernie. "With the fuckin' Krauts on top of us?"

"I'll fix it if you show me how," said Von Leinsdorf.

"I said stay where you are."

Bernie glanced back up toward the road and saw the engineers on the road hustling to attach the charge line to a detonator.

"We're running out of time—"

The whistle of an incoming tank shell split the air. It slammed into the surface of the bridge above them, clouding the air with dust. The blast staggered the sergeant, knocking him against the base of the bridge. Von Leinsdorf picked up his knife and was on him in two steps. He grabbed the sergeant's gun arm and bent it back against the rocks until the pistol fell. He brought up his knife with the other hand, planted it in the sergeant's chest, and rode him down into the dirt, covering his mouth, holding him there until he stopped moving.

Bernie kept the rifle trained on the tangle of their bodies. He was unable to draw a clear target as they wrestled, until the sergeant went still and he had a clean shot at Von Leinsdorf. His finger found the trigger, the second time he'd had Von Leinsdorf in his sights.

The way he cut that rifleman's throat in the cabin.

Bernie had made excuses for him after Von Leinsdorf saved his life. Telling himself Von Leinsdorf had only killed because war or their survival demanded it.

But not that one. Not that poor terrified kid in the cabin.

You need to know what the mission is first, thought Bernie. *Kill him now, there's still others out there trying to pull it off, with no way to stop them—*

Von Leinsdorf looked up from the dead man, saw the barrel pointing at him, and the uncertainty in Bernie's eyes. He raised his hands as he stood up, unafraid, inviting him to take the shot.

Another shell screamed toward them. Bernie turned and ran the rest of the way to the road as Von Leinsdorf dove to the ground. The shell landed to the left of the bridge. Showered with dirt but unharmed, Von Leinsdorf picked up his knife, sliced the main fuse line, and sprinted up the path.

The column of panzers rumbled down the road from the west. The rest of the GIs had fallen back a quarter mile, shouting at the engineers to hurry. Bernie started their jeep, pointed the wheels away from the bridge. The pop of small-arms fire erupted. Bullets kicked up around the engineers as they hooked up their detonator.

"Forget about that! Get out of here!" Bernie shouted to them.

He saw Von Leinsdorf running out from under the bridge, his uniform covered in dust.

"Where's the sarge?" one of the engineers shouted back.

Bernie stepped on the gas as Von Leinsdorf came alongside and jumped onto the running board. They skidded away as another shell exploded behind them on the road. The rest of the Americans scattered in every direction. In a quick look back, Bernie saw the last engineer push down the plunger on their detonator. When nothing happened to the bridge, and a second shell landed near them, the engineers followed the riflemen into the trees. Bernie skidded around the next turn and floored the jeep, desperate to leave the bridge behind them.

Von Leinsdorf fell into the passenger seat beside him. His whole body appeared to be shaking.

"What's wrong, are you hit?" asked Bernie.

Von Leinsdorf turned toward him and Bernie realized he was laughing.

"What's so fucking funny?" said Bernie.

"Why didn't you shoot him when you had the chance?"

"What are you talking about? He had a gun on you the whole time."

"I saved your life, the least you can do is return the favor—"

"I didn't have a shot. Jesus Christ, what am I supposed to do? We shouldn't have stopped in the first place."

"Keeping that bridge open could be the difference for the entire offensive. Did that ever occur to you?" Von Leinsdorf pulled out a cigarette.

"Well, don't mistake me for somebody who gives a shit."

Von Leinsdorf glared at him, then pulled his pistol and pointed it at Bernie's head. "Pull over. Pull off the road and stop right now."

Bernie did as he was ordered, steering onto the first dirt side road, concealed from the main highway by a thick stand of evergreens. Von Leinsdorf told him to stop near the ruins of an old country church. Bernie kept both hands on the wheel, his eyes on the road.

"I'm sorry," said Bernie. "I didn't mean that."

"Are you really that reluctant to shoot an American, Bernie? Before we go any further: You are a German soldier, aren't you?"

"I could've just as easily shot you, too," said Bernie, glancing sideways at the gun. "You think about that?"

"Oh yes. And what would you have done then? How long do you think you'd last after Counter Intelligence takes you for questioning? What sad story would you tell them, Brooklyn? This Nazi/GI took you hostage and forced you to drive all over Belgium? No credibility problem there. But tell us, Private, what about all these forged documents and German uniforms in the back of your jeep?"

"Okay, you made your point."

"The point is they'd break you in an hour. You'd give up your mother. You haven't the backbone for it." Von Leinsdorf looked disgusted. "Get out of the car."

"You said you needed my help, you couldn't do this without me—"

"Get out now."

"Look, put the gun down, all right?"

"Take your hands off the wheel."

Bernie kept his head down, clinging to the wheel, white-knuckled. "Just because I didn't kill that guy? Those other GIs would've heard the shot. What if they came after us? They had ten guys up there, there was no time, the panzers were on top of us. I did what I thought was best."

Von Leinsdorf hesitated. They heard heavy firing behind them. The German advance had crossed the bridge.

"I didn't ask to be here," said Bernie. "I didn't ask for any of this. I don't even know what we're doing."

Bernie glanced over and hardly recognized the man. The shell of civilized personality was gone. What he saw in its place was cold, hard, and sneering.

"I'm sick of your excuses. Get out."

"Why?"

"Because I don't want blood on my jeep."

Bernie climbed down and backed away. Von Leinsdorf followed, pistol raised, into the church's small graveyard. Shells had landed among the old headstones, cratering the field and scattering fragments of worm-eaten coffins and human remains.

"Try to appreciate the stunning degree of your own insignificance. You're here because a politician made a speech, another one rattled his saber, and in this way small men like you are marched out to fight their wars—"

"It has nothing to do with me—"

Von Leinsdorf shoved him forward. "It doesn't matter what you think about it, or what you think about anything. This is a business, and the business of war is killing. It's a job, like baking bread or carpentry—"

"That what they teach you at Dachau?"

"They didn't have to teach me. You learn on your own or you

can't go on. By now you should have figured it out for yourself. That's the lesson."

Bernie backpedaled as Von Leinsdorf advanced straight at him. "What lesson?"

"That it means nothing." Von Leinsdorf screwed the silencer onto the end of his pistol. "You value your sorry little life so highly. Tell me why, because of what? What have you ever done with it? What makes your life worth saving?"

"I don't know, I'm just me."

"How you could possibly know who that is? I grew up in two countries, too, but I never forgot. You've been too busy hiding all your life, making yourself invisible, a nobody so they wouldn't notice you. Because you're ashamed of what you are."

Bernie had no answer. He couldn't even mount an argument, his face burning at the painful truths the man had seen in him.

"None of it matters. That's what you don't know. You have no idea how cheap life really is. You have no idea. What you find when you get to the bottom of it. There's no honor, no dignity, no morality, no spirit. There's just blood and meat. Life is shit. It's *shit*."

Von Leinsdorf leaned forward, inches from Bernie's face, looking haunted and skeletal under his handsome features. Bernie went down to his knees on the charnel house ground, beside a scattering of bones.

"This so-called gift you think is worth saving, that's just a reflex, a bug flinching at a boot. There's no majesty to it. You can take apart a human being as easily as a clock. I worked with a doctor in our camp at Dachau, Dr. Rasher, you know that name?"

Bernie shook his head.

"He organized our research. Identified what we could learn from these subjects. How they react to heat, cold, pressure and pain, wounds and bleeding. It's amazing how little fight they put up. They just hand it to you, that's what we learned: Killing's the easiest thing in the world."

He flicked Bernie's ear with the pistol, and he flinched.

"And the Jews were grateful for it. Because at some level they're aware of this disease they carry. The Jew is an infection. A genetic virus. Once it enters the bloodstream of a society, or an individual, the only remedy is eradication. That's our lasting contribution to science. We found the cure."

Von Leinsdorf knelt down beside Bernie and grabbed his chin.

"You think your hands are clean? Your father works for IG Farben. They make the gas we use to kill them. All of them, Bernie. We're killing all of them."

Bernie felt paralyzed. He couldn't catch his breath.

"I'm no different. I've just had the benefit of a closer look at death. You think I value my own life?"

Von Leinsdorf pointed the gun to his own head.

"This endless series of humiliations and miseries? I'd end it right now if I didn't have this mission. And if I die in its service, at least I'll know it counted for something greater than myself. Can you say the same?"

"Believe whatever you want," said Bernie, shaking so hard he could barely speak. "It's none of my business."

"If you didn't learn the lesson in that basement back there, I don't know when you ever will. What you saw down there was child's play. Open your eyes, man. Declare yourself. This is as real as life is ever going to get. You won't last another day without deciding who you are or what is worth dying for."

"Why make it your problem?"

Von Leinsdorf touched the barrel to Bernie's chest. "Because I'm stuck with you. What am I going to do with you? If I kill you right now no one would mourn. No one would even know. Animals clean your bones, some peasant comes along one day and tosses them into these graves. All trace of you, all memory gone. Even your family will forget. As if you'd never existed."

Bernie saw a stark blackness in his eyes. He tried to steady his voice and ease him back to reality. "You said you needed me. To complete the mission."

"The next time you have a chance to shoot me, take it. If you can ever bring yourself to kill anybody."

Von Leinsdorf slumped, weary, as if he'd lost interest in what he'd intended to do. Then, a change. Businesslike again. He unscrewed the silencer and dropped it in his pocket. He picked Bernie up off the ground, slung an arm around him, and walked him back toward the jeep. Now he took the affectionate tone of a confidant chiding a wayward friend.

"I don't think you're a physical coward, Brooklyn. Just a moral one. But if you do find it in your heart to kill me, you'll kill yourself as well. They'll catch you sooner or later, your American friends. To die in battle is one thing; execution is worse. I tell you from experience. It's not the dying, it's knowing when and where and how. That's the hell of it."

Bernie said nothing, the numbness in his body turning cold. Von Leinsdorf climbed back into the jeep. "Keep driving."

Bernie backed out and steered them onto the main road. They drove in silence for a while.

He's right about one thing, Bernie thought, glancing over at Von Leinsdorf. *I've gone too long thinking about myself, worried about my own life. Not anymore.*

Figure out what he's doing, a piece at a time. And then even if it kills me, I'll find some way to stop him.

22

Supreme Allied Headquarters, Versailles
DECEMBER 18, 1:00 P.M.

T he news from Karl Schmidt's interrogation finally arrived by telex as General Eisenhower finished his strategy meeting in the Map Room. His chief of Counter Intelligence hurried in the dispatch after confirming the contents twice with First Army. Eisenhower scanned the report, that as many as eighty German commandos in American uniform targeting him for assassination might be in Paris, with characteristic calm.

"Just another crazy-ass rumor," he said, handing the pages back.

He was the only officer at Allied Headquarters who reacted that way. Over Eisenhower's protests, his chief of security ordered that the general's quarters be relocated immediately from a comfortable nearby villa into the Grand Trianon Palace in the Versailles compound. Ike relished what little privacy he had, and when he was off the clock, wanted to be left alone. His staff believed the reason for that was Ike's ongoing affair with his British aide-de-camp, a WAC lieutenant and former fashion model named Kay Summersby. When Eisenhower refused to make the move, his chief of staff told him that when his safety was involved, he had to follow orders like any other soldier. By the end of the day, America's only five-star general, commander of the entire Allied theater of war in Europe, had become, in effect, a prisoner of his own forces.

Within twenty-four hours, the Trianon Palace was transformed into a fortress. Two walls of thick barbed wire went up around the perimeter. Tanks and machine gun emplacements were installed at hundred-yard intervals around the compound. Roadblocks were set up for miles in every direction, and an elaborate new pass system was installed overnight. A platoon of MPs was added to the general's personal security detail, and he would be driven in an armored sedan with tinted windows, never using the same route twice. Accustomed to taking long, solitary walks through the gardens of Versailles, Eisenhower was confined to the building with the drapes closed, in case snipers had worked their way within range, while soldiers patrolled the grounds. Ike's protests that these men could better serve the war effort on the front lines were ignored.

"This must be what it feels like to be president," grumbled Eisenhower to a member of his staff.

By nightfall plainclothes Army Counter Intelligence officers in Paris had staked out the Café de le Paix, the restaurant Schmidt had identified as the assassins' rallying point. Machine guns were nested in nearby alleys. Otto Skorzeny's photograph was plastered to walls and lampposts throughout the city. Neighborhood watches organized patrols looking for disguised German agents. Any suspicious-looking GI who wandered into the area was detained and questioned.

Security officers tried using human bait to draw the killers into the open. One of Eisenhower's staff officers, Lieutenant Colonel Baldwin Smith, who bore a striking resemblance to his balding commander, volunteered to move into Eisenhower's vacated villa. For the next few days he dressed in one of the general's uniforms and was driven back and forth in the general's Cadillac along his normal travel routes. Eisenhower himself was neither asked nor told about the substitution.

The fallout from Lieutenant Schmidt's confession affected Allied soldiers all along the chain of command. Although he gave the correct password at a checkpoint, American General Bruce Clarke spent six hours in custody when an overeager MP decided that the general's placing of the Chicago Cubs in the American League constituted proof he was a German spy. Driving back to his own headquarters, General Omar Bradley was stopped half a dozen times and grilled on Midwestern geography, the Notre Dame football team, and the infield of the St. Louis Cardinals.

British Field Marshal Bernard Montgomery, just arriving in Belgium from Holland, was waved down at an American roadblock near Malmédy. As a security precaution, all rank and insignia had been removed from his jeep, which aroused suspicion. Furious at having his authority questioned, particularly by an American, the imperious Montgomery ordered his chauffeur to drive on in the middle of the conversation. MPs responded by shooting out his tires, giving chase, and relieving Montgomery of his sidearm. They held the war's highest-ranking British officer in custody for three hours, until a Canadian colonel identified the apoplectic Montgomery. Exasperated by Monty's habitual grandstanding, Eisenhower reportedly relished hearing about his ordeal in detail.

Soldiers manning the checkpoints were no longer satisfied with passwords, and as the days wore on, their interrogations grew increasingly elaborate. Queries about sports, comic strips, and current Hollywood gossip supplied the most frequent stumpers. Some inventive MPs tried to trip up the putative assassins by demanding they recite poems filled with r's and w's, notoriously difficult for native Germans. "Round the rugged rock the ragged rascal ran" was a favorite.

For all the disruption they caused, these precautions were about to pay tangible dividends.

The French Border
DECEMBER 18, 9:00 P.M.

After driving all afternoon, Earl Grannit and Ole Carlson entered France at a heavily guarded crossing just north of the town of Givet. Grannit identified himself to MPs running the post and made sure they'd received the bulletin about Skorzeny's commandos. They showed him that it had been widely circulated and that more stringent

controls had been imposed. Traffic was backed up on the Belgian side
of the border for a quarter of a mile.

Before pushing on for Reims, Grannit and Carlson were shown
to the mess hall next door for a quick meal. Waiting for their food,
they drank coffee by a window looking out on the post's supply depot on the French side of the line.

"You got a wife, Earl?"

"What do you want to know for?"

"I don't know, I just never asked you."

"I had one," said Grannit.

Carlson waited. "That's it?"

"Yup."

"What did your dad do?"

"He owned a gas station," said Grannit.

"Any brothers or sisters?"

"What is this, the third degree?"

"I'm just making conversation."

"I had a sister." Grannit spotted something out the window. "You
got your binoculars with you?"

Carlson handed them over. Grannit focused them on an American jeep at a gas pump in the supply depot a quarter of a mile away.
Two MPs stood near the jeep, one of them dispensing gas into the
tank. From this distance and angle he couldn't make out any unit
numbers on the jeep.

"Go ask at the post if a couple of MPs came across in the last hour."

"You got it."

Carlson immediately went next door to the border command
office.

Grannit watched the MPs at the gas pump. He scanned the vehicle, looking for details that reminded him of Schmidt's jeep. Nothing
jumped out. Carlson returned a few moments later.

"They came through about twenty minutes ago," said Carlson.
"They had the password and SHAEF passes—"

"Did they check the spelling?"

"He said they had that detail from our bulletin, and that

'headquarters' was spelled correctly. They said they were from SHAEF, working security on the Skorzeny case."

"So they knew about it, mentioned it before they were asked."

"That's what he said."

Grannit saw a third MP returning to join the others at the jeep in the yard. "Anyway, there's three of them."

"You thought it might be our guys?"

"No, Ole, I thought it was Eleanor Roosevelt," said Grannit, lowering the glasses.

"You would've noticed her teeth," said Carlson. "Even at this distance."

Something caught Grannit's eye just as the binoculars came down, and he drew them back up. A fourth MP came out of a side building and climbed into the jeep.

"Hang on, shit, there's four of them."

"But their passes were good."

"Hold 'em up at the gate, we'll check ourselves. Go now."

Carlson hurried back to the post. Grannit hustled out the back of the mess hall into the yard and saw the jeep pull away from the gas pumps. It headed for the nearest exit, an open gate in a chain-link fence a hundred yards away. Heading after them, Grannit broke into a trot.

"Hurry up, Ole," he said.

As the jeep approached the gate, Grannit saw an MP in the guard-house pick up a phone. He stepped outside and rolled the gate shut as the jeep got close. The MP leaned over to say something to the men inside.

The jeep slammed into reverse, spun around, and headed back across the yard toward another exit, quickly reaching top speed. The MP ran after it. Grannit pulled his pistol.

"Hey! Hey!"

The jeep careened straight at Grannit. He lowered the pistol, and emptied the clip. Shots cracked the windscreen and side mirror, but the jeep steered away from him. Ole and MPs from the border post ran out of the main building with guns drawn and angled toward the gate across the yard. A machine gun on top of the post opened up, chasing the jeep with bullets across the yard but not connecting.

With no time to close the rolling gate at the far exit, two guards threw down a line of necklace mines across the opening. The jeep accelerated as it reached the open gate and hit the mines at fifty miles an hour. The mines detonated, blowing off the front tires. The full, oversized gas tank ignited in a fireball, flipping the jeep into the air. It landed upside down, enveloped in flames.

All four men aboard, including their squad leader SS *Untersturm-führer* Gerhard Bremer, died instantly.

23

Pont-Colin, Belgium
DECEMBER 19, 6:00 A.M.

Bernie Oster and Erich Von Leinsdorf spent the night huddled in their jeep, side flaps and canvas roof raised, wrapped in blankets. Bernie was still too cold to sleep. They had driven west from Bastogne until after dark, sticking to back roads; eighteen hours to cover fifty miles, across empty fields, through abandoned or devastated villages. Twice they pulled into heavy woods to avoid American reinforcements entering from France. Using binoculars, Bernie spotted the screaming eagle insignia of the 101st Airborne on their sleeves.

Snow fell steadily through the night, wrapping the forest in silence. For the first time since the offensive began, they'd left the frenzy of battle behind. At first light they rolled down to a heavily wooded ridge overlooking a minor border post that Von Leinsdorf had selected on the map. Through binoculars he spotted two French soldiers manning a kiosk and guard gate spanning the dirt road. No traffic moved in either direction.

Von Leinsdorf fished around in his knapsack for traveling papers.

"I'll do the talking," he said.

Bernie honked the horn and flashed headlights as they drove up to the gate, alerting a middle-aged French soldier, who stepped out to meet them. Von Leinsdorf waved the transit papers at the man as he emerged, and spoke in rapid-fire French. When the soldier asked for a password, Von Leinsdorf lit into him. Bernie didn't understand a word, but it was clear that hearing fluent French from an angry American officer unnerved the man.

Von Leinsdorf held up his dispatch case. *"Je porte les expéditions importantes pour le chef du personnel Américain."*

Von Leinsdorf jumped out of the jeep, red in the face, using names that Bernie didn't need translation to understand. Cringing and apologetic, the Frenchman indicated he needed to show their papers to his superior inside.

"Wait here," Von Leinsdorf said to Bernie.

The sentry led him to their barracks, a squat concrete blockhouse twenty yards behind the kiosk. The Frenchman continued to apologize, backpedaling, tripping over his own feet. Von Leinsdorf waved at him to keep walking and followed, reaching for something on his belt.

Bernie lit a cigarette and waited until the two men entered the blockhouse, then climbed out of the jeep and hurried to the kiosk. He looked around for paper and pen, scribbled a note in English, until he saw the door of the blockhouse open.

Von Leinsdorf walked out, carrying a basket and a bottle of wine. He saw Bernie in the kiosk, studying a sheet of paper next to the window.

"What are you doing in there?"

"Take a look. They changed passwords overnight," said Bernie.

Von Leinsdorf scanned it, a telex from American command.

"Who's 'Dizzy Dean'?"

"He's a pitcher, for the St. Louis Cardinals."

"Well done, Brooklyn. You finally made a contribution."

Von Leinsdorf headed for the jeep. As he followed, Bernie noticed a body lying in the doorway of the blockhouse.

"At least the fucking Frogs know how to eat," said Von Leinsdorf, handing him the basket. "Let's get moving."

Bernie pointed to his cheek as Von Leinsdorf climbed back in beside him.

"What?" said Von Leinsdorf, then wiped his cheek. A spot of blood came off on his hand. "Did I get it?"

Bernie nodded, and started the jeep as Von Leinsdorf took the basket and rummaged through it.

"Not exactly Christmas dinner, but it'll do. Fruit and cheese, a baguette. Guess they already ate the foie gras," said Von Leinsdorf. "First time in France, Brooklyn?"

"Yeah."

"Beautiful country," said Von Leinsdorf, biting into an apple. "Dreadful people."

A phone began to ring inside the kiosk as they drove away.

The Border Crossing at Givet
DECEMBER 19, 6:00 A.M.

The burned hulk of the MPs' jeep didn't cool enough to be searched until halfway through the night. Searchlights were brought out illuminating the yard. Concern persisted that they'd killed four MPs until, near dawn, Earl Grannit turned up some burned German uniforms in a gas canister, and some of the same customized weapons they'd found in Karl Schmidt's jeep. Ole Carlson called Grannit over to look at a still-smoldering scrap of paper he had picked from the debris.

"One of their SHAEF passes," said Carlson.

The top had burned away, obliterating the word "headquarters."

"The guard who cleared them said it was spelled right," he said, troubled.

"Maybe he got it wrong," said Grannit. "You did for a while, and you were staring at it."

"I don't know. Something about it's bugging me."

Grannit asked the captain in charge to make sure every other border post had up-to-date intel about the two men they were looking for. The captain showed Grannit a large map of the French-Belgian border on his office wall.

"There's six crossings between here and the west edge of Luxembourg," said the captain. "Unless they cross on foot."

"They'll go through a checkpoint," said Grannit, studying the map. "They're not going to give up their jeep. We hauled ass getting here; they can't be that far ahead of us."

"Our reinforcements are moving into Belgium along these roads," said the captain. "They'll probably stay in this corridor. That leaves four crossings."

"You have MPs at all these posts?" asked Grannit.

"They were supposed to be there by this morning. We may not have reached all of 'em yet."

One of the MPs working the phones came back to confirm that three crossings had received the bulletin, and that MPs had arrived during the night. No other German teams had been stopped. The second MP was still on the phone.

"What's going on, son?" Grannit asked him.

"I can't get through to Pont-Colin," he said.

"Where's that?"

"Small post, twenty miles south," said the captain. "Used mostly by local traffic. Under French control."

"Get me a map. Ole, bring your breakfast."

The weather improved as Bernie drove out of the hills and made the last crossing over the Meuse as it twisted south through the high plains of northern France. Traffic on the highway from Reims was a solid flow of American military, all headed north, toward Belgium.

"What did you want to be when the war's over, Brooklyn?"

"Alive."

"Aside from that," said Von Leinsdorf.

Bernie glanced over. With a full belly and an open road ahead, the mercurial German had drifted into an unguarded mood, the ugly threats he'd made forgotten. He angled back in his seat, one foot on the dash, hands behind his head, looking up at the overcast sky. Bernie decided to keep him talking.

"I was supposed to go to college," said Bernie. "To figure that out."

"Where?"

"I was thinking NYU. New York University. Maybe study engineering, something like that."

"Yes, it would have suited you. Jolly good wheeze, campus life. I would have gone on to university in England, Cambridge, King's College. That was the plan anyway."

"Thought you'd always been in the army," said Bernie.

"Before the war? No. Politics, diplomacy, that's where I was headed. Peace between nations. Serving the greater good. That was my father's influence."

Bernie saw a shade of feeling flicker across his face.

"Where is he now?" asked Bernie.

"He died. Just after he retired."

"What was he like?"

"A decent man. His talent fell short of his ambition. He needed work to have a reason to live." Von Leinsdorf lit a cigarette, eager to shift the subject. "Is your father alive?"

"There's been heavy bombing in Frankfurt. I haven't heard from them."

"Terrible thing to lose your father."

Von Leinsdorf sounded genuine, as if he still possessed some trace of humanity.

"We were both taken from the life we were supposed to live, Brooklyn. Men our age should have more agreeable things on their minds. We should be out on the town, driving around with a couple of pretty girls."

Bernie looked at him. "Which town?"

"Paris isn't a bad place to start. Ever been?"

"No."

"Maybe once we finish there, we'll cruise down the Rivoli, pick up a couple of those fresh young things in their summer dresses. Champagne dinner at the Hotel Meurice, dancing, a midnight show in Pigalle. How does that sound?"

"Sounds pretty good."

So we're going to Paris. After Reims. That's our destination. Now all I need is the target.

Von Leinsdorf glanced up again. "Looks like it might rain."

"How many squads are working on this with us?" asked Bernie casually.

"Five altogether." He pointed at a road sign as they approached an intersection. "Take a right here."

The sign pointing to the right read "REIMS 60 KM."

Snow stopped falling as Grannit and Carlson parked a quarter mile shy of the post at Pont-Colin, on the French side of the border. Leaving the main highway three miles down, they hadn't passed a single vehicle as they drove up a series of mountainous switchbacks.

They advanced the rest of the way to the crossing on foot, weapons drawn. Grannit eased up to the window of the blockhouse barracks and saw the bodies of two French soldiers on the floor. He signaled Ole to check the kiosk, then went to work examining the scene.

The men's throats had been brutally and efficiently slashed; neither had put up a fight. They'd been cut with a heavy serrated blade, like a hunting knife. Grannit found a footprint in a pool of blood.

A GI combat boot.

"They were here less than an hour ago," he said as he came back out.

"Only one set of wheels came through that gate," said Carlson, pointing out tracks in the snow. "They parked here. Looks like a Willys."

"Two sets of footprints to the blockhouse, only one coming out. The other guy went in there."

Grannit followed a second set of footsteps to the kiosk. Grannit scanned the small room. Carlson stood back and watched.

"There's something going on with these two," said Grannit. "One does the killing. The other guy waited in the jeep outside the hospital. Same thing here. Same pattern."

Grannit's eye settled on a bulletin about Skorzeny's brigade tacked to the wall beside the guard window. He pulled out the thumbtack and saw two holes in the paper.

"They had the alert in plain sight," said Carlson. "Why didn't they stop 'em?"

"They probably couldn't read English," said Grannit. "Look at this."

He showed the back of the flyer to Carlson. The words "REIMS" and "MOVIE HOUSE" had been hastily scrawled.

"Schmidt said something about meeting at a theater in Reims," said Carlson.

"The second guy wrote this."

"Why?"

"I don't know. Get command on the radio. Somebody else has to clean this up."

They ran back to their jeep and Grannit took the wheel. Carlson cranked up the high-frequency shortwave, but all he got was static.

"God damned hills," said Carlson.

"Ole, I don't think I ever heard you swear before."

Carlson's cheeks flushed with color. "These guys really make me mad."

"Keep trying," said Grannit as they drove off. "We know where they're going and they weren't here that long ago. We need road-blocks every ten miles between Charleville and Reims."

24

Verdun, France
DECEMBER 19, 11:00 A.M.

In the middle of the night, General Eisenhower woke to the sound of gunfire just outside his window. His adjutant hurried out of their new quarters at the Trianon Palace in his pajamas and found Eisenhower's chief of staff, Walter Bedell Smith, running around with his carbine. Smith and four other soldiers emptied their rifles into a hedge where one of the MPs on duty said he had heard an intruder. No German assassins turned up, but at first light they found the bullet-riddled body of a stray cat. Eisenhower called the members of his enlarged bodyguard detail together and chewed them out, told them to calm their asses down and keep their fingers off the trigger. They weren't helping the war effort by denying him a good night's sleep. Six hours later, at their home in Fort Benning, Georgia, his wife, Mamie, received a telephone call from a reporter asking if she'd like to comment on the news that her husband had been shot. She spent the rest of the day on the phone frantically trying to track down the false report.

Eisenhower's motorcade left for Verdun early that morning, under heavily armed escort. General Patton was waiting when Eisenhower's motorcade arrived at eleven. Delayed on the road by checkpoints installed to catch the assassins, General Bradley drove in minutes later. They met in a spartan stone room, heated by an old potbelly stove, part of an ancient French barracks overlooking the blood-drenched World War One battlefield. British Field Marshal Montgomery, held up by the MPs near Malmédy, sent a junior officer in his place. The overnight news that greeted them from the Ardennes painted an increasingly bleak picture of the battle. A dozen more towns had fallen under the pounding assault and thousands of American troops had surrendered. Eisenhower sensed the heavy spirits in the room.

"Gentlemen, there will be only cheerful faces at this table," he told them. "From this moment forward, our situation is to be viewed as an opportunity for us, not a disaster."

"Hell, let the sons of bitches drive all the way to Paris," said Patton. "Then we'll really chew 'em up and spit 'em out."

Laughter broke the tension. Over a large map set on the table, Eisenhower laid out the objectives of the German offensive. Under no circumstances could their tanks be allowed to threaten Antwerp. The Meuse was their last line of defense. He asked his generals for ideas, pointing out that because of bad weather they would have to succeed without offensive air support or reconnaissance. Only Patton offered a detailed response. He put three completely different approaches on the table, anticipating every contingency Eisenhower had to consider. The two men had known each other for thirty years, and had long recognized their complementary talents as strategic commander and battlefield tactician. Patton had always hoped they would have a war to fight together so he could play Stonewall Jackson to Eisenhower's Robert E. Lee, and this was that moment. His command of the battle's evolving dynamics and his vision of how to blunt the German advantage stunned everyone in the room.

"Talk us through it, George," said Eisenhower.

"First Army comes at their northern flank. My three divisions from Third Army hit from the south. Long as we hold 'em here they'll stop dead in their tracks."

He pointed with his cigar to the bulge on the map that was forming around Bastogne.

"How quickly can they get in there?" asked Eisenhower.

"Two days," said Patton. "The dumb bastard's stuck his head in a meat grinder. And this time I've got hold of the handle."

The Road to Reims
DECEMBER 19, NOON

"What other baseball players should I know?" asked Von Leinsdorf.

"What do you mean?"

"Who else might they ask about? Like Dizzy Dean."

"I thought that's what you needed me for."

"In case you're taking a piss."

"Well, everybody in America knows the Yankees," said Bernie. "Love 'em or hate 'em, they win the Series half the time."

"All right, good, who plays for them?"

"Bill Dickey, he's their catcher. Great talent. Red Ruffing's their best pitcher. Spud Chandler's a good arm. Joe Gordon at second, Phil Rizzuto's their shortstop. They call him Scooter. Not sure who's playing third this year—"

"Let's concentrate on who you do know. What's your favorite team?"

"Me? Hands down. You're from Brooklyn, it's the Brooklyn Dodgers, hands down."

"All right, so who plays for them?"

"Okay. One guy you gotta know. Biggest name in baseball. Center fielder, Brooklyn Dodgers. Best stick in the game."

"Who?"

"Joe DiMaggio." Bernie watched him closely.

"Yes. I've heard the name," said Von Leinsdorf. "DiMaggio. Center field. Brooklyn Dodgers."

"That's right."

Looking ahead on the highway, they noticed a line of American MP vehicles headed the other way, racing north, lights flashing.

"Pull over," said Von Leinsdorf.

Bernie steered onto the shoulder. Von Leinsdorf steadied his binoculars on the windscreen, looking at the road ahead. When he lowered them he pointed to a dirt road intersecting the highway a short distance ahead.

"Take that road," he said.

"What's going on?"

"They're putting up a roadblock."

Bernie drove onto the side road, while Von Leinsdorf studied the map.

"Take the first left," he said. "Runs parallel to the river. We'll cross farther downstream, come into Reims from the north."

"What if they've got that blocked too?"

"First things first."

"What happened? You think they found those guards at the border?"

"Just drive, Brooklyn."

Grannit and Carlson sped down the highway toward Reims. Roadblocks had gone up as ordered. They'd passed three already, but none had stopped any jeeps answering their detailed description.

"You divorced, Earl?"

"What is it with you and this?"

"You said you *had* a wife. I'm just curious."

"Is divorce such a fucking novelty?"

"It is in South Dakota."

"Marriage and police work go together like a match and a gas tank."

"Sorry to hear it."

"I'm doing just fine without your sympathy."

"I got a steady girl back home," said Carlson, after a while.

"So you said." Grannit glanced over. "You gonna marry her?"

"I was thinking about it."

"Tell me you're not going into police work after this."

"I been thinking about that, too," said Carlson. "I'm getting a pretty good feel for it, don't you think?"

"I got a pretty good feel for falling on hand grenades, but I'm not gonna make a career out of it."

"Well, what do you think I should do?"

"Marry the girl. Stick with insurance."

"It's not like we have that much crime. It's not like, you know, the murder capital of the high plains."

Grannit looked at him. "You gonna stay a volunteer fireman?"

"I guess so."

"So, you feel the need for a thrill coming on, set fire to a barn. You can rush in and put it out yourself. Sell the farmer his insurance beforehand, you win both ways."

"Why didn't I think of that?"

"Stick with me," said Grannit. "I specialize in the big questions."

Carlson laughed, slowing as they approached another roadblock, soldiers waving them down. Because they matched the description of the alert they'd sent out—two Americans in a Willys—it took fifteen minutes to convince the MPs they weren't the men every GI in France was now looking for.

Bernie and Von Leinsdorf skirted the town of Rethel until they reached an unguarded bridge that took them across the Aisne River and an adjoining shipping canal. A light rain started to fall as they passed a memorial for a World War One battle that took place on the strip of ground between the two bodies of water. The road continued to the southwest, parallel to the canal. When they came within sight of the highway south toward Reims, Von Leinsdorf took another look at the connecting road through the binoculars.

"There's another blockade," he said.

"We've got today's password, don't we?"

Von Leinsdorf glanced down the road. He spotted a French military ambulance outside a roadside café. It was early afternoon, lunch hour.

"Park off the road," he said, pointing to the right. "Next to those trees."

Bernie drove toward them. When they got close, Von Leinsdorf stepped on Bernie's foot, on top of the gas. The jeep lurched forward and crashed into the tree, crumpling the hood, sending up a column of steam.

"What the hell did you do that for?" asked Bernie.

"Leave everything. Follow me. Keep your mouth shut."

They walked in the rain to the café where the ambulance was

parked. Von Leinsdorf rushed inside and spotted the uniformed drivers eating at a table, the only customers.

"*Il y est eu un accident*," said Von Leinsdorf, in clumsy, American accented French. "*D'une juste la route. Veuillez nous aider.*"

The drivers followed them outside, asking questions in broken English which Von Leinsdorf, in his feigned urgency, did his best to avoid.

"Where is it?" asked the driver.

"*Nous vous montrerons,*" said Von Leinsdorf. "We'll take you."

The drivers gestured for them to climb in the back of the ambulance, and they drove back down the road until Von Leinsdorf directed them off to the left, where the jeep had hit the tree. The ambulance stopped a few yards away, and the drivers hurried toward the jeep.

Von Leinsdorf followed and shot one of the men in the back of the head with his silenced pistol. The other driver turned when he heard the pop, saw his comrade hit the ground. When he saw the gun in Von Leinsdorf's hand, he fell to his knees, pleading for his life, fumbling out his wallet, showing photographs of his wife and children.

"*Mon frère*, you're talking to the wrong Nazi," said Von Leinsdorf, turning to Bernie. "He actually thinks we're American—would you please just shut the fuck up? *Mettez ceux partis*. Silence!"

The man went quiet. Von Leinsdorf unscrewed the silencer and showed it to him before tucking it away.

"See? I'm not going to shoot you."

"What the hell are we doing?" asked Bernie.

"We need one of them alive," said Von Leinsdorf. Then, pointing to the dead man: "He's about your size, this one's a better match for me. Switch uniforms. Hurry up before there's too much blood on it. Don't ask questions."

Bernie knelt to the task. Von Leinsdorf turned to the survivor.

"*Enlevez votre uniforme,*" he said to him. "*Rapide!*"

The man unbuttoned his tunic. Von Leinsdorf did the same.

"Don't worry, *mon ami*," said Von Leinsdorf, with a reassuring smile. "*Je n'vais pas vous tuer*. Friends, yes?"

The driver smiled grimly as he dressed. Bernie put the driver's uniform on, then worked the dead man's loose limbs into his GI green.

"Don't put your jacket on him, just lay it over his face. Load everything into the ambulance," said Von Leinsdorf, slipping on the other driver's jacket. "Bring back a stretcher."

The second driver had finished changing into Von Leinsdorf's uniform when Bernie returned with the stretcher. Von Leinsdorf joked with the driver that the American uniform looked snug around the middle.

"Too many *pommes frites*, huh? Try them without mayonnaise next time, dummy. Put the dead one in back," said Von Leinsdorf to Bernie; then he waved at the driver, ordering him to lend a hand. "*Aidez-la.*"

Bernie and the Frenchman set the dead driver onto the stretcher and slid it in the back of the ambulance. Von Leinsdorf saw that Bernie had stacked the jerricans holding their equipment in the corner.

"Throw a blanket over those," he said. "Set up another stretcher next to that one."

When Bernie was finished, Von Leinsdorf pointed the driver at the second stretcher. "*Couchez-vous, monsieur, s'il vous plaît.*"

Eager to please, the driver lay down on the stretcher. Von Leinsdorf told Bernie to fasten the straps on the man, as he closed the rear doors.

"You know some first aid, don't you, Brooklyn?"

"A little."

Von Leinsdorf pulled a bottle from the stores of medicine in a footlocker. "Give him half a syringe, just enough to take the edge off."

Bernie took the bottle. Morphine. He prepared the syringe, then knelt beside the second driver, who stared anxiously at the needle.

"It's okay," said Bernie. "This won't hurt you."

"*Il ne blessera pas du tout,*" said Von Leinsdorf, translating.

The Frenchman tensed as the needle went in, then relaxed as the morphine hit his bloodstream. Von Leinsdorf patted his shoulder.

"But I'm afraid this will a bit," said Von Leinsdorf.

He touched the silencer to the man's cheek and pulled the trigger. The bullet tore through his mouth and burst out the other side. Blood spurted, the man screamed and strained against the straps, nearly flipping over the stretcher. Bernie struggled to hold him down.

"Why the fuck did you shoot him?"

"If he's not wounded, why would we be driving him to the hospital?" asked Von Leinsdorf.

"The other one isn't."

"The other one's dead. Why would we need the siren for a trip to the morgue?"

"Well, you didn't have to shoot him in the mouth, for Christ's sake," said Bernie.

"And have our wounded 'GI' spout French at the checkpoint? Think it through. That's why we gave him the morphine. Reduce his suffering, keep him from flopping off that stretcher. You don't speak French by any chance, do you, Brooklyn?"

"No."

"So keep quiet at the checkpoint or I'll shoot you, too."

Von Leinsdorf took the driver's seat, started the ambulance, and steered them back onto the road. He switched on the siren and flashers as they sped past the café. They rounded a curve, following the line of the canal as it turned south, then entered a roundabout, other vehicles yielding when they heard the siren.

South of the roundabout, they approached the American checkpoint. Two MPs stepped into the road, waving them down in front of the guard gate. Von Leinsdorf rolled to a stop. Soldiers were putting up a machine gun emplacement. Other MPs searched half a dozen American jeeps they'd pulled to the side of the road. One MP hurried to the driver's side of the ambulance, another moved toward the rear. As soon as the soldier reached his window, Von Leinsdorf unleashed an agitated torrent of fluent French, gesturing toward the back, shouting over the siren.

"Okay, take it easy, buddy. Where you headed?"

"Hospital," said Von Leinsdorf, in broken English. "Reims."

"What's on board?"

The other MP opened the rear doors. He saw Bernie in a driver's uniform, sulfa packet in his hand, working on a badly wounded man, moaning and covered in blood.

"GIs," said Von Leinsdorf. "Automobile accident. *Un d'eux est mort et l'autre est critique. Nous devons nous dépêche!*"

The lead MP got the okay from his colleague, who closed the rear doors. Both men stepped back and waved the ambulance through. Von Leinsdorf stepped on the gas as the gate went up, and they sped off.

"How's he doing?" asked Von Leinsdorf.

"Great. He just asked for a daiquiri."

"He's not going to die; it's a superficial wound. We need him alive. There may be more checkpoints ahead."

"Ask him how superficial it is."

"Would you relax? It's just a Frenchman, for Christ's sake. Three aren't worth one German. I don't know that the going rate for Americans has been established. Do you?"

Bernie didn't answer. They passed another road sign: REIMS 20 KM.

25

Reims
DECEMBER 19, 7:00 P.M.

Carl Grannit parted the curtains of a second-story window and looked down and across the street at an old, ornate movie palace. Light rain continued to fall, thinning out foot traffic through the small square below. After arriving in Reims in the middle of the afternoon, Grannit and Carlson reported to the commander of the local military police. He placed a twenty-man detachment of MPs under Grannit's command. Half a dozen plainclothes agents from Army Counter Intelligence arrived an hour later, along with a platoon of regular army. Grannit pulled the entire detail together for a five o'clock briefing and broke down their assignments.

American forces used three movie houses in the downtown area to screen movies for Allied soldiers in Reims. Grannit's men had all three under surveillance by early that evening. This one, near the old shipping canal that split the city, was the largest and most popular, and seemed to Grannit the most likely for Skorzeny's men to use as a meeting place. He then commandeered as an observation post an apartment above and across a small square. Undercover men were assigned to circulate through the crowd at each of the theaters. The army detail deployed throughout the neighborhood with orders to stay off the streets until Skorzeny's men were identified. Once they were inside the theater, the soldiers would drop perimeter roadblocks into place and close the net.

The first show was scheduled for seven o'clock, a glossy Holly-wood musical to help enlisted men forget their troubles. Lights on the theater's marquee remained dark, observing blackout restrictions, but Grannit had ordered that the foyer and lobby lights stay brightly lit so that anyone standing under the marquee could be seen from their post across the street.

Dozens of soldiers from different service branches milled around outside, smoking cigarettes, waiting for friends or dates to arrive. Behind-the-line types, thought Grannit, looking them over. He'd learned that the military was like an iceberg; only the small portion above the surface did the fighting. For every front-line dogface under fire in the Ardennes, there were six clerical types like these filling out requisitions in triplicate, calling it a day, and going to the movies. A police force ran the same way, a fraction doing the dirty work while everyone else cleaned up after them. Maybe it reflected basic human nature, this hunger for bureaucracy and order, and which side of that line you ended up on was a matter of luck. Everybody had a job to do. Some were just a whole lot worse than others.

Grannit scanned the soldiers' faces with binoculars, searching for the face of the "Lieutenant Miller" that he'd glimpsed for those few moments in Belgium. A sketch of the man, drawn from Grannit's recollection, had been distributed to everyone in the detail.

"I got a guy bringing over regulation SHAEF passes so I can compare 'em to our forgeries," said Ole Carlson, standing eating a meal they'd brought in from a local restaurant.

"Good."

"Think we'll get to Paris, Earl?"

"I don't know, Ole."

"Ever been?"

"No. You?"

"Heck no. I'd love to see it. See Paris and die, isn't that what they say?"

"I don't think they mean right away."

"Anyway, don't figure I'll ever get this close again." Carlson leaned over Grannit's shoulder to look down at the theater. "I'm heading down there."

"The meet's supposed to happen between nine and twelve. That's not until the second show," said Grannit.

"I'm supposed to meet the guy with those passes. Don't want to miss him."

"While you're there," said Grannit, looking through the binoculars again, "go tell that MP swinging his nightstick around in the lobby like the house dick at Macy's to pull his head out of his ass. In fact, yank that half-wit out of there."

Grannit pointed the man out to him and Carlson headed for the door. "It would be my pleasure, Boss."

Grannit trained the glasses down each of the side streets and alleyways that fed into the old cobblestoned square. The neighborhood sported a flourishing nightlife, a number of hole-in-the-wall bars attracting heavy military traffic. Black-market profiteers flourished in an area with so many potential buyers and sellers. He spotted at least two brothels operating more or less in the open. He'd read in *Stars and Stripes* that in light of the attack in the Ardennes, dancing had been banned in Paris after dark, but young men in uniform still needed to get drunk or laid or both.

His walkie-talkie crackled to life, MPs reporting in from the other two theaters, each less than a mile away.

Nothing yet.

When they drove into Reims, Von Leinsdorf stashed the stolen French ambulance in an abandoned garage in a warehouse district near the canal. He ordered Bernie to exchange uniforms with the dead French driver again. While Bernie's back was turned, Von Leinsdorf killed the second driver with a single, silenced bullet, as if he were finishing some paperwork.

"We're GIs again," said Von Leinsdorf, unbuttoning the driver's tunic, searching both bodies for cash. "Not a moment too soon. I need to be fumigated. This bogtrotter was in desperate need of a bath. Try to run their damn country properly for them and this is the thanks we get."

They dressed in silence. Bernie covered both dead drivers with blankets. Von Leinsdorf emptied the medicine and supplies from the ambulance footlocker into a knapsack.

"Leave the rest," he said. "We'll come back for it."

"What time are we supposed to meet?" asked Bernie.

"Nine o'clock."

"It's only five. What do we do till then?"

"So many questions, Bernie. I'm feeling a lack of confidence in my leadership. You don't hear any complaints from them, do you?" he asked, nodding toward the Frenchmen.

Von Leinsdorf put his black-framed glasses on, straightened his helmet, and opened the back of the ambulance. While his back was turned, Bernie slipped a syringe and a bottle of morphine into his pocket.

"Should I bring my rifle?" asked Bernie.

"We're going to the movies, Bernie."

"Who knows? It might be a western." Bernie jumped down and closed the ambulance doors. He caught a whiff of something foul and sniffed his uniform. "That's great, now I smell like a fuckin' dead guy."

"We could both use a bit of sprucing up," said Von Leinsdorf, handing him a forged seventy-two-hour pass. "Put on a happy face. We're supposed to be on leave."

They walked out into the empty street and a steady drizzle as the last daylight faded. Von Leinsdorf consulted a map with a flashlight as they walked until they reached a shopping district, studded with cafés and shops. Other off-duty GIs circulated in and out of storefronts, so they didn't look or feel out of place. Von Leinsdorf directed Bernie to one of the cafés, where he ordered sandwiches and coffee, in French, paying with francs. They focused hungrily on the food, the first meal they'd eaten all day.

"It may help that they know about us, Brooklyn," said Von Leinsdorf. "He'll have gone to ground. Easier to find."

"Find who?"

"You're persistent," said Von Leinsdorf, admiring his sandwich. "I'll give you that."

Their table offered a view of an open produce market across the street. Von Leinsdorf kept staring in that direction. Bernie saw he was watching a plain young woman browsing through the market with a shopping bag.

"Follow me in a couple of minutes," said Von Leinsdorf. "And, Bernie, don't make me come back for you."

Bernie watched him cross the street and enter the market. He moved down an aisle, a preoccupied shopper checking out vegetables, and then bumped into the young woman. Her bag fell to the floor. All apologies, Von Leinsdorf bent to help her retrieve the items that tumbled out. Within moments he'd engaged her in conversation, taken the bag from her hand, and paid for her groceries at the counter. Bernie finished his sandwich, took what remained of Von Leinsdorf's with him, and followed them as they left the market.

Von Leinsdorf carried the woman's bag as they strolled down the street. When another burst of rain fell, he opened the umbrella she carried and held it over her head as she arranged a scarf around her hair. He maintained a respectful distance from her, holding the umbrella at arm's length, unthreatening and polite as a shy young suitor. Bernie shuffled along on the opposite side of the street, shoulders hunched, rain beating down on his helmet, about twenty yards behind them.

Two blocks later they stopped outside an apartment building. Bernie leaned back into the shadows of an alley across the street. He tried to formulate a plan, but he felt emptied out, cold, and miserable, and his mind refused to offer any clear ideas. From their body language and gestures, it was clear the woman was inviting Von Leinsdorf inside. He refused, she insisted, he agreed, as if it was the only gentlemanly thing to do, then waited while she fished out her keys and opened the door. Von Leinsdorf threw a glance back at Bernie—he knew exactly where he was standing—and followed her inside.

A minute later a light turned on in a window on the third floor.

Drapes were quickly pulled across the window, muting the glow. Bernie glanced at his watch: 5:35. Three minutes later, Von Leinsdorf appeared in the doorway again and waved Bernie over. Bernie trotted across the street to join him.

"Come on, hurry," said Von Leinsdorf, closing the door after him. "Keep quiet. Up the stairs. No one's seen us yet."

Bernie followed him up creaking stairs to the third floor and through the apartment door he'd propped open with a matchbook. Von Leinsdorf closed and locked the door as soon as they were inside. The furnishings looked more prosperous than the building's exterior suggested, tasteful and modern.

"This'll do for us," said Von Leinsdorf. "This'll do quite nicely. Would you like a cup of tea? She'd just put on the kettle."

"Where's the bathroom?"

"Through that door, off the bedroom."

Bernie opened the bedroom door. The woman lay on her back on the bed, legs sprawled, one shoe kicked off, lifeless eyes staring at the ceiling. She'd been strangled with the peach-colored scarf she'd worn on her head, still taut around her neck. Pooled blood had turned her face a bruised shade of scarlet; small capillaries had burst around her protruding eyes. Bernie covered her with a blanket, numb inside, then moved to the bathroom. He closed the door and turned on the faucet, the first running water he'd encountered in days.

The room's austere plainness seemed unreal. A sink, a toilet, hand towels, a bar of soap. The woman who'd used them lay dead, less than ten feet away. He caught a glimpse of his face in the mirror and for a moment didn't recognize what stared back at him, his face black with grime, eyes that belonged to an older, hollowed-out man. As he washed his hands, clots of dried blood dropped onto the porcelain, streaking red when they contacted the running water.

Von Leinsdorf was waiting with a hot cup of tea when he returned. "This'll bring you back from the dead, Brooklyn. Quite the scrounger, this one. She even had sugar and real cream in the icebox."

Bernie took the cup while Von Leinsdorf parted the curtains and looked down at the street. Bernie sat on the sofa, sinking into the cushions, and took a sip of tea. The strong, bitter taste sent a shiver through him. He watched Von Leinsdorf, only a few feet out of reach. His free hand reached down to the syringe in his jacket pocket.

Stick him, and go find help. Make sure the Americans take him. They can make him talk, get the target out of him. They have to. Is it enough morphine to put him under? Will he kill me before it takes effect?

He realized Von Leinsdorf was talking to him.

"Our evening began with real promise, but I soon realized there was no future for us," said Von Leinsdorf, glancing at the bedroom.

"What's that?"

"She had another man in her life. His clothes are in the closet."

"Whose clothes?"

"You know, I never had a chance to ask. Anyway, treat yourself to a bath, then put on a fresh outfit; you're right, you do smell like the grave."

"And wear what? We're supposed to be soldiers."

"That's the beauty of it, Brooklyn. Her gentleman caller was a GI. His uniform's in the closet. Freshly laundered by his little French whore. A sergeant in the quartermaster corps."

He held up a khaki dress cap and twirled it on his index finger, looking at the sergeant's insignia.

"Not overly ambitious, was she?" said Von Leinsdorf. "For a camp follower. No doubt she shacked up with some of our boys before the Yanks showed up with better cigarettes."

"Maybe she saw you as a promotion."

"Frankly, it wasn't a face for an officer's pay grade. I'll fix us something else to eat. I paid for those groceries after all. Finish your tea."

Von Leinsdorf moved toward the kitchen. Bernie stared down at an issue of *Life* magazine on the table beside him. General de Gaulle was on the cover, posed heroically, staring into the distance at some idealized future for France, or at least for de Gaulle. Bernie heard a clock ticking somewhere, far louder than it should have sounded. An alarming sense of dislocation swept through his chest; his heart skipped a beat; his body flushed with heat. He banged the teacup down on the table and staggered to his feet. De Gaulle's face began to wobble. The lines of every object in the room swam in front of his eyes; the air turned rubbery. Von Leinsdorf was beside him in a moment, taking his arm.

"Don't fight it, Brooklyn," he said, his voice distorting. "I put something in the tea. You'll sleep a few hours. Can't have you running off while I'm at the cinema. I'll come back with the others, if they're there. That's a good fellow. After all, you could use the rest."

Von Leinsdorf eased him back down onto the sofa. Bernie was out by the time his head hit the cushions.

The first show ended at eight-thirty, a wave of GIs spreading out from the theater into the surrounding bars and restaurants. The rain had passed through, and the night air warmed slightly under a lowering cover of clouds. Curls of fog spun in off the river, obscuring the square. Carlson and the rest of the men stationed on the ground scanned the faces of the exiting soldiers as they moved toward their evening's pleasures, while Grannit watched from his observation post. No one spotted his "Lieutenant Miller."

A brief lull in street traffic followed before uniforms began to trickle into the square again, lining up for the nine o'clock show. Grannit poured himself another cup of coffee. Ole and the five supervising MP sergeants returned to the apartment for a final briefing.

"Keep your men out of sight until the crowd builds in again," said Grannit. "Stay outside, watch the street. When they're about to start the show, button it up, put a hat on every exit, inside and out. Five minutes into the picture we kill the projector, bring up the houselights, announce we've got a security situation. Then we'll do it by the numbers. Bring 'em out row by row to the lobby, check IDs one at a time."

"What if anybody bolts?"

"Take 'em down," said Grannit. "If they draw a weapon, shoot 'em."

Grannit followed them downstairs. The fog had grown so thick he could no longer make out any faces from the window.

The American deserter William Sharper had spotted the MPs at a border post, abandoned the jeep, and led his squad into France the previous night on foot. After spending the night in a barn, they hitched a ride that morning with a middle-aged French farmer, who seemed thrilled to lend a hand to the American war effort. Before they reached the main highway, Sharper strangled the man and dumped his body in a field. Sharper put on the farmer's clothes, took his wallet and agricultural road pass, and drove his load of chickens into Reims. His other three men hid in the back with the birds. Sharper knew the city well enough to get them to the farmer's market, where they abandoned the truck and blended into the city.

By mid-day, Sharper had found the cinema that he'd suggested for their rallying point. Taking his men to a nearby brothel, he instructed them to play the part of randy soldiers on leave from the front, their easiest assignment yet. He paid for eight hours' time with the four girls in the house and the squad spent the rest of the day upstairs, getting laid, resting, and sleeping. Sharper put so much American cash on the table the madam agreed to wash their uniforms while they relaxed. She thought it odd that the Americans didn't ask for any wine or liquor, but dollars had a way of easing her curiosity.

At eight-thirty, Sharper and his men set out for the cinema, less than three blocks away, in their freshly laundered uniforms.

26

Reims
DECEMBER 19, 8:40 P.M.

on Leinsdorf walked slowly to the middle of the square outside the theater, on the edge of the gathering crowd. He
took out a cigarette and scanned ahead for any unusual police presence. The fog thickened near the waterfront as soldiers
lined up in front of the theater box office. Two MPs stood near the
entrance to the lobby, but didn't look out of place. An American soldier materialized out of the fog, suddenly standing next to him, and
offered a light for his smoke.

"Another Judy Garland picture," the man said, nodding toward
the theater. "Louis B. Mayer's working her like a sled dog. You know
she's not even five feet tall?"

"I might have read it somewhere."

"Just my size. A hot little number, if you like a babe with no waist
and the ass of a ten-year-old boy. She do anything for you, Sarge?"

"She's no Marlene Dietrich," said Von Leinsdorf.

"Are you kidding me? Marlene Dietrich'd eat her like a chicken
leg, spit out the bone."

Von Leinsdorf moved forward, trying to shake the man, but
he fell into step alongside, holding out a hand. Short and fidgety, the
man wore a corporal's stripes and pounded a wad of gum while he
smoked.

"Eddie Bennings, Corporal Eddie Bennings, how you doing tonight?"

"Fine, thanks."

"A free night in France, fresh air, no bullets in the forecast, what could be so bad? I see you're with the quartermaster corps."

"That's right."

Looking ahead through the fog, Von Leinsdorf spotted William Sharper leading his three men into the theater lobby past the MP at the door.

"My line, too. Came in today from Belgium. Makes you appreciate the peace and quiet down here," said Bennings. Then, lowering his voice to a conspiratorial level: "My battalion does a lot of business with the quartermaster corps."

"Is that a fact?"

"And we're always looking for a good man to do business with— you going in to see the picture?"

"Yes."

"Let me spring for the tickets, my treat—you shouldn't have to stand on line, Sarge."

The persistent little man was starting to attract Von Leinsdorf's interest. "What sort of business?"

"I'll get the tickets, we'll have a chat. See if you're interested. Meet you in two shakes."

Von Leinsdorf moved on to the front lobby doors and waited as Bennings jumped the ticket line.

Bernie opened his eyes to a cat rubbing its face on his chin and purring. When he started awake, the animal vaulted off his chest into the kitchen. The room spun violently when he tried to stand. He lurched forward, tumbling over a table and vomiting as he hit the floor. Rolling onto his back, he took deep breaths, opening and closing his eyes, waiting for the ceiling to stabilize. As his fractured thoughts reassembled and he remembered where he was, he raised his watch into view and waited for the hands to float into position. 8:40.

"Shit."

He pulled himself to his feet, made his way into the kitchen, stuck his head under the faucet in the sink, and ran cold water over his neck until his head began to clear. Taking a quick look around the apartment, he spotted Von Leinsdorf's GI field greens lying in a heap on the bedroom floor. The khaki dress uniform that had been hanging in the woman's closet was gone.

He remembered that Von Leinsdorf had mentioned the movie house was near the canal. A memory of the city map swam to the surface. He headed for the door.

Eddie Bennings handed Von Leinsdorf his ticket and they entered the lobby, blending into the crowd.

"Looking for somebody?" asked Bennings.

"Thought I saw someone I knew."

"You want a soda, popcorn or anything, Sarge?"

"No thanks."

"I never got your name."

"Dick Connelly."

"Okay, Dick. You want to talk about my proposition before the picture or after?"

"Now's fine," said Von Leinsdorf, scanning the lobby over the man's shoulder.

"As I was saying, we work with a lot of guys in the quartermaster corps. It's a first-class arrangement."

"Can you be slightly more specific?"

Bennings lowered his voice again and talked out of the side of his mouth, like a gangster.

He's seen too many Jimmy Cagney pictures, thought Von Leinsdorf.

"In the area of surplus supply and demand. Daily necessities. A drink, a smoke, a taste of home, whatever. We scratch their back, they scratch ours; everybody gets healthy, including the average GI who all he's looking for is a little relief."

Von Leinsdorf spotted Sharper standing near a door to the the-ater, his three men walking in just ahead of him.

"You want me to set it to music for you?" asked Bennings impa-tiently.

"I think I get the idea," he said. "Would you excuse me for a mo-ment, Eddie? I want to say hi to my friend."

"Hope I haven't offended you, Sarge."

"You've got a little larceny in your heart, don't you, Eddie?" said Von Leinsdorf with an admiring smile.

"Troubled times. Is that such a terrible thing?"

"On the contrary. It's a character reference. I'll be right back."

Von Leinsdorf took one step toward Sharper, when Bennings grabbed him by the arm.

"Oh shit. Hang on a second. Don't move, Sarge."

Bennings turned away from the doors, then took another glance. "It is him. Fuck. I had a run-in with that guy recently. He's a cop."

"Which one?"

Bennings nodded toward a man near the lobby doors, looking at his watch. A charge of adrenaline shot through Von Leinsdorf. It was the soldier he'd seen near Mallory's bed in the field hospital—the one who chased them.

Von Leinsdorf surveyed the lobby with new eyes, aware of half a dozen other men, in and out of uniform, with that same hard-eyed look. He turned his back to the doors fronting the street. Although he was sure the American wouldn't see through the alter-ations he'd made at a glance, that might change if their eyes hap-pened to meet.

"If I had to guess, I'd say he's looking for me," said Bennings.

"Why is that?"

"Don't really have time for that story right now."

Music blared from the auditorium and the houselights started to dim. Von Leinsdorf saw Sharper head into the theater, unaware of either his or the Allied police's presence. On the side of the lobby nearest to them, he saw one of the uniformed MPs enter the men's room.

"Go to the bathroom," said Von Leinsdorf. "Wait in one of the stalls."

"What for?"

"I think I know him, too. Scratch my back, Eddie, I'll scratch yours."

Eddie headed toward the bathroom, turning his face away from the lobby doors.

Outside, out of breath, Bernie Oster ran up and joined the line at the box office window.

Ole Carlson came out of the auditorium to meet Grannit just after he entered the lobby.

"Think any of 'em showed?" he asked.

Grannit looked around. "We'll find out. You see your guy about the passes?"

"Yeah, got one here. Still doesn't add up, let me show you—"

Grannit looked at his watch. "Talk about it later. Everyone in place?"

Carlson picked up a walkie-talkie. "I'll double-check in back."

He moved into the auditorium just as the music started inside and the last GIs headed for their seats.

Von Leinsdorf entered the men's room, used the urinal, and then walked to a row of sinks to wash his hands. The MP was washing his hands in the next sink over. A muted swell of music reached into the room.

"Sounds like the show's starting," said Von Leinsdorf.

The only other soldier in the room finished drying his hands and exited. As the MP reached for a towel, Von Leinsdorf slid behind him and slipped a piano wire garrote around the man's throat. Yanking hard with both hands, he lifted the man off the ground, then walked him back into one of the stalls. The MP's heels kicked and dragged as he clawed at his throat. His helmet fell off and hit the ground. The stall door banged shut behind them. Von Leinsdorf could anticipate the letting go down to the second. He counted in his head, and as he reached ten, the man went slack.

When the door swung slowly open, Eddie Bennings stood there staring wide-eyed at Von Leinsdorf. The MP's dead body slumped onto the toilet as Von Leinsdorf slipped off the garrote and dropped it into his pocket. He'd pulled so hard the wire had sliced the dead man's throat, a line of blood trickling down his neck.

"Holy shit," said Bennings.

Von Leinsdorf grabbed Bennings and pulled him into the stall. "If you want to get out of here alive, you need to do exactly as I tell you, Eddie. Do you have a problem following orders?"

"Not tonight."

Bernie Oster handed his ticket to the usher at the door and entered the lobby, one of the last men through the doors before they closed. The auditorium doors were still open; he could see the show had started and a newsreel was playing. As he hurried across the lobby, he noticed a number of MPs moving toward the doors behind him from outside, not quite in a line but organized, grouped around a tall officer in the middle of the lobby.

I know that guy, thought Bernie, trying to place him.

He moved to the concession stand and ordered a soda, keeping his back to the tall man. The line of MPs moved in to cover every door out of the lobby.

They found my note. They set a trap.

His eye caught two men walking out of the bathroom to his right toward the auditorium. A soldier followed by an MP in helmet and armbands, nudging the shorter man ahead of him with the butt of his nightstick.

"Let's go, pal, back to your seat," he said.

Von Leinsdorf.

The two men moved into the auditorium. Bernie followed. Entering the darkness, he was momentarily blinded by the illuminated screen, black-and-white wartime footage: destroyers at sea, fighters streaming overhead. Framed against the moving images, two men's silhouettes stood out as they walked down the aisle toward the front of the theater. Bernie waited for his eyes to adjust to the light. His fingers found the syringe in his pocket.

Get close to him. Use the syringe. Slip out in the confusion. MPs are here, they'll take care of the rest.

William Sharper, sitting on the right aisle near the middle of the theater, noticed Erich Von Leinsdorf walk past him. A few moments later he whispered to one of his men to stay in their seats, and got up to follow him.

Grannit waited in the lobby for his MPs to reach their positions at the doors. He looked at his watch again. Three minutes until they stopped the film. His men should be in place by now. He picked up his walkie-talkie to check with Carlson when he overheard a nearby conversation.

"Where the hell's Whitey?" one of the MPs asked another.

"Still in the can," said another, glancing at his watch.

"What's taking him so long?"

Grannit looked toward the bathroom door. Sudden instinct propelled him through the door. The room was empty. He bent down and saw legs in one of the toilet stalls, a man's pants bunched around the ankles. He drew his gun and moved closer. The stall door swung open on a rusty hinge.

Ole Carlson reached the back of the theater stage, directly behind the screen, and put the beam of his gooseneck flashlight on the wall. A small rear door there had been left unlocked and unguarded, inside and out.

"Doggone it. What the heck are they thinking?"

He was about to call the lobby on his walkie-talkie and yell at them to get a body back here covering this door pronto. He turned and looked up at the huge moving images towering above him. He'd never realized you could see movies from the back side of the screen before, a reverse image, like you'd gone through the looking glass.

The newsreel was still running. There was Hitler, and that runt Himmler and the fat one, what was his name, he got Göring and Bormann mixed up sometimes. The crowd booed them. The jeers turned to cheers when the newsreel ended, the MGM lion gave a roar, and the movie began rolling lush Technicolor credits for the Judy Garland picture. He hadn't seen it before. He liked old-time pictures like this, a window back into the simple Midwestern world his parents had grown up in.

Two figures appeared from the left, black outlines against the screen, walking diagonally toward him. His hand went toward his sidearm; then he saw the MP's helmet on the second of the men and relaxed. The MP pushed a GI along in front of him, a shorter guy in a raincoat. He couldn't make out their faces and raised his flashlight.

"This joker was trying to sell hooch in the mezzanine," said the MP.

Carlson pointed the flashlight in the shorter man's face, and he raised a hand to shield his eyes.

"Well, if it ain't Corporal Eddie Bennings," said Carlson. "Seven-twenty-fourth Railway Battalion. Look what the cat dragged in."

Bennings shielded his eyes against the light and didn't answer. Another figure rose up behind the two men, ten paces away, framed against the movie screen.

"Lieutenant Miller, is that you?" asked William Sharper, moving closer. "Lieutenant Miller?"

Carlson's walkie-talkie crackled to life. Grannit's voice. "Ole, he's here. Miller's in the theater."

Carlson reached for his sidearm, but first had to transfer the flashlight to his left hand. In that moment the MP took a quick step toward him. Carlson saw something flash in the man's hand, moving toward him.

Grannit burst out of the restroom and through the doors into the auditorium, pulling his sidearm and shouting at the MPs in the lobby.

"Lock it down! Lock it down!"

Halfway down the aisle, Bernie felt more than saw a man rush past him, nearly knocking him over. He followed him until they'd almost reached the front of the room and the houselights started to fade up.

Behind the screen, Von Leinsdorf pulled the hunting knife out of the man's chest; he'd gone up and under the ribs, into the heart, with the practiced stroke of a surgeon. Looking at the soldier as he dropped, he recognized the round face and close-cropped haircut. This man had been at the hospital with the other one he'd just seen in the lobby. He bent down, rifled through the man's coat, and pulled out his badge and ID, sticking them in his pocket.

"Lieutenant Miller?"

Von Leinsdorf turned to see William Sharper standing above him, anxious and agitated, trying to make him out in the dark. They heard shouts from the auditorium; footsteps pounded toward them down the aisles. Von Leinsdorf pressed the bloodied knife into Sharper's hand, pulled Carlson's sidearm, and pointed it at him.

"Run," said Von Leinsdorf. "Run!"

"What the hell are you doing?" asked Sharper.

Sharper stepped back a few paces, confused, looking from Von Leinsdorf and Bennings to the body on the floor.

"He's a Nazi!" shouted Von Leinsdorf. "Back here, he's a fucking Nazi! I got the bastard! I got him!"

Sharper turned and ran toward the screen, where Judy Garland was making her first appearance, singing and dancing in a hallway. Sharper stopped short, startled by the image, then used the knife to slice a gash in the screen, and as he burst through it, Von Leinsdorf fired three times.

Earl Grannit was climbing the stairs to the stage when Sharper came through the screen. When he heard the shots, Grannit turned on instinct, knelt, and fired twice at close range, spinning the man around. Sharper toppled forward and landed hard on the floor in front of the stage. He wheeled around on the floor, crying out, in death throes. MPs with guns drawn closed in around him from every direction. One kicked the knife away from his hand.

The front of the theater emptied, soldiers crawling over seats, scrambling toward the lobby exits, where MPs with riot guns stepped in and held their ground. Grannit climbed the rest of the way onto the front of the stage, fired a single shot at the ceiling, and shouted to the room.

"Nobody leaves! Get away from those exits! I want every man back in a seat!"

The projector shut down, the music died. A line of MPs and undercover men surged forward from the lobby and the exits to take control of the room. Grannit jumped down to take a close look at the face of the dead GI lying in front of the stage. There were five bullets in him, but he'd only fired twice.

Was it Miller? Maybe; he couldn't be sure. He was the right size, the right body type. But the face? He took a look at the serrated blade of the knife the man had carried, then jumped to the stage and pushed through the slash in the screen.

Ole was lying on his back ten paces away. A young kid, a private, was cradling his head in his hands.

"We need a medic back here!" Grannit shouted back to the auditorium. "Get me a medic!"

He knelt down next to them. Ole saw he was there, felt for him with a shaking hand. Grannit gripped it hard. He glanced down at the wound, saw how bad it was, and how fast he was losing blood. Ole's sidearm lay on the floor beside him, still smoking.

"We get him, Earl?"

"We got him. The same knife he used on the border guards."

"That's good. He was on me before I— He moved so fast— Hurts something awful."

"Take it easy, don't talk, help's coming."

"I can't figure what the hell Bennings was doing with him—"

"Bennings? What do you mean? Eddie Bennings?"

"Oh God, I don't feel good, Earl, I don't feel good."

The private was holding up a syringe so Grannit could see it, asking if he should use it on him. Grannit hesitated.

"Eddie Bennings was here, Ole? Is that what you're saying?"

"I think so. I just never figured an MP . . ." He started to fade, eyes blanking out.

"What MP? What MP?" He shook his head at the private. No morphine. Not yet. "Stay with me, Ole. Stay with me."

Ole's eyes focused again. "Those passes . . . meant to tell you . . . about those passes . . ." Blood bubbled out onto Carlson's lips. Grannit wiped it away with a handkerchief, holding the back of his head.

"Don't talk now."

"Don't think they knew about the mistake . . . Krauts for you, always think they got a better idea . . ."

Grannit nodded at the kid to give him the shot. He leaned in to do it. Ole's eyes met Grannit's in a moment of clarity, his grip grew stronger for a moment, then his hand went slack and he was gone.

27

The syringe shattered when it hit the floor. Bernie dropped his head, a hand covering his eyes, trying not to cry.

"You know him?" asked Grannit. "Do you know him?"

Bernie shook his head. Grannit looked up. There was an open door behind them, leading out into an alley.

"Did you see anything, Private?" asked Grannit. "What he was talking about?"

"I'm not sure what I saw," said Bernie.

"Somebody else was back here with him? An MP? Anybody else? Maybe two men?"

"Yeah, I think maybe."

"Where they'd go, out that way?"

"I heard the door close."

"You a medic?"

"No, sir."

Grannit took the dog tags off Carlson and slipped them into his pocket.

"Come with me," said Grannit, starting toward the door.

"What about him?" asked Bernie.

"Nothing we can do for him now. Come on."

They hurried out the back door into an alley. Grannit had his sidearm pulled, looking in both directions. He pointed to the left.

"Take that way, once around the block, meet back here. Give a shout if you see anything."

Grannit ran off to the right. Bernie headed down the alley like a sleepwalker, his thoughts thicker than the fog.

He knew this man. He remembered him now. The one who'd chased them at the hospital, who came after them on the motorcycle. He didn't think the man had placed him. Not yet, anyway.

Bernie reached the end of the alley and looked in both directions. Visibility was less than twenty yards. No sign of Von Leinsdorf.

Should he go back as the officer ordered him to do or keep walking? The darkness beckoned. He had a chance at least; now that he was free of the German, he could fade into the night. They were focused on Von Leinsdorf now but if he went back to that movie house, there'd be MPs all over him, questions he couldn't answer, then an American firing squad, just as Von Leinsdorf had predicted.

He could use the dead girl's apartment, at least overnight. Find a map, figure a way out of the city. But to do what? Go where? His life in Germany was finished, even if his parents were still alive. He could never set foot there again, not after what Von Leinsdorf had told him about the death camps. He'd heard the rumors, and he'd been around the Nazis long enough to know they were capable of it. Von Leinsdorf had only confirmed what he'd feared was true for years.

A sense of shame overwhelmed him. His impulsive little acts of rebellion in Berlin seemed so puny and inadequate. He could have done more, tried harder to fight them, but all he'd thought of when it really mattered was his own survival. When he faced his own death, whenever it might come, what damage had that done to his immortal soul? If he'd failed so miserably what difference did it make if he lived or died?

The bottom dropped out: Was Von Leinsdorf right? Did it all mean nothing? How could whatever he had left of his life make up for what he'd failed to do, if he didn't take a stand now?

He spotted something lying in a corner of the alley and picked it up. An MP's armband. Nearby a white helmet and billy club had been tossed in a trash can. They'd come this way, Von Leinsdorf and the other man, after they'd left the theater. Bernie looked down the street. The girl's apartment was in that direction. That was where Von Leinsdorf would go first.

To take care of me. Another loose end. Unless I take care of him first.

He heard MPs' whistles blowing somewhere nearby, footsteps running down another street. A manhunt was under way and he re- membered: *They're looking for me, too.*

He ran back toward the theater, until he saw the American officer rounding the corner. Bernie showed him the armband, then led him back to where he'd found it. Bernie watched as he examined the other articles.

"I think I know who did this," said Bernie.

"We killed that man in the theater."

"No, sir. I think it's someone else. Another GI. I followed him to the movie house."

"Why?"

"I saw him hurting this girl, earlier tonight."

"Where?"

"Through the window of an apartment, as I walked by. I'm not sure, but I think he might have killed her. I didn't know what to do so I waited. He came out a few minutes later."

"Where were you headed?"

"Me? I was going to the movies."

"Why didn't you say anything to an MP?"

"I saw him go inside, lost him in the lobby. Then I thought I saw him going behind the screen. That's why I followed him back there."

Grannit just looked at him. Bernie couldn't tell if he believed him or not.

"I think he might've gone back to that apartment," said Bernie.

"Take me there."

"Okay. It's this way."

Grannit called for a radioman to join them and they walked at a brisk clip, Bernie taking the lead. Grannit spoke into the radio most of the way, shouting orders to his men at the movie house.

"What's your name, Private?" the man snapped, as soon as he came off the radio.

"Bernie Oster, sir."

"What unit are you with?"

"Two hundred ninety-first Engineer Combat Battalion."

"Where you from?"

"Brooklyn, sir."

"Which neighborhood?"

"Park Slope."

"North or South?" asked Grannit.

Bernie looked over at him, but couldn't read the man's expression. "North."

"Where'd you live?"

"On Union Street, between Sixth and Seventh Avenue. You know Brooklyn, sir?"

"What'd your dad do?"

"He worked for Pfizer," said Bernie. "Research and development. He was a chemist."

"Was?"

"He's retired now. Turn right here."

Bernie led him to the front door of the woman's apartment building. Grannit ordered the radioman to call in support and wait for it on the street. He forced the lock and Bernie led him up to the third floor.

The door stood open a crack. Grannit drew his gun, gestured for silence, and listened. He silently eased the door forward.

All the lights were off. Bernie couldn't remember if he'd left them that way. Grannit pulled a flashlight from his belt. Bernie watched from the doorway as the beam edged around the apartment. Somehow, before even completing his sweep, the man knew the apartment was empty. He walked in and turned on the living room lamp.

"Stay by the door," said the man. "Don't touch anything."

Bernie stepped inside. Grannit walked straight into the bedroom. Bernie watched him lift the blanket covering the girl's body on the bed. He studied it for a moment, then replaced the blanket and examined the rest of the room. Bernie saw him pick up Von Leinsdorf's old discarded GI uniform from the floor. He glanced briefly at the jacket, ripped something off the shoulder, then dropped it again. Out of nowhere, the dead woman's damn cat rubbed against Bernie's leg. He jumped half a foot and kicked at it.

"Get away. Get away."

Grannit came back into the living room, opened the window, and looked down at the street.

"Is she dead?" asked Bernie.

Grannit marched straight to Bernie, grabbed him by the throat, stuck the barrel of his gun under his chin, and cocked the hammer.

"Two hundred ninety-first Combat Engineers?" he said.

"That's right."

Grannit held up the patch he'd torn from the uniform in the other room so Bernie could see it. The same unit.

"You didn't tell me you were from the same unit," said Grannit.

"Guess I didn't realize—"

"You didn't see him do anything to that girl from the street, the curtains were pulled. You were up here with him—"

"No, only after he killed her," said Bernie, his voice shaking. "He made me come up with him."

"What are you doing in Reims?"

"We were delivering dispatches—"

"Don't fucking lie to me. Tell me what I want to know or I put your brains on the wall—"

"Okay, okay—"

"Your friend just killed my partner, you Nazi fuck!"

Grannit shoved Bernie down into a chair and pointed the gun at him. Convinced he was about to die, Bernie put his hands up and closed his eyes.

"You're with the 150th Panzer Brigade," said Grannit. "Your commanding officer's Otto Skorzeny."

Bernie opened his eyes.

Grannit took a step closer to him. "Your brigade was sent in to take three bridges over the Meuse. Your squad leader gave you a second objective in France. I've got three of your pals we just nailed in that theater ready to ID you. You want to deny any of that to me?"

Bernie shook his head.

"What's your friend's name?"

"His name's Von Leinsdorf. Erich Von Leinsdorf. He's a lieutenant in the SS," said Bernie.

"You came across the line with him into Belgium, with two other men, near Elsenborn. You killed three soldiers at the border crossing."

"He did. And one of ours. He was wounded, Von Leinsdorf shot him."

"Where'd you put the bodies?" asked Grannit.

"He ordered us to drag them into the woods. One of your men was still alive, a sergeant, so I tried to help him—"

"How?"

"I gave him morphine. Put sulfa and a pressure bandage on his wounds."

"You did that? Where'd you go from there?"

"We spent the night near Butgenbach. The next day we scouted that bridge—"

"Why were you at that hospital?"

"The fourth man with us got shot. An American convoy came along and took us there."

"Where Von Leinsdorf killed Sergeant Mallory and your own man."

"I guess he did—"

"You guess so? You were driving the fucking jeep!"

"He didn't tell me what he was going to do, and he didn't tell me after. He never told me anything."

"Why'd you come to Reims?"

"He said we were going to meet the other squads, at that movie theater. That's all I know."

"Where'd you cross the border?" asked Grannit.

"In the mountains this morning. A place called Pont-Colin. He killed the guards. I left a message in the booth to warn somebody, I was trying to stop him—"

Grannit held out a pen and a small notebook.

"Write down your name," he said.

"Which one?"

"Your real name."

Bernie did as he was told. Grannit took the notebook back from him and compared it to a sheet of paper he took from his pocket. Then he held up the note he'd taken from Pont-Colin, the words "REIMS" and "MOVIE HOUSE" on it.

"You wrote this," said Grannit.

"Yes, sir."

"Why did you come to France, what's your target?"

"I don't know."

"Don't lie to me, god damn it—"

"I don't know, I swear to God he never told me. If you know anything, you know more than I do. There's a second objective, but he never told me what it was—"

"Why?"

"He didn't trust me."

Grannit moved closer to him and held up the note again. "Why didn't he trust you? Why the hell did you write this?"

"Because I'm an American."

Grannit stared hard at him. They heard multiple vehicles driving up fast outside. Grannit moved to the window, put two fingers in his mouth and gave a sharp whistle, then waved down to the radioman on the street.

Down to my last chance, thought Bernie.

"I am from Brooklyn, I swear to you it's true, I was born there, I grew up there. My parents are German; they immigrated to New York, then moved back here six years ago. We lived in Frankfurt till they drafted me into their fucking army. I've been fixing cars in Berlin, I've never been in combat, I never shot at anybody; I got pulled into this because I speak English. They didn't tell us what it was about and they killed anybody who didn't go along with it. We didn't even know where we were going until it happened."

Grannit walked back toward him. "What neighborhood in Brooklyn?"

"Park Slope North, like I told you. I was born in Brooklyn Hospital on DeKalb. I went to PS 109 on Snyder Avenue, just off Flatbush. Mrs. Quinn was my third grade teacher. I was supposed to start Erasmus Hall the year we moved away. My best friend was Jackie Waldstein from the south side; his dad worked for the Rheingold brewery in Bushwick. We played ball every day in Prospect Park, on the diamonds by the boathouse."

"What was your address?"

"Three seventy-five Union Street. South side of the street, near Sixth. Big white house, two stories, a porch that ran all the way around the front. We'd sit out there summer nights listening to Jack Benny and Fibber McGee. My buddies and me went to the movies Saturday at Loews Palace near Grand Army Plaza. Matinees, all the serials, Red Ryder, Flash Gordon, kids' stuff. Three times a week I'd take the trolley down Flatbush to Ebbets Field; cost a quarter on Wednesdays for the right-field bleachers. I carved my fucking name in one of 'em with a penknife. If we didn't have the dough, we'd watch the game through this gap under the metal gate in right center. I caught a foul ball from Cookie Lavagetto, he signed it for me after the game, my parents still have the damn ball; I can tell you everybody who ever played for 'em."

Grannit hesitated. "They could've taught you all this."

"They could've but they didn't; I swear to God it's true; I lived it."

Bernie heard footsteps entering the building through the open front door down below.

"Where's the best cheesecake in Brooklyn?"

"Cheesecake? Junior's, on DeKalb and Flatbush; me and Jackie used to go there after school."

"Where'd your mother shop?"

"There was a greengrocer on the corner, corner of Polhemus and Garfield; she went over there almost every day—"

"What was it called?"

"Solly's, Solly's Produce. There was a Laundromat next door, a radio repair shop, then a coffee shop run by two brothers, they were Greek, a long name, lots of vowels in it. My dad used to get that sticky pastry they'd make on his way to work, what do they call it, baklava?"

"There was a candy store across the street."

"I know it, I know it, Foppiano's, this nice old Italian guy, had a big mustache, wore an old worn-out gray sweater every day, kept everything in glass jars behind the counter. Root beer sticks, Houten's chocolates, Black Crows, those little licorice deals? That's where I bought comic books—and it wasn't right across from Solly's, it was di-agonal."

"Tell me something that happened on that street. Something you'd only know if you were living there."

Bernie thought frantically. "When I was a little kid—I don't know, maybe six or seven?—there was a robbery at an Esso station. A girl got shot, I think she was a teenager. I remember it real clear; police were all over the place. I saw them put her in the ambulance, taking her away. Shook me up bad. There was blood on the sidewalk for a couple days."

Grannit looked as if he'd been slapped, and Bernie knew he re-membered it, too. He could hear footsteps on the landing below. The other men would reach the apartment in less than a minute.

"You're from the neighborhood," said Bernie. "You are, aren't you? You're from Park Slope."

Grannit said nothing, but his look confirmed it.

"Jesus Christ, you know I'm telling the truth, what else do you need to hear?"

"I don't know what else."

"Please. I know you don't have to believe me, but I want to help you."

He waited. Grannit just stared at him.

"I'm sorry he killed your partner; I'm sorry he killed anybody, but he's not finished yet, and whatever's coming is going to be worse. Mister, I got reasons to want him dead every bit as bad as you. I've known this guy since he joined the brigade; I know a lot about him, I know how he thinks. If there's anybody in this whole fucking war who can help you stop him, it's me."

Grannit lowered the gun just as three MPs came through the door. He turned to them.

"Miller was here, before he went to the theater," he told them, then pointed to the bedroom. "He killed the woman who lived here, body's in there. Call the police."

"You really want to get the gendarmes involved?" an MP asked skeptically.

"You stay here and handle it. It was a Kraut killed her, make that clear to 'em, the same guy we're looking for. He's an SS lieutenant, Erich Von Leinsdorf. He's dressed like a GI; he's one of Skorzeny's men—get that out on the radio. Make sure these cops know it wasn't an American did this. And get that old uniform out of there."

The MP looked at Bernie again. "We got those three guys downstairs. Like you asked. The ones from the theater."

"Any of 'em talk?"

"Only a little. Two of 'em hardly speakie the English. That sergeant you took out was their squad leader."

"His name was William Sharper," said Bernie. "He was an American deserter."

The lead MP looked at Bernie, even more puzzled, then back at Grannit. "You still want us to bring those Krauts upstairs?"

"No," said Grannit. "Hand 'em off to Counter Intelligence."

"So who's this then?" asked the MP, looking at Bernie again.

"He's a witness. He saw the hitter up close."

"Where you going, Lieutenant?"

"I'm going after him," said Grannit, grabbing Bernie's arm. "And this one's coming with me."

28

Reims
DECEMBER 20, MIDNIGHT

They left the apartment and climbed into an extra jeep Grannit's men had left downstairs. Grannit took the wheel. Bernie directed him to the warehouse where they'd stashed the French ambulance and told him how they'd made their way into the city. The bodies of the two drivers were still inside, but their weapons and the jerricans holding all their equipment were gone.

"He must've come back here," said Bernie. "After he knocked me out, before he went to the movie house."

Grannit wanted to know what was in the cans, and Bernie told him about what he'd seen in three of them: supplies, ammunition, German uniforms. There was one can that he'd never looked into that Von Leinsdorf had always protected. Grannit took a radio call from his detail, updates from the theater. Hearing one side of it, Bernie gathered that Von Leinsdorf had avoided capture. Grannit gave the address of the warehouse to his men, with orders to check it out, then ended the call.

Grannit lifted a box from the back of the jeep and handed it to Bernie. It held an MP's blouse, belt, and armband, puttees for his boots, a white-lettered helmet and nightstick.

"Put those on," he said. "As far as anybody's concerned, you're an MP, working with me on special assignment. Use your real name, don't talk to anybody, don't answer any questions unless you ask me first."

"Yes, sir."

"Don't leave my sight. If you run, if you touch a weapon, if you make one wrong move, I won't wait for a firing squad, I'll kill you where you stand."

"I understand."

Grannit waited while Bernie changed.

"What's your name, sir?" he asked.

"Lieutenant Grannit. That's all you fucking need to know."

"Yes, sir."

When Bernie had finished dressing, Grannit waved him toward the driver's seat. "They taught you how to handle a jeep. Drive back to the movie house."

When Erich Von Leinsdorf and Eddie Bennings walked out the back of the theater, the German turned left and led him down an alley. He had scouted the area earlier before going inside. After dumping his MP equipment in an alley that led deeper into the city, where he knew it would be found, they ran three blocks to the west, jumped a fence, and squeezed through a narrow gap between buildings.

"Where we going, Boss?" asked Bennings.

"Don't talk, Eddie. We're not out of this yet."

They emerged from the buildings onto the banks of the Aisne Canal, barely visible through the fog twenty feet below. They heard police whistles blowing, shouts, and men running through the fog behind them. Von Leinsdorf directed Bennings to a rope fixed to an iron ring hanging down a steep concrete wharf. Eddie glanced over the edge and saw that a small flatboat had been tied off on a narrow ledge at the bottom of the rope. Von Leinsdorf followed Bennings down, untied the boat, and they each took an oar. While Grannit's military detail dropped roadblocks into place on all the side streets feeding into the square, they were in the boat, rowing silently south on the still water.

They stayed close to the shoreline, working their oars without a splash. Unable to see the top of the bank through the fog, they twice heard voices and car engines from above near the edge of the canal. Each time they shipped their oars and drifted until the voices and cars faded away.

They rowed downstream for half a mile, and Von Leinsdorf steered them to the left bank. Another small dock at the base of a quay appeared out of the mist, and he angled toward it, jumped out first, and tied off the boat. A small flight of stairs led up to the top of the bank.

They emerged onto a quiet street under a bridge that spanned the canal and the adjacent river. A single civilian car, a nondescript black Renault, was parked across the street. Von Leinsdorf took out keys and unlocked the trunk. Eddie Bennings had calmed down during the boat ride, impressed by the man's moves under pressure. He'd known a few guys with this kind of cool back home in Jersey—made men, guys he'd always looked up to—but never anybody in the army.

"I gotta say, Dick, whatever it is they want you for," said Bennings, "you got me beat by a mile."

"I didn't have a chance to tell you. Turns out we're in the same line."

"Black market? Can't say I'm surprised."

"I had to take out those MPs. They get their hands on me, it's like this . . ." He slashed his hand across his throat, then lifted a suitcase out of the trunk. "Don't know about you, I'm not that interested in firing squads."

"Brother, I'm picking up your frequency."

"Maybe they were looking for both of us back there. Doesn't matter now."

"Except you saw it coming, set up the boat, left this car here thinking about a way out."

"Helps to cover the bases, Eddie. We gotta lose the uniforms. Here, help yourself."

Von Leinsdorf opened a suitcase packed with everyday outfits. Both men picked some out and changed clothes by the side of the car. Eddie noticed a couple of jerricans sitting in the backseat.

"So, Dick, you a deserter?" asked Eddie.

"I am now." They both laughed. "You?"

"They had my whole battalion in the brig up in Belgium on a black-market beef. The Krauts come across a couple days ago, they tell us we're off the hook if we'll go catch a few bullets on the front line. I said hell yeah, why don't you just fit me for the pine overcoat while you're at it?"

They laughed again, Eddie in an aggressive, Woody Woodpecker staccato, his mouth contorted like the mask of tragedy.

"It was sayonara suckers before they even knew I was gone. This ain't my fight; I got no gripe with the Krauts. A freakin' Chinese fire drill getting down here; I can thank the Krauts for that."

"Why'd you stop in Reims?"

"That was a neighborhood we used to work; lotta freight moves on that canal. Thought I'd make a pass, see if I could pick up a few bucks." Eddie tried on a gray fedora, checking out his reflection in the car window. "That guy who came at us in the theater, he's one of these fellas you were supposed to meet?"

"I never saw him before."

"He called you Lieutenant Miller."

"Obviously he thought I was somebody else."

"Hey, it was him or us," said Eddie. "You won't hear me complaining."

"Who was the other cop, the one in the lobby?"

"That prick busted me the other night, Criminal Investigation Division, a real hard-on. Earl Grannit. New York homicide."

"He's a police detective?"

"That's right. He's on your tail, too?"

"He put some heat on us. I never knew his name."

"Well, fuck him, he can eat our dust," said Eddie. "I was gonna say we head down to Paris, what do you think?"

"You know your way around?"

"Been stationed there since August. Got that city wired. Our battalion was floating on a river of cash."

They heard sirens in the distance toward downtown Reims. When Eddie turned, Von Leinsdorf raised the silenced pistol, ready to shoot him in the back of the head.

"Our train yard's just west of the city, near Versailles," said Eddie.

Von Leinsdorf lowered the pistol. "Versailles?"

"Yeah. I'm telling you, you got to check out Paris. It's a fuckin' free-for-all. A guy with brass ones like you makes a killing in no time."

Von Leinsdorf put the pistol away before Eddie turned around.

"The Free French or de Gaulle or the U.S. Army may think they're running the joint, but nobody's got a handle on it. And the only God they bow down to in that town is the almighty American buck."

"You could introduce me to some people?"

"You got a stake we can use to prime the pump, get things rolling?"

"Sure," said Von Leinsdorf.

"Dick, I'm not pushing banana oil here. A couple weeks we could be running our own show. Just me and you, no brass skimming off the top."

"The army, the MPs, they're going to come looking for us."

"Forget it, I know places we could hole up for months. Local cops want nothing to do with the black market, and they're all on the pad anyway. You make your own law. There's parts of that city the army won't even come into."

"Will these get us there?" asked Von Leinsdorf, showing him some papers from his pocket.

"Road passes, regional business stamps, *laissez-passers*. Yeah, I'd say you got it covered."

"We're Danish businessmen looking into postwar oil contracts," said Von Leinsdorf.

"Let's get rich."

They shook hands, climbed into the Renault, and drove off. Von Leinsdorf had positioned the car less than a hundred yards from an entrance to the bridge that would carry them across the river, toward the highway to Paris. The army wouldn't throw roadblocks up on the bridge until half an hour after they crossed.

Von Leinsdorf glanced at Eddie as he drove. The man amused him, a common thief with a lust for money. So much more useful than Bernie Oster. That he'd left the young American alive remained an irritant, but a minor one. Brooklyn didn't have the skills to survive alone for long on enemy ground. He'd get himself captured or killed. Even if he talked, he knew nothing about the Second Objective; Von Leinsdorf had seen to that. He smiled. Eddie grinned back.

Everybody needed a little luck now and then.

Bernie stayed behind Earl Grannit's right shoulder and kept his mouth shut, as ordered. A few of the other MPs shot questioning glances his way—where had *he* been all night?—but none said a word. Grannit was in charge and he was Grannit's man.

Grannit's temper flared once he'd gathered all his MPs and Army Counter Intelligence men in the theater lobby. The killer and a probable accomplice had walked out into the night and vanished. How was it possible that no one saw them or followed them or picked them up once they left the theater? Forty men looking for one man and "Lieutenant Miller" slipped the net like smoke.

Bernie could feel the other officers' frustration in the tense silence that followed. They had a bona fide deserter from Skorzeny's brigade dead and three men from his squad alive; didn't that qualify as a good night's work? Maybe other German agents had been there, and maybe they'd gotten away, but no one else had seen these two phantom killers in back of the stage or outside the movie house. Not even the three Krauts they'd captured knew anything about them.

It seemed obvious to everyone else in the room that William Sharper had murdered the MP and Ole Carlson. Sharper died with the knife that killed Carlson in his hand. He'd been shot with Carlson's gun. He even looked like the sketch Grannit had circulated.

An army intelligence officer summed up their reservations. "Even if this Lieutenant Miller was here and got away, what can one Kraut do alone in the middle of France?"

"First of all, Carlson didn't shoot Sharper," said Grannit. "He's got no powder residue on his hand. That knife Sharper had in his hand killed two French border guards earlier today. An SS officer named Erich Von Leinsdorf killed those two men. He came into Reims in an ambulance today, killed the drivers, a female civilian, and our two men here tonight. He set up Sharper to take the fall, then killed him and walked away clean when we had him dropped, so don't fucking tell me what this man can't do."

Bernie wondered if anyone figured him as the source of all this, and if so, how he had come to know it.

"I want this sketch of Von Leinsdorf telexed to every checkpoint in France. Expand roadblocks to every road and highway leading out of town. Cover train and bus stations and canvass every street in this part of the city door to door. Do it now."

Grannit stormed out of the meeting; Bernie followed. They spent twenty minutes with a graves detail outside making sure Ole Carlson would be shipped home instead of being planted under a white cross in a French cemetery. Grannit wrote a letter to the man's father to accompany the casket. They were about to walk upstairs to the apartment Grannit used as his command post, when he heard the chug of a diesel motor cutting through the fog on the canal. Bernie followed him to the water's edge. Grannit lit a cigarette and walked along the bank, looking down through a break in the fog at a tug pushing a coal barge downstream.

"He used a boat," said Grannit, angry at himself for not seeing it earlier. "God damn it, he used a boat."

"He won't give up," said Bernie. "He won't stop until you kill him."

"Where's he going? Give me your best guess."

"Paris, I think. He said he spent time there before. He speaks the language like a native. I think he's supposed to kill somebody. Somebody important, I don't know who."

Grannit whistled sharply, and two MPs ran toward them from the movie theater. Grannit offered Bernie a cigarette while they waited. Bernie took it and accepted a light.

"Whoever he's after," said Bernie, "that's his next move."

Grannit didn't answer, but he turned to the MPs when they arrived. "Search the canal, both directions. Cut off the bridges. He took a boat."

They scrambled back toward the theater, blowing whistles to summon more men.

"He's halfway there by now," said Bernie.

"He's going after General Eisenhower," said Grannit. "That's the target."

Bernie felt what little strength he had left rush out of him. He stumbled slightly, and nearly went to his knees.

"Jesus Christ."

"You didn't know that."

"No, sir. He wouldn't tell me anything. I don't know what to say. It's my fault. They're all fucking crazy. I could've stopped him; I should've killed him when I had the chance."

Grannit just watched him. "How many men were assigned to this?"

"He said there were five squads, but I only saw four."

"Not the whole commando unit?"

"No, no, it was a small group. Four squads, four men apiece. How many are left?"

"Not counting you," said Grannit, "one."

"One squad?"

"Just him."

Grannit took out the keys to the jeep. Bernie could see he was thinking about tossing them to him, telling him to drive it around. He could also see that Grannit knew that he knew that Grannit was thinking about it. Grannit put the keys back in his pocket and tossed away the cigarette.

"Paris," he said.

29

Versailles
DECEMBER 19

General Eisenhower returned to Allied headquarters after his meeting at Verdun, and the jaws of the security detail protecting him from Skorzeny's assassins snapped shut. He would not be allowed to leave his heavily defended compound again.

For the first time that morning headlines about the "Battle of the Bulge" appeared in American newspapers, and it quickly became the catchphrase for the entire Ardennes offensive. As the American front continued to deteriorate, Eisenhower made a controversial decision to place Field Marshal Bernard Montgomery in charge of the northern half of the battlefield. In doing so, he transferred authority over two American army groups that had long served under General Bradley to the one British officer almost universally disliked by the American senior staff. Unable to communicate with his generals in that part of the field, Bradley had his hands full holding the southern half of the Ardennes until Patton arrived. Still, Bradley reacted furiously to the perceived slap at his performance and tried to tender his resignation. Eisenhower refused it, arguing that the Germans had surrounded the American divisions in Bastogne. The fight was entering its most critical hours, and Bradley was his man.

Bradley had until recently, and for years prior, been Eisenhower's superior officer, so this loss of command was a bitter pill to swallow, particularly since he knew Ike shared his antipathy for Montgomery.

When Bradley agreed to stay on, as a show of gratitude Eisenhower made arrangements for him to receive his fourth star. Although Montgomery conducted his new command effectively, conflicts that resulted between the senior staffs of the Allies nearly achieved Hitler's objective of tearing their delicate alliance apart. Throughout, Eisenhower maintained his unearthly composure, kept Montgomery in check, and held these two armies together by force of will and his own quiet decency.

Three hours before daylight on December 21, the 150th Panzer Brigade finally entered the Battle of the Bulge under the command of Otto Skorzeny. Realizing that Operation *Greif*'s plan to capture the bridges at the Meuse would never materialize, Skorzeny volunteered his brigade for a frontal assault to capture the key city of Malmédy, where the Allies had mounted a makeshift but tenacious defense. His ten tanks, German Panthers disguised as American Shermans, led the attack from the southwest. They did not enjoy the benefit of surprise; an attack in the Ardennes by a German force dressed as Americans had been anticipated for days. As the tanks approached, they set off trip wires that flooded the night sky with flares. Under the artificial light, American guns entrenched on the far side of a stream opened fire and destroyed four of the tanks. Two more were taken out as they forded the stream. By dawn and into the early afternoon, rallied by Skorzeny's leadership, the brigade fought its way into the outskirts of town, defended primarily by the 291st Combat Engineers. When two companies of American infantry arrived to reinforce them, Skorzeny assessed his precarious position from a hill overlooking the field and reluctantly ordered his brigade to retreat. None of his tanks and less than half of his infantry survived.

That night, while approaching German divisional headquarters near Ligneuville to make his report, Skorzeny's armored car was blown into a ditch by a barrage of American artillery shells. Skorzeny was thrown from the car. Shell fragments peppered him in the legs, and a splinter the size of a small pencil pierced his forehead above the right eye. It caused heavy bleeding and carved off a flap of dangling flesh that impaired his vision. Taken to headquarters for treatment, he refused anesthetics and the doctor's recommendation that he be moved to a hospital for surgery, demanding that they stitch his forehead together so he could return to the field. He would command his remaining troops in a variety of actions for two more days before infection set in around the wound that nearly blinded him and forced his evacuation to a German hospital.

The Ardennes offensive, so far as Otto Skorzeny and what was left of his 150th Panzer Brigade were concerned, was effectively over.

30

Paris, France
DECEMBER 20

The City of Light had turned dark and cold. While the Allies' Liberation of Paris in August raised the spirits of those who had endured the German occupation, the early success of the Ardennes offensive leveled them in a single chilling blow. Amid wild rumors that circulated in the absence of hard news, the specter of Nazi columns marching back in along the Champs Élysées seemed all too easy to envision. Thousands of returning civilians who had just begun to reestablish their lives fled again in panic.

For those who remained, on the eve of what would be remembered as the coldest Parisian winter in modern memory, there was little fuel to heat their apartments and almost no food beyond the barest necessities to put on their table. Unstable gas lines resulted in random explosions that killed dozens every week. Curfews and blackouts, already in place but enforced more rigorously once fighting in the Ardennes began, emptied the streets. The power grid failed at least twice a night and the deep darkness provided cover for a campaign of terror, as the Free French who had resisted the Nazis during occupation took revenge against collaborators. Only two months in office, General Charles de Gaulle's provisional French government clashed repeatedly with the Allied high command, which retained de facto control of Paris as a war zone, and their conflicts strangled the flow of essential goods and services. Anyone with means who sought to remedy their personal or household shortages had no alternative but to traffic in black-market goods.

Every block on every street in every *arrondissement* produced a broker, someone who knew someone who could connect him to the rising tide of illicit goods that flooded the city like an invisible sea. Enterprising citizens traveled back and forth by train to Normandy, returning with suitcases full of Spanish hams, wheels of English cheese, sacks of coffee from Morocco. Whether you were a GI looking to sell his daily ration of cigarettes to a man hawking Lucky Strikes outside the St. Denis Metro station, or a star chef trying to score a hundred pounds of veal for a three-star restaurant on the Rue Royale, the deal could be done if you greased the right wheels. In the Darwinian ecosystem that had sprouted up overnight to meet those demands, ruthlessness and amorality guaranteed success.

Montmartre, Paris
DECEMBER 20

As regular as banker's hours, the man known only as Ververt spent every night from eight P.M. to two A.M. at a table near the kitchen of a jazz club he owned on Rue Clichy at the foot of Montmartre. He chain-smoked cigarettes, nursed one milky glass of pastis each hour, and kept an eye trained to oversee the action on the floor. A squadron of underlings ran interference, screening every supplicant who asked for an audience with their boss. Most problems or requests they were able to handle, but occasionally something crossed the door that warranted Ververt's personal attention. Like the two thousand in American cash sitting on the table in front of him.

Ververt gestured to a couple of chairs. The two men looked and moved like Americans. Soldiers, out of uniform, probably deserters, like so many others who sought him out. Listening to *"le jazz Américain"* from the quartet on stage, the audience was filled with the usual assortment of Allied servicemen, more than 50 percent on any given night. None had any idea they were paying for stolen U.S. Army liquor and cigarettes they should have been getting for pennies on the dollar at their officers' club or PX.

"Is it always this cold in Paris this time of year? I'm gonna complain to my travel agent," said the shorter one, rubbing his hands together. Then, to an appearing waiter: "How about a cup of coffee?"

Ververt could see that the taller man, who hadn't spoken, was in charge but wanted to let the little one do the talking. The second man shook his head to the waiter. His eyes met Ververt's for a moment, before respectfully looking away.

This one is interesting, thought Ververt.

"You speak English, right?" asked Eddie Bennings.

"I speak dollars," said Ververt.

"It's the universal language," said Eddie. "We're working from the same phrase book, my friend."

Ververt looked at the two thousand, without making a move to pick it up. "What are you trying to say?"

The man leaned toward him, in the overly familiar way that Americans mistook for charm. "I believe that you had some dealings with a few of my former associates. Captain John Stringer and other officers from the 724th Railway Battalion."

Ververt stared at him without responding until Eddie felt compelled to take a sudden interest in a book of matches.

"I don't know anyone by that name," said Ververt, pausing to light his next cigarette from the butt of his last. "Even if I did, and it happened that he had recently been arrested along with every other man in your battalion, why would I tell you about it?"

"Because you needed him," said Eddie. "It's left a hole in your supply chain. I worked closely with Captain Stringer, I kept his books, so I know how much business you did together. We never met, but that's how I know about you."

Ververt looked back and forth between the two men, as Eddie's coffee arrived.

"I misjudged you," he said.

"Sorry?"

"I thought you were military police. I am so relieved to learn you're not working undercover," he said, then turned to Von Leinsdorf. "Such a disadvantage in my business. I take everyone at their word."

Eddie seemed bewildered by the man's deadpan cynicism, and looked to his companion.

"What is your name?" Ververt asked the other man.

Von Leinsdorf didn't seem to hear the question, looking toward the stage. "What's with the jungle music?"

"They've played this way in Montmartre for twenty years. *Le tumulte noir*; the tourists come for it. It's as much a part of Paris as our contempt for them."

"I thought the Germans put a stop to it."

"When the Nazis took over, they decided it is degenerate music. A Negro-Jewish conspiracy to undermine the morals of the French, as if they had any, but a more particular threat to the morals of the Germans. Theirs, as you know, are more established as a matter of public record."

"That's rich," said Eddie.

Ververt glanced at him again, then turned back to Von Leinsdorf. "My personal theory is that it reminds the *Boches* of the Jazz Age, Paris in the twenties, and the shame they suffered at Versailles. That's what it's about for them, this Nazi business. We're all paying for rubbing their noses in the shit. So American jazz was banned during the Occupation. The last four years we play only 'French jazz.'"

"The Liberation change that?"

"Now the locals can't get enough. And the soldiers, the Americans, they like it, too. And they like our women," said Ververt, looking out at the audience. "Especially the blacks."

"So why call it American jazz?" asked Eddie. "Sounds the same to me."

"These days if I called horseshit 'American' I could sell horseshit sandwiches. Paris will tire of you soon enough, you'll see. Liberators quickly turn into occupiers."

"You get any British in here?" asked Von Leinsdorf.

"Everyone comes to Montmartre. We create a fantasy here; that sin can be packaged, contained, sold like chewing gum. It appeals to a fundamental part of human nature, whether it's Nazi, American, British, bourgeois, resistance, collaborator."

"I don't see any Brits."

"They're not allowed to wear their uniforms," said Ververt. "Some concern that they mustn't be seen in any *boîte de nuit* that traffics in this alleged black market."

"That's the English for you. Always erring on the side of propriety," said Von Leinsdorf. "They don't approve of premarital sex because it might lead to dancing."

Ververt snorted, his approximation of a laugh.

"Don't they have their own officers' club?" asked Von Leinsdorf casually.

"They've taken over Maxim's," said Ververt. "Do you know it? The Rue Royale?"

"Who's been to Paris and doesn't know Maxim's?" said Von Leinsdorf, with a Gallic shrug.

"It's not the same. The gendarmes arrested the maître d' recently, Albert, a very well-known, a very well-liked local personality."

"For what reason?"

"For extending the same courtesies to the Nazis that he has shown the *haute monde* for twenty-five years. This was not collaboration, it was hospitality. An essential part of his business."

"I'll bet those same gendarmes who arrested Albert," said Von Leinsdorf, "have been collaborating with the Nazis in Maxim's for the last three years. And the only reason was to prevent Albert from testifying against them in the reprisals."

"You see? *Exactement!* The perils of Liberation."

"That's what you can count on in times like these," said Von Leinsdorf. "*Égalité, liberté, hypocrisie.*"

Ververt picked up the two thousand from the table. "Money has no politics. It will outlast ideology."

"Ah yes, but will we, my friend?"

Ververt snorted in appreciation and pocketed the cash. "Come back tomorrow night. Seven o'clock, before we open."

Von Leinsdorf stood up to leave and Eddie followed suit. He

knew that Von Leinsdorf had forged a bond with the man, and that he'd gotten what they came for, but he wasn't clear about how or when it had happened.

"Where do the Brits keep their officers' mess?" asked Von Leinsdorf.

"The Hotel Meurice," said Ververt. "Rue de Rivoli."

"The Meurice. Ah yes. Walking distance from Maxim's."

"You get the idea."

Ververt gestured to his flunkies and they escorted Von Leinsdorf and Eddie away. Von Leinsdorf surveyed the cramped, low-ceilinged room as they moved through the mixed-race crowd that included a number of interracial couples. All eyes were on the tiny stage, where the quartet was heating up, sweat pouring off them under the lights, blacks playing saxophone and bass, white men on piano and bass.

"Hey, Dick, you want a drink?" asked Eddie, catching up with him near the door, flushed with success. "They say it's on the house."

"I don't drink with niggers," said Von Leinsdorf, and walked outside.

The neon sign outside, LE MORT RAT, threw garish red light onto the wet pavement. They turned up their collars against the cold and threaded through the tangled warren of steep, cobblestoned streets toward the small apartment a few blocks away that Eddie had rented with cash after they arrived that morning.

"Have to say, that couldn't have gone much better," said Eddie, breaking the silence. "You see that scar on his face? Bet that wasn't a cooking accident."

"He's a Corsican pimp and a drug dealer and he'll cut your throat the first chance he gets."

"Be that as it may, according to our books the son of a bitch always paid on time for goods received."

"It's one thing him doing business with the army, Eddie; the size of your outfit kept him in line. He knows we don't have that kind of weight behind us. You're sure your boys at the depot can deliver?"

"They're in like Flynn. It's the Christmas train, *le* jackpot of jackpots. Bringing in luxury rations for every dogface in Paris."

"And the branch line runs through Versailles."

"Yeah, I've worked it myself. Don't worry, this is a bull's-eye right down the stovepipe, baby. Pull off this one score, we retire to the land of tits and honey."

"Yes. The American Dream. Hedonism and sloth."

Eddie didn't catch the irony. "Man, it's a beautiful thing."

36 Quai des Orfevres, Paris
DECEMBER 20, 10:00 P.M.

Earl Grannit and Bernie Oster had been sitting on a bench in the cavernous lobby of the city's police headquarters for over two hours. A large electric clock ticked directly overhead, above a bulletin board plastered with sheets of official announcements. Grannit's badge hadn't made much impression on the harried civil servants manning the desks and scurrying through the halls. They watched as uniformed gendarmes hustled in a steady stream of suspects for processing through their overworked justice system. From a detective's bullpen beyond the foyer the clatter of multiple typewriters clashed with the sound of raised voices shouting at each other in French.

"Business is booming," said Bernie.

Grannit lit another cigarette, leaned forward, and ran a hand over his face. The man looked worn to the bone.

"You were a cop," said Bernie. "In New York."

"That's right."

Bernie looked around the room, turning the MP's helmet around in his hands. "Is it any different here?"

"The same shit flowing down a different sewer."

"Never been inside a police station before. Looks like a hell of a job."

"It's a hell of a world."

"Are people just born bad, is that what makes them do this shit?"

"It's a choice. Everybody's always got a choice."

Bernie hesitated. "Von Leinsdorf worked at a death camp."

Grannit looked at him. "What?"

"Dachau's a death camp. They're killing people. Jews mostly, others too. I don't know how many, maybe millions, all over Germany. Do they know about this back home?"

Grannit shook his head.

"Started with them taking people out of the cities. Deporting them to camps. We all knew about that. Nobody did anything. Then this started and nobody wanted to know."

"For how long?"

"I don't know. Maybe two years."

"Von Leinsdorf told you this?"

Bernie nodded. A wave of emotion hit him. "I want to be a good person. But I was in that army. I did what I could, but it wasn't enough. I don't see any way to make that right."

A clerk arrived to collect them. He led them into a warren of cubicles and offices and deposited them outside a door that read LE COMMISAIRE. The clerk knocked; someone inside bid them enter.

A weary, middle-aged man stood behind a desk lighting a pipe. He wore an ill-fitting hand-knit sweater against the cold, waved them forward, and pointed to chairs in front of the desk. A small sign on his cluttered desk read INSPECTOR GEORGES-VICTOR MASSOU.

"My apology," he said. "It took time to find someone of sufficient rank who could speak English. I have only just returned. How can I help?"

Grannit showed his credentials, referring to Bernie only as his associate. He unfolded the flyer with the sketch of Von Leinsdorf and handed it to Massou.

"We have reason to believe this man is in your city as of last night. He's a German soldier disguised as an American, part of Otto Skorzeny's commando brigade."

"Yes. The famous Café de la Paix assassins. We are well aware. There were rumors of paratroops landing outside the city last night. Unverified." From under the jumbled mass on his desk he located another flyer that featured Skorzeny's photograph. "The café is under constant surveillance. It was my understanding your army is handling this investigation."

"We spoke with senior security at SHAEF today as well as

provost marshal of the military police in Paris. They've moved Eisenhower into the Trianon Palace under heavy security. Because only one man is left they feel they have the situation under control. We don't think that's the case."

"How so?"

"We've been involved since this began six days ago. This individual we're looking for is a lot more dangerous than they know or want to admit. They're military men, not police officers."

"As you are."

"New York, homicide. That's your beat, isn't it?"

Massou nodded and puffed on his pipe, his gaze sharpening as he looked at them through the smoke. Bernie saw his polite formality fall away, leaving the same dispassionate, assessing eye that he'd seen in Grannit, a frank, collegial accord between the two men. Massou picked up the rough sketch of Von Leinsdorf again, taking a closer look.

"Tell me about this man," he said.

Grannit gave an account of Von Leinsdorf and his crimes, leaving out Bernie's role entirely. Massou listened without comment, occasionally taking a note. As Grannit finished, he handed Massou a mug shot and rap sheet on Eddie Bennings.

"Von Leinsdorf is probably in the company of this man, an American deserter and black marketer."

Massou looked at Eddie's picture. "Does *he* know who he is with?"

"We don't have a way of knowing that. We believe both men have spent time in your city."

"Then you must have some idea of the legion of places they could hide, yes? A city of ten million, in this kind of chaos? Montmartre, le Marais, Montparnasse. And everywhere scores are being settled. Over five hundred murders since the Liberation in August. Have you ever known such a period in New York?"

"Not while I've been there."

"The number sounds trifling compared to the battlefield, but in cities like yours or mine? Catastrophe, the end of civilization. Entire neighborhoods where our authority has regained no foothold! Paris acquired some lamentable characteristics under the *Boches*. So, re-grettably, did much of the police force."

The phone on his desk rang.

"I have spent these last years in retirement, returning only three months ago—excuse a moment." Massou answered the phone. "*Oui? Oui, oui, mon cher.*" He covered the mouthpiece with his hand and whispered: "Madame Massou." He went back to the call. "*Oui, cher, oui, un cassoulet serait beau. Oui, superbe. J'attends avec intérêt lui. Pas trop tard, j'espère. Est-ce que je puis apporter quelque chose? Oui, cher. Au revoir.*" He hung up. "Please *pardon*, she who must be obeyed, yes?"

"I'll take your word for it."

"If you could experience her cooking, you would understand com-pletely." He looked suddenly to Bernie. "You are not a policeman."

"No, sir." He glanced at Grannit and corrected himself. "Mili-tary, yes, not civilian."

"It is somewhat different in the military. Doing this job on behalf of a nation, you may feel a sense of legitimacy." Massou fastidiously refilled his pipe and lit it again. "The lieutenant and I, you see, we are not a part of proper society. Nor can we be. I may have a wife, a pleasant home, an old cat who keeps me company, but the rest of the time we are immersed in these acts of violence. We study the end re-sult to reconstruct the passions which created it. On occasion we find those responsible."

"You bring them to justice," said Bernie.

"We bring them here. What happens afterward is someone else's department. Murder has and always will have a place in the human heart, but no proper person cares to see this, or think about what we do; they simply want it done. Bodies keep appearing, in different form, day after day, so there are no lasting victories. We go on, too, but the work brings a sadness of spirit."

Grannit's head was down, nodding slightly in agreement. Massou looked at them both, not without sympathy. He seemed to know something was off center between them, but chose not to pursue it, out of professional courtesy. He focused his warm, liquid eyes again on Bernie.

"This is your first time seeing such things," he said.

"Yes, sir," said Bernie, wondering what else this man knew about him from a glance. He felt there wasn't much he'd be able to hide from him for long.

"The Romans had a phrase for it. If you need to catch a devil, set a devil on his trail." He turned back to Grannit, reached forward, and handed him a card. "I will do what I can. Reach me at this number at any time, provided the phones are working. Where are you staying?"

"We hadn't gotten around to that."

Massou hurriedly wrote down an address on a pad. "This hotel is just around the corner. Very small, very discreet, an estimable kitchen. If you don't mind my saying, Lieutenant, you both need a proper meal and some sleep." He ripped off the page and handed it to Grannit. "I'll call ahead."

"Thank you," he said.

"I'm certain you would do the same for me."

31

Paris
DECEMBER 21, 10:30 A.M.

Walking from Montmartre toward the river, Von Leins-dorf turned a corner and found himself standing in front of the Paris Opera. He stopped to stare at the grand white wedding cake edifice, looked around the open square, and smiled at the thought of what he was about to do. He crossed the boulevard, sat down, and ordered a coffee at the Café de la Paix. His eyes scanned across the square and intersecting streets, picking out two undercover operatives in the crowded scene.

Looking for Lieutenant Miller, no doubt, he thought, amused.

When his coffee arrived, he offered a silent toast to Colonel Otto Skorzeny and absent members of the 150th Panzer Brigade. None of the men assigned to watch the square glanced his way. He knew he could have sat there all day without attracting any attention.

Von Leinsdorf wore a conservative overcoat, a dark business suit and hat, and he carried an ivory-headed cane. His hair had been tinted steel gray, and to his three-day beard, similarly bleached, he'd added a presentable white mustache. When he rose to leave, he dropped a few francs on the table, along with the morning edition of *Le Monde*, opened to a prearranged page. If anyone had thought to look at it, they'd have seen a few words hastily scrawled in French in one of the margins. It appeared to be a shopping list. He walked away with a pronounced limp, leaning on his cane. The veteran's service medal he wore on his lapel, a bauble he'd picked up in a Montmartre thrift shop, dated to the Great War. When he rounded the next corner, he looked up and caught a glimpse of two American soldiers on the roof of an adjacent building, manning a machine gun, its barrel aimed down toward the café. One of the soldiers was stifling a yawn. Von Leinsdorf quietly tipped his hat to them and limped away.

He was astonished to see no signs of the impending Christmas holiday enlivening the city's broadest avenues. None of those elegant, swan-necked women in the shopping arcades or haughty restaurants. He had spent Christmas here twice before, once as a London schoolboy with his family and two years ago with the SS, who used trips to Paris as morale-boosting rewards, a tourist attraction for overachievers. The city always wore its brightest colors at Christmas. Now it appeared drab gray and drained of life. Walking through the Place Vendôme, he glanced up at the statue of Napoleon atop its stark central column, fashioned from melted Prussian cannon captured at Austerlitz.

The French beat us that time, Von Leinsdorf remembered grudgingly. *Well, that was once.*

Turning right onto the Rue de Rivoli, he settled on a bench at the edge of the Tuileries, directly across from the entrance to the Hotel Meurice. A line of Allied flags rippled in formation, a harsh wind stirring up a dark, scudding sky. Dozens of military vehicles for ranking British and American officers were parked out front, flying pennants, jutting into the avenue. When Von Leinsdorf had last been here, the hotel served as the German Army's headquarters, until the surrender of the city. An artillery shell had since collapsed two of the arches—covered with scaffolding, under repair—that spanned its classical nineteenth-century facade.

He remembered climbing those same steps for the first time, proud and in awe, his father's sleek leather glove holding his hand. His father was still a high-ranking diplomat and they had been treated like royalty, shown all the sights, squired around the city in a chauffeured car. The happiest days his family had ever known, less than a year before they ended in a single day.

Twelve years later, after the Germans had taken France, he returned as an SS officer on leave, self-made, on his own merits. Everyone in that hotel, in Paris, showed him a respect that not so long before he'd had reason to believe would be denied to him forever. With that visit had come the assurance that his father's disgrace was at last behind him.

The sound of the chair hitting the floor in the next room.

The old man's obsequious, servile smile, the fluttering of his hands whenever a superior turned a corner. How pathetic and defeated he had looked when they found him out. The image still sickened Von Leinsdorf. The womanly tears as his father confessed the secret he'd kept from his wife and son all those years; everything they believed about him a lie. Packing his own bags for exile, unshaven, doubled over, sobbing as he folded every collar and crease like a ghetto tailor, the life already kicked out of him. The shameful legacy of the Jew visible in him from a mile away.

Von Leinsdorf had vowed to forget the man. He would cut the scar from his soul.

The creak of the rope when he walked in and found him swinging from that beam. The old man's pleading eyes meeting his, clawing at his own throat, his life ending with one last misgiving. Von Leinsdorf never moved. He watched him die and then he turned and left the room.

No one had ever worked harder to erase a memory; why would it come back now? Because Paris had fallen? Did that mean all his work had been for nothing? This hotel, the site of the only triumph he'd ever known, was back in the hands of the enemy, Americans and British crawling all over the city, smug and entitled, as if the war were already won.

They would soon be hearing from him about that.

The rattle of a passing bus broke his reverie. He studied the hotel, noting the security outside, the traffic patterns passing through its doors. After twenty minutes he crossed the street and climbed the stairs, leaning on his cane.

Stammering in excited French and broken English, he explained to the guards at the door that an unexploded German shell had been found in his neighborhood. They tried to explain that he needed to report such a matter to his local police or SHAEF's offices near the Place Vendôme. With the wounded dignity of an outraged Great War veteran, his tirade resulted in a spell of breathlessness. The guards assisted him into the lobby to recover, promising he could speak to the next available officer. After bringing him a glass of water, they promptly forgot about him. Von Leinsdorf settled into a chair that offered him a view of the elevators and the front desk. He watched a steady stream of British officers who had taken up residence in the hotel as they came and went.

He waited for an officer of a specific age and size. Such a man hurried through the door at eleven-thirty-five, carrying two suitcases and an attaché case. Von Leinsdorf rose from his chair and hobbled past the front desk, patting his face with a handkerchief, in time to see this British lieutenant, just arrived from London, identify himself, receive his room key, 417, and carry his bags toward the lift.

Von Leinsdorf waited five minutes, then entered an enclosed lobby phone booth and placed a call through the switchboard to room 417.

"Hallo?"

"Is that Lieutenant Pearson?" asked Von Leinsdorf.

"Yes?"

"I've been ringing you for over an hour. This is Major Smyth-Cavender over at SHAEF. Where the blazes are you?"

"I literally just walked through the door, sir."

"Some problem with the flight, was there?"

"A bit delayed, actually, sir."

"Yes, well, RAF's got their own problems. We've had a cock-up down the hall here ourselves, pushed the clock right out of round. How are your quarters?"

"Fine, splendid."

"Beats a damp foxhole by a crushing margin. So listen, Pearson old boy, since there's no rush, why don't you pop round and meet me at Maxim's. Do you know where that is?"

"No, sir."

"Hard by the hotel there; ask at the desk. It's our officers' club for the moment. I'll stand you to a glass and a spot of lunch, act the welcoming committee. Shall we say quarter past noon then?"

"That's only ten minutes, sir."

"Take you five to get there. You can unpack later."

"Yes, sir, right away, sir."

Von Leinsdorf hung up the phone and ducked through a nearby door into a service stairwell. He took the stairs to the basement and moved along a low corridor, following the smell of steam until he found the laundry. No one was there. Stepping into a storage area, he removed his overcoat and jacket and replaced it with a valet's coat, gloves, and hat. He walked into the bustling laundry area and searched through a hanging line of cleaned and pressed military uniforms ready for delivery. After finding what he was looking for, he walked out holding the suit up in front of his face. He waited for the service elevator, followed an Algerian housekeeper pushing a linen trolley on board, and rode it up to the fourth floor. The housekeeper stepped off first. He started down the hall in a different direction, looking at room numbers, then made a show of patting his pocket, groaned, and turned to the housekeeper.

"*Merde, j'ai oublié ma clef de passage. Cher, ouvriez-vous une salle pour moi pour satisfaire?*"

"*Quelle salle?*"

Von Leinsdorf pretended to look at the ticket attached to the suit. "*Quatre cents dix-sept.*"

"*Oui, oui,*" she said wearily.

She led him around the corridor to the room and knocked twice. "Housekeeping," she said.

When there was no answer, she opened the door with her pass key. Von Leinsdorf slipped her an American five-dollar bill. She pocketed it and turned away, sensing that perhaps this was something she didn't wish to know any more about.

"*Merci beaucoup, chéri.*"

He entered, then closed and silently locked the door behind him. He hung the suit on a hook, closed the blinds, and turned on a lamp. He laid Pearson's two suitcases on the bed, opened and quickly searched through them, taking out the man's kit bag. He opened the man's attaché and scanned a cache of letters and documents inside, pleased by what he found.

Walking into the bathroom, he removed his shirt and jacket and studied himself in the mirror. He eased off the false mustache, washed the gray from his hair, the makeup from his face, and used Pearson's razor and soap to give himself a close shave. He pulled a black eye patch from his pocket, covered his left eye with it, then turned to the uniform he'd just stolen from the basement.

"Pearson, old boy, dreadfully sorry, I had one foot out the door and our G2 rings me with the catastrophe du jour," said Von Leinsdorf.

"Isn't that always the way?" said Pearson, rising from the table to shake the major's hand.

Callow, late twenties, weak and sweaty grip. Perfect.

"They've not done you any favors with this table. We call this sector Outer Siberia."

"Really?" Pearson looked around as if he expected to be seized and carted away.

"Don't be afraid to buy yourself a better table. Nothing like the same service here since the gendarmes dragged Albert the maître d' off for crimes imagined. For all their bloody whining, you'd think they preferred feeding the Nazis. Maybe they tipped better. First time in Paris?"

"As a matter of fact it is, sir."

"Not what it was, of course, nor what it will be." Von Leinsdorf snapped his fingers, summoning a waiter. "Best let me order, old thing, or you'll end up with stewed boot on your plate. Garçon, bring us a decent claret, not that swill you decant at the bar, one of those '38 Lafittes you walled up in the basement before the Huns marched in. This is Lieutenant Pearson, just across the pond. Treat him exceptionally well, he's an important man, you'll be seeing a lot of him. We'll both have the tournedos, medium well. *Salade vert apres, c'est ca?*"

Pearson, as he'd expected, was cowed into respectful silence by the performance. Von Leinsdorf tore into a basket of bread. He caught a glimpse of himself in the beveled mirrors on the walls, his image fractured and multiplied, and wondered for a split second whom he was looking at.

"It's all black-market fare, of course, but one can't afford to be a moralist; an army travels on its stomach. What do you know about the G2? Have you met him before?"

"General Strong? No, sir."

"Runs a first-rate shop. One of our finest men. Even gets along with the Americans. Do you know his deputy, Brigadier Betts?"

"Only through correspondence, sir."

"A capable second, Betts. So they're bringing you on board to calculate petrol use or something, have I got that right?"

"To analyze and increase the efficiency of petrol transport and distribution, yes, sir."

"In anticipation of the push to Hitler's front parlor."

"I believe that's the underlying incentive."

"Sounds riveting. Trained at the War College, were you? Sandringham?"

"Actually, no, sir. British Petroleum. I'm on loan."

"Their loss is our gain, we're lucky to have you. How's morale at home? With all this Ardennes business, it's been a week since I've laid my hand on *The Times*."

They chatted about London and the war effort and the exquisite challenges of domestic petrol distribution until their bottle arrived. Von Leinsdorf struggled to keep his uncovered eye open while attempting to appear engaged by this colorless bore. When he poured Pearson a second glass, along with it he emptied a small vial of the medicine that he palmed in his hand.

As they worked their way through the main course, Von Leinsdorf encouraged the man to drone on about the untapped yields of the Middle East while he shoveled in the food rapidly, in the English style, trying to finish his first decent meal in days before the drug took hold. When Pearson dropped his fork, complaining he felt dizzy and light-headed, Von Leinsdorf was instantly at his side and assisted him to his feet. Refusing offers of help from the staff, and berating them for serving his man some questionable beef, he escorted Pearson out the door and four blocks down the street to a side entrance of the Hotel Meurice. By which time Pearson was laughing and mumbling incoherently; Von Leinsdorf got them past the guards with a brief, apologetic shake of the head.

"Too much *vin rouge*," he said.

He collected the key from the desk, moved them into an elevator, alone, and rode up to the fourth floor. Pearson was out on his feet by the time they reached the door to room 417. Von Leinsdorf carried him inside, dropped him on the bed, set out the DO NOT DISTURB sign, and closed and locked the door.

32

Ile de la Cité, Paris
DECEMBER 21, 10:45 A.M.

Grannit's eyes opened and automatically sought out Bernie Oster. He was sitting on the edge of a bed across the room, his right hand handcuffed to the bed frame, smoking a cigarette with his left. Bernie had suggested the cuffs himself before they bunked down, before Grannit had even considered it. For a moment, neither could summon the energy to speak. Grannit checked his watch; almost eleven o'clock. The fatigue that a full night's sleep had only begun to remedy weighed on them even more heavily. They dragged themselves downstairs, and the hotel kitchen laid out its version of an American breakfast: scrambled eggs and mounds of fried potatoes, buttered rolls with dark jam, and thick black coffee. They ate in silence and abundance, then walked out onto the Ile de la Cité and smoked cigarettes in the biting wind while they stood at the rail and looked down the river.

"What's that big church?" asked Bernie.

Grannit took a look. "I think that's Notre Dame."

"How's their football team doing? I don't see the stadium; is it around here?"

Grannit was about to respond until he saw the look on his face. "You always a wiseass?"

"Until Germany. Not a lot of laughs over here."

Grannit turned and looked out over the city.

"I know you have to turn me in, no matter what," said Bernie. "I want you to know I won't ask you not to do that. I don't expect any thanks. I just don't want to die knowing that son of a bitch is still out there."

"Why?"

"Once you told me about the general? A man like him's so much more important. I'm nobody. What happens to me doesn't matter at all."

Grannit didn't look at him.

"What did he say to you about Paris?"

"That he'd been here a lot. It's his favorite city, but he's not that nuts about the French."

"Gee, you think? Where'd he learn the language?"

"English boarding school."

Grannit flicked his cigarette into the river. "That could've prepared him for the SS."

"Got some wiseass in you, too, huh?"

"Must be a neighborhood thing," said Grannit, with as close as Bernie had seen to a smile.

"You never said. Which side of Park Slope you from?"

"South."

"Really? What'd your dad do?"

"Let's stay on Von Leinsdorf."

Bernie remembered something. "Could you get a question to the MPs, have them ask it at their checkpoints?"

"What question?"

"Who plays center field for the Dodgers."

"Most guys won't even know that; it's like a revolving door out there at Ebbets Field—"

"I know," said Bernie. "I talked about it with Von Leinsdorf. He thinks it's Joe DiMaggio."

Grannit stopped short, looked at him, then took out his notebook and jotted it down. "Not bad, kid. So what about Paris?"

"His style, he'd go for the fanciest joints," said Bernie. "Art, culture, he was up on all that stuff."

"I don't think he'll be taking in a museum today."

"Wait a second. He mentioned this hotel he liked once. I got the idea he must've stayed there. A good place to take a girl to dinner if you wanted to get laid."

"What's the name of it?"

"I don't remember."

"There's a thousand fucking hotels in this city," said Grannit.

"I know; it was like a guy's name, I think— Jesus, I'm so tired. Maybe if I saw a list."

Grannit headed back inside the hotel. The concierge handed them a dog-eared prewar Michelin guide from behind the counter. Bernie paged through it while Grannit placed a call to military police headquarters. He was on his way back when Bernie held up a finger, pointing with his other hand to a page of the book.

"Hotel Meurice."

When Von Leinsdorf left that morning for the Hotel Meurice, he told Eddie Bennings to stay inside their rented garret until he returned that afternoon. Eddie promised he would, content to start his day with the K rations they'd brought up from the car. Within ten minutes, prompted by an enticing view of Montmartre and the attention span of a hummingbird, Eddie had talked himself into needing a cup of coffee for an eye-opener—what the hell, it was Paris, he'd only go out for a few minutes—and then there was that bakery he remembered around the corner where they sold those buttery brioche. That led him to look for a newsagent, where he picked up *Stars and Stripes*, see if they had the latest college football scores. The *tabac* next door to the newsstand was open for business so he picked up a pack of cigarettes, and when he saw the attached bar, he thought, *What the fuck, after what I've been through the last few days, what's one beer?*

Three beers later, after exchanging pleasantries with the barkeep, a comely young woman sat down beside him at the counter and they struck up a lively conversation about her enthusiasm for all things American. Taken in by her adorable broken English, and forgetting that he was supposed to be a Danish businessman trying to secure postwar oil leases, he owned up to being American, and twenty minutes later he was banging the living daylights out of the mademoiselle in her room at a fleabag pension.

The trouble didn't start for another twenty minutes, after they'd satisfied their physical needs and shared a few minutes of mutual, if not entirely sincere, postcoital appreciation. As Eddie was pulling on his pants, the young lady revealed that the joy they'd just shared was less the spontaneous expression of mutual affection he'd supposed it to be, so much as a routine, age-old business transaction for which she now expected to be paid accordingly. Eddie took exception, arguing, not without reason, that in order for such an arrangement between two parties to be considered binding it first required that he, the buyer, receive from her, the seller, adequate notification—prior to commencement of services and well before their conclusion—and then give answer to said proposal in the affirmative. The girl, who was seventeen, malnourished, and dumb as a ball-peen hammer, countered that as dazzled as she had been by his all-American personality, she had forgotten to mention it, and although she'd be happy to write off their brief encounter as a freebie, her pimp waiting in the *tabac* across the street would take a much dimmer view. Eddie responded that as far as he was concerned this fell under the category of "that's *your* problem, bitch." He slapped her around to reinforce his position, put on his overcoat, and left her place of business.

The pimp watched Eddie exit the pension, and waited a few minutes while finishing his first coffee of the day. On the short side, and swarthy, he bore a distinct tattoo of a knife between the thumb and fingers of his right hand. When his girl failed to appear, he sauntered up to her apartment. Appalled less by her physical condition and hysterical emotional state than by her failure to collect any cash, he gave her a more severe beating, emptied her purse, and went back to the street. Outraged that this American prick had flouted the conventions of their industry—the little whore claimed she'd been stiffed—the pimp asked the barkeep if he had seen which way the man went, then hurried off in that direction until he spotted his overcoat on a neighboring street. He followed the man until he entered a transient apartment building a few blocks up the hill. A plan on how to collect his debt took shape immediately.

He walked four blocks south to the local police station, behind a nightclub on the Rue de la Rochefoucauld. The bicycle of a corrupt patrolman he bribed to protect his business sat in its usual parking space under the blue lantern outside. As much as it pained him to enter the station, for fear he might be perceived as a snitch, which in fact he was, the pimp did so just long enough to signal the patrolman that he needed a word. They met around the corner, where the pimp told the corrupt patrolman how his girl had just been taken advantage of by either an American GI or more likely a deserter. His behavior fit the profile of a dabbler in the black market, in which case he was probably sitting on a considerable pile of cash, from which the two of them might, without undue effort or risk, be able to separate the fucker. They agreed to pay the American a visit as soon as the patrolman came off duty later that day and then went their separate ways.

In this unwitting way, for want of a cup of coffee, would Corporal Eduardo DiBiaso, aka Eddie Bennings, make his only significant contribution to the Allied war effort.

The Hotel Meurice, Paris
DECEMBER 21, 2:25 P.M.

At 2:25, just before he left room 417, Von Leinsdorf called an office number at SHAEF headquarters that he found in Lieutenant Alan Pearson's address book. Speaking as a convincingly under-the-weather Pearson, he reported that he had taken desperately ill at lunch and would need to spend the rest of the day recuperating in bed. Hoping it wouldn't be too great an inconvenience, he would present himself for duty the following morning. The secretary asked him to hold the line.

"Right, sorry, just checking the schedule, sir," said the secretary. "The G2 will be out at our offices at Versailles all day tomorrow. I'm afraid you'd have to come out there."

Von Leinsdorf tried to sound neutral. "Whatever the general thinks is best."

"Will you be needing a driver then?"

"Yes. If you wouldn't mind sending a car around."

Before ringing off, she filled him in on how and where to present himself to clear SHAEF security upon arriving at Versailles.

An escort right into Versailles. Von Leinsdorf hung up the phone and laughed so hard he had to cover his mouth.

Earl Grannit and Bernie Oster entered the lobby of the Hotel Meurice at two-thirty P.M. After handing flyers with Von Leinsdorf's likeness to guards at the entrance, they were speaking with the front desk when Von Leinsdorf came off the elevator, carrying a small suitcase and attaché, with a British officer's greatcoat over his arm, dressed in the uniform of Lieutenant Alan Pearson. He saw Grannit and Bernie across the crowded lobby on his way to the desk. He turned away, patting his pockets as if he'd forgotten something, and headed back up the stairs. Badly shaken by the sight of them, he stopped in the stairwell to collect his thoughts, then ran back up to the fourth floor. He quickly rearranged how he had left things in room 417 in a way that he thought would solve this unwelcome development, then took a rear staircase to the back entrance, sorting through the problem as he walked away.

They had found the apartment and the dead girl in Reims, and Bernie Oster alive in the bargain. That had to be it. Had he convinced Grannit he was an American soldier? Unlikely, but why else would he still be a free man? Grannit and Bernie Oster together.

He walked back toward the Place Vendôme. Had he said anything to Bernie that could have put them on his trail? Why were they at the Meurice? Had he mentioned staying there during his last trip to Paris? Perhaps in passing. A block away he turned to look back at the hotel, saw no other police or military outside. They would have come in force if they were sure he was there, just as they had in Reims.

The two men had come alone then. He walked on, trying to

weigh how this affected his plan for the following day. The Lieu-tenant Pearson scenario had given him a straight-ahead path to the end, but the identity would be compromised by any thorough search of the hotel. He had to assume that would happen, and couldn't risk using it now.

His mind scrambled after solutions. Pearson had eliminated his need for Eddie Bennings—he'd planned to dispense with him on his return to Montmartre—but now he'd have to keep that scenario in play. And the Corsican, Ververt, as well.

He stepped off a curb without noticing and his foot hit the pave-ment, jarring him. He felt a violent, visceral shift disrupt his mind from his innermost self, and for a moment all thought of the mis-sion was forgotten. His obsessive focus lifted, he was suddenly, keenly aware of the grid of the Paris streets and how much they re-minded him of his own rigid mental discipline; straight lines and an-gles, geometric precision. He saw perfection and power in their clean, spare rigor. Civilization had reached an apex in this miracle of order, and he wanted nothing more than to inhabit them forever, walking down these broad avenues and regimented streets. He felt that if these buildings, all the people, even the streets themselves faded from view, the deep underlying meaning that their physical re-ality masked and could only hint at would be revealed. Patterns that unlocked all the uncertainties of existence. It was a moment of grace freed from time and circumstance, transcendent and full, but it was shadowed by a dawning awareness just beyond his comprehension that something dreadful had been done to him. A yawning darkness opened behind him, hideous forms of primal terror lurched at him out of it. He saw himself being held down in a malformed coffin, squirming to escape unseen hands. His head was missing, then it looked up at him from inside his attaché case, and horror like none he'd ever known lit up his mind—

A horn sounded, a screech of brakes. His attaché hit the pave-ment. He had walked blindly into the middle of a street and nearly been hit by a jeep full of MPs. He waved an apology, picked up his case, and walked on. They watched him go and he felt their eyes on him until they drove away. As quickly as it had come, back in reality, his waking nightmare vanished. He saw the Café de la Paix straight ahead across the street.

The newspaper he'd left on the table was gone. In its place, a pair of gloves and a blue scarf.

The signal. Contact. His mind found navigable points again. Now he could make all the pieces fit together. He crossed the street, and stepped down the stairs to the Madeleine metro station.

Grannit and Bernie spent twenty minutes with the manager at the front desk, who promised them they could question the rest of their staff and the hotel residents. Over two hundred officers billeted at the Meurice, but most were out during the day. Grannit said they were prepared to wait until every last one had been cleared.

Bernie sat near the front desk while Grannit telephoned Inspector Massou. He was out of the office, so Grannit left word to call them at the hotel. He joined Bernie a short time later, waiting for the staff to assemble and keeping an eye on the door in case Von Leinsdorf showed.

As he walked up the stairs at the Abbesses metro station, Von Leinsdorf heard choral music, looked up, and caught sight of a modest Gothic church, St. Pierre de Montmartre, perched on the hill before him just below the Sacre Coeur. The voices drew him forward. He had never had religious feelings—following the Party line, he believed only in the Father, not the Son—but he craved a few minutes in the presence of that music. He slipped inside and stood near the back of the church. A choir stood in a stall below the altar, lit by candlelight, performing a medieval *chanson*. The ancient music fed a hunger in Von Leinsdorf he hadn't known he possessed. The mysterious feeling of peace that had overwhelmed him as he walked the streets crept back into his mind, shadowed by that same black foreboding. He went weak for a moment, breaking into a sweat, and had to brace himself against a pew.

What is this?

A priest appeared at his side. Was he all right?

Yes, yes, he just needed a rest.

Von Leinsdorf slid into a pew and let his eyes drift up and around the chapel. He vaguely remembered that this was the oldest church in Paris. A bank of windows on one side had been shattered by a bomb, and he could see a storm drawing into the late afternoon sky above. He closed his eyes for a moment.

When he opened them again, he saw through the broken windows that the sky had turned pitch black. He glanced at his watch. Over an hour had vanished. He looked around, startled. The music had stopped, the choir was gone. The same priest was talking with a gendarme at the back of the church. Von Leinsdorf got up quickly, gathered his things, and walked out.

ddie Bennings heard him on the stairs before he came through the door. Von Leinsdorf was wearing a long great-coat when he entered their garret and he immediately went into the second room to change. Bennings, who was pitching pennies against a bare wall in the front room, under the light of the room's only lamp, never saw the British uniform.

"Where you been, Dick? I was starting to worry," said Eddie.

"Nothing to worry about," said Von Leinsdorf from the other room. "Making arrangements. What was your day like?"

"Boring. Just sitting around on my ass."

Bennings had decided not to mention his own outing that morning. He picked up *Stars and Stripes* while he waited and made conversation.

"Did you hear they can't find Glenn Miller? They think his plane went down over the Channel."

"When did that happen?"

Von Leinsdorf came out dressed in civilian clothes. He carried a greatcoat and was using a needle and thread to sew a flap inside its left front panel. Bennings glanced at him without curiosity and went back to his paper.

"Don't know. Last few days. On his way to Paris to organize a Christmas concert."

"Was it the Krauts?" asked Von Leinsdorf.

"Had to be. Crying shame, isn't it? You know how many times that guy's music got me laid? I got no quarrel with the Krauts, but I'd like to get my hands on the punks who did this. Man, I'm starving. Haven't been out all day."

"Where did you get the newspaper?"

"Found it downstairs."

"So you did go out," said Von Leinsdorf.

"I went out once, briefly, for a pack of cigarettes."

Von Leinsdorf moved to the window and looked out the curtains. The clouds had lowered and the rain that had threatened was starting to fall.

"Did you speak to anyone?"

"No, Christ, no. You want to get something to eat? What time we meeting him?"

"Seven."

"What time is it now?"

"Half past six."

Von Leinsdorf saw two men standing across the street from the entrance to the building. Both were looking up at the attic window. He turned off the lamp inside the room, retrieved his binoculars, and took a closer look at them.

A gendarme and a smaller, swarthy-faced man, a civilian. Both unfamiliar. Not who he'd expected.

"Something wrong?" asked Eddie.

"I don't know yet."

"So what do you say we grab some grub?"

"We'll get something at the club."

When they walked outside and started down the hill through the winding streets toward Ververt's club, the two men across the street were gone. They arrived ten minutes ahead of schedule, tapped on the front window, and waited for someone to appear. Von Leinsdorf knew they were being followed, probably by the gendarme and his companion, but never caught a glimpse of them. One of Ververt's men opened the front door of the jazz club and they went inside.

Ververt sat at his table near the kitchen. He asked if they were hungry, more hospitable this time, as one of the men set down a bottle of red wine and a platter of bread, cheese, and green olives. Ververt asked to hear their proposal, and he listened carefully, saying nothing while Eddie laid out the details of the Christmas train job.

"How many trucks do we need?" asked Ververt when Eddie was done.

"That's up to you," said Eddie. "We can fill two or three."

"What time do they need to leave Paris?"

"We need a ride to the depot," said Von Leinsdorf. "We have to be there by midnight, so we should be on the road by nine. Have them meet us at the Invalides metro stop. They drop us at the yard, then drive back into Versailles."

"We'll hook up on the spur line at three when we bring the train in to load up," said Eddie.

"How long will that take?"

"Once the train's there, not more than an hour. The trucks should be back in the city by first light."

Ververt looked at his cigarette. "What about security on the train?"

"We've got that covered out of our end."

"And the money?"

"Fifty thousand," said Eddie. "Half now, half on delivery."

Ververt flicked his cigarette, a gesture of disdain. "I don't know what I'm buying."

"We've got to take care of the boys on the train before they'll open it up," said Eddie.

"Why should that be my concern?" asked Ververt.

"Because otherwise we don't have a deal," said Von Leinsdorf.

Ververt poured himself another glass of pastis. He nodded to one of his men, who stepped forward and set a gray strongbox down on the table. Ververt opened it and counted out ten thousand American dollars.

"The rest when we finish loading the trucks," he said.

The money sat on the table between them for a long beat. Ververt closed the strongbox to punctuate the finality of the offer. Finally, Von Leinsdorf reached over and picked up the money.

"Coffee?" asked Ververt.

The corrupt patrolman and the pimp had been taken aback by the appearance of the second man, who arrived at the rooming house soon after they took up their surveillance. They assumed he was another American deserter, and decided to alter their approach. Instead of charging up to the garret, they waited and followed the men, when they left their building, to a jazz club owned by a notorious local gangster. They observed them through a window, sitting down with Ververt. The connection to Ververt made the pimp question the wisdom of taking these two down, but the patrolman, who had collected payoffs from the Corsican for years, felt more certain than before that they were viable targets. These were unknown players with no local standing. Ververt was probably setting them up for a sting, so they might as well beat him to it.

Shortly after seven o'clock at the Hotel Meurice, a British major marched down to the front desk in his bathrobe and registered a noisy complaint about a missing dress uniform that he had sent for cleaning the previous day. Bernie and Grannit were on the house phones, calling each resident officer, working their way through the registration cards, when they overheard the major's tirade.

So did an Algerian chambermaid, who was standing in a nearby line of employees waiting to be questioned by the hotel's chief of security. She stepped forward to say she remembered seeing a valet returning a major's uniform earlier that day on the fourth floor. The major's anger went up a few decibels—he was staying on the *second* floor, so why the bloody hell was his uniform being delivered on the *fourth* floor? The major then answered his own question: because theft was rampant in this bloody hotel, that was why, because of the overwhelming presence in this city of the bloody Wogs.

"Just another reminder that the Wogs begin at Calais," he was heard to say.

The chief of security called Grannit over to hear the maid's story, and inserted himself between them.

The maid, sensitive to the major's racism, mentioned that this valet was a man she had never seen in the hotel before, but not that he'd given her five dollars after she'd opened a room for him with her pass key. She failed to recall which room it was.

Grannit and Bernie pulled registration cards for every officer staying on the fourth floor. Five new arrivals had checked in that day, and Grannit called each room from the switchboard. Two of the men were in their rooms. Grannit identified himself and asked them to come down to the lobby for questioning. Three did not answer. Two of those room keys rested in their pigeonholes on the rack behind the desk, so those men were reasonably assumed to be out of the hotel.

One key was missing, room 417, registered to a Lieutenant Alan Pearson, who according to his card had checked in shortly after noon. One of the clerks behind the desk then remembered that Lieutenant Pearson had come back from lunch shortly thereafter looking the worse for wear from drink, in the company of another British officer who had asked for the key to 417 and then helped him upstairs.

"Who was this other man?"

A major, he thought. Pressed for details, the clerk recalled only that the major wore a black eye patch, although he couldn't say for certain which eye it covered, and that was all he could remember about him.

"That's exactly why he wore it," said Grannit.

Seconds later, Grannit and Bernie were in the elevator, accompanied by the manager and the hotel's chief of security.

Von Leinsdorf and Eddie Bennings walked back up the hill, heads down, collars raised against the cold as the freezing rain gave way to snow. Large, fragile flakes danced down in isolation. Von Leinsdorf stopped for a moment to look up at them.

Like the discharge from the smokestack of the crematorium.

"You all right, chief?" asked Eddie, looking back at him.

Von Leinsdorf had always prided himself on his ability to shut off memories of the camp, all the unwanted pieces of his past, partition them from his waking mind. Now they were punching through those walls with alarming frequency. He didn't know what it signified, but it left him reeling.

"Yes, fine."

They continued, turning the corner into the narrow covered entrance to their rooming house. Von Leinsdorf pulled Eddie back into the shadows against the wall of the building. Moments later, the two men Von Leinsdorf had earlier seen standing outside their building stepped forward. One of them held a handgun and barked at them in French.

"Speak English," said Von Leinsdorf.

"Paris police. Put your hands against the building."

Von Leinsdorf took a step forward, shoving his hands down into the pockets of his raincoat. "I'd like to see a badge first."

The policeman took another step toward them. "Do as you are told."

Eddie started to turn around, but Von Leinsdorf stopped him with his voice. "We're not doing anything until we see a badge."

The policeman seemed thwarted by his lack of respect. The pimp stepped forward with a snarl, unfolding a straight razor from his pocket.

"*Faites ce qu'il dit, chien!*" He took a few threatening steps toward Eddie. "*Vous ne payez pas, ainsi nous vous faisons!*"

"What the fuck is your problem?"

"He said you didn't pay so he's going to *make* you pay," said Von Leinsdorf. "What's he talking about?"

Eddie swallowed hard and blinked, but didn't answer.

"Nobody move," said a distinctly American voice. "Any of you."

A man in a trench coat and hat stepped into view in the street just outside the passage behind Von Leinsdorf, holding with both hands a Colt .45 and a flashlight lined up against its barrel. The gendarme turned toward the newcomer, irritated.

"This is a police matter," said the gendarme.

The man swung the flashlight onto the gendarme. "Put your gun down on the ground and we'll talk about it."

"Who the hell are you?"

"Military police."

"Good news," said Von Leinsdorf, pulling a badge from his pocket. "So are we. Criminal Investigation Division."

Eddie's head swiveled back and forth, trying to keep up.

The officer pointed his light on Von Leinsdorf and the badge he was holding. "Toss that over here. The rest of you put your weapons on the ground and kick them toward me. Right now."

Von Leinsdorf threw the badge toward the feet of the MP. The gendarme and the pimp laid the gun and razor on the ground and kicked them in his direction.

"Get down on your hands and knees," he said.

The Frenchmen obeyed. Before he picked up Von Leinsdorf's badge, the MP slid his light over onto Eddie Bennings.

"Who the hell are you?" he asked.

"I'm with him," said Bennings, pointing to Von Leinsdorf.

"A cooperative witness helping with our investigation," said Von Leinsdorf. "I've got his ID right here. These guys are cops, like they said, and they're dirty as hell."

"That is what *we* are doing," said the gendarme, pointing at Von Leinsdorf. "*They* are deserters, black marketers—"

Bennings glanced down and saw Von Leinsdorf pulling the pistol from his pocket, and a moment later the narrow corridor erupted in gunfire.

At five minutes to eight, the hotel's chief of security knocked on the door to room 417. He identified himself and announced to Lieutenant Alan Pearson that he had an urgent message for him from SHAEF headquarters. Grannit stood to the left side of the door with his pistol drawn. Bernie Oster and the hotel manager waited just down the hall. The door Bernie stood directly in front of opened, and he came face-to-face with a woman on her way out. She looked at his MP gear in alarm, and he saw an officer getting dressed in the room behind her. Bernie held his finger to his lips and she quietly closed the door.

When Pearson failed to answer, the chief of security inserted his pass key with trembling hands and pushed open the door. Grannit pushed ahead of him into the room. Alan Pearson lay in bed, under a blanket pulled up to the chin, his face turned away from the door. Grannit felt for a carotid pulse and then yanked the covers away. Pearson's body had been stripped to his underwear. From the way blood had pooled in the body Grannit knew the man had been dead for at least five hours. He called the others inside, then examined Pearson's arms.

"He was here," said Grannit to Bernie, then turned to the manager. "Call Inspector Massou at the Prefecture of Police."

"I know him," said the manager, grateful for a reason to leave.

"He killed him with an injection," said Grannit, pointing out a wound on the inside of Pearson's arm.

Out of the corner of his eye Grannit saw the chief of security about to open an armoire at the foot of the bed. He spotted a piece of fabric sticking out of a gap at the bottom of the armoire door.

"Don't touch that!"

Grannit crossed to him and examined the door carefully. He opened it a crack and looked down its length, then turned to Bernie.

"Flashlight."

Bernie handed him the flashlight off his belt. Grannit used the beam to illuminate a line of monofilament stretched taut across the opening, then traced it down along the door to the bottom of the armoire, where it connected to the pin of a hand grenade, taped onto a small square pat of dark gray plastic explosive resting on the tunic of the uniform that had been inserted under the door.

"He left something for us," said Grannit. "Call the bomb squad."

When he saw the grenade, the hotel's chief of security turned pale and backed out the door. A moment later they heard him running down the hall outside. Grannit gently closed the door to the armoire and held it there. He looked over at Bernie.

"You gonna have to hold that shut till they get here?" asked Bernie.

"Maybe," said Grannit. "Latch seems a little iffy."

"Want me to do it?"

"You could find some tape."

Bernie turned for the door, then stopped. "If I was gonna run, this would be a pretty good time to do it."

"I can't argue with that," he said.

"I'll get the tape," Bernie said.

Just after Bernie left the room, the phone on the bedside table rang. Grannit looked at it, looked at Pearson's body on the bed, looked at the closet door, and glanced at his watch: 8:25. Bernie returned not long after the phone stopped ringing, with a roll of black electrical tape. They applied the entire roll to the front of the armoire, then tested to make sure the door wouldn't swing open if they let go. When they were sure the tape would hold, they backed away toward the exit. The phone beside the bed rang again. They looked at each other.

"Want me to get that?" asked Bernie.

Grannit sighed, walked over, and picked up the phone, keeping an eye on the armoire.

"Four-seventeen," he said.

"I was asked to call," said the voice. "This is Inspector Massou."

"Inspector, this is Lieutenant Grannit. We're at the Hotel Meurice. Von Leinsdorf was here."

"When?"

"Earlier today, just after lunch."

In a Montmartre apartment, Inspector Massou turned with the phone in his hand and looked out the window, into the passageway of the boardinghouse.

"We've got him here now," he said. "Get downstairs. I'll send a car."

34

The police car deposited Grannit and Bernie outside the entrance to the boardinghouse. The area had been cordoned off by police, their black vans parked up and down the street, flares on cobblestones lighting up the night. Inspector Massou greeted them as they came out of the car and walked them toward the building. He gestured toward an ambulance that was pulling away.

"Two dead," said Massou. "This is one of the men you're seeking?"

He handed Grannit a pair of dog tags. Grannit checked them under his flashlight: Eddie Bennings.

"Yes," said Grannit.

"He died before they could get him in the ambulance."

"Where's Von Leinsdorf?"

"Army Counter Intelligence arrived ten minutes ago. They've got him in the car."

Massou nodded toward the first of two black sedans with U.S. plates. The back door of the first car was open, blocked by a man leaning down to talk to someone inside.

Grannit picked up his pace toward the car, just as the man leaning in closed the door and started toward him, followed by his partner. Both wore hats and belted trench coats, the CIC's unofficial uniform. Grannit showed his badge, ready to blow past them.

"Whoa, whoa, what's your hurry, soldier?" asked the CIC man.

"I need to see that man," said Grannit.

"CIC's taking this, Lieutenant," said the man, showing his credentials. "Major Whiting. Special detail to SHAEF Command."

Grannit trained his flashlight on the man's SHAEF pass. "Headquarters" was spelled correctly. He relaxed.

Bernie ran up alongside the sedan as it pulled away and saw Von Leinsdorf in the backseat. Von Leinsdorf met his eye for a moment, staring at him blankly, without emotion, then looked away before they drove out of sight.

Maybe he doesn't feel anything. Maybe he can't. Even when they line him up to shoot him in the heart. Somewhere in his sick soul he'll welcome the bullet.

Bernie signaled to Grannit that they had the right man.

"We've been tracking him for a week," said Grannit.

"I'm aware of that, Lieutenant," said Whiting, gesturing to his assistant to make a note. "You'll feature prominently in our report."

"Where you taking him?" asked Grannit.

"He'll be processed and questioned at SHAEF headquarters. After that it's up to the G2. We'd like your report, come in tomorrow morning, eight o'clock. Where do you think he was headed?"

"The Trianon Palace at Versailles. Where General Eisenhower's holed up."

"We'll let 'em know Ike can get back to business, thanks to you. Good work, Lieutenant."

Whiting shook Grannit's hand, saluted, and headed back to the second black sedan. His assistant got in to drive, alongside a third man, a uniformed MP.

Massou joined Grannit as they drove away, and walked him through the crime scene.

"An MP came on them here in the middle of a dispute," said Massou. "Between your two men and a Paris patrolman, from the local precinct. He's the other body. I'm told he has been under investigation for corruption. The MP says he drew a gun. They had officers here within fifteen minutes of the shootings."

"The MP that just left with them?"

"They wanted to get his statement," said Massou.

Grannit watched the sedan edge past the police vans and drive away. Bernie stood under the roofline, out of the way, looking out at the narrow, winding streets that reminded him of Greenwich Village set on the side of a hill. The rain that had fallen earlier had turned to snow.

"Did you question him first?" asked Grannit.

"I did, briefly."

Massou borrowed a flashlight and walked Grannit through the alley. "The patrolman had a gun on the two fugitives when the MP arrived. There was some confusion. He said the German, Von Leinsdorf, showed him a counterfeit American badge."

"How do you read it?"

Massou shrugged. "The patrolman waited for them here, under the stairs." With the end of his umbrella he pointed to a couple of cigarette butts near the back wall. "A robbery, or something more complex. The MP hears raised voices, walks into it. Our patrolman panics, shots are fired. Two men die. There's blood on the wall, on the ground. But the monster you're after is in hand, so does the rest really matter?"

"I guess not."

One of Massou's men brought him a glass of beer. "Would you care for something? Wine, or brandy? Coffee perhaps."

Grannit shook his head. Massou extended the invitation to Bernie, who declined.

"My officer's gun was never fired," said Massou. "It seems the MP was quicker on the draw. The only other anomaly is this."

He produced a straight razor from his pocket.

"It was lying on the street. Perhaps it belonged to the dead American, Bennings?"

"Hard to say," said Grannit.

"Just another night in Montmartre," said Massou, wearily. "Chasing a murderer, through the middle of a war."

Grannit pulled his flashlight, bent down, and took a look at a bloodstain on the ground. Working back from there, he found a bullet hole in the wall and dug it out with a penknife.

"It's from a Colt," said Grannit, pocketing the slug. "The MP's gun."

Massou finished the beer and handed the glass back to one of his men. "You should have a look at the apartment upstairs."

Grannit and Bernie followed Inspector Massou upstairs to the apartment. He told them the concierge had confirmed that Von Leinsdorf and Bennings had lodged there for two days. Grannit took a look around, found an empty jerrican in the back room and an edition of *Stars and Stripes*, but little else of interest. They walked back downstairs a few minutes later.

"Is there anything else I can do for you, Lieutenant?" asked Massou.

"I don't know what it would be."

"The driver will take you where you wish to go," said Massou, putting on his hat. "The end of the hunt is never what it should be."

"No, it isn't."

Massou shook Grannit's hand and then turned to Bernie with penetrating but not unkind scrutiny. "It's none of my business, young man, but you're not a military policeman, are you?"

Bernie glanced at Grannit before answering. "No, sir, I'm not."

"I ask to satisfy my personal curiosity." Massou lit his pipe and studied Bernie as he spoke. "To the untrained eye it may seem that what we do, our methods, differ from those we pursue by only a matter of degree. Our authority may be sanctioned by law, but it can seem as harsh as these savages we hunt." He kept looking at Bernie, but the rest seemed directed at Grannit. "In certain instances, perhaps your own, which depend on the judgment of others, there are laws of nature that on occasion supersede those of men. I wish you well."

Massou tipped his hat. As he walked to a waiting car, a military police jeep drove up and the MP on board handed something off to a CID man, who walked it to Grannit.

"Addressed to you, sir," said the officer, handing over an envelope. "Came over in the pouch from London."

Grannit opened the envelope and found a manila folder insider. He opened it and turned on the flashlight. It contained a few clipped and weathered articles from London newspapers. Stories from the mid-thirties about the dismissal of a high-ranking diplomat named Carl Von Leinsdorf from the German embassy. There was a photograph of the man and his wife and teenaged son. Bernie could see Erich's face in the boy, smiling and untroubled. A briefer article, accompanied by a photograph of the father, mentioned the man's suicide in Stockholm a few months later.

"Is that him?" asked Grannit, nodding to the photograph.

"Yes."

"Doesn't mention why his father lost the job."

"From what I heard," said Bernie, putting it together, "I think they found out the father was Jewish."

"Don't know why they make such a big deal out of it." Grannit took the folder back. "So am I."

Bernie took a moment to register that.

"We stopped him, anyway. That's what matters."

"I gotta take you in, Bernie."

"I know."

"We could wait till morning."

"Let's get it over with."

SHAEF Headquarters, Paris
DECEMBER 21, 11:00 P.M.

They rode in the backseat as the same police driver steered them through the night streets toward SHAEF headquarters in the Place Vendôme.

"I'd like to try and write my parents," said Bernie. "Would you let me do that before . . . ?"

The rest of his question hung between them.

"Where are they?"

"I don't know. I don't even know if they're still alive. They live in

Frankfurt, at least they did a couple months ago. I'd like to let 'em know I tried to help. Help the Americans."

Grannit looked at him. "We can do that."

"Always thought I'd see the neighborhood again. I dream about Park Slope all the time, you know? That's where I always go. Think that means I'm really an American, deep down, if I dream that way?"

"Maybe so, kid."

"That's something, anyway," said Bernie, watching the city go by out the window. "Beautiful place, isn't it? Doesn't even look like anybody lives in it."

"It'll outlive all of us."

"You have to put cuffs on me when we go in, Earl?"

Grannit thought about it. "No."

"I'd appreciate that."

They pulled up outside of SHAEF headquarters, a ponderous bank building fronted by massive columns, commandeered after the Liberation. Grannit gestured for Bernie to get out first, then followed him, tipped his hat to the driver, and the police car sped off. Grannit took Bernie by the arm and they walked up the steps to the entrance. A heavily armed detail of MPs patrolled the front.

"Don't say anything," said Grannit. "I'll lay it out for 'em and do the best I can. When they weigh in your cooperation, we can get some—"

"Don't make any promises," said Bernie. "I appreciate it, but I know it's not up to you. I'll take whatever's coming."

When they reached the top of the stairs, Grannit showed his badge to the guards at the door. "I need to talk to the CO, whoever's got the watch."

"What's this regarding, sir?"

"The 150th Panzer Brigade."

"Follow me."

They entered the dimly lit lobby and waited while the MP went into the offices. Stripped of decoration, windows blacked out, the cold marble of the massive room extended to the edge of their vision. They stood under one of the columns and waited. Civilian aides and junior officers trafficked through the room, still bustling near midnight. They all wore the familiar blue SHAEF pass on a chain around their neck.

Bernie felt a cold chill run down his neck. A shaking started in the pit of his stomach and spread outward. He blinked, having trouble seeing. His mind raced, involuntarily calculating how many days and hours he had left to live. Von Leinsdorf had been right about that, too: It was worse knowing when you were going to die.

He noticed Grannit's back suddenly straighten. Grannit pulled a charred piece of blue paper from his pocket and looked at it, then moved out to one of the junior officers crossing the room. Grannit stopped him, took the man's blue SHAEF pass in his hand, and examined it.

The letters e and a in "headquarters" were transposed.

Grannit stopped another person crossing, to look at his pass, then another and another. Bernie went to him as the last person moved off. He looked stunned.

"What's wrong?" asked Bernie.

"There is a mistake on the passes. But the army never corrected it."

"The blue one?"

"Did they give you one of these?"

"Yeah, and we got new ones in Belgium from the *Abwehr*—"

"After you came across?"

"Von Leinsdorf said their forgers didn't notice the mistake in time to fix it. He said these were the ones we were supposed to use."

"And they were spelled correctly."

"That's right."

"But Schmidt's wasn't corrected," said Grannit.

"Then you must have caught him before he could pick them up."

"God damn it, that's what Ole was trying to tell me. The fucking passes."

"What about them?"

"How many squads did Von Leinsdorf tell you were working on this?"

"Five."

"The men who took Von Leinsdorf had the corrected passes," said Grannit. "We only caught four teams."

"You're saying that MP, those guys from Counter Intelligence—"

"They're the fifth squad."

A young lieutenant came out to escort them into the CO's office. Grannit grabbed him by the arms.

"Has a suspect in the Skorzeny case been brought in during the last hour?" asked Grannit.

"I don't know—"

"Well, how fast can you fucking find out?"

The young lieutenant ran back toward his office. He returned at a trot leading his CO, a dyspeptic captain, who assured them that if any German operative in the Skorzeny case had been brought in, he would've been the first to hear about it.

"Is there anywhere else they would've taken him?"

"Maybe the SHAEF offices in Versailles."

"I need to use your phone," said Grannit.

Invalides Metro, Paris
DECEMBER 21, 11:00 P.M.

Ververt's two men had been parked outside the Invalides metro station in an empty bakery truck for an hour when a black sedan with U.S. military plates pulled up alongside. Two men climbed out, one in the uniform of an MP, the other in civilian clothes, who brought along a suitcase he lifted from the trunk of the car. One of Ververt's men opened the back panel door and they climbed inside. The black sedan sped off. Once the back panel of the truck rolled shut, the driver headed west toward the highway along the river, out of the city.

Paris City Morgue
DECEMBER 22, 12:30 A.M.

Inspector Massou was waiting for them at the front door. He led Grannit and Bernie downstairs to the examination room. An attendant pulled the sheet off a body lying on a slab, next to one bearing the body of the dead French patrolman.

"This is the man who was wearing Bennings's dog tags," said Massou.

He had taken four gunshot wounds to the chest. One had gone clear through. He'd died quickly. About Bennings's age and with similar coloring, he had a tattoo of a knife on the back of his right hand.

The coroner showed Grannit the bullets he'd taken from the body. They matched the one Grannit had dug out of the alley wall. Each bore the same distinctive rifling as the silenced shots that had hit Sergeant Mallory.

"This isn't Bennings," said Grannit.

35

Versailles
DECEMBER 22, 3:00 A.M.

Eddie dozed off in the back of the truck during the ride out from Paris, which was slowed by the snowstorm blanketing the city. Von Leinsdorf pretended to sleep, listening to the two men up front speaking in French. They said little, but he gathered enough to know they'd been given orders from Ververt to kill them as soon as the goods from the train were on board their truck.

Von Leinsdorf woke Eddie as they neared the supply depot in Matelot. Bennings directed them to their rendezvous point near the back gate of the train yard. Moments after the truck came to a stop, Von Leinsdorf shot each of the Frenchmen in the back of the head with his silenced pistol.

"What the hell," said Bennings.

"They had orders to kill us, Eddie," said Von Leinsdorf. "I heard them on the drive."

"What the fuck we supposed to do with Ververt now?"

"Live in hope our paths cross again so we can make it up to him. I've arranged for the men who helped us out of Paris to meet us at the drop. They'll take the delivery off our hands and pay us on the spot. We're done."

Troubled that he still lacked a satisfactory explanation for exactly who those men were, Eddie followed Von Leinsdorf into the train yard. Eddie's two contacts in the depot's railway battalion were waiting, as instructed, inside the gate. Eddie sounded anxious, but they were used to that, and in the dark of the train yard they couldn't see the sickly sheen of sweat on his face. The GIs led them to the Christmas train, waiting on a side track near the edge of the yards. Von Leinsdorf paid them out of Ververt's advance, and beyond that they showed no interest in the aftermath of their transaction.

Von Leinsdorf helped Eddie up into the last boxcar holding the luxury goods, and the train rolled out of the yard just after twelve-thirty. Eddie propped himself up against a stack of whiskey boxes in the corner. He watched Von Leinsdorf set down and open his suitcase, turn on a flashlight, and go to work.

"How long to the drop?" asked Von Leinsdorf.

"An hour, maybe more, depending on the switches," said Eddie. "Trouble you for a smoke?"

"A million cigarettes in this car and you're bumming one off me?"

"Old habits die hard."

Von Leinsdorf tossed a pack of Luckies over to him. Eddie fumbled through his pockets.

"Shit, sorry, you got a light?"

Von Leinsdorf moved over to him, taking out his lighter.

"This is a one-night career, Eddie. We collect our end, work our way down to Portugal, and buy passage home out of Lisbon."

"I can't wait to get back to New York. You can have fucking Europe, they're all out of their minds. There's some important guys I want you to meet in the city, Dick. Connected guys."

As Von Leinsdorf leaned down with the lighter, the car jolted sideways and he stumbled slightly and bumped into Eddie. When he straightened back up, Eddie was holding a pistol at his head.

"Now you tell me what the fuck is going on," said Eddie. "Or you're not leaving this car."

"Eddie, Eddie, I thought we understood each other."

"Fuck you. I bring you into this, now you try to hijack my job? Think I don't know a double-cross, bringing these new guys in—"

"Eddie, I told you, they're buddies from my old outfit, you can trust them—"

"Where'd they get the uniforms, the badges, the cars, all that shit, how'd you pull it off?"

"We have the resources of an entire army behind us."

"What unit are you with, and I want the truth."

"The 150th Panzer Brigade. Munich."

"Munich. That's a good one."

"No, seriously."

"I don't know what the fuck you're talking about, but I'm getting to the bottom of this before we stop this train."

"Do you mind if I change clothes with you?" asked Von Leinsdorf, back at his suitcase, unbuttoning his jacket and loosening his tie. "We don't have much time."

"What the fuck are you talking about? I'm gonna shoot you in a god damn minute. You're not changing anything."

Von Leinsdorf looked at his watch. "How's your hip, Eddie?"

"What about my hip?"

"Look at it."

Eddie looked down at his leg. A syringe was sticking straight out of the side of his right hip. He hadn't even felt the needle go in.

"Jesus, what did you do?" asked Eddie. "What the hell did you do?"

"Can you move your legs?"

Eddie tried. Each felt as if it weighed a hundred pounds; he could barely budge them. "What the fuck?"

"Drop the gun. Your hand won't work now anyway."

Eddie tried to squeeze the trigger, but his fingers wouldn't move. The gun fell to the floor. The progressive numbness branched in from his limbs toward the center of his body. Eddie gasped for air, his lungs aching for breath.

"What . . . what . . ."

"Don't fight it, Eddie. You'll only make it worse." Von Leinsdorf walked back across the car holding another syringe.

"What you doing?"

"That last one killed you. This one will keep you alive."

The Road to Versailles
DECEMBER 22, 4:40 A.M.

Massou left the siren on even after they left the city, even though the roads were empty. Another detective drove, riding next to him up front. Grannit and Bernie sat in back. Grannit gave him an uncorrected SHAEF pass to use when they arrived.

"Why correct the passes?" asked Grannit quietly. "Why would Skorzeny do that?"

"It's like your partner said," said Bernie. "The Nazis always think they got a better idea. That their way's the only way, and yours is wrong, no matter what."

"Our mistake and they had to fix it anyway. Couldn't stop themselves even when it gave 'em away. Arrogant fucks."

"And I can tell you," said Massou, turning around, "contrary to what you may have heard, they never made the trains run on time either."

Versailles
DECEMBER 22, 5:15 A.M.

Snow continued to fall as the American supply train rolled onto the side track forty-five minutes behind schedule. Once the train had stopped, the boxcars containing the luxury goods and the one trailing it were uncoupled. The rest of the train slowly chugged forward again, onto the main track, and out of sight.

The side door facing away from the compound slid open. Von Leinsdorf dropped to the ground and closed it behind him. The southern perimeter of the vast Versailles compound stood less than a hundred yards away, on the far side of a row of tall cypress trees and a service road that hugged the exterior fence line. Carrying a small knapsack, Von Leinsdorf stepped to the trees and walked south a quarter mile away from the train cars. He surveyed the double line of fence and barbed wire ahead of him and saw no movement up and down the service road.

He sprinted across the road, used bolt cutters to hack a small opening through the lines of barbed wire, and slipped through it into the compound. He ran forward into the shelter of a stand of evergreens. The heavily falling snow quickly erased his footsteps as he headed deeper into the trees.

Versailles
DECEMBER 22, 5:20 A.M.

After clearing security, Grannit and Bernie entered the provost marshal's office, a large, drafty room in the château at Versailles. Grannit presented his dossier on Von Leinsdorf to the provost's second in command and a junior officer from Army Intelligence, who looked like he'd been dragged out of bed. The men listened patiently while Grannit explained that they believed Von Leinsdorf had been taken from police custody in Paris by an undercover German squad posing as U.S. Counter Intelligence officers. They might try to gain access to Versailles with Von Leinsdorf as their prisoner, or perhaps posing as the British lieutenant he'd killed at the Hotel Meurice. Without telling them how, Grannit also mentioned that these men now knew that General Eisenhower had been moved from his regular quarters to the Trianon Palace.

Appearing to take their report seriously, the two officers reassured Grannit that security surrounding Versailles and the general had been elevated to extraordinary levels following the initial threat of Skorzeny's commandos. Eisenhower had spent every minute of the last few days inside the Trianon Palace, almost a mile across the gardens inside the compound. They appreciated this new information, but the idea that any alleged or actual assassin could endanger the general there was inconceivable, no matter what guise he arrived in or who was escorting him. They also mentioned that in just the last few hours, thanks to CID's efforts, the recent arrest of Skorzeny's last squad in Reims had resulted in a lowering of the threat assessment. The general was chomping at the bit to get back to his usual hard-driving schedule. With that, the senior officer indicated their meeting was at an end.

"You men are welcome to bunk down here if you like," said the major. "Or grab a meal before you head back to town."

Grannit knew it was an order, not an invitation.

"Would you mind if we had a look around?" asked Grannit.

"Around the grounds?" asked the major. "It's five in the morning."

"The compound covers over fifteen hundred acres," said the intelligence officer. "There's an entire battalion stationed around the perimeter. A bedbug couldn't get into Ike's quarters without our knowing it. You think you're going to find something out there we've missed?"

"No. I'm really beat. Thinking it might help me sleep."

"Why don't you wait until after the war's over and come back as a tourist," said the intelligence officer, out of patience.

"No, that's all right, they're welcome to take the grand tour," said the major. "We'll arrange an escort as soon as someone's up and around. Save you the price of a ticket down the road."

Two MPs walked Grannit and Bernie through the palace's long corridors to the officer's mess. A long buffet table of breakfast food for early risers was being laid out by the kitchen staff. Grannit pulled cups of coffee from the silver urn and stood with Bernie next to a wall of windowed doors looking out onto the fabled gardens. The first light of dawn filtered into the eastern sky. Snow fell softly outside, accumulating in powdery drifts around the steps of a broad terrace outside, lending the marble of the columns an otherworldly glow. Bernie glanced through an old tourist brochure with a map of the grounds, then looked back at the two MPs, sitting at a table near the door.

"They're not going to leave us alone, are they?"

"No."

"I could try to distract 'em."

"Don't push it, kid. You got too much to lose."

"So we're just going to leave it up to them," said Bernie. "The army and the MPs—"

"We did our job."

"We didn't finish it."

Grannit looked at him, not disagreeing. He tried the door and to his surprise found it open. He held up a pack of cigarettes to show to their MP escorts at the rear table, then pointed to the terrace. The MPs nodded. Grannit stepped outside and Bernie followed him.

Standing under a portico on the terrace, they lit cigarettes and shivered against the cold. In the faint predawn light, they could just discern the enormous outline of the château spreading out around them. When they'd arrived earlier, it had been too dark to see the massive scale of the buildings.

"What a joint," said Bernie, looking at the map on the brochure. "Guess some big shot built this for himself way back when, was that the deal?"

"Labor was a little cheaper."

"No unions."

"In New York, they'd still be pouring concrete."

Bernie smiled. Their MP escorts stepped out to join them and borrow cigarettes.

Eddie Bennings's eyes opened with a jolt. He was lying in the dark and couldn't move, but he felt something cold and metallic in his hands. He identified it as his own automatic pistol. He heard the sound of a car engine approaching outside. His finger inched toward the trigger.

The GIs patrolling the compound perimeter heard a gunshot, then another. They pulled off the road and listened. Another shot. They appeared to be coming from a train car parked on the spur line to the south of the fence. They drove the jeep close and approached cautiously, with weapons drawn. Two boxcars sat on the tracks. The doors of the first car stood open, boxes of ammunition stored inside. They heard a muffled voice issuing from the second car, then noticed that the door was partially open.

. . .

A call came in on the MPs' walkie-talkies about an abandoned train car that had been found near the southern perimeter. The officer reported that shots had been fired and they were moving to investigate. One of the MPs listened on his walkie-talkie as the officers advanced on the train.

Grannit leaned in to listen.

With weapons drawn, the two soldiers slowly rolled open the rear boxcar door.

If they'd been alive long enough to register it, they would have caught a brief glimpse of Corporal Eddie Bennings lying on the floor of the car, bound hand and foot, a gag in his mouth, and a pistol taped into his hands. His body was surrounded by a chain of small gray bricks connected by fuses. Eddie looked up at them and screamed through the gag just as the opening door snapped a small cable, which set off a detonating cap and fired the fuses attached to the plastic explosives packed around his body.

In the next instant the explosion atomized Eddie Bennings, the two officers, and the boxcar. The explosion set off an even bigger secondary blast in the adjoining boxcar, which carried a full load of artillery shells. An arc of flame shot two hundred feet in the air, and the concussive blast knocked out windows in a row of suburban houses over a thousand yards to the south. Along the perimeter of the Versailles compound, American soldiers manning the guard-houses and entrenched defiles saw the flames, heard the explosions, and left their positions to investigate.

The MP escorts on the back terrace heard the explosion distort through their walkie-talkie. An unnaturally bright glow caught Grannit's eye on the southern horizon. A moment later a muffled thump echoed across the flat landscape in front of them like distant artillery. Bernie turned in time to see a lick of flame above the distant tree line and hear a second, larger concussion. Both their MP escorts rushed down the stairs toward the explosion, pulling their weapons. "Go back inside!" shouted the MPs. "Back inside now!"

Grannit waited until the MPs were out of sight. Then he took a spare pistol from his pocket and handed it to Bernie.

"Fuck that," he said, and started down the steps. "Bring the map."

36

The Trianon Palace, Versailles
DECEMBER 22, 4:30 A.M.

General Eisenhower woke at 4:30 A.M. after a restless night. He showered and dressed, then walked down from the small flat he was using as a bedroom in the Trianon to his office. His orderly served him coffee while he looked over the night's accumulated cables from the Ardennes. He looked at his watch; the Third Army's counterattack across the southern front of the Bulge was just getting under way, but it would be hours before any meaningful reports reached his desk. A full briefing was scheduled for ten. He looked out the window at the snow that had fallen throughout the night, worried about how much was coming down in Belgium and if it would hamper Patton's advance.

He picked up a pen and legal pad, prepared to compose the most important letter he'd written in weeks. Eisenhower had announced the night before that he wanted to issue an Order of the Day, a commander's prerogative he seldom exercised. Addressed to every Allied soldier in the European Theater, he wanted to send an inspirational message to rally their spirits as they faced this crucial hour. He had asked his staff to compose a draft for him by morning, but he'd tossed and turned all night because he knew he needed to write such a vital communication himself. With the pen in his hand, the words stalled; he could hear the tone he wanted, but nothing flowed.

On his desk he noticed that an order had come through

overnight to SHAEF high command, lowering the threat assessment
from Skorzeny's commandos. Welcome news. He told his orderly to
bring his hat, scarf, and overcoat. He was stepping outside. After
three days cooped up in this eighteenth-century cuckoo clock, he
knew a walk in the gardens at sunrise would clear his head.

By the time the explosion drew most of the security detail toward
the southern perimeter, Von Leinsdorf was half a mile inside the
compound. Under thick clouds, the blanket of fresh snow on the
grounds amplified the first hints of dawn, giving the light the peculiar
quality of emanating from the ground up. The storm had passed,
but a lingering mist gave the air a granulated texture, as if viewed
through cottony gauze. Von Leinsdorf walked just inside the tree
line, following the linear shore of a large, frozen rectangular body of
water to his left. The woods were empty, the air still as glass; all he
could hear was his own breathing and the plush turning of the powdery snow underfoot. He had memorized the maps Skorzeny had
given him before the mission, but the snow had erased all low-lying
landmarks and made it difficult to orient himself. He knew he was
skirting the Great Canal, but it wasn't until he reached this perpen-
dicular intersection with another hard-edged line of water that he
placed his location on the grid he'd built in his mind.

He stopped at the edge of the tree line, double rows of symmetrical beech and linden, and looked both ways. The arms of the canal,
a grand cross, stretched out in all four directions nearly to the horizon. He could vaguely sense the outline of the main château loom-
ing up a slope a mile to the right. That meant he was headed north,
toward the Trianon Palace. Not another soul in sight. He stepped
out of the trees and crossed the canal. Halfway across the ice, he
stopped, overcome with sudden awe. He had reached the geometri-
cal center of the park, where the perfect balance and majesty of its
architecture all flowed from this axis. In formal perfection, lines
from every point of the compass converged where he was standing.
Despite the urgency of his mission, he was stunned by this faultless
ordering of space and angle, land and water and air.

After the brutality and chaos of the last week, his mind resonated in harmony. The secret meaning he had detected the day before hidden in the design of the Parisian boulevards broke through here in explicit expression. The landscape's spiritual precision meshed in his mind with the sure prospect of completing the mission he'd been given, and he knew in that moment that fate would guide him to the finish.

It would happen here, within sight of the palace where they'd signed the treaty that began Germany's long, slow humiliation at the hands of the Allies a quarter of a century before, setting in motion the chain of disasters that had brought him to this place and time. The insult would be answered at its source. Meaning and culmination merged in him as one, even in the same breath, an exaltation that caused his soul to soar.

The panzers would march on Antwerp. He would complete the Second Objective. The death of the American commander would fatally split the Allied alliance.

He continued on to the northern shore of the canal. Safely inside the cover of the tree line, he stopped and opened the attaché case. The ID cards he carried would get him close enough to the building to detonate the explosive device inside, but he was prepared if a better opportunity arose. He quickly screwed a wooden stock to the handle of the machine pistol and then attached the silencer and scope to the barrel. The assembled gun slid into the pocket he'd sewn inside the front left flap of his overcoat. He closed the coat, picked up the case, and continued walking.

Bernie tried to keep Grannit in sight before him as they sprinted through the snowbound gardens, past emptied round ponds and statuary and strange conical trees, down broad steps and around a frozen fountain. A long avenue opened up straight ahead of them leading to what looked like a frozen canal that extended beyond the end of the lane as far as the eye could see. They covered the ground between a dense narrowing of trees to another larger, empty circular pool. Startling sculpted figures, a godlike creature being drawn by wild horses, burst out of the snow in its center. On the far side of the pool, they reached the edge of the canal and Grannit stopped for a moment.

"Where's the Trianon?" he asked as Bernie caught up to him.

Bernie quickly placed them on the map, found the Trianon Palace, then pointed toward the first of two diagonal lanes branching away from the canal to the right at a forty-five-degree angle.

"That way. About half a mile."

Grannit looked back in the direction where they'd seen the explosion, calculating distances and times. He looked straight down the canal, then pulled a small pair of field glasses from his pocket and pointed them in that direction.

A single set of footprints in the pristine snow, crossing the canal.

"Get there as fast as you can," he said. "Tell them he's coming. Go on!"

Grannit pulled his pistol and started toward the second diagonal path that ran closer to the canal. Bernie kept pace with him until the paths diverged, and he took the one bearing right. They ran at the same pace, Bernie glancing to his left, watching Grannit until the bare trees between them grew thick enough to obscure his view. Bernie slipped once on a patch of ice below the snow, and when he got back on his feet Grannit had disappeared.

Grannit sprinted down the symmetrical pathway, chuffing for breath, his lungs burning in the frigid air. He stopped briefly when it intersected with another diagonal that angled back toward the center of the water. He looked both ways, then pressed forward, the northern terminus of the crossbar of the Great Canal coming into sight at the end of the path.

Von Leinsdorf stopped in the woods just short of the water's northern shore. Fifty yards beyond the end of the canal a series of empty fountains cut into the slope of a gentle rise, framed on either side by curved staircases that led to a flat terrace and gardens on the upper level behind the Trianon. A solitary figure was walking through the snow in the formal gardens on that terrace, moving in and out of sight behind an intermittent line of trees and high hedges. Von Leinsdorf dropped his attaché case and pulled the rifle from the slot in his coat. Keeping the man in view, he walked steadily forward into a small grove of conical evergreens, dropped to one knee, and focused down the barrel through the telescopic sight.

The figure came into focus, his face turned away. A middle-aged man wearing an American officer's cap, walking with a slight limp.

Grannit sprinted to the end of the diagonal pathway, where it reached the canal, saw the line of footprints continuing to the north, then spotted a leather case in the snow beside them twenty yards to his right. He hurried to it, opened the case, glanced inside, and knew who had brought it here. Movement against the white snowfield drew his eyes farther to the right.

A soldier in an overcoat kneeling in a nearby thicket held a rifle, pointed at the northern terrace.

The officer on the terrace turned, and Von Leinsdorf glimpsed Eisenhower's face. As he squeezed the trigger and heard the muffled snort of the silencer, he felt a sharp slap on the back of his left thigh and a jolt of searing pain rocked him forward. His bullet fired off-line, kicking snow off a branch above and to the right of the general. In that frozen moment, as a gunshot cracked the clear cold air, Von Leinsdorf realized he'd been shot from behind. He spun around onto his back, saw a man advancing toward him, pistol in hand, and fired the rifle at him. The shot caught the man between the neck and right shoulder and punched him off his feet.

Bernie had nearly reached the end of the path to the Trianon Palace, the barbed wire and defensive gun emplacements around the building in his sight, when he heard the single shot ring out through the trees in the distance to his left. He stopped and looked both ways, then turned to his left, the direction Grannit had gone, and kept running.

When Von Leinsdorf looked back up at the terrace, the general was out of sight behind the line of hedges. Von Leinsdorf limped out of the trees toward the staircases and fountains beyond the canal. By the time he reached the bottom of the stairs, he could hear shouts coming from the terrace above. Looking to his left, he noticed a gap in the back of the empty fountain complex and remembered something pleasing from his study of the maps.

Grannit pulled himself to his feet. His right arm hung uselessly at his side, the collarbone shattered, pain exploding along the arm, through the shoulder, and up into his neck. He bent down awkwardly to pick up his gun with his left hand and staggered after Von Leinsdorf, following a trail of blood and footprints in the snow. At the base of the stairs, the trail veered to the left into some empty fountains at the foot of the slope and toward a narrow three-foot gap at the bottom of the back wall, where it met the base of the hill. Grannit advanced to the opening, bent down to look inside, and saw smooth concrete walls below. He stuck the gun in his belt and lowered himself with one hand toward the edge, inched himself back over the lip, and then let go and dropped about four feet, stifling a cry of pain as he landed on a smooth concrete floor.

He had landed in an ancient reservoir below the fountains and terraces, emptied of water. A series of low keystoned arches branched up to form the ceiling from rows of square pillared foundations, stained by ageless watermarks. A distant light source illuminated the symmetrical edges of the pillars as they marched away in both directions. The air felt glacial and stagnant, as if it hadn't been disturbed in a hundred years. Grannit pulled his gun and stood up, nearly to his full height under the center point of the arches. He listened and heard nothing but a distant, steady drip of water. He saw no movement or shadows in either direction. He set down his gun, switched on the small flashlight and held it between his teeth, then picked up the gun again.

The trail of blood continued ahead of him on the smooth stone floor. The reservoir seemed to have no end, extending into infinite darkness. He advanced slowly, following the blood from pillar to pillar with the light. His right arm felt dead, hanging as if by a string, its every involuntary movement shooting pain out through his upper body that took his breath away. He crept forward, half a step at a time, cautiously approaching the edge of each pillar before inching into the open again.

He heard footsteps moving ahead of him in the dark, then the sound of a scuffle, followed closely by two booming gunshots and a groan. He heard something heavy hit the ground.

"I got him!" he heard an American voice yell. "I got the son of a bitch!"

The fragile beam of the flashlight caught the edge of something moving two pillars ahead. Grannit leaned out, took the light into his good hand, focused it along the trail of blood, and followed it. His eyes blurred, refusing to focus, and he knew he was going into shock.

"Can I get some fucking help down here! He's still alive, I got him!"

Grannit saw the soles of a man's boots around the corner of the pillar. He took another step forward and saw the man in the overcoat moaning in pain, writhing on the ground in a spreading pool of blood. An MP stood over Von Leinsdorf, holding his gun pointed down at the body with both hands.

"Anybody there, god damn it! I need help!"

Grannit rubbed the back of his hand across his eyes, trying to will them to work. He took the gun back into his left hand, held it along with the light, and stepped forward with the barrel raised. It looked as if Von Leinsdorf had been shot in the face; he was covered in blood, his hands reaching up frantically to his head as he moaned in pain.

"Don't fucking move again!" said the MP, lowering the gun at him.

"Where'd you hit him?" asked Grannit.

"Head and neck, I think. I had patrol down here," said the MP. He pointed deeper into the darkness. "There's a door connects to the basement inside. I heard the shot outside so I came through. He jumped out at me; I was lucky I got some shots off."

"Is the general all right?" asked Grannit.

"I think he is, I think they got him back inside. Who the fuck is this guy? One of those Germans?"

"That's right," said Grannit, staggering as he leaned toward one of the columns.

"Jesus, you're hit, too. Cover him, I'll get help. Where the hell is everybody?"

Grannit rubbed his eyes again. He thought he saw a bloodstain on the back of the MP's left leg as he took a step toward the door in the darkness.

"Hold up," said Grannit.

"Come on, man, you're hurt—"

"Who plays center field for the Dodgers?" asked Grannit.

"What, are you fucking kidding me?"

"Just answer the question."

"Joe DiMaggio."

Grannit pulled the trigger. Von Leinsdorf spun around and dove to the ground, squeezing off three shots from his .45, deafening in the enclosed space. The first bullet caught Grannit just above the hip and drove him to the ground. His good arm braced to break the fall, his elbow cracked as it hit the concrete, and his gun and flashlight skittered a few feet away from his hand.

Von Leinsdorf stepped forward into the light, holding the Colt in both hands. Grannit's shot had grazed his ribs. He touched the blood, assessing his injury as he advanced slowly toward Grannit, staring at him with a mix of rage and curiosity. Grannit tried to inch his left hand toward his gun, but his legs wouldn't work properly and the area under his hip grew slick with blood, preventing any traction. Von Leinsdorf stopped three feet away.

"What do you want?" he asked. "What do you want?"

Grannit didn't answer, but didn't look away.

Von Leinsdorf raised the gun to fire point-blank at him when the reservoir exploded with a series of deafening shots that merged into one long, continuous blast.

Bernie advanced steadily toward Von Leinsdorf as he emptied the clip, and every shot caught him square in the back. The German jerked forward, spun to his left as he dropped the gun, tried to grab a pillar to hold himself up, then slid to the ground and onto his side. He looked up at Bernie in disbelief. Bernie stood over him, held his look without flinching, pointed the gun at his forehead, and the trigger clicked again, the clip empty. And in that instant the dark light in Von Leinsdorf's eyes finally went out.

Bernie tossed the gun away and knelt down beside Grannit. He didn't like what he saw.

"They're coming," he said. "You're going to be all right. They'll be here soon."

"How's the other guy?"

Grannit nodded toward the man in the overcoat. Bernie went to check on him, a young military policeman.

"He's gone," said Bernie.

"Get out of here now," said Grannit. "Before they find you."

"I'm not leaving you here."

"Go on—"

"Forget that. Forget it. I'm not leaving you alone."

Grannit closed his eyes and struggled to breathe. They could hear shouts and footsteps entering a far end of the reservoir, voices echoing over the stone. Grannit pointed toward the left pocket of his coat.

"Here. In here."

Bernie helped him reach in, and they pulled out Ole Carlson's dog tags. Grannit pressed them into Bernie's hands, held his hand over them, and squeezed hard.

"You're with me, Bernie," said Grannit, fading away. "Tell 'em you're my partner. We came here together. We finished the job. You tell 'em that."

"All right."

"He dropped a case near the water. Make sure you get it first. There's papers in there you can use."

"Okay, Earl."

"Promise me you'll do that."

"I promise."

Grannit closed his eyes, but didn't loose his grip on Bernie's hand until the first soldiers arrived.

37

L̲ate on the morning of December 22, General Eisenhower issued his Order of the Day to all the Allied troops in Europe, his first public acknowledgment of the seriousness and scale of the Battle of the Bulge.

> *The enemy is making his supreme effort to break out of the desperate plight into which you forced him by your brilliant victories of the summer and fall. He is fighting savagely to take back all that you have won and is using every treacherous trick to deceive and kill you. He is gambling everything, but already, in this battle, your unparalleled gallantry has done much to foil his plans. In the face of your proven bravery and fortitude, he will completely fail.*
>
> *But we cannot be content with mere repulse.*
>
> *By rushing out from his fixed defenses the enemy has given us the chance to turn his great gamble into his worst defeat. So I call upon every man, of all the Allies, to rise now to new heights of courage, of resolution, and of effort. Let everyone hold before him a single thought—to destroy the enemy on the ground, in the air, everywhere—destroy him. United in this determination and with unshakable faith in the cause for which we fight, we will, with God's help, go forward to our greatest victory.*

Later that same day, for reasons that have never been adequately explained, the extraordinary security detail surrounding General Eisenhower at the Grand Trianon in Versailles was ordered to stand down. He soon returned to his former patterns of free movement behind the lines and among his forward troops.

On the morning of December 23, the weather over Belgium and the Ardennes Forest cleared. For the first time in the week since the battle had begun, combined Allied air forces took to the sky and entered the fight against the invading German armies with devastating effect. Within three days, elements of Patton's Third Amy reached the exhausted American defenders who had resisted the ferocious siege of Bastogne. Hitler's last gamble had reached its high-water mark. Within days, his bold offensive would devolve into a desperate retreat toward the German border to save what remained of his battered divisions from utter destruction. Although intense fighting would continue for weeks into the New Year, generating for both sides the highest casualty rate of the entire war, initiative and momentum had shifted back toward the Allies for the final time. Less than five months later, at SHAEF's field headquarters outside Reims, German field commanders signed the official articles of surrender.

After watching his staff struggle and fail to produce a satisfactory statement to commemorate the moment, with characteristic modesty General Eisenhower summed up the entire war effort in a single sentence:

"The mission of this Allied force was fulfilled at 0241 local time, May 7, 1945."

38

Brooklyn, New York
OCTOBER 4, 1955, 2:00 P.M.

Each afternoon, outside the urgent-care wing of the Veterans Administration Hospital on Seventh Avenue, nurses wheeled their patients out onto a western-facing plaza overlooking a public golf course, to soak up the last heat of Indian summer. The play-by-play broadcast of the World Series could be heard from a dozen different radios, the voices of Red Barber and young Vin Scully setting the scene. After losing two of the last three championships to the despised Yankees, the Brooklyn Dodgers had once again carried the Series into a seventh and deciding game.

When Bernie arrived for his visit, he expected to find Earl on the plaza, but didn't see him there and went back to look for him in his room. A young, friendly nurse whom he didn't recognize was working the floor. They met just outside of the room, as Bernie glanced in at Earl.

"How's he doing today?"

"Feeling a little poorly this morning," she said.

"You're new, aren't you? What's your name?"

"Charlene. I've been here a few weeks."

"Charlene, I'm Bernie."

Bernie held out the small bouquet he always brought to brighten up the room and asked if she could help him find a vase. He walked with her to the nurses' station.

"Where you from, Bernie?"

"Here. Brooklyn."

"Yeah? Me, too," she said. "Mr. Grannit doesn't get many visitors."

"I come by every Sunday."

"See, that's why, I don't usually work weekends."

"Anyway, kind of a local holiday today, isn't it? For a Tuesday."

"For any day, you kidding? I'm living and dying with every pitch."

"You want to listen to the game with us? We'll put it on in his room."

"Thanks, I'll be in and out. Just about everybody in here's got it on the radio."

"They say you could walk from one end of Brooklyn to the other today and never miss a pitch," said Bernie.

"I believe that."

She held out the small vase she'd filled with water, and he nestled the flowers inside. She noticed the worked-in dirt and grime on his hands and under the nails. They walked back to the room.

"You a relative, Bernie?"

"No, just a friend."

"I don't believe Mr. Grannit has any immediate family, does he?"

"Not that I'm aware of."

They entered the room. Earl sat propped up in the bed, his face turned to the single window. He showed no sign that he'd noticed their arrival. Charlene set the flowers on the bedside counter. Bernie switched on the radio, and the sounds of the warm-up show came across, Red and Vinny running down the lineups as the crowd settled into Yankee Stadium. Bernie pulled up a chair beside the bed.

"What do you think?" asked Bernie. "You think today's the day, Earl? I really think we're going to do it. With Podres going for us, he had their number last game. I don't think they can touch him."

Earl's right arm sat folded up beside him, atrophied and useless. He had some movement in the left hand, to signal for things he wanted or needed. Bernie and the staff had learned how to read most of those requests. This time, as the game started, he gestured in a way Bernie couldn't decipher. Finally, he realized Earl wanted to hold his hand for a while as they listened. Earl looked directly at him, which he didn't usually do. His features had been twisted by the series of strokes he'd suffered, and some days his eyes stayed dull, but today Bernie could see a spark. When Gil Hodges singled in the game's first run in the top of the fourth and Brooklyn took the lead, Earl slapped his hand on the bed a few times and nodded his head.

It looked like a sure thing. Podres was too strong. This time they were going to do it. After fifty-five years Brooklyn was finally going to win the Series.

Three weeks later, two days after Earl died, Bernie received a call at the station from an attorney named Jack Meyer, who worked out of a small storefront near Grand Army Plaza in downtown Brooklyn. He mentioned that he was handling the details of Earl's estate and had a couple of questions for him. Bernie arranged a time to see him during his lunch hour and took the trolley to his office.

Meyer worked alone in a cramped single room, piled halfway up the walls with accordion files and loose paperwork. A round, balding man in his mid-sixties with a welcoming smile, he welcomed Bernie in and gestured toward the chair in front of his desk, the only other place to sit.

"Apologies in advance for my filing system," said Meyer. "I'm a few weeks behind on my paperwork."

Bernie said he didn't mind, uncomfortable as always in an encounter with any form of authority.

"If you don't mind my asking, how did you know Earl Grannit?" asked Meyer.

"We met during the war."

"Did you serve together?"

"Not in the same unit. But that's where we met."

"Where are you from originally?"

"Brooklyn. That's what we realized. That we were from the same neighborhood."

Something of Bernie's reticence came across. "I don't mean to pry," said Meyer. "I'm just trying to understand the relationship. I knew Earl's father; I represented the family for many years. I never heard Earl mention you."

"He was never much of a talker," said Bernie.

"No," said Meyer, with a warm smile. "But he made the most of the words he let go of."

"Yes, sir. After the war, we stayed in touch. When he had the stroke, I started helping out at the gas station. I'm a mechanic."

"I see."

"Earl had a rough time of it."

"I know he was badly wounded over there. Took him years to recover."

"See, I don't think he ever really did."

"It's a blessing his suffering is over," said Meyer. "So our business here today is short and simple. If you knew him as well as you say, you won't be surprised to hear that Earl took very precise care of his affairs."

Bernie smiled slightly.

"I have his will here. He's left everything to you."

Bernie couldn't speak for a moment. "Excuse me?"

"You're his sole heir. Don't run right out and move to West-chester; there's not a lot, aside from the gas station and a few savings bonds."

"I thought . . . He had no other family at all?"

"He had a sister growing up."

"Where is she?"

"She was killed. There was a robbery at the station. Some punk emptied the till, she walked in on him. A long time ago now, over twenty-five years. She couldn't have been more than twelve or thirteen."

Bernie's own vivid impressions of that day came flooding back and his eyes filled with involuntary tears. He could even pick a young policeman out of the crowd in his memory who might have been . . .

"As I understand it, Earl had just joined the police force. Had to work a double shift that day when he would normally have been at the station. Terrible, terrible business. They never found the killer. Family never got over it. Two years later Earl's father dies of a heart attack. His wife went the next year. There's one theory that she killed herself. Didn't he ever tell you any of this?"

"No, sir. He never did."

"Well," said Meyer, sympathetic to Bernie's show of emotion. "He was a hard man to know."

Bernie composed himself before he spoke again. "You have no idea what he did. Over there. Nobody knows what he did. More than any man I know. Did he ever tell you what happened?"

"No. And I never asked. Nor, in putting this document together, and this is a little awkward, could I find any mention of your service record. No entry or discharge. Nothing with the Veterans Administration." He let that sink in for a moment, then turned to a legal pad. "I did verify that your family lived in Park Slope, as you say. Then it appears you moved away for some time in '38? Eight years later you're back in the area. Alone. Living in a one-room apartment. Unmarried. No trace of your family."

Meyer appeared to be waiting for an explanation, but when none was forthcoming he showed no disappointment.

"The fact is Earl Grannit vouched for you," said Meyer. "And that is as far as my curiosity extends. I require your signature here, and here."

Meyer set two copies of the will down in front of him and handed Bernie a pen.

"I owe him my life," said Bernie, about to elaborate.

"Please, feel no obligation to say anything more. Earl obviously had his reasons as well."

Bernie signed the documents. Meyer efficiently gathered them from him and showed him to the door.

"Anyway, one hopes that's what we've learned about what happened over there, isn't it?" he said. "In those black hours."

As Meyer looked at him over his glasses, behind the easy congeniality, Bernie wondered exactly how much he did know.

"What's that, sir?"

"What we were fighting for. And against."

"Yes, sir."

"Not every hero came home with a medal."

They shook hands, and Bernie stepped out onto the quiet tree-lined street, a chill in the wind, the leaves just starting to turn, and walked all the way back to Park Slope.

On May 19, 1945, near Salzburg, Austria, where he had led his commandos into the Alps to mount a final defense, *Obersturmbannführer* Otto Skorzeny turned himself in to American forces. News of the surrender of "the most dangerous man in Europe" created a sensation throughout the Continent, America, and the rest of the world. When General Eisenhower learned of Skorzeny's capture, he sent his personal chief of security to interview him and ordered a film crew from Army Counter Intelligence to record the interrogation. Eisenhower reviewed the resulting footage personally, but his reaction was never made public. Skorzeny would spend the next two years in prisoner-of-war camps at Nuremberg and later at Dachau, awaiting trial in the Allies' war crimes court. Although he was universally described in newspaper accounts as "the man who tried to kill Eisenhower," Skorzeny skillfully defused the accusation through the English-speaking press. Charming and formidable, easily the most charismatic of the surviving Nazi hierarchy, in dozens of interviews he claimed that he had never seriously intended to assassinate the Allied commander, adding, with a sly smile, that if he had, "no one would have been left in doubt about what I was trying to do."

Despite working steadily for the next two years, Allied officials were unable to produce any written orders or compelling eyewitnesses who would testify to Skorzeny's direct involvement in the plot to kill Eisenhower. Skorzeny had received his orders directly from Hitler, and had made certain that no paper trail survived. The only other men with direct knowledge of the Second Objective had all been killed in combat or shot by American firing squads. Only the interrogation of the unfortunate Karl Heinz Schmidt and a few others testified to its existence, and those files would remain classified by Army Counter Intelligence for the next fifty years. The reason for that had something to do with the fact that, while in custody, after weeks of fruitless interrogations about Operation *Greif* by Allied interrogators, Skorzeny was visited by the legendary Bill Donovan, head of the Office of Strategic Services, forerunner of the CIA, and Skorzeny's opposite number on the American side. Donovan recognized a kindred spirit in Skorzeny, and although no record of their discussions remain, they were apparently amiable and far-reaching. What they shared in earnest, besides an appetite for spy craft, was a serious dread of the Soviet Union and its emerging designs on Eastern Europe. Shortly after their encounter, all pursuit of charges against Skorzeny in the Eisenhower assassination attempt was dropped. For a while, frustrated prosecutors considered including Skorzeny with the dozens of soldiers and officers responsible for the massacre of American troops near Malmédy, but the idea was dismissed for an obvious lack of evidence.

Skorzeny was finally brought to trial before a military tribunal in 1947 on a lesser charge that his deployment of German commandos disguised as Allied soldiers during the Ardennes offensive constituted a war crime. Press from around the world gathered to cover the proceedings. With the help of a tenacious American defense attorney, Lieutenant Colonel Robert Durst, Skorzeny argued that every side in the war had at one time or another employed the exact same tactic. If his actions were considered a war crime, any similar Allied effort would have to be held to the same criminal standard. At the eleventh hour, Skorzeny's attorney called a surprise defense witness to the stand, a decorated British RAF war hero who testified that he and his commando unit had worn German uniforms on a number of missions during the war. The tribunal acquitted Otto Skorzeny of all charges. Afterward, the thwarted and furious chief prosecutor told the press: "I still think Skorzeny is the most dangerous man in Europe."

Although technically free, Skorzeny remained in American custody while they debated what to do with him. Attempts by the Soviets and the Czechs to extradite him for war crimes in their own tribunals, where he faced certain execution, clouded the issue. While those efforts were tied up in the courts, he was finally transferred to a German detention camp in early 1948. A few months later, with help from agents of the recently formed Central Intelligence Agency, three former SS officers arrived at the camp disguised as American military policemen and presented forged documents that authorized them to transport Skorzeny to a hearing at Nuremberg the following day. The American soldiers on duty signed the release, and Skorzeny walked out of the prison in the custody of the disguised MPs. He promptly disappeared. When his absence was discovered and his cell searched later that day, officials found a letter Skorzeny had left behind, addressed to the German court, explaining his actions:

> *After the capitulation of the German Army, Mr. Chairman, I, as a soldier, which is all that I was, freely gave myself up with a trust in the justice of the victors without making any effort to avoid my responsibility. For over two years I tried to clear myself and restore the honor of my name to the world. The American military tribunal in Dachau cleared me of all charges and therewith declared to the public that I had acted and fought purely as a decent soldier and had only done my duty to my Fatherland. In spite of this official release I was kept under arrest. The American authorities offered me the choice to go to either a DP camp or a German internment camp. I chose the latter in the hope of finding only justice before a German court and have prepared myself for months for these proceedings. However, I will not allow myself to fall under a one-sided, outside influenced decision and thus lose the honor which was restored to me by the American court. For these reasons I have withdrawn myself*

from further German court proceedings. If I'm given an opportunity to come before a German court which stands only under the law and is strong enough to resist the hatred exerted from outside sources as is worthy of German justice traditions, I will immediately place myself at your service. As a German who fought for his country, as did every German man, I have only one wish: to live in honor in my Fatherland.

Yours sincerely, Otto Skorzeny

Hindsight makes it clear that in the utilitarian opinion of Bill Donovan and the CIA, Skorzeny possessed more value as a living intelligence asset than a dead war criminal. Although rumors reported his whereabouts all over the globe, one of the world's most sought after fugitives spent the next two years living in Paris, where he regularly dined at the Café de la Paix. Recently declassified documents confirm that he was now working on behalf of the Western Allies, gathering intelligence against the French Communist Party. After his identity was revealed in France, he published his memoirs and moved back to Germany, where he lived under an assumed name for a few years, before finally settling in General Franco's fascist Madrid. He would spend the next twenty-five years straddling an unsettling line between Western intelligence informant and godfather to the surviving remnants of the *Waffen*-SS, known initially as "The Brotherhood" and later more notoriously as Odessa. During that time, drawing on his early training as an engineer, Skorzeny founded a technical consulting company and amassed a considerable personal fortune. He amplified that fortune with a number of less savory business ventures, among them industrial espionage, assassination for hire, and international arms dealing. Throughout these years Skorzeny lived the social life of a dissolute playboy, romancing dozens of glamorous socialites and minor royalty, including, for a time in Argentina where he worked as a consultant with that fascist regime, Eva Perón. Operationally conceived on the back of Skorzeny's World War Two commando force, to this day Odessa remains the original prototype for the modern terrorist organization.

When he finally succumbed to cancer in 1975, Otto Skorzeny was laid to rest in a Madrid cemetery. In surviving footage of the funeral, a band plays "*Deutschland Über Alles*" while the aging members of his organization offer their dead leader a sustained Nazi salute as his casket lowers into the grave.

A Note on Sources

The 150th Panzer Squad, Operation *Greif*, and all the details about training at the Grafenwöhr camp are based on fact, most of which remained classified by American Military Intelligence for fifty years after the end of World War Two. Much of what the Allies learned about the objectives of the operation during the Battle of the Bulge, including the plot to kill General Eisenhower, came from a captured German commando named Karl Schmidt. Two American-born soldiers took part in the attack; one was a deserter by the name of William Sharper. Another of the German commandos, the son of a diplomat, had learned English while growing up in England.

Less than half of the men who trained at Grafenwöhr and served in Skorzeny's Brigade 150 survived the war. The casualty rate among the commando group, Company Stielau, approached 75 percent. Of the twenty members of the commando group who took part in the Second Objective, eighteen were either killed in action or captured and executed by American forces during the Battle of the Bulge.

The remaining two men have never been accounted for.

Los Angeles, California
November 2006

ACKNOWLEDGMENTS

Many thanks to my agent, Ed Victor; editor in chief Will Schwalbe; my editor, Gretchen Young; and my expert researcher, Jennifer Bidwell.

© Tom Lascher

MARK FROST is the bestselling author of *The Match*, *The Greatest Game Ever Played*, *The Grand Slam*, and the novels *The List of Seven* and *The Six Messiahs*. He received an Emmy nomination for the acclaimed television series *Hill Street Blues*, was co-creator and executive producer of the legendary ABC television series *Twin Peaks*, and in 2005 wrote and produced *The Greatest Game Ever Played* as a major motion picture from Walt Disney Studios. Mark lives in Los Angeles and upstate New York with his wife and son.

Also from

MARK FROST

"Frost...has a gift for dramatizing historic golf matches."

—NEW YORK TIMES BOOK REVIEW

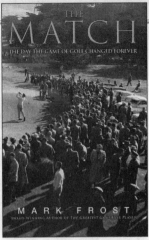

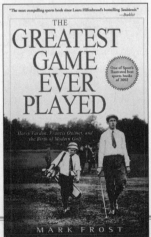

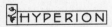